# THE FOREST AT THE HEART OF HER MAGE

## HIYODORI

# *Contents*

## Part One
### Nui City



## Part Two
### Outpost Twenty-Four

## Part Three
### The Devouring Forest



## Part Four
### A House in the Mountains

## Part Five
### The Heart of the Forest

# PART ONE

*Nui City*

# 1

Months passed before Tiller Koya discovered the first draft of her dead grandmother's will. It was handwritten on a single slip of grid-lined paper. Concealed deep in a drawer packed full of paisley-print pajamas.

The pajamas smelled like Baba Sayo, but they had also gotten musty enough to give Tiller a coughing fit.

She straightened up, paper in hand. She forgot about organizing the rest of the dresser. She forgot about the drawn curtains, the afternoon sunlight that clawed its way in through tiny gaps.

The writing was wavery yet neat, each character carefully slotted in its allotted box. The sheet of paper had been smooth and flat when Tiller first extracted it. Only now, clutched in her fingers, did it turn crumpled and damp.

The final notarized draft of Baba Sayo's will had instructed Tiller to keep her ashes in a plain ceramic container—one previously used to hold bread flour. No need to set up an extra household shrine, it said.

Her official will requested little else. In the end, it gave all of Baba Sayo's assets (not that she had many) to Tiller. Her only surviving heir.

The hidden paper from the pajama drawer said something very different.

There Baba Sayo described the sacred mountains deep in the Devouring Forest. The fire caves where Koya villagers would travel to deposit their dead. She pleaded with the Lord of Circles—a god from outside the Forest. A god she'd never had much faith in.

*Don't steal me away for your cycle of hellish rebirth*, she wrote. *Return me to the Forest. My only wish is to become a thistle growing from the stones of our secret mountain, and then to vanish.*

*Don't feed me your cheap promises of a neverending water-wheel of life. I don't want it. Give me my eternity in the Forest. Give me my forever death together with every forester who came before me.*

Before Baba Sayo died, Tiller had attempted to ask her more about her wishes. She always responded gruffly.

"I don't want anything special," she'd say. "Hmph! Don't waste your money on a pretty urn. I won't care when I'm gone."

Twenty years ago, they'd all left the Devouring Forest together: Baba Sayo and Tiller and every other Koya villager. They were among the last of the foresters to leave.

With the exception of Tiller, most of the seventy villagers had already been quite elderly. Even back then. Now Tiller was thirty. She'd watched over half of them die.

In the Koya Foundation group home, she'd arranged for a dedicated room with a spectacular nondenominational shrine. The best you could get in any sort of senior housing.

She'd used the Foundation's money to purchase land for a private cemetery, too. No bodies were buried there. All foresters hoped to be burned as soon as possible after dying. But Tiller wanted to give them markers. And to show city folk that foresters could adequately imitate their traditions.

For twenty years, neither Tiller nor any of the other exiled villagers had set foot anywhere near the Devouring Forest.

Those two decades mattered little now, here in Baba Sayo's humble apartment.

Tiller looked at the mushroom art hung on the walls: large slabs of dried bracket fungus that Tiller and her twin brother had etched with ambitious designs when they were little.

She thought of the view beyond the curtain-covered window. A six-foot gap, and then the concrete surface of the taller building across the alley.

Baba Sayo used to sit by that window, swollen-knuckled hands motionless on the armrests of her perversely uncomfortable wooden chair. Without moving a finger, she would claim that she was painting.

Tiller always offered to bring her supplies. Baba Sayo would raise her puffy hands as if showing off a hated pair of gloves. "I'm no artist," she'd say. "Not in real life."

She would look out the window all day and paint woodland murals on the blank wall across the street with her mind. She was a forester to the end.

They'd been forced to leave for the sake of survival. The Forest had grown much too dangerous for human settlements. But foresters still longed for it, consciously or unconsciously. All of them.

Tiller folded Baba Sayo's paper and slipped it in her pocket. She eyed the unmarked white jar holding Baba Sayo's remains.

She wondered what it would take to survive a trip all the way to the sacred mountains in the deepest part of the Forest. To carry that jar of ashes to the fire caves. To grant Baba Sayo the proper death she'd secretly longed for.

An entire division of soldiers from the Outborder Corps?

Cutting-edge combat machina requisitioned from the southern islands?

No, she decided. She was a forester by birth. She didn't need to bring an army.

Not only that—in her years since leaving the Forest, Tiller had undoubtedly survived more assassination attempts than anyone else in the entire city. Foresters and regular Jacian citizens alike.

She could survive a one-time trek through her homeland. She'd bring her usual tools to defend herself. She wouldn't ask for much else.

All she needed was a mage.

# 2

FEW MAGES WERE eager to volunteer for what they viewed as a death march. Not even those affiliated with the Outborder Corps.

Tiller offered the largest cash reward she could muster. But this was a private mission; she couldn't draw from Koya Foundation funds. Her personal savings weren't substantial enough to make mages leap up and throw away their lives.

Tiller planned on coming back alive, of course. Both she and her mage guardian, if she ever found one. But she couldn't blame them for doubting her.

Twenty years ago, the Forest had turned so deadly that even native foresters got forced out.

Now, to make matters worse, the Forest was spreading. It crept south more rapidly every year, consuming farm after farm. The depths of the woods might not be anything like what Tiller remembered from her childhood.

As an adult in Nui City, Tiller had by necessity become skilled at dodging attempts on her life. (Not a common problem for most people.)

She'd also gotten very good at lobbying.

Most of her work stayed behind the scenes. She hired charismatic publicists on behalf of the Koya Foundation. While Tiller negotiated with lawyers and big-time donors, her spokespeople made heartfelt public appeals about the plight of exiled foresters.

This time, she couldn't hide behind the Foundation. She was doing this for Baba Sayo. Not for the entirety of Koya Village, or for the whole stranded population of foresters in general.

Baba Sayo had raised her all alone, and in return Tiller had brought her nothing but terror and trouble.

She would give Baba Sayo her forever death in the sacred mountains at the heart of the Forest. She would secure the help of a mage even if she had to lie through her teeth to make it happen.

In the receiving room of an Outborder Corps garrison, Tiller began to worry that her lies might not suffice.

"You think you can make the Forest stop spreading," said the colonel.

He appeared to be around the same age as her and had a rather delicate build. More of a strategist than a physical combatant. Tiller wished she'd ended up facing a meathead instead.

"I can't make any promises." She attempted to strike the appropriate balance of confidence and humility. "But you know what I am."

She pointed at her hair. At her black wig, rather.

She always wore a lace-lined wig when going out and about. For the same reason that she always kept the curtains drawn at home when taking it off.

"I do know what you are," the colonel agreed. "A much rarer breed than other Forest refugees. The last of your kind. How does Jace benefit from sending you back to the Forest to die?"

Tiller gazed at the topographical map on the wall behind the colonel. She took a sip of bitter coffee as she considered how to answer.

Jace, Jace, Jace. Everything had to be about Jace. An archipelagic nation consisting of eight major islands and thousands of smaller ones.

The map showed no hint of other countries or land masses. Just Jace and the surrounding sea. The familiar islands and their swarm of tiny companions stared back at her.

Technically Tiller, too, had always been Jacian. Tiller, too, was a citizen. Just like Baba Sayo, and every other former Forest dweller. The Forest grew in a remote area of Nui, the northernmost and least populated of the major islands.

But she had never felt particularly Jacian. Either before or after moving to the city. The Forest may as well have been its own empire, its own universe. Even the branch of the military that monitored it was called the Outborder Corps—the same branch that patrolled the edge of Jacian territorial waters.

"I'm not going to the Forest to die," Tiller said. "And I didn't come here to waste your time." She kept her tone friendly. "I heard that mages in your unit volunteered to join me."

For the first time, the young colonel's composure flickered. Eyes downcast, he rotated the saucer beneath his coffee cup.

"Only one mage volunteered," he said. "She isn't officially in my unit. She isn't in anyone's unit."

"Can you offer me an introduction?" Tiller asked.

Silence.

"I enjoyed corresponding with your commander. She's been very cooperative. She said you would be, too."

He adjusted his uniform collar. "You seem like a decent operator. I'm sure you can handle mages well enough." (Empty, baseless praise.) "But I promise you, you've never dealt with a mage like this one."

Tiller waited a moment before speaking. Just to make sure he was finished raising objections.

"Are there any foresters in the Outborder Corps?"

"Not that I know of."

"Then you'll just have to trust me," she said. "I can navigate anywhere in the Forest. I can find a way to make the Forest stop invading occupied land. Let me meet your mage."

"I've been in the Forest far more recently than you have," the colonel said sharply. Despite his elegance, he wore the scars to prove it. Shiny white streaks spattered his hands and neck and jaw.

Tiller whipped out her trump card again. "Your commander—"

"Did the commander give you my name?"

"Colonel Istel."

He sighed.

"This mage you want to meet—she isn't quite a formal member of the Corps. Besides, she's extremely good at making herself scarce."

"She won't make herself scarce if she volunteered to help me," Tiller said sensibly.

Colonel Istel didn't seem reassured. "Several squads will join a Corps event tonight."

"A party?"

"You could call it that. At any rate, the woman you're looking for loves parties. I doubt she got an invite. But she'll find a way to be there."

"What's her name?" Tiller asked.

"Carnelian Silva."

"Quite a name."

"She lives up to it."

"How will I know it's her?"

"I'll point her out," said Colonel Istel. "She'll be the one that everyone stops to glare at."

# 3

IN HER DAILY LIFE, Tiller strove to appear as unobtrusive as possible. She wore relaxed clothing in neutral colors, and dark wigs that matched the hair of most others around her. She walked neither too fast nor too slow. She was an expert at matching the pace of a crowd.

Despite this, she had a lot of practice at dressing up for fancy events. Mostly fundraisers.

The Koya Foundation had received some grants from the government here and there. But the vast majority of the endowment came from private donors. There had been a time when Tiller did nothing but frantically help plan charity dinners, auctions, galas....

It was dark out by the time she arrived at the address the colonel had given her.

The mansion was in the city. But it stood on a generous plot of land, surrounded by an old-fashioned walled garden. The neighboring houses loomed equally large, though they had more modern silhouettes.

A placard by the gate marked the building as a historic site. Owned by the city government or a local society, Tiller guessed, and leased out for events.

Stiff-faced guards let her in. Nearly every other attendee wore military dress uniforms: mages and operators and laypeople alike.

The mages were easy to pick out, with their long multi-layered mantles and gloves and hoods.

Even in plainclothes, they would've been recognizable by the radioactive-looking glow of magic they each held deep in their torsos. An area that Tiller thought of as the pit of the stomach. Although in reality, magic cores were positioned closer to the small of the back.

Operators—those, like Tiller and Colonel Istel, with the ability to tame mages' willful magic—were harder to tell apart at a glance. The insignia on their uniforms depicted a snake. Or perhaps it was meant to be a dragon.

Either way, those who bore neither the light of magic nor the mark of the snake would have to be laypeople. Magically speaking, that is.

Statistically, most Jacians were born as laypeople. Neither mage nor operator. Most lived without the burden of magic. It might ease their lives in subtle ways, but they never felt its weight.

Refined chamber music wafted through rooms full of antique furniture. Glass mosaic tiles carpeted the ceiling, glittering with the unselfconscious gaudiness of ages past.

Vials of sunvine oil hung like teardrop earrings from fussy chandeliers. They tinkled in the way of wind chimes when too many people walked beneath.

Tiller sipped plum wine on the rocks and made light conversation. She let anyone who spoke to her assume that she was a civilian employee in the Outborder Corps. Some kind of administrator, perhaps.

No one here seemed drunk enough to attack her simply for being a forester. But why risk trouble when she could pass as one of them: a Jacian born on normal Jacian soil?

All she had to do was avoid mentioning her last name. *Koya* would instantly out her as a forester.

Certain family names tended to be very Forest-specific. Thanks to the Foundation's success, Koya was the most famous of them all.

Still, it was a relief to find Colonel Istel. Of all the attendees, he alone knew her full name and what lay beneath her pitch-black wig.

"Sorry," he told Tiller. "Nel—Carnelian always arrives late."

Tiller shrugged. Social tardiness wouldn't matter much once they were deep in the Forest.

"Mind if I ask a personal question?"

"I might mind," Tiller said, "but you can try asking."

"Are you easily swayed by a pretty face?"

"Is that relevant?"

"Yes," he said. "Very relevant. Some can't help but think the best of beautiful people."

"I never trust strangers," Tiller replied. "I'd be dead if I did. Beauty has nothing to do with it. Assassins can be charming and beautiful, too."

Colonel Istel studied her for a moment. "Perhaps you'll be fine, then."

This was not, happily, the sort of ball where people danced. Men and women gathered around small tables, engrossed in old strategy games.

Colonel Istel invited Tiller to play a round of cards. Having nothing better to do, she obliged. But she kept getting distracted by the scene across from them.

Uniformed Corps members clustered in a smoking room sealed off by a ceiling-high sheet of glass. Magic-tinged vapor rolled off the walls all around them. They paused to breathe it in, then blew it out through long slender pipes, shaping elaborate smoky sculptures in the hazy air.

It was rare to see Jacians permitted to exploit magic for solely recreational purposes. At least here in Nui, perhaps smoke sculpting was an old enough tradition to get a pass.

"Your turn," said Colonel Istel.

Tiller looked back down at the cards in her hand. She'd already forgotten the rules of the game.

Laughter cut through the muted voices around them.

For some reason, that brief laughter hit the floor like a bolt of lightning.

The harpsichord player and other musicians faltered, then valiantly regrouped themselves. Even the people in the smoke-sculpting room stopped to stare out through the glass wall.

Colonel Istel massaged his forehead and muttered something along the lines of: "Will she ever learn to keep her voice down?"

Tiller didn't need any help figuring out which one was Carnelian Silva.

She came through the entrance with her arms draped grandly around two amused-looking operators. For a few confused seconds, Tiller thought she must be extremely tall—but no, she just had that much more presence than anyone else in sight.

She wore the same gloves and elaborate mantle as other military mages. But she kept her hood off, and her mantle hung wide open. All she had on beneath was some sort of shiny leotard or bodysuit. One scarcely adequate to the task of keeping her covered. Courtesans dressed more modestly to hand out leaflets near the red light district.

"Is she an exhibitionist?" Tiller asked. She felt no qualms about looking. Everyone else seemed to stare twice as hard.

"Don't ask me," muttered the colonel. He glumly set down his cards.

On the other side of the room, Carnelian Silva demonstrated a trick that involved balancing a wineglass on her fingertip (no magic). More operators and laypeople drifted over to join her.

Not a single fellow mage set foot anywhere near her. They watched silently from beneath their hoods, glass stems pinched with tight fingers.

Meanwhile, she tilted her head back and held her arm up as high as it would go, pouring garnet wine in her own wide-open mouth like a sadistic sommelier. She didn't spill a single drop.

Well, no mystery about why the other mages seemed to hate her.

Common wisdom held that mages were wild party animals by nature. Volatile and needy. Weak against mind-altering substances. Easily influenced by crowds and cults. Ravenously lustful for all manner of stimulation.

None of this had ever rung true for Tiller. There had been no mages back in Koya Village, anyway. Every mage she'd met in Nui City had been very quiet and buttoned-up and by-the-book—all battling to disprove the ages-old stereotypes.

Carnelian Silva, in contrast, clearly cared not a whit for what anyone thought of her.

She twirled a long metal pipe like a baton. Despite its thinness, it must have been quite heavy. She tossed and caught it with a flourish. A few operators laughed and clapped.

"I've been practicing," Tiller heard her say breezily.

She swept off into the smoking room. The glass barrier parted like a curtain to admit her, then swooshed shut.

Suddenly, just inside the foggy glass, she stopped and turned.

Gnarled smoke sculptures lurked behind her. A miniature tree. Twisted serpents. With each passing second, they warped into increasingly unrealistic shapes.

Carnelian Silva looked steadily through the glass.

She looked straight at Tiller. Her face bore no tinge of either invitation or repulsion. It was indeed the sort of shockingly symmetrical face that might stop hearts dead or—on a passing whim—jolt them back to life.

Then she swiveled again, pipe in hand. Her long mantle swished through the ambient haze. She vanished into the back of the smoking room as if getting swallowed up by a snowstorm.

# 4

EVERYTHING COLONEL ISTEL told Tiller had come true. Despite her rowdy entrance, Carnelian Silva turned out to be annoyingly good at disappearing.

The next time Tiller lost sight of her, the colonel suggested keeping an eye on the chamber musicians.

She didn't understand why until she heard singing. A woman's voice, light and clear and resonant.

Tiller lacked the technical knowledge to judge whether this was a professional-caliber voice, but she instinctively liked it.

No. Not just that.

At home she didn't even own a melodium. She'd never bought tickets to a concert. Music had little presence in her life outside the Forest, and she'd never felt its lack.

Now, though—she stopped thinking. She listened. She forgot why she'd come here.

The lyrics held no meaning for her: they were bloody, jingoistic. The vocals were what transfixed her. Silvery and weightless, soft and full.

It sounded nothing like Carnelian Silva's speaking voice.

Tiller didn't make the connection until—tracing the gazes of everyone else who'd shut up to listen—she saw how Carnelian had infiltrated the ranks of the musicians.

She sang toward them, as if in an impromptu practice session. Not toward any would-be audience.

A lively audience gathered anyway, blocking Tiller's view. The music took on a jaunty tone. They'd switched to a folk tune praising the strength of spring wind.

Yet there came a time when the singing stopped, and the instrumentals continued alone.

Tiller stood on tiptoe. Carnelian was nowhere to be found.

Searching proved fruitless. Tiller almost wondered if she'd snuck out of the party altogether.

Eventually Colonel Istel advised her to look for Carnelian in the garden.

Outside it was chilly and oppressively quiet. A mild night, for late winter, but Tiller buttoned her coat up to her throat. The black sky held no moon or visible stars.

Strings of glowing sunvine beads had been tossed about the bushes. They offered just enough visibility to avoid breaking an ankle.

Some of the lights turned out to be winter fireflies. They rose and floated away to a safe distance as she passed.

These were a rare and lucky sight. This species of firefly—the one every Jacian knew—steered clear of the Forest. And there had always been fewer of them throughout all of Nui than on the other great islands. Especially here in the city.

A wooden chair hung from the bough of an old tree. Carnelian Silva was a motionless silhouette on one side of the swing. She faced away from the house, and from Tiller.

She tilted her head back before Tiller had a chance to greet her.

"You found me," she said.

Her voice didn't ring through the garden as her laughter had rung through the game room. It had little in common with her singing, either.

"Were you waiting for me?" Tiller asked. "Do you know me?"

"Alder mentioned you."

"Alder?"

"Alder Istel," Carnelian said. "The colonel."

Tiller had begun to shiver the moment she stopped walking. She hugged her coat around herself.

Carnelian didn't. Her mantle still fell open, exposing those long bare legs. Sunvine beads wound about the swing ropes and the branches above, too. Golden light glistened on the surface of her leotard.

"Aren't you cold?" Tiller asked.

"It won't kill me." Carnelian patted the seat beside her. The swing was sized for two. "Alder—Colonel Istel said you'd like to recruit me for a mission to the Forest. Sit down, why don't you? Let's talk it out."

"I'll stand," Tiller said.

"Don't be intimidated. I only bite on request."

"That branch looks like it might snap at any second."

"You're a forester, aren't you? Ask it if it's safe."

"I can't talk to trees," Tiller said flatly.

"I was being facetious."

"A lot of people believe it."

Tiller generally did her best not to associate with her neighbors. In the past, those who figured out she was a forester—usually after learning her last name—would flag her for help with anything they deemed remotely wild. They wanted her to keep rabbits out of their vegetables. To locate lost cats. To revive dying houseplants. To make crows and raccoon dogs stop attacking the garbage heap.

Back when Tiller had a personal bodyguard, her bodyguard would've put a firm stop to those sorts of requests. Nowadays she had to dodge them herself.

"Sorry," Carnelian said. "It was a poorly conceived joke. I know foresters don't have that sort of special connection with nature. No more so than anyone else."

Tiller nodded. "Not outside the Forest, anyhow."

By now her eyes had adjusted to the candle-soft illumination of all those decorative sunvine beads. She moved in front of Carnelian, facing her, in lieu of joining her on the swing.

Carnelian had rumpled feathery hair, the ends just brushing her shoulders. The sort of cut that looked casual at a glance, but in reality was probably quite complicated.

It was a wolfish silver-gray. Slightly darker at the roots. One of the most difficult colors to achieve and maintain with dye. Tiller assumed it was dyed, anyway. Like the colonel, Carnelian seemed near Tiller's age. Somewhere around thirty. A bit young to have gone naturally gray.

This was not a woman of cheap tastes. She wore the same brand of watch as the Koya Foundation's richest donors. Even her strapless leotard, with its cheap gaudy shine, appeared on closer inspection to be cleverly tailored to her form. Not the sort of thing you could buy off the shelf.

A low-ranking military mage wouldn't take home much of a paycheck.

According to Colonel Istel, she wasn't even a full-fledged member of the Outborder Corps. She acted more like an understudy. A stand-in who only joined the most dangerous missions, the ones that every other mage sought to avoid.

Where did Carnelian Silva get her money?

Then again, what did it matter? Tiller didn't care if Carnelian Silva had won the lottery or inherited a family fortune or taken bribes or worked sketchy side jobs for the mafia.

She only cared about two things.

One: would Carnelian Silva—like so many others—attempt to kill her?

Two: and if not, would Carnelian Silva help her carry Baba Sayo's remains all the way to the heart of the Forest?

Tiller blew into her fingers to warm them.

"Nice wig," Carnelian said.

Tiller stilled, hands clasped by her mouth. Carnelian crossed her legs and leaned back in the weathered swing chair.

"Most people don't notice. Or if they do," Tiller amended, "they're too polite to mention it."

"No one's ever accused me of being overly polite," said Carnelian. "But I'm sure you're right. Most people can't tell. I only see it because there was a time when I got really fascinated by analog makeup and wigs and such."

"Analog?"

"Non-magical."

"Seems redundant," Tiller said. "Cosmetic magic is all illegal."

The government wouldn't let precious magical resources get diverted to frivolous uses.

Carnelian laughed, low and short. It couldn't have been more different from how she'd laughed inside the party. "Surely you've seen that the law is more porous for some people than for others."

On that note, Tiller had been surprised to find her out here alone. Not a single operator nearby to keep an eye on her.

Looking around the garden, though, she realized that subtle magic surrounded the entire estate in a framework like a birdcage. She hadn't noticed it when the guards first ushered her in. Or perhaps it hadn't been activated till later.

Now, wiry lines of shadow-dark magic criss-crossed the sky high over the roof, and formed a lattice around the garden walls. Easy to miss unless you knew what to look for. A barricade to spare neighbors from the noise of the festivities.

And, perhaps more importantly, to prevent unattached mages from wandering out of the venue on their own.

"So," Carnelian said. "What's beneath your wig?"

"That has nothing to do with whether we go to the Forest together."

"Doesn't it?" Carnelian tilted her head. She wore the smile of someone who was used to getting their way.

"What did the colonel tell you about me?" Tiller asked slowly.

"Want me to guess your real hair color?"

"No."

Tiller took a step back from the swing. The ground was treacherous with tree roots.

Carnelian rose to her feet, unhurried. Again she momentarily seemed very tall. In truth, even her heels didn't give her much of an advantage over Tiller.

The wooden swing rocked gently behind her, making a creaking so soft that Tiller thought she might've imagined it.

Carnelian extended a gloved hand, reaching for Tiller's hair. For her wig.

"Stop," Tiller said.

The hand retreated.

"I'll be risking my life if I join you on your quest for—whatever it is you seek in the Forest," Carnelian said. "Isn't it only fair for me to know who I'm following?"

Tiller, meanwhile, would risk her life simply by attempting to exist as her true self in public.

No law compelled her to keep secrets. She could remove her wig and walk the city streets without shame. She'd done it before, many years ago. No one would stop her if she did it today.

No one would come save her, either. Her bodyguard had already died for her.

"Don't even think about trying to yank my wig off," Tiller said. She watched Carnelian's fingers. "If you know anything about good wigs, you'll know that there's glue involved. It'll get ugly."

Carnelian didn't appear to be listening. Her gaze slid to the shadows beyond the garden wall.

For all the apparent wealth of the neighborhood, it lacked proper street lamps. Each household seemed to have assumed responsibility for their own outdoor lighting. Some was blindingly harsh, and some virtually nonexistent. The gulf between properties became a river of darkness.

"Is someone following you?" Carnelian asked.

Tiller whirled.

She saw neither movement nor magic. Her heart beat high in her throat.

"You're paranoid," Carnelian said softly, "but perhaps not paranoid enough."

Something tapped Tiller on the shoulder. She looked back.

Carnelian held her long metal pipe. She'd drawn it from a loop sewn to her mantle. It had been hanging there all this time like a sword hooked to a belt. Muted sunvine light crept into the crevices of its obscure silver etchings.

"A fine thing, isn't it?" said Carnelian. "Military-issue equipment. Not just for carving smoke sculptures."

"You use it to brain people?"

"Only as a last resort. But I could most certainly have brained you in the back of the head just now. You left yourself wide open."

"No, I didn't," Tiller said. No need to admit weakness.

Anyway, no would-be attacker would turn on her right outside a house filled with seasoned members of the Outborder Corps.

"How would you like to be paid?" Tiller asked, gathering herself.

"To be honest, I don't need your money. I can take it or leave it."

"Never heard a soldier say that before," Tiller retorted. "You aren't even an officer."

Carnelian turned the slim pipe in her fingers. Then she tossed it high in the air. It cartwheeled magnificently before landing with a solid smack in her waiting palm.

She hung the pipe from her mantle again. Her gray hair looked golden from all the sunvine beads littering the gloomy tree overhead. "Won't you ask me what I want instead?"

"Just tell me, then."

"I'll go with you anywhere if you do me one favor."

Carnelian looked her in the eye. Tiller, taking it as a challenge, looked back without blinking.

The wooden swing creaked dolefully, even though the air hadn't moved a millimeter.

Carnelian's expression remained deathly serious.

"Marry me," she said.

# 5

THE ONLY THING Tiller understood was that Carnelian hadn't been joking. Rather than debate her out in the garden, Tiller decided to appeal to a higher authority.

Carnelian followed her inside, unbothered. Tiller located Colonel Istel. She started to explain what Carnelian had sought as payment.

He blanched and promptly dragged both of them into a roped-off part of the basement.

The door closed heavily behind Carnelian, the last to drift through. It was almost as cold here as in the nighttime garden. Tiller began to regret hanging her coat up.

On the way down to the basement, Carnelian had somehow managed to acquire multiple drinks. As well as several lipstick smudges on her right cheek.

Colonel Istel wheeled on her, incandescent with rage. "You *proposed*? Lord, I should've known you were up to something."

Carnelian threw an arm around Tiller's shoulders. "It was love at first sight."

Tiller shrugged her off. Colonel Istel looked ready to pop a vein. "All you love is making trouble!"

"What are you," Carnelian said, "my father? My big brother?"

As the two of them bickered, Carnelian appeared to play a private drinking game. She took a swig whenever Istel's yelling got emphatic enough to make him spit. She was quite adept at dodging.

Tiller backed up to the wall and waited for them to exhaust themselves. This had the added bonus of keeping her outside the range of Istel's spray.

Foresters were keenly aware of how much the Jacian family registry system could impact one's life. When they dwelt in the Forest, none of them had been officially registered.

One of the greatest struggles of migrating had been convincing the local government to set up a brand new register for each village family. It had proven particularly difficult for Baba Sayo and Tiller and Doe—Tiller's bodyguard at the time, and her surrogate big sister. None of them were blood relatives.

Family was perhaps even more important for mages.

The burden of magic was far too dangerous to be borne all alone. In past times, the government would've confiscated young mages and deposited them in properly equipped facilities.

Nowadays, magical children didn't get automatically taken away. But parents who didn't feel up to the task of nurturing a mage still had the option of surrendering them to the state.

This bore no lasting stigma. It was noble and admirable to think yourself capable of raising a mage. But most people couldn't take it. Even with significant financial support from the government.

Until mages came of age, their parents (not to mention other relatives on the family register) would remain fully liable for any harm they might cause. With or without magic.

That all would change when a mage turned sixteen. Even if their family had initially chosen to keep them. Sixteen was the age at which the state would assume liability for them as burgeoning adults. They would be purged from the family register, their parents released of all responsibility.

Solo mages—unattached to any family register—had their lives tightly controlled by the state. Where they worked, where they lived—the state decided it all. But if they ever caused a magical accident, if they ever snapped and went berserk, only the state would take blame for it.

Carnelian, presumably, was one such unattached mage. Which meant she had only one path for earning greater personal freedom: bonding or marrying her way into a non-mage's family register. Her partner (along with the rest of their family) would then become wholly responsible for her. A lifelong guarantor.

Bonded and married mages had so many more options open to them than the unattached. They still had to apply for approval, but they could take on nonmagical types of work. They could choose not to work at all. They could travel freely, following their spouse or bondmate to any of the other islands in Jace.

It wasn't hard to imagine why Carnelian might be eager to marry someone. Anyone.

It also wasn't hard to imagine why she hadn't yet found any takers. This woman was the riskiest-seeming mage Tiller had ever seen in her life. And she couldn't be bothered to make the slightest attempt to disguise it.

Carnelian and Istel's sniping had begun to get repetitive. Tiller reached back and rapped her knuckles on the wall. It resounded like a gong, much louder than she'd intended.

The voices ceased.

"What is this place, anyway?" Tiller asked, hoping to distract them. "A root cellar? A boiler room?"

There was a staleness to the air, but it didn't have much of a smell.

"This is an old house," Carnelian answered. "Isn't it? Historic. Meticulously preserved."

Glass in hand, she gestured behind Tiller. "It's got to be a mage pantry. Every grand manor would have one. See those coffin-shaped slots? They used to stash sleeping mages there, back in the day."

Tiller's Forest-centric upbringing had left her clueless about a great deal of general Jacian history. But even she was familiar with the concept of a mage pantry.

She eyed the sunken portions of the wall. They did look just about the right size to store a malnourished adult body. Jacian society used to control mages far more severely in the past.

She turned to Colonel Istel, who had pulled out his military field scarf. It was printed with a brilliant rendition of the Jacian islands, all green and gold and blue. He dabbed sheepishly at the corners of his mouth.

"Carnelian Silva guessed what I am," Tiller said. "Very quickly. She knew I was wearing a wig. Did you tell her?"

He looked uncomfortable. "No. I swear not."

"You're sweating."

"Because she's an enormous pain in the ass, that's why!"

"Well, I never," tutted Carnelian.

"I only mentioned you being a forester," he said to Tiller. "She made a lucky guess."

"Not a guess," Carnelian corrected. "Simple deduction. You told me she came from Koya Village. I already knew that Koya Village was where the last living—"

Tiller broke in. "Don't say it here."

Carnelian spread her hands. It was a miracle that she hadn't spilled any drinks yet. "Whatever you want. So—will you marry me? I promise I'll be a spectacular magewife."

"It isn't entirely up to me," Tiller said.

"Don't equivocate."

"Even if I were fully on board, we'd need approval from the government."

"You've survived the Forest, and you've survived society." She pointed at Tiller's wig. "You're an endangered species, in a manner of speaking. I think the government would be willing to throw you a bone."

"The screening process can last for months or years. I've heard stories."

"You don't have that kind of time," Colonel Istel cut in. "In fact—"

"That doesn't sound good," Carnelian commented.

He glowered. "Let me finish. It was just decided this evening. Sixty days from now, Central will send out multiple war chalices. Their mission: scourge the Forest back to its original boundaries."

Tiller felt as if she were underwater. "What?"

"You'd better aim to get in and out of there before then. For your own safety. Everyone will celebrate if you find out how to prevent the Forest from spreading all over again. But it's already spread much too far."

The mage pantry had no windows. A few sickly blue water-lights drooped from the ceiling, globules like fruit rotting on the vine.

Tiller imagined chalices hovering over the Forest. Those insatiable Jacian machines of war. Oozing hungry magic.

No pilot ever flew a chalice more than once. Their maiden flight marked their retirement. To enter the cockpit of a chalice was to accept a death sentence. For a few minutes or hours, you would wield unimaginable power. And then the great machina would grind you up and swallow you whole. Time for the next pilot in line to take over.

Chalices might be able to erase the parts of the Forest that kept slouching closer and closer to Nui City, annexing rural fields and towns and reservoirs and resorts.

But what would they leave behind? And what would happen next? What if the Forest came back with a vengeance? How many more pilots would Central sacrifice to hold it at bay?

"I used to dream of being a chalice pilot," Carnelian murmured.

"What?" Tiller said again, as if she'd forgotten how to use other words.

"I applied over and over," Carnelian said pensively. "Thought I'd be perfect for it. They always rejected me."

Istel scoffed. "The Bureau of Mage Management won't let you throw your life away on a whim."

"They keep letting me join operations in the Forest. Even this time—"

"You know that's different." His impatience was audible. "In the Forest, you always have a chance of coming back alive. It might be slim, but there's a chance. No one ever emerges alive from a chalice."

He looked at Tiller. "I can't say I endorse marrying her."

"Hey!" Carnelian cried.

"Also, this sounds like a textbook case of marriage fraud."

"No fear," said Carnelian. "We'll nurture our love in the Forest."

Istel spoke to Tiller instead. "If you apply to get licensed for marriage, you'll need testimonials. When the time comes, good luck with convincing me that you care for one another as more than a meal ticket."

He paused before hauling open the heavy door.

"Look," he said. "You'll need special training if you're going to act as Nel—as Carnelian's operator. You aren't at all prepared to deal with her magic."

He jerked his head at Carnelian. "Show her once I'm gone."

# 6

The sound of the door banging shut echoed between them.

For a room called a pantry, it felt barren. But better to see it empty than stuffed with comatose mage bodies, as in older times.

"Nel," Tiller said. "The colonel's name for you?"

"Nellie," Carnelian pronounced. "You can call me that, too, if you like. I love nicknames. Any thoughts on Tillie?"

"I refuse."

"It'd be so cute. We'd match."

"No, thank you," Tiller said.

"Ah, well. We've got the rest of our lives to get used to it."

"That'd more convincing if we'd met more than an hour ago."

"It was love at first—"

Tiller tapped the side of her face. "And if you didn't have another woman's lipstick all over your cheek."

"You don't kiss your friends on the cheek? How sad." Carnelian rubbed at the problem spot with gloved fingertips. It made her look vaguely bruised. "I have no idea how this got here."

"Doesn't sound like it was from a friend, then."

"What can I say? I know a lot of people. Too many to keep track of them all, honestly. It's hard being popular."

Tiller exhaled. The noise of it grated on her ears.

It felt eerie not to hear any hint of footsteps or chamber music leaking from the party above. The mage pantry must've been almost entirely soundproof.

"Silva," she said.

"Call me Carnelian."

"What are you trying to achieve by getting married?"

Carnelian tossed back the dregs of her last remaining drink, then set the glass on the floor. "What do you mean?"

"What do you want to do with greater freedom?" Tiller asked.

"I'll think about that when I get it," she said. "Haven't you ever wanted something for the sake of having it?"

"If we get married, you'll still be tied to me."

Carnelian grinned. "I'd rather be tied to you than the state."

"In other words, any living human would do. As long as they could obtain permission for marriage."

"Yes. More or less." Carnelian cocked her head. "Don't take it as an insult."

"I don't know you well enough to take offense," Tiller admitted. "What did the colonel want you to show me?"

"Look at my magic core," Carnelian said.

Tiller looked.

The light gathered low in her torso appeared strangely diffuse. Blurred, as though seen through a defective pair of binoculars.

Tiller's magic perception was distinctly average. She couldn't tell why

Carnelian watched her with such an air of expectation. The fogginess of Carnelian's core did seem strange, sure. But wasn't it normal for magic cores to vary in size and shape from mage to mage? Just like how no two human bodies would ever end up being exactly the same. Not even identical twins.

She gave up. "I'm looking," she said. "What about it?"

Carnelian took a step closer. Then another step.

If Tiller backed up any further, she'd entomb herself in one of the wall-slots once meant to hold insensate mages.

"How much experience do you have as an operator?" Carnelian asked. "How many mages' magic have you touched?"

"That's—none of your business."

"It will be," Carnelian said, "if we're forced to fight for our lives in the Forest."

"Maybe you should've thought things through a little longer before proposing to marry me."

Carnelian shook her head. "Neither of us has any other choice," she said gently. "I'm the only mage the Corps would consider assigning to join you. I'm certainly the only willing volunteer."

"And you've never managed to persuade anyone else to take you as their magewife."

Carnelian wagged a finger at her. "Yes, that. You get it."

Tiller edged sideways to open up a little more breathing room between them. "So why me?"

"Because I have leverage," Carnelian said. "You need me."

Unfortunately, this was true.

The Forest had changed tremendously since Tiller grew up there. Nowadays even long-time foresters considered it uninhabitable.

And she couldn't get away with creeping up to the very edge of the Forest and tossing Baba Sayo's remains over the border.

She had to bring Baba Sayo all the way to the sacred mountains. An area that even foresters had mostly avoided, back in the day. They'd ascended the mountains only to offer up their beloved dead, or for rare special occasions. Ritual self-sacrifice. Seasonal fire festivals. Pilgrimages to mark some rite of passage.

To weather the hazards of the Forest and reach the mountains at its heart, she needed a mage.

If Carnelian Silva was her only viable option, then she needed Carnelian.

The water-lights that sagged down from the ceiling had started trembling, palpitating under the pressure of unheard vibrations.

Tiller forced herself to meet Carnelian's gaze.

"I can make a good-faith effort to marry you after we leave the Forest," Tiller said. "If that's really your only request. But I don't want to be bonded."

"Then we're perfect for each other," Carnelian said immediately. "There's a reason I only brought up marriage. Not bonding."

"Most real couples do both. If they can."

"We're not a real couple, are we? Me, I just want to get married on paper. For legal reasons. You know how it is. If you're worried about being magically tied to someone for the rest of your life—well, you've got nothing to worry about from me."

Mage-operator bonding required mutual consent. Unlike a marriage, it was also impossible to end early. A bond would last until you or your bondmate died—whichever came first.

Marital spouses didn't need to be magically bonded. Bondmates didn't need to be legally married. But combining the two would give a magewife much greater security in their place on the family register. You could divorce a spouse and still be stuck as lifelong bondmates.

Tiller had her own reasons for not wanting to bond any mage, ever.

On the other hand, she couldn't see why Carnelian Silva wouldn't seek out that extra insurance.

When Tiller questioned this, Carnelian reached down and patted her shimmery leotard. One hand on the small of her back. The other on her lower abdomen.

"I'm a defective mage," she said simply. "I'm incapable of bonding anyone. But I have to take this off to show you."

"Take what off?"

Carnelian patted her leotard again.

Tiller hastily turned around. "Make it quick," she said.

"Do you avert your eyes when you go to a bathhouse?" Carnelian sounded amused.

"I don't go to public baths. We didn't have them back in the Forest."

"Your loss. But surely you went swimming in rivers and such."

"Maybe we saw each other naked sometimes," Tiller said, "but in the village, we were family. We'd known each other all our lives."

"We won't be strangers once we're wed. We'll be family, too."

Responding only seemed to encourage her. Tiller said nothing further.

That glittering bodysuit must've been what smeared her perception of Carnelian's core. Some Jacian technology was extremely effective at camouflaging magic. Tiller didn't know much about the exact mechanism.

A zipper came undone. The sound of it vibrated off the plain concrete walls of the mage pantry.

Carnelian had long since finished her drinks, but a stagnant scent of alcohol continued to permeate the unmoving air.

Tiller stared into the empty holes carved out for mages.

How old was this building? A century? Two centuries?

There would have been a time when mages got packed down here like kindling. There would have been people—the vast majority of the population—who figured that as long as the buried mages remained unconscious, using them as a magical fuel source wouldn't cause any quantifiable suffering.

Tiller had left the Forest when she was around ten. At thirty, she'd now spent over twice as much time living outside the Forest as she'd spent growing up inside it.

Many aspects of Jace still seemed culturally odd to her, all the same. The pride they took in their long, convoluted, and bloody history. Their worship of pilot-consuming chalices.

By now she was used to it, but that didn't mean she fully understood.

What could be so bizarre about Carnelian's magic, anyhow? She clearly didn't mind being the center of attention. What made her magic core and branches so abnormal that she felt compelled to disguise them?

Every mage had a core: a metaphysical concentration of magic located in a spot near their lower back.

All that changed from mage to mage was the number of branches that extended tentacle-like from their core. Each branch could be assigned a different magic skill. The more branches a mage possessed, the more versatile it made them.

Of course, mages also differed in how adept they were or weren't at manipulating their branches: learning and executing particular magic skills, or snipping off magic cuttings to be shipped away for implementation elsewhere.

"I'm guessing you've only had rudimentary training as an operator," Carnelian said from behind, her tone conversational.

"Right." Denying this would only cause greater difficulties down the line.

"Istel must've caught on, too. He seemed concerned by your total lack of reaction to my magic. Even when veiled, it doesn't look entirely normal."

Most Jacian operators made a career out of managing mages. The government strongly encouraged this, sometimes to the point of requiring mandatory periods of service.

In fact, all of society had a vested interest in maintaining the operator talent pipeline. They were vital to preventing mages from going feral.

But Tiller, together with scores of other refugees, had come from the Forest. She'd gotten a hardship exemption. She'd devoted herself entirely to the Koya Foundation. Which was all that kept many former Koya villagers from starving.

No. She hadn't laid hands on any mage's magic in years.

"I learn fast," she said.

"The top operators in the Outborder Corps struggle to make sense of my magic," Carnelian replied. "Colonel Istel included."

Her voice brightened. "Turn back around, now. I won't flash you."

Tiller peeked gingerly over her shoulder. The leotard lay crumpled at Carnelian's feet. In exchange, she'd drawn her mantle shut around her like a robe. The small room felt unpleasantly clammy.

Magic—no longer muted—shone from Carnelian's torso. It shone straight through the dark fabric of her mantle.

She didn't have one single core, like every other mage in the world.

She had—

Tiller almost forgot how to count.

One, two, three, four....

She had nine cores crammed in her body.

Each with a different number of branches jutting out of it, in the way of veins and arteries extending from a human heart. Too many total branches to count at a glance. More than twenty? Less than fifty?

Mages could be born with that many branches. It wasn't impossible, though most mages had only a couple at most.

But no mage was ever born with more than one core.

"How?" Tiller said dumbly.

"How indeed."

"You—"

"I'll tell you the full story if we get engaged. Maybe around the same time you tell me why you wear wigs."

Carnelian paused politely. "Or has this sight turned your appetite? Don't want damaged goods?"

"I didn't say that."

"Right," Carnelian agreed. "You can't afford to be picky."

She held her mantle demurely closed as she stooped to retrieve her leotard.

"So what do you say?" she asked. "Do we have a deal? I've always dreamed of becoming a loving magewife."

"I thought you wanted to be a chalice pilot."

"A person can have more than one dream, you know."

Tiller took a deeper breath.

It felt very surreal to be holding a conversation with a nine-core mage. As surreal as it might feel to converse with a person who'd grown nine heads.

The feeble water-lights dribbled a spectral blue glow down across Carnelian's otherwise colorless shag of hair, her heart-shaped face, the smug dimples skulking by the corners of her mouth.

She peeped up at Tiller through her lashes, hands toying with her leotard as if to emphasize the fact that she wasn't currently wearing it.

"I'll marry you if we survive the Forest," Tiller said heavily. "Don't hold me responsible if you end up regretting it."

This was her only chance to bring Baba Sayo home. Carnelian Silva seemed full of complications. But no matter what it might mean for her future, she couldn't afford not to pay Carnelian's price.

# 7

After the Corps party, Tiller came home to Baba Sayo's apartment. In the first few weeks after Baba Sayo died, she could hardly bear to set foot there. Nor could she bring herself to get rid of it.

Eventually she broke the lease on her own apartment. She moved in together with Baba Sayo's lingering scent.

It wasn't the first time she'd experienced such an all-consuming grief. Yet it would surely be the last. She had no one left to lose now.

She would mourn the other elderly Koya villagers as they passed one by one, but not like this. Never again like this.

She went through her usual routine after getting back. She locked the door behind her. She checked each room for signs of intrusion.

She remained on high alert throughout. But she kept remembering the sound of Carnelian singing, sliding nimbly from low notes to lighter notes, free and ethereal. It took far too long to scrub that voice from her head.

Once she finally felt ready to relax, she swept back her black wig. She applied adhesive remover all around her hairline. The lacy edges of the wig began to release from her scalp.

Beneath it she'd been wearing a disposable wig cap, which she pulled off and tossed in a bin. Afterward she took her time cleansing excess glue residue from her skin, as well as from the perimeter of the wig itself.

Her now-freed hair was longer than she would've liked. Long enough to tickle her face if she didn't clip it out of the way. But it had a habit of growing back faster the more she cut it. This length worked as a reluctant compromise.

From root to tip, Tiller's natural hair was the rich blue of a midsummer sky.

Dye it black in the morning, and all the dye would drip out of her hair and down onto her shoulders by noon. Shave her head in the morning, and it'd sprout back shaggier by the end of the day.

She'd experimented with countless hair-bleaching chemicals. She'd covered her head with wimples, hats, and all kinds of wigs.

The problem was not the hue of her hair. Plenty of city-dwellers dyed their hair interesting colors. The problem was what it meant.

Most people barely knew what a blue was. Most people thought they'd gone extinct ages ago, or had never existed at all. They lumped blues together with dragons and elves: creatures which might once have existed in some form, which had inspired plenty of folklore, but which no sensible modern citizen would think of as *real*.

Some, however, knew that blues were real people—human beings like any other. Extremely rare, and born at random in the Forest.

Some knew the old stories. For example: mages who sacrificed a blue would gain unfathomable power. Operators who sacrificed a blue would gain a magic core of their own, thereby becoming a perfect complete being, capable of both using magic and fully controlling themselves without the need for any outside assistance.

Rumors. Fairy tales. Tiller believed none of it.

Hunters came for her anyway. Nowhere in Nui City was safe once people found out that you were the last living blue.

Which was why Tiller could count on one hand the number of times she'd brought a stranger home. But a scant few days later, she found herself letting Carnelian Silva into Baba Sayo's apartment.

"Didn't think you'd be wearing a wig in your own home," said Carnelian.

"We'll be going outside soon enough."

Tiller went to the kitchenette to finish making tea: brown-roasted corn steeped in boiling water. A simple Forest village drink. She could hear Carnelian humming from the room beyond.

She made Carnelian sit at a small scarwood table. The mugs she set out bore a shaky pattern of Forest leaves, painted by Baba Sayo in some kind of arts-and-crafts class for seniors.

Carnelian had shown up in a sweater dress and over-the-knee boots. Other than that, she still bore the accoutrements of a magc affiliated with the Outborder Corps. The long hooded mantle. The finely fitted gloves.

"I was wondering if you'd be in a leotard again," Tiller remarked.

"Would you have preferred that?"

Tiller declined to answer.

Carnelian's multiple magic cores once again appeared to have merged into a single vague blur. An illusion wrought by something she wore. Perhaps she had a corset or girdle designed to disguise her magic in the same way as the leotard from the other night.

Tiller, clad in another one of her neat black wigs, felt an odd sense of kinship.

Carnelian looked avidly around the apartment as she drank her tea. "Would've thought you had plainer taste."

"My grandmother picked the decor."

"Does she live with you?"

"She's gone."

"Sorry to hear that."

"I moved in afterward. Didn't feel like changing anything."

Baba Sayo had gone a bit wild with textiles after leaving the Forest. She'd loved the vibrant dyed prints that got shipped up to Nui from the southernmost islands. Clashing patterns had been the least of her worries.

Perhaps out of necessity, she'd come to love all kinds of things that hadn't been readily available back in Koya Village. Vintage paper stamps. Fancy metal buttons. Traditional Jacian music boxes. Porcelain statuettes.

"It's an interesting mix," Carnelian said, with more tact than Tiller would've expected.

"For the record," Tiller told her, "you're almost an hour late."

Carnelian yawned. "Sorry. Guess we need to rush."

"Not at all. I told you to come much earlier than necessary."

"You tricked me!"

"You showed up late to the Corps event."

"That's just one data point."

"You showed up late today, too," Tiller said. "I was right to hedge my bets."

Carnelian scowled. "I hate waking up early."

"It's past ten in the morning." Tiller set down her mug. "So we have plenty of time."

"To do what?" Carnelian leaned forward, elbows on the table, suddenly bright-eyed. "Oh, I see. Is this your way of putting the moves on me?"

"No," Tiller said firmly.

Fifty-eight days remained before military chalices would be unleashed to bombard the Forest—killing numerous pilots in the process.

But Colonel Istel wouldn't authorize them to leave until Tiller went through at least two weeks of intensive training with an expert operator. In the afternoon today, Carnelian was supposed to take Tiller to meet her designated tutor.

Before then—

Tiller looked up from her drink. Carnelian was gone from her seat. With the nonchalance of a master snooper, she'd flitted all the way over to the small Forest-style shrine set up in an inconspicuous corner.

"Is this for your grandmother?" Carnelian asked. "If I'm to be your wife, I'd better pay my respects."

Tiller inhaled steam from her cup before answering. "My grandmother didn't want a household shrine," she said. "No grave, either. All she wanted was to be cremated immediately."

"Right—foresters dislike decay. Understandable," Carnelian said. "So do I."

"Not many people love decay, do they?"

"True. And yet they let expired food rot in dumpsters." Carnelian shuddered. "I much prefer forester standards of cleanliness. Who's the shrine for?"

"Two people. My twin brother. And my bodyguard."

"They both—?"

"Not at the same time. But yes. They're both dead. It all happened years ago."

"Was your brother a blue, too?" Carnelian asked.

"Why do you think he got killed?" Tiller said.

She was the only person left alive on her family register. Her twin brother Gren never got recorded there in the first place.

He never made it out of the Forest.

Tiller and Gren had looked close to identical when they were really little. But differences soon emerged.

She'd bet anything that a living Gren would've grown up taller and better-looking than her. Maybe taller and better-looking than their bodyguard Doe. Or Carnelian here, with her soulful gray eyes and saintly face.

Sometimes she'd convinced herself that Doe and Baba Sayo wished they'd gotten stuck raising Gren in the city instead. Gren had been a quick reader, a precocious student of every topic that caught his interest, a disciplined and organized thinker, and more patient than Tiller deserved.

Two decades later, to think of Gren was to hold her hands over the pale coals of a dormant fire. Even without visible flames, grief remained hot enough to make the air buckle. It might sear her, it might melt and fuse her skin, but she would die in the cold of her brother's absence without it.

"I called you here," she said to Carnelian, "to share something private."

Carnelian straightened up and turned away from the shrine. She didn't say anything flippant.

"It would be nice if I could find a way to stop the Forest from spreading," Tiller continued. "But that isn't my only reason for wanting to walk all the way to the sacred mountains."

Carnelian appeared unsurprised. "I figured there was something more to it."

"Why?"

"If you had a hunch about how to make the Forest stop overflowing, why would you wait so long to try to help?"

"I had responsibilities in the city," Tiller said stiffly. "Forest refugees to take care off. A nonprofit to run. I had to get my affairs in order. Isn't that explanation enough?"

She couldn't parse Carnelian's expression.

"Do you think Colonel Istel suspects my motives?" she asked.

"He's no idiot," Carnelian replied. "Don't give him any reasons to dig deeper."

"This needs to stay between us," Tiller said.

"Consider me sworn to secrecy."

She told Carnelian of her plan to bring Baba Sayo's ashes to the sacred mountains at the heart of the Forest. She'd bring Doe's ashes, too.

No matter how guilt ate at her, she wouldn't divulge this to any of the other ex-villagers. She couldn't guarantee success. And anyway, she couldn't carry the remains of every single forester who'd ever died outside Forest borders.

That must be why Baba Sayo hadn't put it in the final version of her will. She'd have known that Tiller would stop at nothing to grant her wishes. She'd have wondered: why me? Why should I be the only stranded forester to get my heart's desire?

If they could speak again, Tiller would tell Baba Sayo: because I say so. She would be selfish for her grandmother, who had never been selfish in life.

Together with Doe, the two of them had worked day and night to get the Koya Foundation up and running. To establish group homes for Koya villagers with nowhere else to go. To distribute modest pensions to elderly foresters who wouldn't qualify for benefits from the Jacian government.

Nowadays, the Foundation could run itself even if Tiller spent a few weeks away from Nui City.

Not that she'd ever taken any vacation time before. It simply hadn't occurred to her. She'd never had a reason to stop and rest. Until the very last of them died out, there would always be more foresters in need.

# 8

CARNELIAN'S REACTION: "Sounds like as good a reason as any."

Tiller collected their empty mugs. "I'll be asking you to risk your life in the Forest. Didn't want to lie about why."

"That's what I like about you," Carnelian said opaquely. "No worries. I feel thoroughly informed."

Colonel Istel had been oddly secretive about the operator he'd asked to give Tiller a crash course in mage maintenance. The only information she'd received was the time of her first appointment. And the fact that Carnelian would take her there.

They entered one of the vast pedestrian bypass tunnels that criss-crossed below the city: echoing spaces deformed by magic, where a single step could in effect transport you an eighth of a mile.

Even many lifelong city folk suffered a sort of queasy pressurized motion sickness down in the bypass tunnels. The public bathrooms linked to the tunnel walls came with delicately labeled vomit troughs.

Still, the convenience was hard to beat. Tiller swore to herself that this time she would make it in and out without incident.

They only had to walk underground for less than a minute. They emerged in a commercial district, one with buildings standing tall enough to block sunlight from the streets. Decorative trees and flowers grew from enormous pots installed along the sidewalk.

Tiller had assumed Carnelian would bring her to one of the city's military garrisons. Or an office occupied by the Bureau of Mage Management. Or some other specialized operator training facility.

Instead Carnelian led her to a high-end hotel.

The lobby was heavily guarded, and as curiously quiet as a house of worship. Watchdogs the size of ponies sat like bronze statues on grand pedestals. Tiller only knew they were alive because they blinked.

Carnelian leaned on the counter and whispered to the concierge.

Tiller waited by the fountain at the center of the lobby, which made almost zero noise despite its thirty-foot plumes. A marble woman with enormous antlers struck a triumphant pose amidst transparent curtains of water. She brandished two swords, standing victorious atop an extravagant pile of intricately carved enemy soldiers.

The hotel staff checked this and that. Carnelian presented them with her military ID, plus a sheaf of paper covered in vermilion and indigo stamps. Tiller had to collect similar seals of approval whenever she prepared documents for the city government.

At last a guard ushered them to a magically concealed elevator at the opposite end of the lobby.

"Do you know this person we're supposed to be meeting?" Tiller asked Carnelian once they were alone again.

"Not well," said Carnelian. "Only met her about a month ago."

"What's she like?"

"The best operator I've ever encountered. No contest. But—"

"But what?"

"I can't imagine her making a very good teacher."

The elevator slid open. After passing several sticky veils of security magic, and knocking to be let in through double doors, they found themselves in a penthouse suite with floor-to-ceiling windows.

The woman who had admitted them was startlingly short. Around the same size as Baba Sayo. Although she was clearly much younger. Maybe somewhere in her mid-thirties. Her oversized sweatshirt completely swallowed her hands.

"You again," she said to Carnelian.

She spoke with a mud-thick foreign accent.

Tiller stopped dead in her tracks.

As a forester, she'd always felt like something of a foreigner. But the Forest was nevertheless located on one of the Jacian islands, and the nation considered her a native-born Jacian. No question about it.

As far as she knew, Jacian borders had been closed all her life—and had in fact been officially closed for far, far longer than that.

She'd never heard of anyone who'd met a real live foreigner. She'd certainly never met one herself.

"Yeah, yeah," Carnelian said to the little foreign woman. As if there were nothing unusual about having a rendezvous with a potentially illicit visitor from the continent. On the top floor of a luxury hotel, no less. "Me again. Your favorite patient. I brought you the lady Colonel Istel was talking about."

"Who?" asked the foreigner.

"Istel," Carnelian enunciated. "Alder Istel. The colonel." She pointed at Tiller. "He told you about her. Didn't he?"

The foreigner stared up at Tiller. Her hair was a mixture of stark black and white streaks. Perhaps even more distinctive: the large patch over her right eye socket. The pale fabric had a stylized eye hand-drawn on it in thick brown marker, complete with stubby lashes and a curving aristocratic brow.

"You know any Continental?" she asked Tiller, still in Jacian.

Tiller shook her head. She spoke the forester dialect and standard Jacian. Neither of those had anything in common with the Continental language.

The foreigner groaned.

Still, their self-introductions went more or less smoothly. With a few inevitable misunderstandings along the way.

The foreigner turned out to be from a country called Osmanthus—none other than Jace's greatest historical enemy on the continent. She'd arrived as part of the first diplomatic mission in a very, very long time.

She called herself Asa Lantana. Last name first, in the way of Osmanthians.

She passed Tiller a business card printed with letters in an illegible foreign script. Carnelian looked over Tiller's shoulder and murmured: "*A. L. Consulting.* The rest is just a bunch of slogans."

Asa Lantana's Jacian was, to be frank, excruciatingly difficult to understand. Half the time, Tiller had no idea what she was talking about. But she seemed to quickly grasp what Tiller attempted to say in reply.

Carnelian, who apparently knew a sprinkling of Continental, sometimes interjected a word or two of help.

At least in the beginning. Soon enough, Carnelian wandered off to the penthouse kitchen and uncorked a long-necked bottle of sparkling wine.

"Is it okay for her to serve herself?" Tiller asked nervously. She was afraid to contemplate how much that single bottle might cost.

Asa threw herself down in an armchair. She shrugged expansively. "Not my money."

"Whose is it, then?"

Asa pointed skyward. Did she mean her higher-ups? The Jacian or Osmanthian government?

Tiller decided not to question it.

In Jace, magic was considered a precious resource. One that needed to be shared fairly, although by nature it randomly concentrated in the hands of a few.

Mages were duty-bound to contribute their magic to the greater good. Likewise, those capable of serving as operators had a duty to help control and administer magic. To forge a better society for one and all.

From what little Tiller knew, Osmanthus was very different. A mage-run tyranny. Downright dystopian in its treatment of anyone born without magic—operators and laypeople alike.

She wondered if Asa Lantana, an Osmanthian operator, was starting to prefer life here in Jace.

"Carnelian Silva!" Asa yelled at the kitchen. "Correct me if I say anything stupid."

"Aye, aye, captain," Carnelian called back. She raised her glass in a mock toast.

Asa pointed at herself. She pointed at Tiller. "You and me. We're the same thing."

"Operators?"

"In my home country, we're healers. Mage healers. You Jacians call it mage maintenance. Mage supervision. Mage goring."

"Mage what?" Tiller said.

"Governance?" Carnelian guessed, coming up behind her.

She tried to pass Tiller a glass. Tiller shook her head.

"Yes," Asa agreed. "Mage governance."

She snatched up the glass of wine that Tiller had refused. She took a dainty cat-size sip, then curled her lip and set it aside.

"In Osmanthus, we call it mage healing. Mage treatment. A kind of therapy. Magical pain relief."

In both countries, Asa explained, operators performed similar tasks.

In both countries, mages who never received proper treatment would eventually lose themselves. They'd go berserk—an event that might prove deadly for dozens or hundreds around them.

Jacian operators saw themselves as bringing discipline and order to the painfully tangled magic branches of unruly mages. Mages and their magic were by nature prone to disorder and rebellion. They couldn't help it. Even if all it did was bring them additional suffering.

The job of an operator was thus neverending. No matter how many times you sorted out the messed-up tendrils extending from a mage's core, soon enough you would have to do it all over again.

Without operators to undo the knots in their magic, mages would eventually tangle themselves to death. When they inevitably went berserk in the process, they would magically maim anyone in their path. Innocent bystanders. Beloved pets. Their own children or parents.

Thus the old Jacian saying: magic is a fatal poison. Operators are the only antidote.

And another: a mage without an operator is like a battleship without a captain.

After her lecture, Asa Lantana proceeded to interrogate Tiller about the basics of mage maintenance. Or healing, as Asa called it.

Tiller's answers kept making her put her face in her hands.

Eventually Asa sprang up out of her armchair. She dove for a dish of chocolate bonbons on the coffee table. She furiously unwrapped them, shedding colorful foil every which way. She devoured three or four in a row before offering any to Tiller, who thought it better to decline.

Then she waved Carnelian back over to join them.

Carnelian obliged. By now she appeared thoroughly tipsy: floaty, rosy-cheeked, sleepy-eyed.

She hadn't been drunk at all at the party, Tiller realized belatedly.

"You," Asa said to Tiller, "are not qualified. You are not qualified to untangle a measly two-branch mage. Much less one with nine different cores. My god, what a mess. I don't care what special foghorn you came from—"

"Forest," Carnelian said. "She came from the Devouring Forest."

"Whatever." Asa shot Tiller another sideways look. "Hope you're good at learning by cannibalism."

"By ... observation?" Tiller guessed.

"By swallowing. By absorbing. By sponging!"

"By osmosis?" Carnelian suggested.

"Sure, that," Asa said, as if she'd abruptly stopped caring.

She ordered Carnelian to take off her girdle.

Carnelian fussed with something inside her sweater dress.

An undergarment fell down to her knees. The light of her nine separate cores shone free.

Up till this point, Asa's face had been highly emotive (albeit mostly scowling or frustrated or twisted in disgust). Yet as Carnelian shrugged off her mantle and turned around to show them her back, Asa's expression smoothed into blankness.

Mysteriously, even her overexaggerated foreign accent beat a temporary retreat. "This is a crime against humanity," she said as she gazed at Carnelian's cores.

"You tell me that every time," Carnelian answered lightly, facing the window.

"The man who did this—"

"He's long dead," Carnelian said.

"Does she know?" Asa asked. "Have you told her?"

"Who, my future wife?" Carnelian looked back at them both. Her mouth quirked. "Don't you worry," she added to Tiller. "I'll tell you the full story sooner or later. Let's not speak of it now, though. Don't want to bring down the mood."

Tiller had deliberately avoided asking. There were plenty of things she hadn't told Carnelian, either. For instance, she didn't see any reason why Carnelian would need to know the full story of her and her brother.

Carnelian knowing about it wouldn't ensure them safe passage through the Forest. Carnelian knowing about it wouldn't bring Gren back to life.

Part of her was curious, of course, about how a mage could end up with multiple cores. But she wouldn't pry any deeper.

Asa Lantana didn't ask Carnelian to lift her dress. Her right hand hovered over the gray knit covering the small of Carnelian's back.

This was a show of strength. Most operators found it much easier if they could make direct contact with bare skin.

Asa's fingers twitched as if in a dream. It hardly looked intentional. But in response, something began to change in the dozens of crooked branches flowing like tributaries into Carnelian's nine cores. They loosened and uncurled, became pliant and smooth.

A dramatic transformation. Asa had made only the smallest of motions to prompt it, but her gesture must have been precisely calculated to cause the desired effect. To prod one innocuous magic branch, and cause a perfect chain reaction in all the others.

"I have no idea how to replicate that," Tiller said frankly.

Asa sighed.

"She was hoping you might turn out to be a secret prodigy." Carnelian confided. "Then she could avoid having to teach you all the tedious details."

"One branch at a time," Asa said to Tiller. "Your turn now."

# 9

CARNELIAN WAS surprisingly stoic. Tiller would've expected her to complain more about getting her magic poked at for hours.

She asked for occasional stretch breaks, and seemed miffed when Asa sequestered her wine. But other than that, she tolerated their ministrations without any sign of discomfort.

For mages, getting worked on by an operator could feel like the magical equivalent of a deep-tissue massage. Most found it difficult not to let out a groan or two.

"Don't praise her for it," Asa muttered while Carnelian was in the bathroom. "She has a higher pain tolerance than most. Maybe she doesn't feel much of anything from her little moons. Can you tell which is the one she was born with?"

"Which core?" Tiller said. "No."

"You can see from how the branches respond to you," Asa told her. "Next time, look harder."

Tiller still couldn't see it.

But it did make sense that Carnelian, like any other mage, had been born with only a single core of her own.

Then something had happened to change that. In her childhood? Or much later?

Normally, combing out the knots in a mage's magic had the twofold effect of reducing their risk of berserking, and also reducing the pain their own magic induced in them.

The more tangled a mage got, the more they suffered. Tangling would happen over time whether or not they actively used magic. It was an unstoppable force of nature, like dust collecting on floors. But wielding magic would accelerate the process.

Tiller didn't need Asa Lantana to spell out the implications for her. There were definite downsides to partnering with a mage who had lower pain sensitivity.

They would be less adept at detecting the signs of their own tangling. They wouldn't know to ask for help when they needed it. They might not realize when they were on the brink of berserking. They might keep trying to use more magic anyway. They wouldn't know when to stop and run back to their operator for maintenance.

Such mistakes could prove fatal in the Forest.

Tiller strove to stay focused throughout that first training session. For the most part, she succeeded. But there were moments when the view from the grand hotel windows caught her eye.

When Tiller walked down in the streets alone, her primary objective was always to avoid getting ambushed.

Direct attacks had been rare in the years since Doe died to protect her. The government had made an admirable effort to debunk the old rumors about what you could gain by slaughtering a blue.

Tiller kept her guard up all the same. Some people would always believe what they wanted to believe, no matter what. And eventually they would show up to kill her.

Because of her intense focus on staying alive, there were certain aspects of the cityscape she rarely noticed. Not on a conscious level, anyhow. Seen from above, they became far more obvious: barricaded lots, unfinished construction, blocked streets. All randomly placed.

One of the buildings right across from this very hotel was swaddled in protective scaffolding, which in turn had been covered in sheeting like a colorful shroud.

The sheeting had an enormous black sign printed on it. A warning symbol in the shape of a vortex.

Everyone in Jace knew that design. It was as iconic as the skull and bones stamped on a bottle of rat poison.

Had Nui City been so littered with vorpal holes back when Tiller first came from the Forest? Surely it hadn't been this bad twenty years ago. It was hard to say for sure, though. She'd migrated right after Gren died. Despair blotted out most of her memories of that time.

You could rebuild after a hurricane. But there was nothing to be done for vorpal holes: ravenous holes in reality. They spawned wherever they pleased, without any advance warning. Stray animals or children who fell through a vorpal hole would never come back.

All you could do was wall the holes off—using both physical barricades and magic—and pray to the Lord of Circles that no monsters would emerge from the other side.

A high-end hotel like this would be ruined if a vorpal hole happened to manifest inside it. Even if the structure remained intact, even if the hole never spat out a single beast, guests would flee and never come back.

Tiller wondered if they had vorpal insurance. Probably—but it would be ungodly expensive.

After a long, repetitive afternoon of practice, Asa released them in the early evening. Carnelian, who had sobered up with remarkable speed, said she'd be staying downtown to play slots.

"Slots?" Tiller echoed.

"No slot machines in the Forest, are there? Better get it out of my system while I still can."

"I didn't sign up to marry a gambler."

"What, it doesn't suit me?"

"That's not—"

Carnelian winked. "I won't blow my own money. Gotta stop by a pawn shop first."

She reached into the pocket of her mantle and pulled out a handful of designer silverware.

A bold move, considering that the two of them still stood in the shadow of the hotel.

Tiller gaped. "You took that from—"

The silverware disappeared back inside Carnelian's pocket. She put a finger to her lips. "Asa Lantana knows I'm grabby. Her government's already paying for her to stay in a five-star suite. A few souvenirs won't hurt the budget."

"Theft is theft," Tiller said.

"I think of it more as a tip. A minor kickback. My reward for putting up with you two manhandling my magic all afternoon." Carnelian shrugged, unrepentant. "Do let me know if my Forest princess ever wants to learn how to gamble."

"I'm not your—"

Carnelian sailed off without listening, waving a merry farewell.

Over the next two weeks, this became a pattern. After each visit to practice mage maintenance techniques with Asa Lantana, Carnelian went gambling.

When Tiller asked how much she'd won or lost, she would smoothly change the subject.

Petty theft aside, Tiller still had no idea how Carnelian got her money. The jewels in her many earrings seemed real, and she often showed up with a designer handbag in tow.

Tiller herself had never shopped from a boutique in that price range. But she knew the signs. She'd learned the language of wealth from her time spent hobnobbing with prospective donors to the Koya Foundation—merchant families, socialites, the old nobility.

In between training sessions, they gathered supplies. Carnelian was supposed to help, but Tiller ended up doing most of the work herself.

On the floor of Baba Sayo's apartment, she spread out her weapons of choice. A basher: a tall staff embedded with rods of stone. A sheathed machete to strap to her hip. A selection of yo-yo knives. An antique phage herder's crook, two heads taller than her. She would probably need to leave that one behind.

She examined the scarwood shaft of her basher under the brightest light in the room, looking for cracks. She took her time oiling the black blade and blond wooden handle of her machete.

She honed each cutting edge on her old whetstone. Stroke after stroke, a bitter nostalgia welled up in her.

Sharpening knives used to be one of her childhood chores in the Forest. Later on, for some years after coming to the city, she'd worked every day as a street sharpener. Blowing her bamboo flute to call customers.

Every time they saw each other, she kept asking Carnelian to provide a full list of her skills.

To use magic, mages first needed to learn specific skills from a teacher. They had to imprint those skills on their magic branches one by one. One skill, one branch.

At the population level, the average number of branches per mage was well under two. Many mages had only one branch. No mage could choose to acquire any old skill they liked, either. The Bureau of Mage Management would assign them skills for maximum efficiency, so no vital industry ended up underserved or overcrowded.

Carnelian carried far more branches than the average mage. Surely she'd been obligated to imprint a suitable skill on each of them. Given how she'd participated in past missions to the Forest, Tiller assumed much of her magic would be oriented toward combat.

But she still needed to know Carnelian's exact skill profile. That knowledge would shape their strategy for dealing with a sudden attack or an unexpected injury.

"You must have a list on file somewhere," she said, losing patience. "Should I ask the colonel?"

"No, no, I'll write it up for you," Carnelian assured her. "Give me time. I've never made a proper resumé before."

She didn't possess any military-issued armament, either. (The sole exception seemed to be her fighting pipe.)

Tiller offered her Doe's old selection of swords and daggers. At first Carnelian shook her head, saying she could create her own weapons on the fly. Tiller insisted: what if she got too sick or tired to readily use magic? But Carnelian still demurred. In that case, she claimed, her pipe would suffice.

They agreed to revisit the issue of battle equipment at their last stop before the Forest.

After leaving the city, they would make their way across the countryside, heading for the military outpost positioned closest to the current border of the Devouring Forest. There they would pick up their stash of supplies before crossing over into Forest territory.

The Jace Postal Service, pride of the nation, had a direct line to every military base on all the islands. Which meant they could mail nearly everything they needed straight from Nui City to Outpost 24. Including dangerous goods like weaponry as well as water purification tablets, towels, condensed soap, field rations, pain ointment, glowsticks filled with sunvine oil, and other sundry necessities.

Carnelian counted the ration packets stacked for mailing in Baba Sayo's apartment. "Did you forget how large the Forest is?" she asked. "That isn't nearly enough for two people."

"The rations are just for you," Tiller told her.

"What'll you do? Starve?"

"The Forest provides for foresters."

She remained confident of this, even after twenty years away.

"We won't make much progress if you spend all day foraging for berries," Carnelian warned. "And I won't help you hunt."

"I don't eat much meat, either," Tiller said. "Don't worry about it."

Carnelian threw up her hands. "Don't blame me if you start wasting away."

Toward the end of their preparations, Carnelian surprised Tiller by asking about the Koya Foundation. "I thought most nonprofits are understaffed," she said. "Your Foundation won't fall apart without you?"

"In the early days, it might have," Tiller conceded. "We're in a better place now."

"What changed?"

"Money."

"What money?"

"From an anonymous donor."

"Like a secret admirer?"

"Our first significant benefactor," Tiller said. "They refused to be named. But they let us make a big announcement about the gift. It's true how money calls money. Other prospects became much more approachable after they heard about that one huge donation."

"Money calls money," Carnelian said. "If only that held true for gambling."

She got up and went to open the curtains. Tiller winced. She'd given up on telling her to keep them closed. Carnelian had this compulsion to let in natural light whenever possible.

After days of being covered in camping tools, the apartment floor looked bare and lonely.

"Was your mystery donor a mystery even to you?" Carnelian asked.

"Even if I knew their name, I wouldn't tell you."

"Damn. I was wondering if it might be someone I knew."

Tiller went to the sink to wash their finished cups of corn tea. From the kitchenette, she could still see Carnelian basking in afternoon rays from the window. She occupied the same spot where Baba Sayo used to sit alone for hours.

# 10

Tiller had one last task to take care of before leaving Nui City. Originally she'd planned on going alone. But once Carnelian heard about it, she invited herself to tag along.

Still, Tiller thought she was hallucinating when she found Carnelian waiting outside Baba Sayo's apartment at eight in the morning.

"You're on time," she said blankly.

"Of course." Carnelian's voice was crackly, shot through with sleep. "I'm famous for my punctuality."

"I wasn't planning on using the tunnels," Tiller warned her. "It'll take a while to get there."

Carnelian shrugged. "Oh, well. No bypass tunnels in the Forest, either."

Today she wore a short red sheath dress beneath her military mantle, again with over-the-knee boots. Tiller would refuse to be held responsible if the walk hurt her feet.

The morning cold retreated as soon as they started moving. It was peak season for plum blossoms, white and bright pink on low gnarled branches. Tight-closed buds dotted the later-blooming cherry trees.

Only after the plum and cherry petals had all fallen would roe flowers begin to unfurl.

Roe blossom trees were the most distinctive of all. They shed shaggy bark onto the sidewalk in long leathery strips, leaving their trunks striped like a tiger's hide. Tiller and Carnelian kept stepping over damp piles of it. The bark dropped year-round and was much more of a hassle to clean up than autumn leaves.

Despite their jewel-like appearance, summer roeberries stank worse than ginkgo fruit. They also lasted much longer.

No other city in Jace had made the mistake of lining so many streets with such troublesome trees. Season after season, Nuians loved to complain about them. But they also flocked to watch when the roe flowers bloomed in a virtuoso riot of yellow and orange.

"We'll miss the cherry trees at their peak," Carnelian said. "And the roe blossoms beginning to open."

"Mm."

"And then we'll miss the Feast of Chalices."

"Might make it in time if we rush back from the Forest," Tiller said. "But don't count on it."

"It's my favorite holiday," Carnelian said mournfully.

"Why?"

The Feast of Chalices was a national day of rest meant for commemorating lost pilots. Tiller would've expected Carnelian to gravitate to something less somber in origin. Although most people did treat it like a regular seasonal festival.

"I used to fantasize about becoming one of those dead pilots they were celebrating."

"So the propaganda worked on you," Tiller muttered.

They made a number of detours to avoid blocked roads. The same warning sign popped up over and over: the symbol of a black vortex.

If vorpal holes kept appearing at this rate, Tiller thought, the streets of Nui City would be utterly impassable in a matter of decades. Then everyone would get forced down into the bypass tunnels—which, though not immune to vorpal holes, seemed to develop them somewhat less frequently.

Carnelian yawned as she clopped along in Tiller's wake. Her boots made much more noise than Tiller's flats. Her dress was such a saturated color that even pedestrians far down the block would sneak looks at her.

After two weeks of commuting together for lessons with Asa Lantana, Tiller had begun to get used to this. Carnelian soaked up attention like a sponge.

At first her flashiness had made Tiller nervous. Then again, if everyone stared so intensely at Carnelian, no one would take much notice of the dark-wigged woman beside her.

"Why'd you want to come today?" Tiller asked. "You could have slept in."

"So no one in the Corps could try to foist off any last-minute work on me. There've been a bunch of vorpal beast sightings in the suburbs."

"You won't get called on for backup?"

"I've got more important duties to execute," Carnelian said piously.

"Like what?"

"Guarding you," Carnelian replied, and promptly tripped over a pile of roe bark.

Tiller caught her before she face-planted. Carnelian laughed, unembarrassed.

Some bodyguard she was. Doe—who'd been a layperson, neither

mage nor operator—could've tied Carnelian into a pretzel without even trying. No need to rely on magic.

The largest temple in the city was called the Temple of Combat and Chains. It had no standard circular gate of stone. Instead, the trees lining the path up to the complex had been trained to form a tunnel.

A true tunnel, and a perfectly round one at that. The convex curves of the trunks lined up like the ribs of a snake, forming a long and meandering cylinder. The upper boughs had been plaited into a latticed roof, swelling together in a way reminiscent of braided bread dough.

"Didn't take you for the religious type," Carnelian commented.

"I'm not," Tiller said.

"Then why spend your last day in the city at a temple?"

"My grandmother taught me that when you visit a god's territory, you pay your respects. It's just as important to greet them on your way out. Otherwise, leaving the city would be like fleeing a dinner party without saying a word of goodbye to your host."

"But you're not a visitor," said Carnelian. "You live here. You're Jacian. The Forest is as much a part of Jace as Nui City."

Not everyone saw it that way.

Rather—Jacians believed that the Forest was Jacian territory. It was located on one of the Jacian islands, after all.

Few foresters would bother arguing differently. Yet at the same time, at least half the island's population deeply resented foresters who received even a smidgeon of government help. Hence the Koya Foundation. Hence its heavy reliance on the generosity of private donors.

Tiller and Carnelian had little company inside the tree tunnel, though there was room for dozens of people to pass abreast. It was still early morning on a weekday, and most of the other temple-goers appeared to be slow-moving senior citizens. No gaggles of children on school trips.

A few of the grannies they passed did double-takes at Carnelian, confused by her outfit. That scarlet dress of hers was far brighter than the military mantle she wore atop it.

Beyond the tunnel lay an old historic dueling ring. Long out of use (except during the occasional festival) but preserved for posterity.

Gladiators used to come to the temple to pray for good fortune. Then they would head down into the arena to die.

Throughout the open grounds, roeberry trees grew in circular clusters. The shape of a fairy ring. So much soft bark covered the gravel that it felt like walking on a pile of animal skins.

Slow, dull drums thumped from somewhere deep inside the temple buildings. Hints of a ceremony closed to the public.

Tiller went over to the round collection barrels. She took out her change purse to make an offering.

"Wait," Carnelian said. "Don't waste your money on the Lord of Circles. Waste mine."

Tiller contemplated this for a moment, then decided not to argue. She accepted Carnelian's coins in cupped palms, a veritable rain of shiny new grails. Then she turned and poured her handful of grails down through the slots at the top of the largest barrel.

"This, too, is a form of gambling," said Carnelian. "Hope the Lord of Circles appreciates our tribute. Maybe his priestesses can treat themselves to something fancy."

"Family money?" Tiller asked as they moved away from the arrangement of barrels.

Carnelian laughed. "You think I have family? My poor parents surrendered me to the state as fast as humanly possible."

"Hard to imagine where else you'd get enough money to be careless with it. Your entire fortune can't come from stolen hotel spoons."

"Would be pretty impressive if it did."

"So I thought you might be an heiress. Either that, or—"

"Or?" Carnelian asked. She looked sideways at Tiller. She wore a small closed-lipped smile. Her dimples were ghosts.

The only other person in sight was a severely hunchbacked old man. He stared at the main temple hall as if searching for the source of the steady drumbeat.

A large sign with a vortex symbol blocked the garden path up ahead. Tiller stopped. Carnelian came to a halt right behind her.

"Or?" Carnelian repeated, half as quiet as before.

"Or someone paid you off," Tiller said, emotionless.

"Right," Carnelian agreed. "It's not family money. So maybe I took a bribe, or collected half my reward in advance. Maybe I have other motivations for volunteering to join you. Aside from the prospect of becoming your lovely magewife."

The trees here were so quiet that they seemed frightened, smothered, their trunks wrapped tight in clear film and burlap to shield them from winter cold and summer pests. Tiller felt a similar tightness around her torso.

"If it were true," she said evenly, "you wouldn't be so foolish as to hint at it."

Carnelian didn't move. "You've been wary of me since the day we met. Rightfully so, I suppose."

"Why are you saying this?"

"There are still a lot of people who would love to have your head as a trophy. Even here in Nui City. The mafia has never taken kindly to foresters, much less blues."

Carnelian put her hand on the warning sign telling them to beware of vorpal holes. She learned in closer.

"They don't have to believe in the legends about what killing a blue can do for them. They might not buy a word of it. But they want you anyway. It's the same as how most game hunters don't kill to eat anymore. They do it for sport."

Tiller's hand closed around the nausea pellets in her pocket. She always carried at least one self-defense tool.

"Were you ever a hunter?" she asked.

"Of game? Of vorpal beasts?"

"Of bounties," Tiller said. "Human ones."

"If I were," Carnelian answered, "I'd wait till we got very close to the Forest. Or perhaps I'd wait till after we were already inside. Who can come running to save you if you scream in the Forest?

"I'd incapacitate and abduct you," she continued, as if describing her plans for a Sunday afternoon date. "I'd pass you off to my employer. Or perhaps to the highest bidder. Maybe one day I'd see your head mounted in their basement."

"Nice story," Tiller said woodenly.

"Anything to entertain my wife."

"You can't marry a stuffed head."

"Don't tempt me." Carnelian pulled back. Her gloved hand left the sign of the vortex. "But it's just as you say. Surely I wouldn't mention any of that if I were actually going to do it."

"Is this your way of telling me to stop watching my back?"

"You can relax a little around me, at least," said Carnelian. "Isn't that why you hired me?"

"It isn't that easy."

"What can I do to make it easier?"

"Stop making up hypothetical scenarios about my severed head."

Tiller led the way back toward the main circle of buildings. Scraps of bark absorbed all sound made by their footsteps.

"Do foresters eat seafood?" Carnelian asked.

"There are bodies of water with fish in the Forest."

"All right. Let me take you out tonight. I'll treat you to the best sea urchin in the city."

"It's your money to waste," Tiller said.

Carnelian beamed. "You're so understanding."

Turtle doves hid all over the wooded park around the temple grounds. They cooed louder than the equally hidden drums.

These cultivated trees—surrounded by mulch or trimmed grass, naked of underbrush—were nothing like the Forest.

Tiller could see why Baba Sayo had hated coming here. The smell in the air was a watered-down memory of something wilder.

Heavy chains hung like jewelry from tree branches and pagoda eaves. Out in the garden they were mostly bare metal—dark rusted iron, aged copper. The largest ones on the temple buildings had been painted gold and turquoise and brilliant vermilion.

For the Feast of Chalices, children would donate thousands of colorful paper chains to adorn the tree tunnel, to stream from all the temple roofs and outdoor lanterns.

An old folktale said that the entire temple had once tried to uproot itself and flee from rumors of foreign invaders. So the people of the time chained it in place.

Subsequent history proved that Nui was the safest of all the major Jacian islands. Virtually immune from outside attacks.

One by one, Tiller and Carnelian plucked leaves from the temple's oracle tree. A diviner by the temple shop took the leaves and used a slender twig to inscribe their fortunes.

Carnelian didn't want to show her fortune to Tiller. She brooded over it for a bit, then tucked the leaf in her mantle.

"You don't really believe in the Lord of Circles, do you?" she said to Tiller once the diviner was out of earshot.

"Not really, no."

"Neither do I. And what's a fortune but words on a leaf?"

"Did yours say something bad?" Tiller asked.

"Just average," Carnelian said shortly. "You?"

"Life-Changing Luck." The best prediction possible. "I always get the same thing." Tiller pointed at her wig. "My grandmother had a theory that my nature confuses the system."

"Damn. I knew it was rigged."

The scent of incense lingered outside the shop, and all around the base of the oracle tree. It kept tickling Tiller's nose even as they headed back toward the great snaking tree tunnel, ready to leave the Temple of Combat and Chains.

She toyed with the nausea pellets in her pocket as if rubbing a handful of marbles.

Suddenly Carnelian stopped, tugging her back.

"Tiller," she said.

Her face wore a carefree smile. Her body language remained casual. Her voice had gone low and wary.

# 11

"ACT NATURAL," Carnelian said.

"How?"

"We're in love. Besotted. Just look at us."

They'd paused by the old open-air combat arena. Worn stone steps formed tiered seats marching down to the earthen ring below.

Carnelian took Tiller's hand and tugged her over to the top step. She pointed at the combat ring as if delivering a lecture on its long history.

Tiller looked, but there was nothing to see. No footprints. Only dust.

Carnelian tilted her head closer and said very quietly: "There's a tick on your leg. Don't look at it."

"Like ... a deer tick?"

"Not a real one. Magical. Manufactured. Don't try to find it. Don't try to touch it."

It was very hard not to glance down.

Now Carnelian caught both her hands and faced her. She gazed at

Tiller as if she were really in love, as if every moment were bliss. "So far, so good. You're very calm."

Her clipped tone clashed with her adoring expression. It felt like a ghost had borrowed her body to deliver a prophesy.

"I'm used to bodyguards giving me sudden warnings," Tiller said. "Are we surrounded?"

Carnelian laid a loving hand on the side of Tiller's face. Her palm was cool and dry. "Keep your eyes on me."

Tiller obeyed. She hadn't seen any other temple visitors since the old man over by the central circle of chained structures. Small birds chittered irritably in dark treetops beyond the arena, some still bare from winter.

"It would've helped to know your skill set," she told Carnelian. "I'm still waiting on that list."

"Now you get to see it in action. I—"

Numbness engulfed Tiller's right leg.

No, more than numbness. It was as though her leg had been sheared from her body, had ceased to exist. Even the downward pull of its dead weight had been utterly extinguished. She staggered into Carnelian.

Urgent fingers dug at her shoulders. Carnelian's magic dropped down around the two of them with the finality of a stage curtain.

Then the ground, too, vanished.

They rematerialized in front of a sign marked with a vortex. Carnelian held Tiller up with an arm around her waist.

Heaps of curling roeberry bark made the ground look soft. Tiller couldn't feel it under either of her feet now. The trees around them dripped with rusting chains.

"You can't port any further?"

Her voice came out weak and breathy, not at all the way it had sounded in her head.

She struggled to remember how to use her lungs. Hostile magic radiated from her insensate right leg. The rest of her body threatened to shut itself down piece by piece, defenseless.

They were still on temple territory. Just a three or four-minute stroll from the combat ring. Carnelian heaved her behind the sign of the vortex and propped her up against a nearby stump.

"My porting skill only works for short distances." Carnelian bent over Tiller and pushed the fabric of her right legging up to her knee. "And only for places I've been in the last twenty-four hours."

"Then—"

"I didn't go anywhere near this district yesterday. If I use magic to port us out of here, I'd have to start by jumping us right back the way we came. Closer and closer to your apartment. Best not to lead them there."

That red dress of hers was definitely not meant for crouching in the woods. She glanced up at Tiller. "Can I take off my gloves?"

"Why ask me?"

"You're my operator right now," Carnelian said patiently. "Consider yourself my commanding officer. Can I take off my gloves?"

Military mages wore various limiters to reduce their lethality. The mandatory gloves, the many-layered mantle—each piece could function like the safety on a gun.

Tiller wrestled with her tongue to force words past deadened lips. "Do it."

Carnelian pulled off her right glove in a single smooth motion, as if drawing a sword. It fell to dangle from a cord clasped to her mantle.

A sunburst of magic struck at Tiller's senses.

"You just told them where to find us," Tiller said, or tried to. "Even the most magic-blind layperson would notice—"

Carnelian really did hold a sword now, long and transparent. A slender curved blade like pure ice.

"They have a tick on you," she said. "They'd find us soon enough anyway. Don't move, now. And don't scream. This will hurt."

She knelt. She placed the edge of the blade flush against Tiller's bare calf.

Hard to imagine it hurting—it didn't feel like anything, neither cold nor hot. Tiller stared down at her own bent leg as if it belonged to a stranger.

Carnelian moved her magic sword. A swift sawing pull, as if shaving off a mole. Immediately afterward she let go of it. The sword vaporized midair, gone as soon as her fingers stopped touching it.

Tiller's leg came back to life with a vengeance. She hunched forward to clutch at it. If she clenched her teeth any harder, she'd crack her molars. The air of the woods smelled all wrong, rusty and empty and tame.

But she didn't scream.

Carnelian touched her back. They ported again, this time to the foot of the oracle tree.

The drums inside the temple buildings kept up their ponderous beat. The scent of incense had thinned, though, and the diviner on duty was nowhere in sight.

Carnelian pulled Tiller to her feet. She opened her palm to show a brown dot the size of a freckle, crushed and misshapen.

"An immobility tick," she said. "They want you alive."

"Great," Tiller deadpanned.

"I thought there were too few pilgrims here. It's early, but not the crack of dawn."

"They must've cleared the grounds."

"Perhaps with the temple's cooperation."

"The temple would do that?"

"For a reputable group of hunters, yes."

"You know who's hunting me," Tiller said.

Carnelian blew the broken tick off her palm. "The Parasite Guild."

"That's ... unexpectedly literal."

"The tick is their symbol. Their calling card. They've been around for generations."

"Where do you know them from?"

"Government operations. Inside and outside the Forest. They're usually very respectable. So respectable that I'm not surprised if you've never heard of them. Normally they—shit."

Soapy bubbles shimmered in the air, small and large, drifting closer on the wings of an unnatural breeze. The kind of bubbles you might see groups of children playing with on warm weekends.

The bubbles circled wordlessly around Tiller and Carnelian. Tightening like a whirlpool. In a matter of seconds, they had coalesced into the equivalent of an abstract cage.

"These interfere with porting," Carnelian said. "Among other things. May I take off my mantle?"

"Do whatever you need to," Tiller told her. "Strip naked, if it helps. You don't have to keep asking me."

"There are some areas where even I know better than to break protocol."

Carnelian handed Tiller her mantle and gloves.

The bubbles jostled closer, radiant with a magic too complex to parse at a glance. Tiller had to huddle up against Carnelian's back to avoid them.

Her right calf throbbed from its artificial tick bite. Her scalp felt hot and smothered beneath her wig, infested by an unreachable itch.

The mantle was heavy in her arms, even heavier than she'd expected. Did the military sew weights in these?

"They'll make a move soon." Carnelian spoke in just above a whisper. "As soon as they think we're helpless. Cry out right before the bubbles touch you. Loud as you can. Right before, you hear me? We're done for if the bubbles make contact."

"Right before," Tiller repeated. She turned carefully, her back pressed to Carnelian. The rainbow-skinned bubbles crept inexorably closer. "Won't be much longer."

"If you need to...."

"What?"

"Do whatever you need to do to stop me."

She didn't get a chance to ask Carnelian what that meant. Tiny pearly bubbles surged forward like charging soldiers. She cried out, high and ragged and almost too late.

<h1 style="text-align:center">12</h1>

THE FAUX SOAP bubbles popped. Simultaneously combusted. The cage they'd formed vanished from the air, negated.

No—something had shredded them. A crimson whirl of magic and motion.

The distant temple drumming died out.

Carnelian stood there in her short red dress and long boots, legs planted apart, breathing heavily.

Tiller refocused her magic perception.

A phantom limb hovered over Carnelian's right arm, a presence like the prismatic glassfish that haunted Forest ponds. It was long and clawed and much too large for her body. The ends of its talons curled down by her knees.

She wore a strangely chagrined look on her face.

Three shadows moved in unison beneath the evergreen oracle tree. Masked figures in brown-gray camouflage and darker body armor. They all carried firearms. Their feet didn't quite touch the bark-blanketed ground.

Carnelian tensed. Tiller caught at the back of her dress.

"They're projections," Tiller said. An illusory distraction.

Carnelian's eyes remained fixed on the men and their guns. "When I move," she said, "hit the ground."

No time to argue. Carnelian lunged. Tiller flung herself down beside a threadbare cluster of bushes. Roeberry bark cushioned her landing.

Carnelian, too, dropped lower. Her monstrous phantom claw snaked forward on its own, stretching away from her, swift as a cracked whip. It raked through the armed projections, shredding them like mist.

Then she dove sideways at Tiller, her spectral claw dissolving. Something hit the base of the oracle tree, missing her by inches as she moved.

Tiller twisted deeper into the bushes. Panicked adrenaline submerged her in an instant, dark and distorted. She hadn't felt this way in over a decade.

Twelve years ago, Doe had ordered her: stay hidden. Don't make a fuss. Don't come out, no matter what.

Twelve years ago, Doe had started bleeding out inches from Tiller's hiding spot.

Right there in the old suburban house where they'd started the Koya Foundation. Right there in the first place outside the Forest that Tiller had learned to call home. Right there, while Tiller cowered, hunters did anything they could think of to make Doe tell them how to find her.

"There's a sniper," Tiller said, choked.

"I know."

Even before Carnelian spoke, the air behind her remade itself. A pattern rippled through it. A kaleidoscopic bloom akin to frost flowers on glass. It all happened in a matter of nanoseconds. The shield solidified into a matrix of translucent hexagonal facets, complex as the compound eye of a dragonfly.

Something struck it and stopped, frozen as if trapped in glue. Another followed. Then another. Then silence.

Carnelian, crouching, swiveled with her hands out. Her shield faded in an undulating chain reaction, one hexagonal cell after another. Bullets plopped into her palms.

Tiller grabbed at her to pull her down. "They'll—"

"They won't shoot again," Carnelian said, unmoved. "And if they do, I'll block it. Have a little faith."

Tiller glared. "Faith has nothing to do with our odds of survival!"

Carnelian tossed the black lumps in her palm like a street conjurer about to start doing coin tricks. "They weren't shooting to kill. These are porting bullets."

She squished one between her fingers like soft clay. She ripped it in half, and it crumbled.

She lobbed the other spent bullets into the bushes behind Tiller. Then she dusted off her hands.

"If they hit us, they'd transport us to a secure location. The hunters would have us right where they wanted us. But we wouldn't be dead.

"Besides," she added. "If I'm good at one thing, it's shielding. They've seen that now. The Parasite Guild are pros. They won't double down on a failed approach."

She offered a hand to pull Tiller up.

Tiller accepted, rising shakily. "I got your mantle dirty." It had fallen in the bushes when she dove for cover.

"No matter," said Carnelian. "It'll get dirtier in the Forest. Now"—she rubbed her hands together—"time to hunt the hunters."

Tiller went still. "You made it sound like they're pulling back."

"Yes. We've got to chase them."

"If they're pros like you claim, they won't strike in busier areas. They can't block the temple off all day, either. We should take this chance to get out of here."

"No," Carnelian said simply.

She walked over to the oracle tree. She pointed at two bullet marks. One right at the base, which Tiller had heard whizzing past them. One higher up on the trunk, which Tiller hadn't noticed at all.

"The Parasite Guild is fully capable of following us out of the city," Carnelian continued. "Can they do much in the Forest? Nah. But there's a good distance to travel before we get there.

"So why give them a chance to regroup? I mean, they'll regroup either way, so why make it easy on them? Let's give them more of a setback."

"Thought I was supposed to be your commanding officer," Tiller said.

Carnelian's fingers traced the marks on the oracle tree. They weren't as deep as one might expect. More like dents than proper bullet holes.

Given that the tree and its divining leaves hadn't been teleported to an undisclosed location, the porting bullets must've been keyed to only work on mammals. Or perhaps only on human beings.

Again, Tiller attempted to make Carnelian see reason. "Asa Lantana said that you need more maintenance than most mages. You just used multiple skills in succession. You should—"

"Submit to you for a maintenance session?" There was a curious note in Carnelian's voice. She smoothed the front of her dust-streaked dress. "Let me tell you—the mages she usually deals with are a lot weaker to pain than I am. I'll be fine. You can tune me up after dinner tonight."

"Don't think we'll have time for fine dining," Tiller said.

"That depends on what happens next, doesn't it? Excuse me."

Having excused herself, Carnelian turned aside and spat in her palm.

Tiller blinked, baffled.

"Homing pearls," Carnelian explained.

She'd spit out a handful of glistening pebbles the size of baby teeth, brown and irregular.

Tiller said the first thing that came to mind: "Those don't look like pearls."

"They call it that because you hock the stones out of your mouth. Like how people vomit jewels in fairy tales. Look—I didn't invent the skill. I just learned it."

Carnelian took her fistful of so-called pearls and swished it through the air where the magically projected hunters had stood, guns at the ready.

The illusion had been ruined with a swipe of her ethereal claw. But the residue of its magic still hung about the oracle tree like stray dust motes.

"Good enough," Carnelian murmured.

She opened her fingers. The homing pearls zoomed away like freed bumblebees.

"We don't know how many of them are still in the area," Tiller said. "We don't know what kind of weapons or tools they've got."

"Oh, I can guess," Carnelian said airily. "I told you I've fought beside them before. I've seen quite a bit of their arsenal."

"What if they're armed like their reflections?"

"With a bunch of guns? No problem."

"Can you stop multiple people shooting at once? From different directions? Human reaction times can't possibly—"

Carnelian was smiling. Her dimples deepened. "I blocked the sniper, didn't I?" she said. "Good situational awareness can work miracles."

She tucked her arm through Tiller's and began walking. Back toward the combat ring and the tree tunnel beyond it.

"Let's make it look like we're about to slink away to safety," she said. "Anyway—I was supposed to be a super soldier, you see. I was supposed to be able to take on armies. Unfortunately, I'm not all that great. I'd have trouble dealing with a well-defended submarine. And I'd be helpless against a chalice."

"That doesn't make me feel any more confident."

Carnelian flicked a brief look down at herself. At the place in her lower abdomen where her multiple cores lay obscured—hidden by whatever specialized garment she wore beneath her close-fitting dress.

"They hoped for me to be one of the greatest war mages of all time," she said casually. "A rival for the most powerful mage over on the continent."

"The one called the Kraken," said Tiller.

"The one called the Kraken," Carnelian agreed. "In comparison, I'm afraid I've been nothing but a disappointment. But I'm damn good at stopping bullets. My trainer used to take me to firing ranges and shoot at me till I messed up my shielding. Good times."

Massive chains wound like strangling pythons around the trees that marked the entrance to the meticulously cultivated tunnel. The glaring pale sky bore only a faint burnt-out hint of watercolor blue.

Tiller hugged Carnelian's bundled-up mantle in her arms. She was growing tired of its weight. "I still think we should leave."

"Well, where's the fun in that?"

Carnelian kept pulling her toward the shadows of the tall tunnel. Step by step. Arm in arm. Spotters from the Parasite Guild must've been watching them go.

They moved under the bent and braided trees, out of the light. The air instantly felt like winter.

Another step, and Tiller's foot took a fraction of a second too long to meet the ground.

She stumbled. Carnelian caught her.

She'd almost tripped headfirst into a sign with a black vortex. Carnelian's magic had whisked them back to the woods around the temple perimeter.

"We're going in circles," Tiller said under her breath. Her heart beat too hard. She didn't care for sudden porting. "We should just—"

Carnelian stepped smoothly around the sign. That long clear sword flashed in her hand again. She threw it forward as if releasing a captive bird. It flew away on its own, streaking out of sight.

Moments later, shouts followed. Men crying out. Words Tiller didn't recognize. Call signs? Code phrases?

A small suppressed smile tugged at the sides of Carnelian's mouth again. It seemed genuine.

"Stay close," she said. She seized Tiller and dashed toward the voices.

They ran together in a straight line through the trees—no dodging, no zig-zagging.

Someone fired shots. Carnelian's hexagonal patchwork shield coalesced midair before the sound smacked Tiller's ears, before she recognized what was happening. The hexagons burst into being and faded, over and over.

The shields crystallized exactly where the bullets hit, and melted away an instant later.

Three men. No, four. Five? A coating of magic coruscated across their camouflage-pattern clothing.

One was on the ground, Carnelian's sword spearing his belly.

More shots rang out. It happened so fast that Tiller couldn't see where they came from. Carnelian's shields rendered them meaningless.

Behind the hunters: a vorpal hole shaped like a ragged grin, a partial eclipse of the sun. The hole that the painted sign had warned them to stay away from.

A lopsided mess of chain-link fencing attempted to corral it, but parts of the fence lay trampled. The edges of the hole stretched almost all the way through a hoary confused tree, taking a bite out of its trunk that could never begin to heal.

With all their futile shooting, the hunters seemed to be attempting to edge their way back around the fence, around the vicious hole in reality. Perhaps they had a escape portal placed in the woods beyond.

Carnelian held her right hand out, fingers splayed. Her icicle-colored blade wrenched itself out of the fallen hunter. His body arched and bucked with the force of it.

The sword hurtled back to her. Her fingers curled shut around the glassy hilt.

"Those pearls hurt, didn't they?" she said. "How many of you got wounded?"

One of the standing hunters made a gesture. Tiller didn't know military hand signs in detail, but it appeared to carry a meaning adjacent to surrender. A proposal of nonaggression. *Let us both depart in peace*.

"Not that you ever had a chance of hitting us," Carnelian said, "but Lord, do I hate being shot at."

She dismissed her sword with a flick of her wrist. "Those homing pearls have more than one use, you know. Come to me."

The five hunters flew up and crashed into each other as if magnetically drawn together, heads banging, torsos thumping. The man who'd been impaled by her sword was no exception. They dropped in a groaning pile of tangled limbs.

Tiller thought, inanely, of the sculpture in the lobby of Asa Lantana's hotel. The stacked pyramid of defeated enemy bodies.

Carnelian walked over to the dazed hunters. She grabbed the topmost man and heaved him off with a grunt. She dragged him toward the seething vorpal hole, past the collapsed portions of the ineffectual fence.

Dark blood painted fallen leaves and strips of bark on the ground behind them.

Tiller followed. Her hand tightened around the nausea pellets in her pocket.

"I'm sure you know how to cut your losses," Carnelian said to the hunters. She braced herself, hauling the wounded man closer to the vorpal hole. "Satisfy my curiosity. Who hired you?"

An incomprehensible absence awaited on the other side of the vorpal hole. It hurt to look at. It was a wound in space and time, a wound that didn't belong there, as wrong as the bloody hole her sword had tunneled through his torso.

If his little finger touched that nothingness, his little finger would vanish, never to return. If she put his arm through the hole, his arm would be eradicated without a sound. If she put his head through the hole, he would in that very instant be reduced to a decapitated corpse.

Carnelian pushed his masked face closer to the hole. The rest of the hunters twitched in place. They seemed incapable of getting up. They hadn't even begun crawling out from beneath one another.

Tiller remembered the house where Doe had died. She remembered hiding in her cubby in the wall, plastered over with purchased magic that made it nigh-impossible to notice. A cubby that in past times might have been used to store a convenient household mage.

She remembered hiding there while they tortured Doe for answers that would never come.

"Oh, come on," Carnelian said.

She gave the bleeding man a brisk shake. It nearly plunged his ear into the vorpal hole.

"You're in the Parasite Guild, my friend. You're tougher than this. Surely you've been through worse. Surely one of you can string together a few words for me. Help me out here."

"Carnelian." Tiller stood right up against the chain link fence. She forced her voice not to shake. She beckoned Carnelian over.

She couldn't risk doing anything drastic. Not while they teetered on the edge of that senseless hole.

Carnelian cocked her head. Eventually she sighed. She unceremoniously dropped the hunter right in front of the vorpal hole.

She stalked over to Tiller. "I'm a bit busy," she said. "What?"

"Got something for you."

Tiller flicked a nausea pellet through the fence. It hit her square in the chin.

Carnelian's eyes widened. The small pellet stuck to her like chewing gum in hair.

The nausea pellet merged with Carnelian's skin, sinking deeper and deeper till no visible trace of it remained.

She staggered. She spun around. She collapsed onto her hands and knees.

"You told me to stop you," Tiller said as Carnelian heaved her stomach out onto the ground already soaked deep maroon with hunters' blood.

# 13

THE DAY BEFORE visiting the temple, they had gone in for their final session with Asa Lantana.

As afternoon stretched into evening, Asa sent Carnelian off to the hotel bar. She went happily, giving a mischievous salute as she made her merry way out of the penthouse suite.

"Don't you need to watch me tune her?" Tiller said.

"I've seen enough."

Asa sat cross-legged in her usual armchair by the ceiling-high windows filled with sunset.

Her eyepatch of the day featured fabric with humpbacked white clouds against a weak gray sky. Tiller had yet to see her recycle a pattern.

On the side table next to her rested a bowl of pistachios, and a second bowl to hold their shells. She began cracking them open without eating them.

"I hear," she said, "all you Jacian operators get taught the same move to use on bad mages." She gave Tiller an expectant look. "What's it called?"

Unlike the sky of her eyepatch, the real sky behind Asa was a rich dusky rose fading into orange. Her stomach grumbled loud enough for Tiller to hear it. Pistachio shells clinked softly as they piled up in her trash bowl.

"Is this a technique I haven't shown you yet?" Tiller asked, perplexed.

"It's a way to cause mages pain."

"Oh." Now she got it. "Compression."

"How did they teach it to you?"

Tiller tilted her head back, searching her memory.

Compression had not been a concept in the Forest. Then again, there hadn't been any mages living in Koya Village. Not for a long time. The last one had left well before Baba Sayo started caring for Tiller and Gren. So there was no one for operators to do maintenance on. No one at risk of berserking.

Only once had Tiller ever encountered a mage in the Forest. She hadn't known what was coming. But in the end, that one meeting led to disaster.

She went through mandatory operator training only after everyone left the Forest and settled down in Nui City.

Her teachers explained that if a mage turned defiant, if they didn't know what was good for them, if they showed signs of opposition—

Sometimes you might need to use compression. To crush their magic branches like tissue paper. To deliberately make their tangling worse. To subdue your mage with disabling pain.

A wise operator would use it sparingly. Operators needed to make responsible choices for both themselves and the mages in their care.

Everyone knew that there were few things more dangerous than a mage who couldn't listen to orders. Yet the very act of compression, of deliberately hurting their magic, would push them temporarily closer to the edge of going berserk.

It was like kicking the machine you were supposed to fix. Sometimes shock treatment might work, but you'd better follow up immediately with proper maintenance—with actually repairing your damaged mage.

"Promise me you won't do that to Carnelian Silva," Asa said.

Her clumsy foreign pronunciation made Carnelian's name sound childish. Almost cutesy. It was rather charming, especially in combination with the morbidly earnest look on her face.

"What, use compression on her? I wasn't planning on it."

The doorbell rang. They both flinched. Then Asa went back to shelling her pistachios. "I called room service." She seemed to be waiting for Tiller to let them in.

Tiller dutifully went over to admit a cart covered in small plates. Asa ordered her to taste a little of everything.

"Trying to poison me?" Tiller asked. She was only half kidding.

"Every time," Asa said, "I beg them to make it less spicy. Every time! They smile and bow. I bow back at them. Everyone's happy. Now tell me: does it taste spicy to you?"

Tiller broke off a small morsel of a crab cake. She nibbled on pink pickled radish.

"Zero spice," she said truthfully.

Asa used a dessert fork to stab a single flake of the crab cake. She swallowed. Seconds later, she made a noise like a cat getting its tail shut in a door.

She drank water, then lavender wine, then water again. She groped for the bowl on the table and crammed shelled pistachios in her mouth.

"You're like Carnelian," she told Tiller as she crunched on her pistachios. "It's spicy as hell, but you don't taste it. Carnelian doesn't feel much even when her magic is tangled from root to tip."

"This is extremely mild by Jacian standards," Tiller said as politely as she could. "I don't think the chefs would be able to water it down any further. At that point, they wouldn't even consider it cooking."

"I know people who would love it here," Asa muttered. "Listen—that's why you can't use compression on Carnelian. Don't try to shock her into obeying you."

"Her spice tolerance is too high?"

"It won't work on her. Unless you hurt her magic badly enough to make her snap."

"Sounds risky."

"Too risky. You can't let her lose control."

"I don't have any experience with neutralizing berserk mages," Tiller admitted.

"Of course you don't." Asa threw up her hands. "Even worse—she's got nine cores. You'd be done for."

Tiller began picking at more snacks from the food trolley. It all tasted quite bland to her. But the spread seemed liable to go to waste if she left it alone with Asa Lantana.

As the sunset sky dimmed, its colors leeching down below the jagged black skyline, water-lights embedded in the walls and ceiling glowed awake one by one.

"Is there nothing I can do if she starts to lose it?" Tiller asked.

"They ever teach you how to throttle?"

Tiller nodded. Throttling a mage's magic meant pinching it as one might pinch a hose, cutting off the flow of water. Executed correctly, it would prevent them from using any magic whatsoever. At least until you let go.

Asa wasn't finished yet. "You won't be able to throttle a multi-core mage," she said. "No way. I only know a couple operators in the whole world who could pull it off. Me included."

"So if I can't use compression, and I can't throttle her—"

"If she ever gets out of control, you're gonna have to subdue her some other way."

"How?"

"Psychically."

"...Physically?"

"Yeah. Before you can start sorting out her magic." She motioned Tiller over and made her take a palmful of shelled pistachios. "If I were you, I'd load up on sedatives. See if your military can supply anything useful."

"I'll ask around," Tiller said.

"She'll tell you she doesn't need that much maintenance. She might even believe it. But you've got to do maintenance every time she uses any of her skills. Even just one.

"Don't let her go to sleep that same night without getting tuned. If she executes multiple skills in a row—you've really got to drop everything and tend to her as soon as you can."

On the evening following their visit to the Temple of Combat and Chains, Tiller repeated these words to Carnelian. They were back at Baba Sayo's apartment after hours spent filing reports with the city constabulary.

Needless to say, they hadn't gone out for dinner.

"I may never eat again," Carnelian said, rubbing her stomach.

She certainly had a flair for the dramatic. Granted, it had taken much of the afternoon for the effects of the nausea pellet to finish wearing off.

"We can have sea urchin another time," Tiller told her.

She made Carnelian face the mushroom art on the wall. Meanwhile, she poked at Carnelian's lower back, sorting out the crimped and crooked parts of her magic. It was a frustrating process, like picking at tangled yarn with fingernails too short to really dig into the knotted bits.

Carnelian entertained herself by commenting on Tiller's old childhood scribbles like an art critic. "This piece is far superior to the rest," she said, indicating a slab of dried mushroom hanging a little further off to the right. "Such meticulous etching. Such intricate ferns. What creature is that—a weasel?"

"A civet," said Tiller. "My brother drew that one."

"Ah."

Unlike Asa Lantana, Tiller needed the immediacy of bare skin to do mage maintenance. The extra barrier of clothing made it too difficult for her to effectively push and pull at all the magic branches that lay buried beneath. They curled and rippled inside Carnelian like arteries too free-spirited to lie still.

Afterward, she zipped Carnelian's dress up and picked her girdle off the floor. "I won't be wearing wigs in the Forest," Tiller said. "You shouldn't wear these, either."

"My goodness. You want me to go full-on nudist?"

Tiller shook the girdle for emphasis. "This stuff. Your—what you use to make it look like you've only got one core."

Carnelian took the girdle. She tugged at its sides as though stretching dough for a flatbread. "I suppose it doesn't matter if we're all alone in the Forest."

"Because of how it blurs your magic, I can't tell if your branches are getting more tangled. You might end up in a really bad state—you might need emergency maintenance—and even if I were right next to you, I wouldn't perceive it. That's incredibly dangerous."

"The Forest is full of dangers," Carnelian said. "But sure, that makes sense. If you're so determined to make me stop wearing underwear, I suppose I have no choice but to listen."

Tiller didn't bother reacting. Instead, she wondered: how many other people knew Carnelian had multiple cores?

Any operators who ran maintenance on her would inevitably find out. But if she'd worn concealing garments on past missions with the Corps, most fellow soldiers might remain clueless.

If people could see her cores at a glance, they'd stare. They'd be irrepressibly curious. It would be the first and last thing anyone asked her about. Everyone would brood over the implications.

Maybe it wasn't that different from being born with blue hair. Tiller could certainly understand the urge to use camouflage.

Carnelian was a mage, though. There were inherent risks in camouflaging the state of her magic. She could slink right up to the brink of berserking without anyone knowing it.

And yet the Corps let her conceal herself anyway.

Perhaps the powers that be didn't want all and sundry wondering why she carried multiple cores. Or where they'd come from. Or how she'd gotten them in the first place.

Suppressing speculation had been deemed more important than guaranteeing the safety of those around her.

"I can guess the basics of how you ended up with extra cores," Tiller said.

Carnelian stopped moving. Then, calm and deliberate, she finished threading her arms through the sleeves of her mantle. She took her time putting her gloves back on.

"If you're right, that'll save me the trouble of explaining it." She gave a theatrical little shiver. "You certainly keep it cold in here."

"Parts of the Forest get much colder."

"You're sponging off your neighbors," Carnelian said tartly. "They heat their rooms, and it bleeds over to your place. How cozy, you think. Well, it's all thanks to them."

"You were a government project," Tiller said. "You told me at the temple. Jace wanted a mage who could hold her own against the continent's Kraken. But your extra cores had to come from somewhere."

"Indeed." Carnelian laid a hand on her stomach, over her close-fitting red dress. "Was it an immaculate birth? Is there a classified facility somewhere capable of manufacturing artificial magic cores? Were they extracted from vorpal beasts?"

"Every single one of your cores looks perfectly normal and human," said Tiller. "You just happen to have too many of them. If they were extracted from anywhere, they were extracted from other people."

The warm aura of sunvine lamps illuminated the cold room, the silence between them, Tiller's spare wigs mounted on featureless mannequin heads, Carnelian's stocking-clad feet. Baba Sayo had always eschewed water-lights whenever she could.

Tiller knew better than to ask what had happened to the original owners of Carnelian's eight extra cores. She'd heard stories—most of dubious veracity—about top-secret government experiments with magic core extraction.

The gist of it was that most mages would die as soon as you cut out their core. Those rare few who survived were never quite the same. Core loss nearly always led to some kind of death: physical, mental, or both.

"Is the experiment over?" Tiller asked.

Carnelian turned to stare at her.

"You don't have to answer," Tiller added. "I'm not asking formally. I'm not asking as an operator."

"No," Carnelian said. "No—that's not what threw me. Sorry. Yes—it's over. They're quite done with me."

"So you're free."

She laughed. There was a startled edge to it.

"Free of anyone expecting me to become something great, yes. Free of the pressure to go down in history as a new national hero, yes. I'm much better off than most. But I'm still an unattached mage. By default, I'm still wedded to the whims of the state."

14

# 14

The moment Tiller used a nausea pellet on Carnelian at the temple, the hunters had started to stir again.

Perhaps they'd been feigning impairment. Perhaps they'd genuinely been too dazed to get up. Either way, their recovery happened as soon as Carnelian doubled over, retching. They rose to collect their worst-wounded man—the one who her sword had pierced like a crossbow bolt.

"I've got more pellets," Tiller said to them. "If you want to test how it feels."

The hunters said nothing in response. Even if they'd attempted to speak, Carnelian's vehement gagging would have erased it.

They carried their bleeding man a short distance away. Deeper in the woods, though not entirely out of sight. There they activated a disposable portal and vanished all at once, swift and efficient.

A brief wind came through the trees in their wake, rattling the fence around the vorpal hole. The long rusted chains dangling from high branches let out tortured-sounding squeaks.

Carnelian's back still hadn't stopped heaving. Tiller knelt to do some initial emergency maintenance.

Later, she called over a few local constables. She avoided going to the temple staff for help.

Once Carnelian was coherent enough to get up off her knees, they filed a formal report. Then they went to see Colonel Istel at a garrison on the far north end of the city.

This required venturing down into a bypass tunnel. Tiller almost had to bail out halfway through. She kept remembering the sound of what the nausea pellet had done to Carnelian.

During their debriefing, Tiller did most of the talking. Carnelian lay on a sofa, looking wan. She refused Colonel Istel's offer of refreshments.

Istel seemed surprised that they'd gotten attacked in broad daylight. Tiller didn't find it so peculiar, though it had been years since the last time anyone targeted her so brazenly.

By night she was usually back at Baba Sayo's apartment—which, magically speaking, had better security than the average bank vault.

"The Parasite Guild doesn't normally take jobs like this." Carnelian still sounded weak. "They're quite law-abiding, as far as hunters go. Someone must have paid them a lot. And told them very little."

"You know them, too?" Tiller asked Colonel Istel.

He frowned. "They often do work for the city or the Corps. Just last year, they helped take down one of the big mafia families from the southern islands. But that's another story."

Tiller pictured the immobility tick on her leg. The mysterious bubbles. "They used a lot of strange tools."

"They have their own private mages for weapons production. They marry or adopt mages to get them added to a relevant family register.

"In that sense, they work much like the oldest mafia clans. Specialized magic skills getting passed down from one generation of mages to the next. But at least the Parasite Guild adheres to all the legal requirements about sharing their skills with the government."

"Half their tools don't function nearly so well in the Forest, anyway," Carnelian said from her couch.

"Few things do," muttered the colonel.

Later that night at Baba Sayo's apartment, bathed in the radiance of sunvine lamps, Tiller finished performing maintenance on Carnelian's magic.

Afterward she attempted to send Carnelian home. To wherever she lived. One of the wealthy districts on the far side of the city, most likely. She'd have to traverse the bypass tunnels to get there.

Yet Carnelian turned up again less than half an hour later, a duffel bag slung from her shoulder. Tiller, who had already removed and cleaned her wig of the day, was sorely tempted to ignore her.

Carnelian smiled sweetly on the other side of the apartment door peephole. Tiller pulled on a knit cap and reluctantly let her back in.

As soon as she crossed the threshold, Carnelian plopped her duffel bag on the floor. "Thought I'd stay with you tonight," she announced. "If you'll have me."

"Why?" Tiller said, bewildered.

Carnelian raised one finger as she spoke, then another. "First, for security reasons. The Parasite Guild ought to know better than to attack you here. You've got this place locked down like a fortress. Still, a little extra protection won't hurt. Second, I think we're both well aware that if I'm alone back at my own place, there's an extremely high chance that I won't make it in time for the train tomorrow."

"You want me to be your human alarm clock?" Tiller demanded. "That's it? That's your reason for coming all the way back here?"

"Were you hoping for something else?"

Earrings that glittered like tinsel grazed Carnelian's shoulders. She'd left her short red dress at home: the one she wore now was long and gauzy, better suited for summer.

"I have no idea what you mean," Tiller said with dignity, but by then Carnelian had already moved on. She poked her head into the kitchenette, lured by the scent of the roasted corn tea Tiller had started brewing after she left.

"I love this stuff," Carnelian exclaimed. "Can I take some?"

"Help yourself," Tiller said, giving up.

She went about the rest of her night as if she were alone. Well, mostly. Carnelian sat in Baba Sayo's chair and watched with avid interest as Tiller took off the cap she'd donned to answer the door.

"It's a beautiful color," Carnelian told her.

"I'm not flattered." Tiller raked irritably at the sides of her hair.

Carnelian drank more tea with a smile. "Ever considered growing it out?"

"What would be the point? I wear wigs every day."

Few people could boast of having seen the hair of a living blue.

The largest natural history museum in the city kept old clippings on display. Alongside a few ultra-rare preserved corpses with stringy blue strands still attached.

Baba Sayo had forbidden Tiller from going to look at them. Don't buy a ticket to gawk together with all the city folk, she'd said. Imagine if it was Gren in there—imagine if they'd made him a botched mummy. Imagine if they'd made him part of their permanent collection.

There were some things Tiller wouldn't have known how to explain to her. Lately, the Koya Foundation's best-performing fundraisers had all been held at that very museum.

Now there was no longer any risk of Baba Sayo finding out. Now there was no reason for guilt. Now there was no one she wanted to try to show her best self.

She hid in the bedroom to change to fluffy pajamas. Unlike Baba Sayo, she preferred the plainest clothing she could find. Few colors, and no patterns.

"Cute," Carnelian said upon seeing her emerge clad in the brown-gray hues of a turtle dove.

"That sounds sarcastic."

"I only ever say exactly what I mean." Carnelian beckoned her closer. "C'mere. I brought a present for my future wife."

She handed Tiller a necklace of brass teeth. Human-shaped teeth, loose on a thin chain. They clinked together like gambling dice.

"Um," Tiller said.

"Too touched for words? That's quite all right. Sometimes I get moved to tears by my own thoughtfulness."

"Is this a prank?"

"Of course not. We're promised to each other, aren't we? I've known many loves, but I've never given anyone teeth before."

"I would hope not," Tiller snapped. "Why *teeth*? Do I even want to know?"

The sunvine lamps flickered like candles.

"Why teeth?" Carnelian repeated.

Infuriatingly enough, there was a note of legitimate confusion in her voice. She glanced about as if hoping to find the answer concealed somewhere among Baba Sayo's many clashing drapes.

Then she returned her gaze to Tiller. "You don't know? You've never heard of this? You left the Forest twenty years ago. Surely—but you must have—"

"I spend most of my time with foresters, or discussing forester business. You can't expect me to be familiar with every obscure Jacian tradition."

"It's the traditional gift from a magewife to their spouse," Carnelian said. "Up here in Nui, and most of the other islands. At least about as far south as Central."

"Teeth?" Tiller uttered.

"Teeth. In the past, mages like me would've pulled out a couple of actual adult teeth. A real sign of commitment. Nowadays we use replicas."

Tiller pinched the necklace's small metal clasp and shook it in the air. The brass teeth jingled. They looked rather too large for Carnelian's mouth. "You're telling me these are supposed to be yours?"

"Of course. I had a mold taken and everything."

"You're lying," Tiller said.

Carnelian put a hand on her heart. "You wound me."

"We've known each other for two weeks." Tiller rattled the teeth again. "Which means you had two weeks to get this made. With your time management skills? Impossible."

They stared at each other until Carnelian looked away, her long earrings glimmering sheepishly. "I may or may not have bought it at one of the big city flea markets."

"Great," said Tiller. "So you want me to wear a total stranger's teeth."

"It's a symbol of my eternal devotion."

"I'll put it in my luggage," Tiller said. "But I'd rather martyr myself to the Lord of Circles than string these replica teeth around my neck. Thanks for the present."

Trust Carnelian to give her something absolutely useless rather than the one thing she kept asking for: a complete list of Carnelian's skills.

She attempted to compile the ones she'd seen Carnelian use at the temple. Short-distance porting. A long clear sword drawn from thin air. A grotesquely large and flexible phantom hand. Homing pearls— small black rocks—spat from her mouth. Multifaceted shields.

She asked what Carnelian called these skills. The military must have given them some manner of official designation.

In response, Carnelian rattled off a string of incomprehensible codes.

"Not gonna be able to remember those off the top of my head," Tiller said.

Carnelian pulled a face. "I know. That's why it's been taking me so long to make a list. I keep trying to think of cooler names for them."

"You'd better finish writing me that list on the train."

Carnelian didn't make any promises. She did, however, stop making excuses. She also began to show every indication of planning to spend the night in lingerie. Or even less. Tiller made her wear Baba Sayo's paisley pajamas instead.

"I'd rather sleep nude," Carnelian muttered. The sleeves were too short for her, but she dutifully donned the full matching set.

"The bed's only got room for one," Tiller said, in one last attempt to make Carnelian rethink this. "My grandmother was a small woman."

"That's all right. I can sleep anywhere. Maybe I'll take that chair by the window."

Said chair was sized for Baba Sayo and cobbled together from stiff wood, with zero padding. "Knock yourself out," Tiller told her. "But don't you have a bunch of girlfriends you need to visit before leaving the city? Or boyfriends. Or gambling buddies."

Carnelian crossed her arms, but she couldn't pull off looking stern while squeezed into too-small psychedelic paisley. "What an awful thing to say to your fiancée. You're the only one for me, darling. I even gave you my teeth."

"Those are most definitely not your teeth."

"Sure they are. In a spiritual sense. I paid good money for them."

Tiller told her goodnight and headed off to bed without looking back.

In lieu of a door, the bedroom had a hanging fabric divider with vertical slits incised in it for easier passage. The cloth bore a pattern of pretty Forest bison and albino bats—clearly designed by someone who had never been to the Forest in person.

In real life, both the bison and the bats were much larger.

Tiller had expected Carnelian to fuss more. To grow bored with the long night, the stiff chair, the lack of heat, and the fact that no one was paying attention to her. Yet Carnelian remained remarkably quiet out in the main room.

Something woke Tiller around two or three in the morning. Too late for much noise to filter up from the street. Too early for dawn light to leak in.

She rose, without knowing why. She moved silently to the bedroom entrance and poked her head out through the slits in the fabric divider.

The chair by the window was empty.

Carnelian sat on the floor in front of the shrine in the corner. But she wasn't looking at it, not at the moment. She had her head in her arms.

A strange place to go.

A strange way to sleep.

Tiller's wariness had eased somewhat after Carnelian defended her at the temple. Yet she couldn't help but think that Carnelian might be playing a longer game. No better way to win someone's trust than by pretending to protect them.

Even if she weren't in cahoots with the Guild, Carnelian herself might harbor designs on the power that could be gained by sacrificing a blue. Or she might be getting paid by someone who would eventually demand that she hand Tiller over on a silver platter.

In that case, Carnelian would still have every motivation to fight off the Parasite Guild to keep her prey.

All that money of hers had to be coming from somewhere.

Carnelian herself had alluded to this possibility. But that openness, too, could've been a tactic to throw Tiller off the scent. To preemptively disarm her.

The only people Tiller had ever trusted without reservation were her twin, her bodyguard, and her grandmother. Gren, Doe, and Baba Sayo.

All three of them were now dead.

The fastest way for Tiller to join them would be to believe the things people told her. To take everything she saw at face value. To give her trust out unstintingly, without holding anything back.

She watched Carnelian lift her head from her arms. She wondered how much Carnelian could see in the darkness.

She waited a moment longer, then asked: "Want to open the curtain?"

Carnelian jerked. She clambered to her feet by the family shrine. More clumsily than usual, as if her legs had started falling asleep.

Tiller pointed at the window. "You can't sleep with it covered up, can you?"

"I—" Carnelian took a few careful steps back from the shrine. She lowered her voice. "I can sleep on the train."

"And make me drag you around like a big lump? No, thanks."

Tiller went to the window and flicked the curtains open. Moonlight, starlight, and ambient street light tumbled in to languish wanly on the scratched-up floor.

Carnelian put a hand to her forehead as if feeling for a fever. She wore her daytime gloves again, and her full mage mantle as well. Hood and all.

Perhaps Baba Sayo's pajamas weren't warm enough on their own. Tiller ought to have offered her a second or third spare blanket.

She felt Carnelian looking at her hair—uncovered, raw in its blueness, mussed from sleep.

She in turn found herself studying Carnelian's cores. For once they were wholly undisguised. A minor constellation trapped in her abdomen like dying fireflies clustered at the bottom of a jar, too tired to float.

Carnelian turned, suddenly, and bowed her head to the family shrine.

Baba Sayo's ashes observed from behind, resting unobtrusively in their ceramic flour jar on an unlabeled shelf. Her remains—hers and Doe's—would be the very last thing Tiller planned on packing when morning rolled across the city.

"I'll bring you back safe," Carnelian said. "I'll bring you home to them."

A dramatic proclamation, as was her wont, but her voice lacked its usual flair.

"What's home?" Tiller asked. "The city? The Forest? And who'll I be coming home to? They're all dead and gone."

She shook her head before Carnelian could say anything more. "You claimed you could sleep anywhere. Prove it."

She pointed back at the humble wooden chair where Baba Sayo had spent her last days. At least until she lost the strength to sit upright, the ability to hobble out of bed.

Moonlight gilded every dent and bump and scar—on the chair, on the floor, on the walls.

"You'd better be well rested if you're going to keep protecting me," Tiller said. "The Parasite Guild is nothing compared to the dangers of the Forest."

Beside her, Carnelian gazed mutely at the blank concrete canvas of the neighboring building beyond the window.

Beneath her hood, her hair was a soft weary silver on the sides of her neck. Night stripped the color from her garish borrowed sleepwear. All that remained was the muddled pattern of a labyrinth with no way in or out.

# PART TWO

*Outpost Twenty-Four*

THE TOP OF A VERY HIGH MOUNTAIN FOR HER MAGE

# 15

IN A SHOCKING turn of events, Carnelian was the first to rise. Tiller found her haunting the kitchenette in a silken robe, boiling corn tea as if she'd done it all her life.

"Did I teach you how to make that?" Tiller asked.

"I learned by watching."

"You didn't need me to wake you."

"I can wake up just fine on my own," Carnelian said. "But I have trouble with rushing."

Indeed, she moved so slowly that Baba Sayo could've beaten her in a race around the apartment.

Soon Tiller ended up waiting by the door, fully packed, tapping her foot. She had a camping backpack with everything nestled in its place. She'd taped up the jars holding Baba Sayo and Doe's ashes and wrapped them in clothes for extra padding. Now all she needed was for Carnelian to get on with it.

"What were you looking at last night?" she asked.

Carnelian flexed her fingers in her gloves, testing their fit. "I have no idea what you're talking about."

Tiller pointed. "You were on the floor in front of my family shrine. We had a conversation."

"I've been known to walk and talk in my sleep." Carnelian glanced up. "Did I say anything rude?"

"No ruder than usual."

Tiller hadn't bothered packing any of her finer wigs. The one she wore now was a cheap synthetic piece. The hairline wouldn't look as flawless as a proper lace-lined wig, but that wouldn't matter much out in the wilderness.

It was her first time seeing Carnelian in full uniform. Her outfit included a tunic over trousers, tactical belts, a vest, long sleeves, and far too many other layers and components to comprehend at a glance.

On top of it all came the familiar mantle and gloves, along with pointed lacquer ear cuffs. Plus her silver fighting pipe hooked at her side.

"Now I see why you're slow to get ready," Tiller said as they took their bags and set off.

"I look good, though, don't I?"

"No comment."

Thanks to the bypass tunnels, getting to the far northern end of Nui City took only a couple of minutes. But none of the tunnels extended beyond the city borders. To head deeper into the countryside, they would have to board a train.

They had a lot of time left to kill before the next departure.

Carnelian tried to sneak into an underground bar near the train station. Tiller grabbed her by the hood and hauled her back up the steps.

"We've got nothing else to do," Carnelian said dolefully.

"Appreciate the scenery," Tiller ordered.

Side by side, they looked about in silence.

Plum blossoms peeked out from behind residential fences a block away. The sounds of construction echoed everywhere—drills, shouts, metallic banging. In an empty lot overgrown with weeds, a pair of tiny children pushed earnestly at stacked cinderblocks.

The city was always full of construction, morning to night. Roads getting blocked or rerouted to work around vorpal holes. Old houses getting demolished and new houses popping up like springtime bamboo shoots in their place.

Few people wanted to live in a second-hand residence. *It's a used house*, they'd whisper in the same tone as *used underwear*. They would much rather knock it down and construct a brand new dwelling on the same lot. It was land that held true value in Nui City, not the swift-depreciating homes that crowded atop it.

Eventually Carnelian convinced her to go in some of the station's souvenir shops. They examined elk leather craftwork and vials of locally produced liquor. Carnelian bought one marked up to a price that Tiller would never have paid for a ten-course meal, much less a few measly sips of syrupy alcohol. And that was after the discount she'd obtained by flirting with the overeager clerk.

"Don't look at me like that," Carnelian said, indignant. "It's a gift."

"For who?"

"My good friend Alder Istel."

"Does he drink much?" Tiller asked. He'd seemed fairly reserved at the Corps party a few weeks ago.

Then again, anyone would've come off as reserved next to Carnelian.

"Not as much as he should," Carnelian said. "He's got a lot of stress in his life."

"Most of it caused by you, I'd bet."

"How'd you know?" Carnelian wiggled her small bottle. The aged pickled roeberries at the bottom bounced slowly off one another, then settled back down into a dubious pile of sediment. "I'm a good friend, aren't I? I may cause him trouble, but I do what I can to help."

"Not sure if that's something to brag about."

Down on the platform, they watched freight trains pull in and out. The passenger trains were slower and more decrepit. Not to mention much less busy. Most commuters into town lived within a walk or bike or skimmer ride away from the bypass tunnels.

In terms of sheer land mass, Nui was among the largest of the Jacian islands. But it had the smallest population—and everywhere except for Nui City, the population kept shrinking precipitously. People fled rural areas for the city. Or they fled the island altogether.

The Devouring Forest had once occupied less than a fifth of Nuian territory. Over the past few decades, it gobbled up border towns and farmland, expanding its share to almost a third.

"Ever thought of leaving Nui?" Tiller asked as they boarded their train.

The inner walls were dark blond wood, the seats a faded mossy green. The fabric smelled powerfully of mildew. They were utterly alone in their compartment.

"Leaving for good?" said Carnelian. "No. Not seriously. You?"

"I'm a forester." To Tiller, that was explanation enough. No longer could anyone live safely in the Forest. But staying on the same island still felt better than uprooting herself to cross the Amber Strait.

"You're not, though," she added. "Don't see what's holding you back. Especially if you used to want to be a chalice pilot."

Carnelian propped her elbow up on the narrow windowsill. The train grudgingly chugged forward.

"Oh, I've been off the island before," she said. "I've gotten summoned to Central plenty of times."

"What for?"

"You know. Mage duties. Can't say I ever thought of moving down south."

"Just not interested?"

"It's too hard to blend in. People from southern islands consider Nui to be some sort of lost wilderness backwoods. To them, even our biggest city is the boondocks. They think our accent sounds stupid. They think we're all superstitious hicks. A lot of them don't even consider us fully Jacian. Not like the rest of them. Not in a cultural sense."

She shrugged one shoulder. "It goes both ways. Here up north, we obey orders from Central. But we don't necessarily show a lot of respect for their reasoning."

The train window framed the classic icons of Nui City. The old tiered castle mounted on improbably tall and spindly stilts, pretending to float in the air above the populace. A colossal statue of a chalice on a cliff over tilled fields.

The statue was intended to give off the impression of a watchful guardian. With the way it stared across at the distant castle, it looked more like an invasive monster gearing up for one last attempt to claim the city.

The train passed abandoned farm silos, a defunct elementary school, pastures full of thick-legged stock-elks.

After much urging, Carnelian finally scribbled down some notes about her branch skills.

She had terrible handwriting. It wasn't a comprehensive or tremendously informative list, either. Tiller had no idea how this woman could possibly have set about studying for the Outborder Corps audition, which was supposed to be extremely rigorous.

Even if she did pretend to study for a day or two, how had she managed to pass it?

"You didn't write anything about porting," Tiller said.

"I only wrote the skills I'd feel confident using in the Forest. Porting is a no-go."

"Your version of it only covers short distances. Thought that'd be less risky."

"Most fatal magical accidents in the Forest involve porting. It just doesn't work well."

"Not at all?"

"Not even the best mages in the Corps could pull it off safely. And I'm certainly not one of their best."

Carnelian proceeded to describe what had happened when one of her colleagues tried to port out of the Forest in a wild panic. The story ended in a wet steaming shower of body parts.

Tiller handed the paper back. "Write about the skills you're less confident in, too. Just for the sake of completeness. I won't ask you to port in the Forest."

The updated version did include an explanation of Carnelian's porting skill. That one was straightforward enough, limitations and all.

Other skills only got more confusing the more she tried to explain them. One had something to do with concealment. Or with hunkering down in a bunker, in the way of a trapdoor spider. It let her seal off passages, making it so that she alone could reveal the entrance.

*But it really only works for me, and I haven't used it in years*, she wrote in the margin. *Great for siege situations. Not so useful for traversing the Forest.*

At the very end she'd jotted a few words about a basic type of levitation. It sounded like a softer telekinesis. Too low-velocity for lobbing projectiles at an enemy. Still, Tiller could imagine plenty of other uses.

"This floating skill might come in handy," she said.

"...It's pretty unstable. Wouldn't want to activate it in the Forest, anyway."

Tiller read through the full list again. Only then did she understand why it struck her as being so strange.

Regardless of field, most mages got assigned to work as specialists. Their skills might not be particularly useful in isolation. Instead they would serve a key function as part of an assembly line, or in conjunction with the rest of a complete team.

"None of your skills are inherently cooperative," Tiller said. "Or did you omit those?"

"Never had any to begin with. They envisioned me as a human weapon. Capable of devastating armies all on my own, with only the aid of an operator." Carnelian snorted. "They dreamed a little too big, I'd say."

"But you can only use one skill at a time."

Or so Tiller assumed, based on how she'd deployed them at the temple. Strictly consecutive. Never two or more at once.

"I never did get the hang of parallel processing. Just don't have it in me. They could stuff me full of other people's cores, but they couldn't make me any better at the absolute basics of being a mage. Such a shame."

"You don't sound too torn up over it."

Carnelian smiled as if recalling an inside joke. "Life becomes a lot easier when people give up on you."

"Does it?"

"I love having it easy. Why struggle when you don't need to? Why suffer?"

The train lurched.

Carnelian sprang up, gripping the edge of the window. Tiller stayed in place.

This felt like an issue with the train itself, not an earthquake. But whatever the cause—when one shake came, another would usually follow in short succession.

She tugged at Carnelian. "You might want to—"

The train lurched again—much harder and louder—launching Tiller like a battering ram into the back of the seat in front of her. Then it rocked to a complete stop. A feeble creaking faded away into silence.

# 16

Somehow, Carnelian had avoided losing her balance. Tiller drew herself up, adjusting her wig, and twisted to stare out the window.

She saw nothing resembling a station or a crossing. No trains approaching on the opposite track. Nothing but banks of dead grass and vigorous thick-stemmed weeds.

The sky looked bluer and deeper here than in the city. The shadowy silhouettes of distant mountains seeped up from the horizon like water stains.

They waited a few more minutes. Passengers from other compartments let the train staff herd them off to one side of the tracks. There weren't many of them, and most seemed resigned to their fate.

Carnelian, clad in her official Outborder Corps attire, managed to get the crew to divulge more information about the sudden stop.

A vorpal hole had manifested near the tracks. Perhaps last night. Perhaps this morning. There'd been some confusion about whether scheduled trains were still cleared to pass. Now new orders had come down from on high. No trains, regardless of whether they carried travelers or cargo, were to proceed any further along this route. Passengers would be escorted to the closest countryside town, many miles back.

Tiller and Carnelian thanked the train attendants. They collected their bags. They started walking in the opposite direction, ignoring the chattering of the stranded riders and the curious whispers of the crew.

No one attempted to stop them. Carnelian looked like a full-fledged Corps mage. Tiller, by association, must've given the impression of being her operator—and therefore a Corps member herself. Even if she didn't dress like one.

Sunlight burnt away any lingering traces of winter chill. Amber bees floated about their heads, bright and translucent, beads of living sap.

Carnelian made a show of taking a deep breath. "I do love the smell of the country," she said.

Istel and his commander had requested that they stop by Outpost 24 (the military base nearest to the Forest) before proceeding onward. They needed to collect the supplies and weapons they'd mailed ahead, anyhow.

If the train had carried them to its final stop, it wouldn't have taken much longer to reach the outpost. Now they'd be stuck walking the rest of the distance along the tracks. An extra two or three hours, if all went well.

Could've been worse. Since Carnelian's porting skill could only jump her to places she'd already physically visited in the past twenty-four hours, they really had no choice but to hoof it.

"Want to play a game?" Carnelian asked.

"Not really."

"Want to hear a fun fact, then?"

"You seem excited to tell me," Tiller said.

"We've met before."

Neither of them stopped walking. Tiller kept a firm grip on the straps of her backpack. "Sure you're not thinking of someone else?" she asked. "I don't do one-night stands."

"I do meet a lot of interesting people that way," said Carnelian. "But no. That's not it. You can't remember?"

"You seem like you would be hard to forget."

"Well, it might be stretching the truth to say we *met*. We never exchanged names."

Tiller considered the possibilities. Unseasonably early white butterflies skittered past, seeking wildflowers that had yet to awaken.

"Something to do with the Koya Foundation?"

"Right on," Carnelian said in tones of admiration. "You got it. I saw you at a charity gala years ago. Never forgot your face, though."

"Why were you there?"

"The folly of youth. I took a brief interest in philanthropy."

"And then what happened?" Tiller inquired. "You got into slot machines instead?"

"My repertoire goes way beyond slots," Carnelian said. "I can hold my own in far more sophisticated games."

"Has your gambling ever turned a profit?"

Carnelian pretended not to hear her.

They followed the tracks across a stone viaduct spanning a precipitous yellow-green valley. It was high up enough to glimpse the serpentine barrens off to the east: a patchwork of harsh grasslands with poor soil ill-suited to farming.

Beyond the bridge, Carnelian wistfully suggested turning west. Keep going long enough, and they might reach a hot springs town in the coastal mountains.

Of course, that would take far more than a day to reach on foot.

They kept heading north along the tracks. Tiller hummed under her breath to pass the time. Most of the melodies that came to mind were the sort tootled by old-fashioned neighborhood merchants—bean curd sellers, traveling knife sharpeners.

Whatever sounds she made never quite reached the level of outright singing. Carnelian seemed unlikely to know the same tunes as her. If she were going to sing on the road, she didn't want to sing alone.

An hour went by. Then another. Tiller strained for a glimpse of the final station. The primitive rails on the ground seemed to stretch on forever, implacable.

Carnelian stopped. She put an arm out.

Tiller stopped, too. She kept her mouth shut.

Carnelian: "Do you hear that?"

A bird cried piercingly in the distance. But Carnelian seemed to be thinking of something else. She put a finger to her lips. A cold wind stirred the brush.

She leaned in closer, as if worried about being overheard. "Can I—?"

"Go on," Tiller said, matching her pitch. "Take off your gloves."

The gloves came off. Carnelian's long clear sword drew itself from the air. Its blade bent sunlight like a heat mirage given flesh.

"Hunters?" Tiller asked.

"Seems too fast for the Parasite Guild to have caught up. I made sure they weren't on the same train as us."

Tiller took Carnelian's duffel bag and trundled along behind her. Carnelian pointed wordlessly at signs of a struggle further down the tracks. Unnaturally shattered trees, scorched and splintered as if struck by lightning. Directionless motes of used magic wafting about like polluting smoke.

"Might be a vorpal beast," Tiller said.

"Maybe."

They'd passed the new vorpal hole a while back. It hadn't been visible from the tracks, but they'd seen multiple warning signs—a whole flock of them, hastily installed, bearing the usual vortex-shaped icon.

"I used to dream of being a hunter," Carnelian confided. "Thought I could die a glorious death to vorpal beasts."

"Was this before or after you aspired to become a chalice pilot?"

"Both, I suppose."

"So you've always been this morbid."

"I've always been myself," Carnelian said. "Plus or minus a few extra magic cores."

The last stop came into view. It was a humble structure, just barely holding its own against the encroachment of nature.

A ramshackle restaurant huddled against the side of the train station, almost entirely overgrown by brambles. A weathered sign advertised local tea, fried dumplings, hot noodles, cheap meat buns.

It appeared to be closed for the day, or perhaps forever, but someone had diligently cleared vines away from the windows. Dolls of angels, demons, and clowns rested inside, shoulder to shoulder, faces pressed up against clouded glass.

Sword out, Carnelian yanked Tiller into the woods around the tracks. These were young trees, still battling for dominance of space and light.

"People," Carnelian said tautly. "Not beasts. If it gets bad, I'll port us back the way we came."

"They might expect that. They might lay a trap."

"I know. Put those bags down. You're making yourself a bigger target."

Something rustled. Overhead, a woodpecker drilled away in brief staccato bursts. Hints of an indescribably foul odor clung mustily to the air, as if a wild animal had sprayed musk all over the foundation of that dark old restaurant. Carnelian held her sword in both hands now.

# 17

"Nellie?"

A male voice.

Carnelian spun around. The glassy sword nearly left her fingers—it surged like a water bird about to take flight—but she seized it harder at the last second, reeled it in.

In a single swift step, she inserted herself between Tiller and the people behind them. Three people in total.

One was Colonel Istel. He wore a field uniform and an expression of profound consternation.

Carnelian dismissed her sword with a flick of her wrist. She put her gloves back on.

A pair of mages flanked Istel. One male and one female, but otherwise eerily similar. They looked like city joggers who'd taken a wrong turn into the woods. All they had on were athletic leggings and hoodies and one glove each.

They couldn't have been dressed less like Carnelian, with all her layers and buckles and straps.

They were both taller than Istel. They both wore neat little purple-tinted glasses. They were mirror images of each other, right down to their flipped asymmetrical haircuts, each shaved on one side and sleekly braided on the other.

They had limpid olive skin which suggested that they never slept less than nine hours per night.

"Nellie!" cried the woman.

"Nellie," said the man.

"Do I know you?" Carnelian asked warily.

"She forgot," the woman said to the man.

"We were just children back then," he replied. "We look different now."

"Sing for us," the woman told Carnelian. "We always loved your voice."

Colonel Istel cleared his throat.

As the highest-ranking operator in this group of five, he ostensibly had authority over all the rest of them. Tiller included. She'd gotten permission to bring Carnelian as a guard to the Forest, but Tiller herself was still a mere civilian.

The twin mages loomed amiably on either side of Colonel Istel. The man rested an arm on his left shoulder. The woman linked elbows with him. Squished between them, Istel appeared to be on the verge of developing hives.

"Auditors from Central," he said, more to Tiller than to Carnelian. "They'll be staying at the outpost till chalices arrive to scourge the Forest outskirts. They're part of Central's ... advance preparations."

"We have names, you know," said the woman.

"I was getting there!" Istel made a futile attempt to wrench himself away from them. "Auditor Lapis," he said, jerking his head at the woman. "Auditor Aeris." This time he indicated the man.

Tiller's eyes went to the design on their hoodies and gloves. A bold spiral—the sort you might see painted by a large calligraphy brush. The mark of Central.

She'd almost gotten it confused with the vortex-shaped hazard symbol meant to indicate vorpal holes. Or with the convoluted serpent insignia worn by Colonel Istel.

But that snake on his uniform was meant for operators, and these two were indisputably mages. Their cores gleamed with a clean healthy light. They had four magic branches each, impeccably maintained, not a single wayward twist or tangle among them.

"The colonel was worried about you," Auditor Lapis said to Carnelian. "He took us to scout out the new hole by the tracks. A small swarm of vorpal beasts emerged overnight, it seems."

"All is well," said Auditor Aeris, low and cheerful. "We slaughtered them."

The auditors had distinct southern accents, clear and cultured.

Of course, to Nuians, everyone from the other islands was a southerner. These auditors spoke with pronunciation as close to the ideal of standard Jacian as any living human could get. Tiller and Istel and Carnelian must've sounded terribly backwards to them.

"Had any episodes lately?" Auditor Lapis asked Carnelian. Her tone remained bright.

Carnelian shifted in place. "I don't—"

"Just don't try so hard," Auditor Lapis advised her. "Loosen up."

"Things only go wrong when you push yourself," said Auditor Aeris. "Giving up is always safest."

"Or you could work your stress out by singing."

"That's a great idea, actually."

"Music does wonderful things for the psyche."

"We're always happy to listen."

Carnelian looked murderous.

"Colonel Istel," she said, hard and formal. "Can we talk for a second?"

He appeared grateful for an excuse to shake off the auditors. He and Carnelian strode over to the abandoned shop lurking next to the station. They whispered to each other in front of the dark doll-lined window.

When they edged too close to the wall, brambles caught at their clothing. Carnelian tore herself free with visible irritation.

"Confused?" Auditor Lapis asked softly.

"I don't need to know everything," Tiller said. Which was true. Why concern herself with the endless push-and-pull of tension between Central and the Outborder Corps and the local Nuian government?

In another day or two, she and Carnelian would be alone in the Forest. Simple survival would become their most immediate concern.

"Let's give them more privacy," Auditor Lapis said.

She put a hand on Tiller's back and nudged her further from the station, toward a clearing that turned out to be a neglected playground.

Vines dragged at a seesaw as if trying to hoist it into the treetops. Sculpted whales and wild boars teetered on thick spiral springs. All the paint had flaked off their faces, leaving behind a florid mask of rust.

Auditor Aeris had followed close behind. "Ever met an auditor before?"

His voice was deep and smooth. In another life, it would've been well-suited for crooning lullabies.

"No," Tiller answered.

"So we're your first," said Auditor Lapis. "Such an honor."

Neither seemed higher in rank than the other. Tiller settled on addressing them both at once. "You asked Carnelian if she'd had any episodes recently. Episodes of what?"

Auditor Lapis tilted her head one way. Auditor Aeris titled his head the other way. "Take a guess," he said.

Together they peered at Tiller over the delicate rims of their lavender glasses.

A wet stench permeated the clearing, as if it were too secluded for morning dew to ever fully evaporate.

She thought of Carnelian saying: *Do whatever you need to do to stop me.*

She thought of Carnelian dragging a hunter closer and closer to the fatal maw of a vorpal hole, unmoved by his bleeding.

Carnelian hadn't questioned why Tiller used a nausea pellet to stop her. They hadn't spoken much of it afterward. But that didn't mean Tiller thought nothing of it.

Her objective remained unchanged. She would bring Baba Sayo and Doe back where they belonged. Carnelian's bloodthirsty side seemed unlikely to interfere with that core mission—as long as she didn't turn on Tiller herself.

No signs of that so far. But things could always change in the Forest.

"To be clear," said Auditor Lapis, "we like Nellie. We like her very much. We're different from all those prudes in the Corps. You know the type."

"Do I?"

"Mages trying so hard to flaunt their sophistication. Their restraint. Their ability to cooperate."

"They waste so much energy tamping down their true nature," added Auditor Aeris. "Mages are weak-willed and hungry. We're feeble-minded creatures, really. Driven by instinct and fleshly desires. Why not embrace it?"

"You could say that about a lot of people," Tiller replied. "It's not exclusive to mages."

"Tell us what you really think," he said. "You don't have to be polite."

So she did. "You two are in a position of real power, aren't you? They let you travel all the way from Central without an operator?"

One at a time, they grinned. Both had large gaps in their teeth.

"Think of it this way," Auditor Lapis said. "Central is our core, and we are but branches."

"Delicate tendrils," Auditor Aeris chimed in. "A cat's whiskers."

"A cephalopod's tentacles."

"An insect's antennae."

"Cilia."

"Nerve endings."

"Observers."

"Sensors."

"Feelers."

Auditor Aeris gave a satisfied nod. "Yes, that sounds right. Feelers. We're here to feel our way around and report back the unvarnished truth of it. We don't editorialize."

"Do a cat's whiskers editorialize?" asked Auditor Lapis. "Surely not." She turned to Aeris. "If we have true power—"

"—It lies in the fact that we've got so little clothing to remove."

He raised his naked left hand. Lapis raised her naked right hand. They spread and curled sleek fingers.

"We aren't weighed down by excess restraints. We can use certain forms of lethal force at our own discretion. That's rare for mages, I guess."

"Some would call us inquisitors," Auditor Lapis said.

"Or executioners."

"But basically, we're the same as your Nellie. We're just here to have fun."

Tiller tried to look around them, to see if Colonel Istel and Carnelian were done whispering yet. With the smooth coordination of pack animals circling prey, the auditors shifted to block her view.

She resigned herself to entertaining them. At least the location felt fitting: a creepy lost playground for dealing with oversized children.

They had to be in their early twenties. Close to a decade younger than her and Carnelian. But their preternatural confidence made them seem ageless.

"Are you twins?" she asked.

"Blood relatives, you mean?"

Auditor Aeris put a hand on her head. On her synthetic wig.

"Were you and your brother twins?" he asked.

So they already knew exactly who and what she was. No way to keep secrets from the authorities down in Central.

Tiller lifted his hand off the top of her head. The spring-mounted animals on the far side of the playground, deprived of children willing to ride them, gawked at her with flayed and eyeless faces.

"Of course we were twins," she said. "We—"

Auditor Lapis popped up on her other side. "Sure about that? Did you ever get tested?"

"No, but—"

"You were both blues. So? Your adoptive grandmother found you and a boy around the same age. She found you living feral in the Forest. Your hair was the same color. You looked similar enough. You acted inseparable.

"Naturally she assumed you were siblings. Fraternal twins, to be precise. But where's the proof?"

"We aren't twins, by the way," said Auditor Aeris. "We aren't related in the slightest. We did grow up together in the same facility, though. Dogs resemble their owners, or so people claim. Maybe nurture makes us similar."

"Gren was my brother," Tiller said. A slow acidic rage wicked its way up to sear the lining of her throat. "Gren was my twin."

The auditors exchanged a look. "Believe what you like," Lapis told her. "Our job is to remain impartial. Our job is to wallow happily in the facts. Pigs in mud. You've already decided on one story for yourself. We see the other possibilities. It's all equal to us."

"No one asked you to—"

A crystal-clear sword dropped like a falcon from the sky. It plummeted hilt-deep into the mud at the center of the playground.

Tiller's first reflex was to jump back. The auditors caught her and held her in place.

The magic sword melted into an opalescent puddle, then seeped down to become one with the dirt.

Carnelian and Colonel Istel stood at the entrance to the clearing.

"Surely that was unnecessary," said the colonel.

Carnelian ignored him. "Leave Tiller be," she called to the auditors. "She's not used to dealing with the likes of you. If you absolutely must bother someone, bother him." She pointed at Istel.

Istel gibbered. "You little—"

"You got assigned to babysit them, didn't you? Get them out of our hair."

Auditor Lapis put an arm around Tiller's waist. Auditor Aeris put an arm around her shoulder. The same pincher maneuver they'd used on the colonel earlier.

Tiller started to wiggle free. Their arms tightened like a snare trap. They both looked straight at Carnelian.

"We've never met a blue before," Lapis said.

"And she's the only one left to meet. The only one still alive," Aeris continued. "What's the big rush? You aren't leaving for the Forest tonight, are you? We've got time."

They smelled the way they looked: like mid-workout athletes, youthful and healthy and a touch overripe.

Tiller inhaled—through her mouth, not her nose—and said in the tone of an operator commanding a mage: "Hands off me."

They immediately obeyed.

Neither her words nor her voice held any special power. They'd already disregarded her subtler attempts at resistance.

But there was no way these elite mages would be permitted to roam so far from their home base if they hadn't been thoroughly trained to heed the orders of the nearest operator. When it really mattered, anyhow.

"Stop picking fights," Colonel Istel said wearily. It wasn't clear whether he meant the auditors, Carnelian, or both.

Tiller trotted over to Carnelian. "Better go collect our bags," she said.

No response.

"Carnelian?"

For a fleeting moment, a skeletal clawed shape enveloped Carnelian's arm. It passed like a cloud crossing paths with the moon.

"I wonder," Carnelian said meditatively, "did I get that much joy out of stirring up trouble when I was younger?"

"Have you completely outgrown it?" Tiller asked.

"Maybe not." Carnelian studied the backs of her bare hands. She must've wrangled permission from Istel to remove her gloves again.

# 18

The colonel guided them to a hidden portal near the final station. It was a door behind the counter of the defunct restaurant full of dolls. He unlocked it with his snake emblem.

Beyond the portal door—though physically many acres away from here—lay Outpost 24.

Colonel Istel briefly pointed out the barracks, the armory, the dining hall, the command center.

The buildings stood in a semicircle around an extensive patchwork of practice arenas. The largest: a wooded section of land the size of a sprawling city park. A pale imitation of the Forest.

The Jacian flag, which bore a stylized goblet, followed them everywhere. It flew from flagpoles and windows. It appeared in murals on the sides of buildings. It all seemed rather excessive to Tiller—but then again, she wasn't the intended audience.

Sunvines grew thick overhead in the dining hall, roots tangled around crossbeams, all but covering the glassy ceiling. They cast warm light down on clusters of uniformed soldiers who ate briskly, without much talking. Most appeared to be laypeople. They carried neither magic cores nor the same snake badge as Istel.

The not-twin auditors wandered off while Colonel Istel and Carnelian and Tiller served themselves lunch.

"Feels a bit empty here," Carnelian remarked.

The soldiers stuffing their faces in the dining hall were the first living people they'd encountered in the entire outpost.

"Most everyone's headed out for patrols or training," said Istel.

"Then why is the commander here?" Carnelian asked.

"She's not here at the moment."

"Didn't she say she wanted to see us?"

"She'll be back tonight. Try not to do anything foolish in the meantime."

"I never do anything foolish."

"What about the auditors?" Tiller inquired, curiosity getting the best of her. "Why hang around here if nothing's happening yet?"

"Please don't ask me to explain their whims," Istel said gloomily.

Tiller and Carnelian intended on setting off for the Forest the following day. So they would only stay one night at the outpost. Colonel Istel showed them to their assigned rooms in a humongous guesthouse near the command center.

They stopped by the mailroom to gather all the supplies they'd sent in advance from the city. They carried their haul back to Tiller's bedroom and got to work on consolidating and repacking.

Being a forester—even one who'd spent the last twenty years in a faraway city—Tiller required neither rations nor a way to produce clean water. The Forest would feed her without harming her.

Carnelian, on the other hand, needed to bring as much food as she could carry. No matter how Tiller rebalanced their respective loads, Carnelian seemed to end up with heavier bags.

Tiller sat back on her heels. "Listen," she said. "I grant you blanket permission to take off anything you want. Your gloves, your cloak—anything weighing you down. You'll have an easier time in the Forest if you simplify your outfit."

Carnelian glanced up. She'd been fussing with her first aid kit, trying to find the best place to wedge tins of pain ointment. "So you're saying you want me to wear less."

"I'm being serious."

"I do appreciate the thought," Carnelian said. "Bad idea, though. The Outborder Corps doesn't make us mages wear all this just because it looks cool."

"It doesn't."

"Ouch. Still. The more restraints a mage has in the Forest, the better."

Carnelian got to her feet and stretched, demonstrating how much flexibility she had even in full uniform.

"It's more practical than it might appear at first glance. The layers are light, and thoughtfully tailored. I seemed comfortable enough during our little hike today, didn't I?"

A stiff wind came through the open window, carrying a faint odor of barbecue or burning brush. It smelled ever so slightly like Baba Sayo's village food: seared slowfish, batter-coated burntree leaves, roasted pulpfruit, pickled willow-berries.

But of course no one here at this outpost would risk eating anything foraged from Forest soil. No matter how close or convenient it might seem.

The breeze churned on, washing away Tiller's nostalgia.

As she sorted out their weapons, she remembered something she'd been meaning to ask about for a while now.

"You don't have any scars," she said.

Colonel Istel had a spiderweb of stark white marks that went all the way up to bisect his chin. Doe and Baba Sayo had sported their share of telltale scars, too. The soldiers chowing down in the outpost cafeteria had been visibly scarred. So were all the active Corps members at the party where she'd met Carnelian.

"Don't see any scars on you, either," Carnelian said absently. She picked up one of Doe's old swords, safely sheathed, and held it out as if trying to guess at its weight.

Tiller pushed up her left sleeve and showed Carnelian a series of smeared scars near the crook of her elbow. Her skin was blanched in patches that looked like four messy outspread fingers.

"My brother and I didn't get attacked as much as other foresters," she said.

"Something about being a blue?"

"Maybe. But we weren't immune. So what about you? You've been on multiple missions to the Forest. Where are your scars?"

Carnelian proceeded to examine Doe's scabbard much more closely than she needed to. "As you've seen, the one thing I'm extremely good at is shielding."

"Good enough to never let a phage touch you?"

"Never," Carnelian said. "But—and I'm guessing you won't be too happy to hear this—I'm a lot weaker when it comes to shielding other people. More than once, I've been the only person to survive an operation in the Forest. A lot of Corps members call me cursed."

"More than once?"

"There was a time when I dragged myself out of the Forest, the sole survivor from a crew of twenty. Then I joined a salvage mission to help clean up after all the casualties. Guess what happened?"

Tiller said nothing.

"Everyone who went on the second mission died, too. Except me. Unbelievable. They actually put me on trial for that one. Not that I can blame them. Did Istel mention any of this?"

"Not in detail."

"Do you regret recruiting me yet?"

Tiller got up and took Doe's sword from her. She moved it to their *maybe* pile.

"No one else volunteered," she said. "You were willing to come. That makes you the perfect candidate."

"For a price. Hope you haven't forgotten."

"At least it's a price I can pay."

Carnelian sighed. "Lord. I can't believe those brats got married before me."

"Who?"

"The auditors."

"They're married?"

"Not to each other," Carnelian said. "To high-ranking operators back in Central." She pointed at her mouth. "Didn't you see? They're missing half their teeth."

Tiller's gums ached in sympathy. "You told me that no magewife rips out real teeth for marriage anymore. You said that's a much older custom. Nowadays everyone uses replicas."

"They must be real strict traditionalists down in Central, huh?"

This was around the time when Carnelian appeared to tire of being helpful. She gathered up the contents of their *no* pile—weapons deemed excessive or redundant; clothes set aside for their return to the city. She offered to go stick it all in storage.

Tiller didn't expect her to come rushing back. And she didn't. Perhaps she'd run into an old acquaintance, or one of her many past conquests. Perhaps she'd found someone playing a card game.

On the plus side, little work remained. Tiller did one last inspection to make sure the ceramic containers holding human ashes were safely situated in her bag.

The sky outside the open window had gone overcast in what felt like an instant. The same as a mood darkening for no reason. Inexplicable sadness flowing in to fill the unguarded space of an empty room.

As they crossed the outpost grounds, she'd craned her neck for a glimpse of the Forest. The simulated wilderness of the training ranges blocked her view.

Despite that, she could feel the Forest much closer now. A kind of subliminal magnetic call. A voice heard by her blood and her bone marrow, not her ears.

That formless feeling seemed much more tangible than the carpet under her knees. She wouldn't have been surprised if the guest room around her turned out to be a flimsy set made from cardboard. Or if the whole city she'd spent twenty years in had never fully existed.

Even unseen, the Forest was stronger. The Forest was realer.

That was why she would have trouble answering if someone asked her whether she'd missed it. Yes? No?

The Forest had always been and always would be so much bigger and so much more all-encompassing than her own puny memories, her own meager existence, her own tender grief.

She missed Gren. She missed Doe. She missed Baba Sayo. She missed—with perhaps an even fiercer sense of brutal deprivation—the self she'd been before each of them died, now forever lost.

Did she miss the Forest? It was too huge and too absolute and too eternal to evoke such emotion. At least not in Tiller.

Less than half a year ago, Baba Sayo had died peacefully. If only in the sense that no one had outright killed her.

Death was a lonely and laborious task for a body unable to comprehend the stages of its own slow chaotic failure. It was a frightening task for a body that felt trapped in the wrong part of the world, a body that sought only to return to the sacred mountains. Like every forester before her.

Twelve years ago, in a quiet second-hand house in the suburbs, Doe had gotten tortured to death by a pack of hunters searching for Tiller.

From Tiller's childhood in Koya Village to her adolescence in Nui City, Doe had always been the bravest warrior she knew. And the most heavily scarred.

But even the worst monsters of the Forest had more grace and civility than the monsters of the city, the ones who spoke human words and laughed with human voices.

Twenty ... no, twenty-one years ago—

Tiller and Gren had just turned nine. That was what everyone mutually decided on, anyway. No one knew their exact real age or their exact real birthday.

No matter: they were the only children in Koya Village, and the only blues. They soaked up adoration as their birthright.

They wore their blue hair free and loose in the Forest. Occasionally they tried to fool the other villagers by switching places. It never worked on Doe or Baba Sayo—or on most people, really. They weren't identical twins to begin with. But some of the elders had extremely poor eyesight.

They put on little skits and plays to entertain the village adults. Gren came up with stories and dialogue. Tales of dragons and demons and the old lost kingdom of blues.

Tiller acted out his sagas with heartfelt zeal and a plethora of fake tears. They loved tragic deaths, ironic betrayals, runaway kings and brides, all manner of melodrama.

"Where the heck did you learn this stuff?" Baba Sayo would grumble.

The other villagers showered the twins' shows in applause. They had no competition, after all. They were the only new entertainment in town.

It ended like this.

A mage came to the Forest.

A man they'd never met before.

A man called the Scholar.

He came at a time when Doe wasn't there. When the aging village had very little protection. He took Tiller and Gren. He spirited them away to a secret room in a secret house with only a red-haired boy in a cage for company.

Did they see other children? Never. Sometimes they thought they heard voices. But for the most part, it was just Tiller and Gren and the boy in the cage.

Then one day, the Scholar took the red-haired boy from the room. The cage stood open and empty. The boy never came back.

Gren's turn came next.

Why did Tiller survive? Why did the Scholar sacrifice Gren first? Because Gren seemed smarter, more valuable—a truer blue? Because Gren pleaded with the Scholar to kill him before Tiller?

No one remained to tell her the answer. Gren and the Scholar and the red-haired boy—all of them were long gone now. Everyone except Tiller.

Why hadn't she thought to volunteer herself instead? Why hadn't she convinced the Scholar to slaughter her first? Why had she dully watched them go, the red-haired boy and then Gren, as if watching the inevitable progression of a pre-written stage show?

Even if she were powerless, even if she were all of nine years old, why hadn't she kicked and fought and screamed to change the script?

The answer came to her in daydreams and nightmares, in punishing daylight and cold panicked slumber.

*You loved your miserable life more than you loved your own brother.*

Gren was different. In dying to spare her, he proved his worthiness. He proved his goodness. He protected his undeserving coward of a sister.

She became the last living blue only because she was the most selfish, the least courageous, the least worthy.

Sometimes she hated Gren for showing her that. In the act of leaving her, he'd forced her to learn who and what she really was.

She could never forget it. She could never go back to the time before she had that truth implanted in her, bright as a mage's core, a blazing accusation that burned colder and stronger in the darkness of solitude.

One of them had been strong when it mattered, brave and heroic and selfless.

One of them had been the good twin, and it had never been her.

Doe blamed herself for leaving the village vulnerable. Baba Sayo blamed herself for not keeping the twins closer.

Everyone berated their own failings; everyone attacked themselves with vigor. No one had the good sense to blame Tiller.

Alone in an unfamiliar bedroom, twenty-one years after the kidnapping, she touched the chilly ceramic jars that concealed her most precious cargo.

There was nothing left of Gren to bring home. But at least she could try to do right by Baba Sayo and Doe. Her grandmother and her sister. Though none of them shared any blood.

# 19

A DOG BARKED near the window.

Tiller went out and found Carnelian playing with it: a huge lumbering sheepdog. It had a long gray coat very similar in hue to Carnelian's rumpled hair.

She threw comically oversized branches for the dog to fetch. It loped about with the enthusiasm of a lance-bearing knight.

"Whose dog is that?" Tiller asked. "The commander's?"

"Who knows? It just lives here on base."

This was the oldest breed of dog in all of Jace, the kind you might see depicted on clay pots from thousands of years ago. Even today, many remained hard at work on countryside farms.

There hadn't been any dogs in Koya Village. Or anywhere in the Forest, for that matter. To young Tiller and Gren, dogs and cats and domesticated sheep and pigs and cows had been like exotic mythical creatures. Nothing thrilled them more than to glimpse a sand-colored spitz sniffing its way about the now-defunct Market at the Edge of the Forest.

"You seemed surprised to find me playing fetch," said Carnelian. "What'd you think I was doing, putting the moves on scullery maids?"

"Are there scullery maids here?"

"I don't even know what a scullery maid is, come to think of it."

Eventually Carnelian dragged herself away from her canine friend. They'd promised to dine with Istel's commander, who had been instrumental in arranging for them to pass unimpeded into the Forest.

Normally, a civilian operator like Tiller wouldn't be able to borrow a military mage—even a part-time one like Carnelian—on a whim.

Normally, the Outborder Corps would seek to stop civilians from going anywhere near Forest land.

No one had legitimate business there anymore. Nearly everyone seeking to enter turned out to be poachers or mafia associates. The rest were simply looking for a remote place to die.

"Have you met the commander?" Carnelian asked.

"Not in person. I wrote her a few letters."

An unprecedented expression crossed Carnelian's face. As if she'd taken a swig of a drink and found her glass full of ants.

Tiller didn't understand what about the commander could possibly seem so repulsive. Then she saw where Carnelian's gaze had landed.

The sheepdog had wandered over to sniff at the base of an azalea bush. More specifically—at the deflated carcass of a small six-legged rabbit.

Was it the extra set of legs that horrified Carnelian, or the deadness of it? Surely she'd seen this type of rabbit before. They flourished in the Forest, scurrying and hopping quick as spiders, scaling trees with the finesse of a squirrel.

Carnelian turned her head from the dead rabbit and said, without further elaboration, "It'll be just us and the commander at dinner tonight."

"Colonel Istel isn't coming?"

"The commander tasked him with entertaining the auditors. He's supposed to keep them out of trouble."

"He must be thrilled."

Carnelian laughed darkly. "He won't be bored."

"How long have you known them?"

"We met a few times when I got called down to Central. They used to be these skinny little kids. Hardly said a word to anyone. I liked them a lot better back then."

The commander's private dining room turned out to be high up enough to afford them a glimpse of the Forest. It hulked expressionlessly on the horizon, a low black strip like an army massing to attack.

A flock of antique glass chimes hung motionless from the high ceiling. The wallpaper, which bore a subtle pattern of interlocking goblets, was presumably intended to evoke patriotic thoughts of the Jacian flag. The whole room smelled of sweet citrus.

The commander of Outpost 24 stood taller than Tiller and Carnelian. Taller than most women Tiller had met in her life, with the possible exception of Doe.

She wore a tight-cinched top with the same snake insignia as Istel, and bell-shaped, floor-length skirts that emitted inexplicable creaking sounds when she walked.

And like most other people on base, she had phage-marks: melted white swathes of scar tissue. In her case, there was little left but intense scarring from the corners of her mouth all the way to her ears. Twin patches shaped like a pair of white handprints. A phage must've grabbed her face in the middle of battle.

The thick scars made her difficult to read. She may as well have been wearing a mask. She greeted the two of them with elaborate courtesy, and inquired about the state of the Koya Foundation with what seemed like genuine interest.

Carnelian was uncharacteristically quiet. She had yet to reach for her wine. But Tiller had never been one to let the reluctance of others deter her from eating.

She could appreciate that her plate was full of rarities. Sticky clouds of real blue-black rice. Fleshy fava beans the size of her thumb. Thin strips of bison meat drenched in a spicy mahogany sauce. Purple-red pulpfruit, a salad of yellow moss-sprouts, cedar-smoked peppers, candied venison jerky from wind-deer.

She left the meat mostly untouched, but gladly devoured the rest.

It didn't taste anything like Baba Sayo's cooking. Still, it was a valiant attempt at reconstructing something vaguely in the neighborhood of Forest village food. Like trying to hum a song you'd only ever heard floating from the window of a stranger's apartment.

The ingredients couldn't have come directly from within the Forest itself. If they did, both the commander and Carnelian would be getting deathly ill right about now. But they were all authentic, and not the sort of thing you could procure from large-scale commercial suppliers.

The commander's chefs must've gone to tremendous lengths to prepare a meal that matched their notion of forester tastes.

Tiller praised the food. The commander thanked her graciously, then looked across at Carnelian with an air of concern.

"Nellie," said the commander. "You aren't feeling well?"

Carnelian bristled. "Silva," she said. "Call me Silva. You call all your subordinates by their last names."

Tiller scraped up a spoonful of sauce and ate it like soup. It seared her tongue and lips in a distant, pleasant sort of way. A foreigner like Asa Lantana would probably have found it unbearable.

She took a few cautious sips of wine as she listened to Carnelian snipe at the commander like a moody child.

Were they related? No—Carnelian was an unattached mage, an adult ward of the government. She'd said she'd been very young when her parents gave her up. Which meant she hadn't been on anyone's family register for decades.

It would be deeply unethical for an operator in the commander's position to have a dalliance with a lower-level mage. Then again, the commander might not always have been a commander. Carnelian's sullenness would make a bit more sense if they were exes.

Since Carnelian wasn't contributing much, Tiller found herself obligated to pick up their end of the conversation.

The commander self-deprecatingly called herself the commander of a dying base. The Forest kept approaching like a slow, slow tsunami. They would have to abandon the outpost in another half a year or so. Unless the Forest's southern progress came to a sudden and total halt.

In the twenty years since every last forester abandoned their ancestral home, no one (native-born or otherwise) had set foot in the deepest parts of the Forest.

Even back before the exodus, foresters had entered the sacred mountains only when they had no other choice.

Tiller nodded with all sincerity and told the commander that she truly believed the sacred mountains held the key to quieting the Forest's rage. Perhaps she needed to perform one of the secret rituals, she said.

(If any such ritual actually existed, Baba Sayo had never bothered sharing the details.)

Tiller was not a gifted actress. But when she needed to, she could do a good enough job of telling people what they wanted to hear. This skill had been crucial for soliciting donations to the Koya Foundation.

"The clementines," Carnelian said suddenly.

All this time, she had barely eaten. Tiller and the commander looked where she was looking: at the antique sideboard embellished with intricate bone inlay.

Atop it, flanked by flickering candelabras, rested a decorative silver fruit bowl piled high with small orange clementines.

"Would you like one?" asked the commander.

"They're rotting."

"A fraction overripe, perhaps, but—"

"They're rotting," Carnelian said again.

Tiller excused herself. She rose from her seat. She went over to the sideboard and picked off the top layer of clementines.

They looked fine at a glance, but felt wet on the bottom. The rich sweet stench in the room intensified.

The second layer of clementines—and all the ones beneath, probably—were going soft, their skin turning dark orange and damp. In some places, the peel had white spots. In some places, it had all but liquefied.

"These might be a little too far gone," she said.

"You knew," Carnelian said to the commander. "I smelled something off the second I stepped in here. You knew these were turning."

The commander shook her head. "Nellie—Silva—I truly didn't. Fruit can turn so fast. You know how it is. Good in the morning, bad by night."

"You were testing me," Carnelian said rigidly.

The commander's smile remained fixed in place. Or maybe, with the density of her scars, she lacked the finer flexibility needed to modulate it.

"Let's step outside," she said. "I didn't bring you here to make you suffer."

She led them down into an outdoor garden. Lights on the ground illuminated the twisted branches of small plum trees, which grew not much taller than the commander herself.

Tiller thought of how Carnelian had stared at the dead six-legged rabbit.

When Carnelian brought a carton of strawberries to Baba Sayo's apartment, she'd been very insistent on eating them all in one sitting.

"Watch out," she'd said. "Good strawberries start going bad the second you turn your back."

When she saw piles of trash waiting to be collected from the street, she held her breath and made a wide berth around them, like a child passing a graveyard.

She'd nodded with approval at how Tiller stashed sacks of food waste in her freezer, rather than let it decay in a room-temperature wastebasket.

Foresters had a cultural aversion to rotting things, to all forms of gradual decomposition. There was a reason Baba Sayo had requested an immediate cremation. Even in the version of her will that made hardly any other demands.

Carnelian didn't have the excuse of being raised as a forester. And Carnelian's revulsion seemed far more extreme.

Tiller had stepped out to wash her hands after touching the disintegrating clementines. Yet she hadn't been nauseated simply by existing in the same room with them, inhaling air infused with their overripe perfume.

They gathered around a garden table, sitting on ceramic stools that looked like thick inverted vases. The commander had more refreshments brought out to them. Mostly drinks—plum wine, rice wine. Roeberry bark cushioned the ground below their feet, soft as a pile of furs.

"I thought you would be sad to miss all the flower-viewing parties this year," the commander said to Carnelian.

"This isn't much of a substitute." Carnelian proceeded to down a too-large gulp of rice wine. It had no effect on her face. She may as well have been drinking water.

"Look." The commander pointed past the plum flowers. "The whole poet's trio is starting to bloom. I've only ever seen it happen here. Might be the influence of the Forest."

The poet's trio: plum blossoms, cherry blossoms, roe blossoms. From February to May, they flowered one after another. Two of the three might see some overlap, depending on the year, but nowhere in the country did these trees naturally bloom all at the same time.

"The poet's trio never blooms together," Tiller uttered.

A common saying, and a useful one at that. *You can't have everything you want.*

The commander smiled and toasted her.

After a brief conversation about key differences between life in Nui City and life in the countryside, Tiller requested final permission to depart the following day.

The commander sipped her wine slowly. "There's going to be a storm tonight."

"I'm sure it'll pass by morning," Tiller said.

"No—it could continue well into tomorrow. Wouldn't feel right sending you off in the middle of that. Stay one extra night."

This was unexpected.

She attempted to catch Carnelian's eye. Carnelian seemed preoccupied with rolling fallen petals between her finger and thumb, crushing them into tiny pink logs like cigars for a cockroach.

"We can't impose on you any longer," Tiller told the commander. "We're working on a deadline. Only forty-five days left till the chalices come from Central."

The commander sighed. "Life is just full of deadlines, isn't it?

Still—what's one more day? The accommodations won't cost you, and I'll make sure you're well fed."

"We appreciate your generosity," Tiller said. "But this whole base is funded by taxpayer money. Doesn't seem right for us to take advantage of you any longer than we have to."

"Imagine if you succeed in making the Forest stop its advance," said the commander. "Then every little expense would seem worth it. Not that it costs much to host you for another night! Trust me when I say that there's plenty of room in my budget."

"If the storm ends by morning—"

"There might be clean-up afterward," the commander said smoothly. "In fact, I promise there will be. Both on base and nearby. Fallen trees. Train track inspections. Might get quite busy. Do you know why I'd prefer to send you two out during calmer times?"

"Why?" Tiller asked. The commander hadn't left room for her to say anything else, and Carnelian wasn't helping.

"We recently declared catastrophe ROE."

"ROE?"

The commander had pronounced each letter individually. Not like the roe trees flowering yellow in the garden.

"Rules of Engagement," Carnelian said flatly.

The commander nodded. "Phages have been creeping right up to the Forest border," she said. "It can be quite difficult to determine who is a threat, and who isn't. For their own safety, Corps personnel are authorized to attack suspected phages on sight."

The Forest monsters known as phages were always shaped like human beings.

"I see," Tiller said. And she did. A cherry petal floated atop her plum wine. She plucked it free with delicate fingertips. "Even if we're authorized to enter the Forest—"

"Any unplanned encounters with the Corps could turn deadly," Carnelian finished. At last she looked up. "How long do you plan on keeping us here?" she asked the commander.

"One extra day," the commander said gently. "Let the storm pass. Let the chaos settle down. I'm just trying to set you two up for success. It would be terrible if you had a tragic accident right at the start of your journey."

"Yes," Carnelian muttered. "Just terrible."

# 20

It rained that night at the outpost. At first it fell placidly enough to leave the guest room window cracked open. Tiller breathed the smell of rain sinking into gravel, cobblestones, soil, the sides of the building.

She shut the window after the wind picked up.

As she shut it, she could've sworn she saw someone clambering up over the lintel of the room next door.

Carnelian had said very little after the commander released them. She'd complained of a headache, then headed straight for bed. She'd had three times more alcohol than Tiller and the commander put together, but she didn't show it.

Tiller looked at her own face in the rain-studded black window. She hadn't removed her wig yet. Her scalp itched with discontent.

She reluctantly stripped down to an undershirt and leggings. Might as well wear something that would dry quickly. The leggings had only shallow pockets, but did include a strap where she could hook a pair of yo-yo knives. She opened the window again and pulled herself out into the nighttime cold.

Tiller and Gren had shimmied up and down the great cedars of the Forest every day as children. In comparison to that, an old-fashioned building like this was practically designed to be scaled, with all its convenient eaves and lintels—rough enough to grip onto even when painted with rain.

The mild-angled roof consisted of huge reddish stone tiles coated in a scuzz of lichen and slimy moss. Everything looked deep gray in the dark without moonlight or starlight.

Tiller only began to shiver after hauling herself all the way to the top. She rubbed rain-spattered arms, flexed wet unsteady fingers.

She walked across the broad roof ridge. A colorless shape stood silent before her.

Carnelian. Who seemed unsurprised to see her. Who held steady in the storm as if getting rained on were a perfectly ordinary form of recreation.

"Does it ever feel like he's still with you?"

"Who?" Tiller asked warily.

"Your brother."

Tiller held her tongue. The answer was not as simple as a straightforward *yes* or *no*. She didn't see why they had to discuss her brother here and now, either.

"I had a brother, too," Carnelian said without prompting. "Also long gone. Did I ever mention him?"

"No."

"We were blood siblings, and we knew it. Not like those auditors. Our parents surrendered us together. Made no difference in the end, of course. My brother's been dead for decades. Wow," she added, with a touch of irony. "We have so much in common."

"Except for being complete opposites," Tiller said. "I'm an operator. You're a mage. I'm from the Forest, and I'm a blue. You're not either of those. You're wealthy," she went on, warming up. "I count my grails much more carefully. You've left Nui before. I've never set foot on another island."

Carnelian chuckled. "And here I thought you were going to pick on me for gambling and having flings."

The view might have been impressive on a clear day. But with weather this inhospitable, they couldn't even see the rest of the outpost. Hopefully someone had brought that sheepdog indoors.

"Your mantle's getting soaked," Tiller told her.

"There'll be plenty of time for it to dry," Carnelian answered, accepting the change of topic. "The commander plans on trapping us here as long as she can."

"She seems supportive enough on the surface."

Carnelian considered the sleeve of her mantle as if wondering why it insisted on drinking up rain. Wind gusted with malicious force—determined hands trying to shove them off the side of the roof.

"You have a history with the commander," Tiller said. "Bad breakup?"

At last Carnelian stopped looking like a statue, beautiful and immobile, paralyzed before the burgeoning storm.

She raised her chin. "I don't sleep with *everyone* I meet," she pronounced.

"Only half?"

"Well under thirty percent. I'm extremely discerning."

"Then what's your problem with her?"

"It won't matter once she lets us out of here."

"I'd like to know," Tiller said. "If it's something severe enough to make you come brood like a tragic hero from the Crying Age."

"I..." Carnelian pushed at wet hair with gloved fingers. "I was asleep," she said slowly. "Or at least half-asleep. I always wear my mantle and gloves to bed."

"Always?"

"I have to. I'm prone to sleepwalking without them. And worse than that—sleep-maging.

"By the time I came to my senses, I was already up here dripping. I accepted my fate. I'm used to waking up in strange places. Then I heard your voice. There's no deeper meaning to it."

"You climbed the side of the building in your sleep?"

"Of course not." Carnelian pointed at an access hatch behind her. It stood cracked open, letting rain in. "I assume I came from there."

The sound of the wind retreated as Tiller's mind flipped in place. Cold no longer held her rigid. Fear could be a very warm and lifelike thing.

"I saw someone climb out your window," she said. "Minutes ago. I thought it was—"

Without saying a word, Carnelian seized her hand.

Carnelian's porting magic snatched them away from the slippery roof. They landed in a room with tile underfoot.

Flat bathroom tiles. Mostly dry. Bare of moss and mold.

They were together in a single modest stall of a utilitarian shower room. It looked like the one down the hall from their guest quarters.

A ventilation fan whirred in the ceiling, almost loud enough to drown out the sound of rain. The lights were off. Tiller could see nothing beyond the door of frosted glass.

She made eye contact with Carnelian as best she could in the dark, trying to ask if it were safe to speak.

The answer seemed to be yes.

"I don't get it," Tiller said. "Of all the places you've been since yesterday—why bring us here?"

"My range isn't just places I've been in the last twenty-four hours," Carnelian whispered back. "I've got a physical limit of—well, I doubt I could take us as far as the last train station."

"Not in a single port. But with a series of smaller hops—"

"To what end?" Carnelian asked. "You didn't have enough of getting rained on and smacked around by the wind? You're shivering."

"No, I'm not," Tiller said sternly. Mind over matter.

She extracted her hand from Carnelian and patted delicately at her damp wig. Thank goodness it was a cheaper synthetic one.

Her feet squelched in her shoes. They'd both left dark muddy prints all over the pale stall floor. "You brought us here to hide?" she asked.

"And strategize."

"So whoever I saw leaving your window wasn't a guest of yours."

"A guest?" Carnelian asked sharply. "For what?"

"Do I have to elaborate?"

Carnelian took her by the shoulders and turned her away from the frosted door. This stall was most definitely not designed to accommodate more than one person.

"We're engaged," Carnelian said. "I gave you my teeth."

"You keep calling them your teeth, but—"

"You know what I mean. You think I'm still luring other women back to my room?"

Was this the conversation they needed to be having right now?

Light must be leaking in from somewhere. Or maybe Tiller's eyes had gotten used to the meager gleam of the tile grout. It was soft as moonlight, a subtle form of emergency illumination that would only prove noticeable in complete darkness.

"If we're engaged," she said, careful to keep her voice down, "it's purely for practical reasons. You have no reason to change your personal habits. You know I won't mind."

"Start caring," Carnelian snapped. "If only for the sake of appearances."

"Since when do you care about appearances?"

Carnelian indicated her gloves and mantle. "Permission to remove this wet crap, please."

"Granted."

Perhaps this was why she'd chosen to port them to a bathroom.

"At some point," Carnelian said as she plucked off her gloves, "you'll have to convince the government that you actually want to marry me. At this rate, we'll get fined for fraud before we even fill out the first set of papers. That'll be nice for you, but a raw deal for me. I risk my life for you in the Forest, and what do I get?"

She hung her mantle on the shower head. Beads of water dripped from the hem. All she had on beneath it were shorts (that scarcely qualified as such) and a bra tank. Nothing to obscure the distinct auras of her nine cores. She really had been meaning to pass out and sleep the night away in her bed.

"I have plenty of experience with pretending," Tiller said.

Pretending to care what donors thought about how the Koya Foundation used its funds.

Pretending to listen when people who had never breathed Forest air in their lives presumed to tell her what foresters needed and how foresters felt.

Pretending to be happy in front of Baba Sayo. Happy enough to make up for the fact that Gren and Doe were gone, and that the city was full of people who would never understand them.

Pretending not to fear for her life.

She put a hand on the waistband of Carnelian's small shorts.

It must've been a very cold hand. When her thumb touched the bare skin above Carnelian's hip, Carnelian flinched and backed up into the knobs jutting from the tile wall.

"I'll give you what you asked for," Tiller said steadily.

Carnelian looked at her with large unguarded eyes. There was a power in the beauty of that face, a pull as insidious as a riptide. A hypnotic force that would make people want to go easy on her, laugh off her foibles, forgive her sins, do anything for a smile. Like hypnosis, it would work better on some than on others.

Tiller remained unmoved.

She inched closer—the stall left very little space to maneuver—and said with zero emotion: "I can make the right bureaucrats believe that I want you, I need you. I can make them think I'm obsessed with you. But let's wait to focus on that until we come back from the Forest."

Carnelian caught at the hand on her side—then immediately let go, as if she'd burned herself.

As if she'd forgotten she was no longer wearing gloves.

"You're still shivering," she said, looking away.

"Nothing to be done about it."

Carnelian pulled her mantle down and hung it around Tiller's shoulders.

Tiller started to complain on reflex. Before the words fully left her mouth, she realized that though the outside surface of the mantle had gone all glossy and heavy and wet, the inside remained dry. And confusingly warm. As warm as the brief skittish touch of Carnelian's fingers.

"You're not a mage," Carnelian said brusquely. "The magical restraints won't affect you."

Head bent, she fastened the mantle shut over Tiller's collarbone. It took her a curiously long time to get it right.

"Didn't think you were particularly experienced," she said as she fiddled with it.

"At what?" Tiller asked blandly.

Carnelian's hands stilled for a second, then rallied to finish securing the front of the mantle. "You know," she said.

"I'm asking because I don't."

"Matters of the heart."

"That can mean a lot of things." Tiller spared a glance for the shower door, as opaque as ever. "Did you want to stay here all night? We should go get backup."

"No."

"...No?"

"First we should try to catch the intruders ourselves."

"Intruders," Tiller said. "You think there's more than one."

"There's always more than one."

"And you think we should confront them ourselves? Completely on our own? We're on a military base. You could port straight to the commander, to Istel, to dozens of other soldiers. If ever there were a time to seek outside help—"

Carnelian reached past Tiller to nudge at the stall door.

It creaked. Of course. The sound felt as loud as a siren.

"Question," Carnelian said. "How many of those troops did you see in person today? Anyone outside the dining hall? Anyone at all?"

Tiller couldn't answer.

"There you go. Strange, isn't it? All this space, and so few people. With how much the commander harped on about the storm, you'd think she'd call everyone back much earlier in the day."

Carnelian pushed the door open further. Another long, long creak rent the air.

The fan in the ceiling kept buzzing. Rain and wind thumped at the small high bathroom windows like a fugitive desperate for shelter.

"Maybe it's coincidence," said Carnelian. "Maybe everyone had business elsewhere. A big training exercise down on the plains. Vorpal beasts to exterminate along the coast. Who knows? The Outborder Corps always has their hands full."

She bent closer to Tiller's ear. "Even so—even if everyone were away for innocent reasons, you think it's that easy for an unauthorized intruder to slip inside a military outpost? Just like that? And how'd they know which rooms were ours?"

"You think they had help," Tiller said.

"Inside help."

"You don't want to seek backup because you don't trust anyone here." Tiller paused. "Not even Istel?"

"I consider him a friend," Carnelian replied. "But surely you of all people know that sometimes you've got to suspect your friends."

The tiles had gone slick with muck from their shoes and rainwater from their clothing. They stepped carefully, silently. Carnelian steered Tiller toward the exit with a hand on her back. The gridlines of pasty grout shone with the faintness of dying stars.

"Might be able to wring a few clues out of them if we catch them in the act," Carnelian said.

"Or we could end up strolling into a trap."

Carnelian pulled her mouth into the shape of a smile. Her eyes remained unchanged. "We're already in it. What makes you think the trap wasn't sprung the moment we came here?"

"To the bathroom?"

"To the outpost."

# 21

CARNELIAN MUST'VE slept-walk her way to the roof before anyone broke into her room.

"Good thing you got out of there," Tiller said. "Even if it wasn't on purpose."

"Good thing *you* got out of there," Carnelian retorted. "They would've come for you next. Bet they didn't expect you to sneak outside in pouring rain and slither up the wall like a roach."

Her plan of action: go back down the hall together and check their assigned rooms. Carnelian's first, then Tiller's.

"You could port us in," said Tiller.

"That could go well," Carnelian said. "Or it could backfire. If it were just me, I'd go for it. But I've got you to look after."

The carpet in the hall outside the guest rooms bore a pattern of a lonely demon battling endless human armies.

Tiller and Carnelian didn't try to stay hidden. They walked softly together along the carpet, arm in arm, as if returning from a casual nighttime stroll. It would've been more believable if not for the raging storm.

Their respective doors looked no different from before. No hint of sound came from either room except the muffled noise of wind and rain.

Tiller thought she smelled something off, but it might've been the rankness of her own wound-up tension. Hopefully she wouldn't stink up Carnelian's mantle.

Although it should've been much warmer here than outside, the thin sweat springing up all over her skin made her go colder than ever. And shaky to boot, as if she hadn't eaten all day.

Carnelian's sleepwalking self had apparently not seen fit to lock her door. She drew her glittering sword from the air without comment. She held it ready in her right hand while she opened the door with her left.

The hinges squeaked meekly. The room appeared empty—but horribly ransacked, with clothing strewn like dead leaves all over the floor.

Tiller froze at the threshold. "They were searching for something."

Carnelian blinked. "What? Oh, no, this is exactly how I left it when I went to sleep. No one's moved a thing."

"What are you, a wild boar?"

"Would you love me as a wild boar?"

"I wouldn't marry a wild boar," Tiller said, "if that's what you're asking."

"But I would be such a beautiful specimen. I'd win all the top prizes at local fairs."

It was difficult to avoid treading on fallen undergarments. At least it seemed relatively harmless, as far as messes went. No food crumbs or festering used towels.

"Are you this bad at home?" Tiller asked. "Or did you throw clothes around to vent your frustrations with the commander?"

Carnelian turned to scan their surroundings, her sword still drawn at the ready. "Bad at what?" she asked absently.

Tiller chose not to elaborate.

The curtains were open, but the windows were firmly closed. Raindrops squiggled down lightless window-glass, worms racing to a finish line that lay somewhere far out of sight.

Over the bed hung a painting that looked disturbingly like a vorpal hole.

Carnelian had begun muttering to herself. "—could've drugged us at dinner. One or both of us. Too worried I'd notice? No—maybe there *was* something in my food. If not in my drink. She seemed displeased with me for eating so little. And I felt like real shit afterward. But—"

Something huge and heavy hit the bed.

Tiller's heart seized up in her chest. Carnelian shoved her back, away from the bed, and her body blindly obeyed.

For an instant it was like being with Doe again. Doe who was tall and strong and who always knew exactly what to do. Doe who had never wavered, not even when home invaders hurt her in unspeakable ways, not even when all she had to do to make them stop was tell them about Tiller hiding inside the wall three feet away, every bone in her body quaking, biting down on her hand to hold back vomit.

Carnelian's sword flashed, then lowered. Sharp remnants of some other mage's magic flickered in the air.

Someone had dropped—ported—a body into Carnelian's bed.

It filled the whole mattress and then some, longer than an adult man. Its hooves jutted off the sides. Its enormous antlers clawed at the headboard. Maggots and organs and a stomach-convulsing stench spilled freely from the long, long slit in its distended belly.

A wind-deer corpse.

Carnelian swayed.

Tiller tugged at her. "Port us. Port us out of—"

Carnelian shook her head.

Not all the maggots were mere maggots. Some had human magic welded to them, tidy little cuttings from a hardworking mage. Or a whole sweatshop full of mages, grimly trimming the same cuttings off their branches over and over and over.

Tiller had heard of skills meant specifically to interfere with the magic of others. A sticky field to prevent porting, for instance. That might be what now emanated from these maggots, together with the ghastly smell of liquefying death.

They might have to burn this whole room to purge the odor. The bedding already looked thoroughly soaked.

At first Tiller tried to pull Carnelian back toward the door. These maggots—rather, the anti-porting magic they played host to—seemed like far too potent a tool for civilian hunters.

She fought to hold her breath. Her eyes stung.

Carnelian's sword slipped from loose fingers and plunged itself halfway through the floor.

The problem with the dead wind-deer was not simply its payload of magic-carrying maggots. Or the fact that its rot had shocked Carnelian into going borderline catatonic.

The real problem: it was almost certainly intended as a distraction. The way a pickpocket might bump you to distract from their accomplice nabbing your wallet.

Which meant it would ultimately be too risky to leave through the door. That was exactly where the mind behind the wind-deer meant to drive them.

Carnelian couldn't port, and Tiller lacked the strength to clamber out the window with a full-grown woman on her back. They were trapped here.

She pulled Carnelian's mantle over her nose and mouth. The outside was still clammy, and had begun to smell of wet dog. Still far preferable to the death-steeped reek that had closed in around them like drowning waters, filling the room from floor to ceiling.

"Your claw," she hissed at Carnelian. "The shredder."

That phantom claw had decimated the encroaching bubbles and illusory hunters at the temple. It was a skill meant for crude destruction. For mauling the magic cuttings wielded by others.

And it was their only path to reclaiming the ability to port to safety. Carnelian would have to force herself to swipe at the port-stifling magic on those maggots. To shred it to bits.

Either way—they might be safer near the dead wind-deer than shrinking away from it.

Someone would show up any second now. They wouldn't come leaping from the torn belly of the deer as if popping out of a cake. They wouldn't emerge from the one spot that kept inexorably drawing attention to itself, both with its squirming maggots and its gag-inducing stink.

She pushed Carnelian closer to the bed. This way the maggots would be easier for Carnelian to slash at. Assuming that she had the presence of mind to manifest her shredding claw. Assuming that the wind-deer wouldn't make her faint dead away.

Carnelian's arm shot sideways, her fist clenching the air.

She lowered her hand and opened her fingers.

A dark brown tick scurried down her palm, latching onto the base of her wrist.

Carnelian cursed.

"Bad reflex," she said hoarsely. "It came flying off the covers."

Her legs crumpled beneath her. She ended up on the floor, her shoulder slumped against the side of the bed. Tiller hastily dragged her away from the dark stains spreading ever closer.

Real ticks couldn't fly, much less jump. This was the same type of device they'd used on Tiller at the temple.

It must've mingled with the maggots, its unique spark of magical cargo indistinguishable from theirs at a glance. Waiting for someone to get close enough to trigger its launch.

Could there be more lurking in the swamp of the deer's melting guts? Maybe. But these immobility ticks seemed like a highly specialized tool, comprising cuttings from multiple mages. Not quick or easy to produce.

Tiller unclipped her yo-yo knives from the strap on her hip. She grabbed Carnelian's wrist. She attempted to scrape the tick off.

Part of it crumbled. The rest burrowed deeper still. She'd have to draw blood to get rid of it.

She couldn't keep track of everything at once. The dead wind-deer, the window, the door, the clothes on the carpet, Carnelian's limp tick-bitten arm.

Carnelian's floor-impaling sword had dissolved like ice melting. It left behind a slender open scar, a peephole to the room below.

If there were other immobility ticks hidden nearby, they might be lurking under one of Carnelian's discarded girdles. Obscured by the same force that blurred her magic cores.

An enemy could've used that convenient camouflage as cover for more magical traps. Ticks or otherwise. Damn her for being so messy!

She gripped Carnelian's wrist harder. No resistance. She readied the point of her small knife to dig out the rest of the immobility tick. Carnelian breathed audibly, as if struggling not to be sick.

The rain whooshed louder. The window and the door simultaneously came open, then closed again.

Tiller's hands faltered. It was like trying to open a jar in a dream. The sort of dream where you already knew everything was fated to go wrong.

There were two hunters. One from the window. One from the door.

Of course they couldn't port in or out, she thought numbly. The maggot-magic stopped Carnelian from absconding with her. It would also stop the hunters themselves.

They'd have to physically drag Tiller out of the room. They'd have to get far enough away from the wind-deer to open an escape portal without interference.

That's what they'd have to do, at least, if their goal was to take her alive.

With slippery fingers, she dug the end of her yo-yo knife under Carnelian's skin. A motion like trying to shuck an oyster. Carnelian flinched—slowly, dazedly, as if sedated. Strands of blood leaked down toward the crook of her elbow.

The tick's carcass ricocheted onto the bedspread. Tiller hoped she'd flicked out most of it. Blood filled her sweat-slick palm, and Carnelian didn't seem any freer.

Scant seconds had passed since the hunters first penetrated the room.

They wore something very similar to the outpost's civilian staff uniform. They were masked, which must've helped protect them from the eye-watering stench.

Tiller hurled her yo-yo knives. She didn't even graze them, and the knives never made it back to her hand.

She started to scream. No one leapt to cover her mouth. Did the port-suppressing magic stop sound from escaping down the hallway, too? Or had they gotten rid of all possible witnesses?

The hunters already had Tiller cornered. It was not a large room.

Even if she abandoned Carnelian, there was nowhere else to go except the wall beside the bed.

She wove a shaky path backwards. Away from Carnelian. Away from the hunters. They barely glanced at Carnelian, who had gone as still as the slaughtered wind-deer.

Doe used to teach her that every millisecond of bought time had meaning. Even if you didn't know what you were buying time for.

Time was the difference between life and death. The slimmest, most inconsequential fraction of it could—once measured and weighed—turn out to be unspeakably precious.

She hit the corner of the bedside table. She kept breathing through her nose as little as possible.

Then, abruptly, she understood why this felt so wrong.

The hunters were approaching too slowly.

They'd slipped into the room with such rapid precision. They could've been at Tiller's side in an instant, seizing her arms to handcuff her. Or to slap a second immobility tick on her, if they had one at the ready.

Instead they circled with the patience of scavengers.

They wanted her to back up. They wanted her to retreat in this specific direction.

Tiller stopped herself too late. Something soft—almost intangible—touched the side of her face.

She'd walked right into it. She jerked, and it fell to coil around her wrists. A nigh-invisible leash.

# 22

TILLER'S MIND FELT two steps behind the rest of her.

The thing she'd stumbled into had dangled unseen from the ceiling. Like a minuscule caterpillar hanging down from a long silken thread. An automatic trap that bore only the faintest shimmer of magic.

It could get away with being fragile and unobtrusive because you had to touch it to activate it—and now she was hooked like a fish, magic cinching her wrists together.

The end of the ghostly leash had tossed itself to the nearest of the two hunters.

Tiller attempted to brace herself. She only lasted a moment before her body lurched forward.

The masked hunter reeled the leash in. Tiller stumbled into Carnelian, slumped soundless on the floor by the bed.

She tripped over Carnelian's legs. She fell flat on her face. The hunters pulled her up and toward the door.

The magical force of the leash was as unsparing as the rain lashing the window. A nauseating stink filled her as soon as she caught her breath.

Panic wrung at her. Once they got her away from their maggots, they'd be able to port her far beyond anyone's reach.

She didn't have time to sit around waiting for rescue, or for death. She had only forty-five days to lay Doe and Baba Sayo to rest.

That might sound like long enough to take a couple detours. But time had a way of sneaking past you in the Forest. It could careen at speeds unheard of in the city.

She told the hunters she would pay them much more than their current employer.

Being professionals, they showed no reaction.

She tried to snatch at her fallen yo-yo knives. The leash snapped her hands away.

She struggled more furiously at the threshold, kicking and snapping her teeth—not that they had any exposed flesh to bite.

A mesh hood came down over her head, something akin to a beekeeper's covering. It swallowed every last sound that burst from her lips.

Every defining moment in her life came back to this same abject helplessness.

When she was thirty—not too many months ago—she'd used up her savings to hire home aides as Baba Sayo deteriorated.

Nothing wrong with that. Except for the terrible and baseless conviction that she should've looked encroaching death in the eyes and done it all herself. The massages to clear swollen tissue and exhausted lungs. The endless cycle of food and laundry and medication. The exhausting labor of bathing a body in the process of betraying itself, a body that bitterly resisted everyone's attempts to maintain a hygienic environment.

When she was eighteen, she'd hidden behind a wall while Doe choked and twitched and gurgled and finally—finally—died.

When she was nine, she'd been locked in a room with Gren and a empty cage, a cage that had once held a boy with no name.

After sixty-three days of imprisonment, the Scholar came to take Gren away. It's okay, Gren had said to calm her. You don't have to fight.

She immediately believed him. Because she wanted to. Because it relieved her.

She didn't question why he didn't mention anything about coming back. She didn't try to go with him. She didn't clutch at him to slow their separation. The boy in the cage would've bellowed for Gren more furiously than she did.

No, Doe told her later. No matter what anyone says, you always have to fight.

It was like she'd never escaped that room. She'd never escaped her nine-year-old self. In the end she was still alone there, the sole survivor— and a supremely undeserving one, at that.

With Gren and Doe and Baba Sayo gone forever, the whole world might as well be that distorted room without anyone left.

The hunters weren't going out of their way to hurt Tiller. But they weren't going out of their way to be gentle, either.

The door stood open, and she was halfway out of the room. She bucked, trying to headbutt the hunter holding her leash.

The hunter smoothly redirected her. Her mesh-covered skull slammed the door frame.

She staggered. Pain came after the impact, as delayed as thunder from a faraway storm.

She was in the hallway, and she was hopeless. She couldn't remember where she was supposed to go. She might've howled in rage or fear. The magic of the mesh hood absorbed every sound.

One of the hunters turned to close the door behind them. There was something almost polite in the way they reached for it. They had the air of a cleaning crew leaving a hotel suite. Brisk and efficient. Nothing to see here.

"Hey," said a voice from the room. "That's mine."

The voice sounded like death.

The hunters didn't miss a beat. One spun to lob something through the gap in the cracked-open door. Then they slammed it shut.

A magical weapon? A grenade? Tiller's body stiffened before her rattled brain knew what to think. Her head throbbed as if consumed by a hangover.

Nothing happened. Nothing except for a faint pinging, more magical than aural in nature.

It was the sort of sound you might expect to hear coming from nighttime stars, if stars had a voice.

It was the sound of something striking Carnelian's multifaceted magical shields.

The hunters shoved Tiller down the hallway, down the carpet with its design of raging armies. She dug her feet in as best she could. She couldn't tell how far the anti-porting field extended. Every last millimeter might make a difference.

A claw came shooting out through Carnelian's closed door. It was like the arm of a mythical dragon. It made the hall resemble a dollhouse. But it was woven from muscular ropes of fog.

It didn't leave the walls in shreds. It kept erupting ghost-like from the door, tearing toward Tiller and the hunters without actually tearing anything up.

The hunters leapt back. The clawed arm rammed its way between them and Tiller. The fog felt like nothing.

As the claw passed, the magical leash around Tiller's wrists snapped in two. She flung herself back toward the guest room. As the door came open, she ran headfirst into Carnelian.

Carnelian wiped her mouth with her left wrist, then nudged Tiller behind her.

The wraith-like claw came shooting back to merge with her right arm in the way of a tape measure retracting. It didn't linger. A blink later, and it had erased itself both from Tiller's sight and her magic perception.

"Your hair," Tiller said, dumbfounded. "What—"

The immaculate silver was gone. Carnelian's hair had turned a color like blood.

Maybe it *was* blood. It still looked wet. But the transformation extended from root to tip, and none of it bled down to stain the skin of her face or neck or ears.

"It'll pass." Carnelian's voice was still gravelly. She looked at the hunters. "You were about to steal my mantle," she told them. "Any idea how much those things cost?

"And don't look, but I just vomited out the entirety of my nonexistent dinner. I think the contents of my stomach have gone into—into negative digits. Into debt. Oh, come on!"

She cried that last part as one of the hunters drew a gun on her.

Her shields formed in the air again. It was like watching a jigsaw puzzle come together piece by piece, hexagonal facets blooming in fractal swirls.

They bloomed around the hunters. Not in the shape of a box or a bubble or a coffin. The shields hugged them like a biohazard suit, snapping into place before either hunter could move to escape.

They remained frozen. Living statues. Masked faces rigid behind the contours of the clear shields locking them in place.

One still had their arm raised, gun at the ready, unable to use it.

"Can they breathe?" Tiller asked tentatively.

"We'll find out in a few moments, won't we?" Carnelian gave her a reproachful glance. "What about me? Think I had a easy time of it breathing next to that wind-deer?"

Tiller took a few wary steps closer to the hunters. After about a minute of observation, she concluded that Carnelian wasn't in the process of killing them. Not yet, anyway.

They were still breathing, though not deeply. They had just enough spare room to squeeze out a blink or two.

She turned back to Carnelian. "When you said *That's mine*, you meant your mantle?"

It was still draped over Tiller's shoulders, though it had gotten rather skewed in her tussling with the hunters.

Carnelian looked at her oddly. "Did you want me to mean something else?"

In lieu of answering, Tiller stared. As Carnelian spoke, the red had left her hair.

It was like watching a fire fizzle out. In fact, the gray hue that her hair returned to was a color very much reminiscent of cremated human remains.

Carnelian touched the side of her head. "See? Told you it'd go back to normal."

"That isn't much of an explanation."

"Life is full of mysteries," Carnelian said glibly. She turned and coughed into her elbow. "Lord, I want to wash my mouth out. Careful where you step, now. Don't even remember all the places I spewed while they were wrestling you out of there. You seemed a little too busy at the time to notice."

She waved her hands like a road worker directing pedestrians. The prismatic shields moved, and carried their human burden with them.

Thus the trapped hunters sailed through the doorway back into Carnelian's bedroom.

When Carnelian lowered her arms, they dropped out of the air onto the bed, one on each side of the wind-deer. It looked as though they were cuddling it.

Their landing had made a horrible noise, wet and visceral. But the shields hugging their bodies remained intact.

"Seems a little vindictive," Tiller said.

"It's their carcass. They can deal with it. Anyway, they aren't actually touching anything gross. They ought to thank me for my shields."

"Is this why the Corps hasn't made you a full-time member? Because you have issues with dead bodies?"

"Think it's ironic?" Carnelian sniped. "Believe me, you wouldn't be the first. It's not death that gets to me, though. It's the rot. At least it won't pose a problem for us in the Forest."

True. The Forest enforced its own unique cycles of death and renewal, sacrifice and rebirth. It wasn't completely devoid of decay. But a wind-deer that perished in the Forest would never end up in a state like the one on Carnelian's bed.

"I gotta wonder how your would-be kidnappers knew about my one big weakness. Who told them the best way to incapacitate me, hm?"

It sounded like Carnelian already had a culprit in mind.

"Someone close to you," Tiller guessed.

"Want to try naming names?"

"I'm still wondering how you overcame it," Tiller said. "You seemed dead to the world even after I gouged your tick out."

Carnelian blew out a weary breath. "Let's get away from this smell first."

They trekked back to the shower room down the hall. Carnelian gargled water from one of the sinks, then began fiddling with her damp silver-gray hair in the mirror above. "I don't have multiple personalities," she informed the mirror.

"I wasn't saying you did...?"

"But sometimes my other cores—the cores that weren't originally mine—get a bit pushy. I mean—they push me harder than I'm capable of pushing myself. It's hard to explain."

There was a nervousness in how she tugged at the ends of her hair, the chunks curving by her jaw and her neck. "They don't speak to me," she appended. "They don't have identities. Or desires of their own. Or names. Not anymore." She abruptly pivoted away from the mirror. "You know those stupid kiddie shows at carnivals? The hero shows."

"Not really," Tiller said. "But go on."

"It's always a hero versus a villain. Very black-and-white. And the hero is younger and smaller and weaker. But the hero has friends. The villain has none. When the hero cries for help, their friends—and the audience— send them strength. Then they miraculously get more powerful. They miraculously beat the bad guy."

"The power of love and friendship."

"Right. There's no such thing in real life. Except—I have these relics of other people left inside me. Sometimes it feels like they come together. They give me that extra strength of will."

"Like the hero's friends."

Carnelian laughed bitterly. "They weren't all my friends in real life. If only. I barely even met most of them. Some of them, I—"

She stopped herself.

"Did one of them have red hair?" Tiller asked. "Is that why it changes color?"

"*I* had red hair," Carnelian said. "Used to, anyway. As for why it comes back when I overextend myself—beats me. Why were you born with blue hair? Why not brown? Why not purple?"

"Life is full of mysteries," Tiller acknowledged.

"I'll tell you this much: it isn't always a good thing."

"What isn't?"

"That thing you call the power of love and friendship. Whatever extra strength I leech off the guests inside me." Carnelian gestured vaguely at her lower stomach.

"Out of all of them, I'm the weakest and most pathetic. I'm the first to want to give up. To seek a path without fighting. To slink away and let other people take care of things. Where's the harm in that? But sometimes they make me press onward. Even when it hurts.

"When that extra strength wells up, I don't have the option of rejecting it. I can't control when it comes to me—I can't invoke it. And I can't say no to it. Willingly or not, they all died to be inside me. Even if I wanted to, I couldn't dishonor them by refusing their gifts.

"They make me rise up like a hero in one of those scripted shows. Taking a stand isn't fun, you know. It's actually pretty awful. Most of the time, it happens too late for me to save anyone except myself."

Her lips quirked. "Which is how I ended up being the only one to survive all those Forest expeditions. My other cores banded together and forced me to fight harder than I ever could on my own. Every time. No matter how hopeless it got. By then there'd be no one else left alive to see it happen."

She went back to the sink and splashed water on her face. Then she bent down by Tiller. She used the inner fabric of her own mantle as a towel.

*That's mine.*

The rawness of her voice had made her words sound like a curse.

Tiller closed the spigot of memory. She closed it tight. They had countless other problems to deal with, and the storm outside was only growing louder.

# 23

THEY RELUCTANTLY returned to Carnelian's guest room. The stench seemed worse than ever. Carnelian started gagging before they even opened the door.

The sealed-up hunters and the leaky wind-deer were still squeezed together on the bed. Something about their pose made the whole tableau feel like a particularly dreadful piece of contemporary art.

On the plus side, no one other than the wind-deer seemed to have died yet.

A cluster of metal shrapnel formed an inexplicable ring on the ground. Tiller asked what it was from. Carnelian shrugged.

"They threw something through the door at me, remember? Wrapped it in shields before it went off."

Her eyes seemed to be watering from the smell of the room. She fetched a magic-obscuring girdle and fastened it grimly around her middle. After she finished, Tiller handed back her mantle.

She almost asked if Carnelian were ready for porting. But she realized her mistake before she spoke.

Carnelian could only deploy one branch skill at a time. As long as her shields kept detaining the hunters, she wouldn't be able to port anywhere. Or use any other forms of magic. Even if her claw had already eliminated the anti-porting field carried by the still-squirming maggots.

This time, Carnelian locked the door when they left. She brought her pointy lacquer ear cuffs, attaching them with the air of a horse grudgingly letting a bit slip to the back of its mouth.

Tiller assumed her next move would be to call on Colonel Istel or the commander. Either to requisition help with clean-up, or—as she'd begun implying—to accuse one or both of them of masterminding the attack.

The communication magic grafted to the ear cuffs wasn't Carnelian's, after all. It appeared to be a mesh of cuttings procured from other mages. She could activate it without being forced to first take down her shields.

But Carnelian didn't use her earpieces yet. She took Tiller's elbow and ushered her to the lower floors of the dim guesthouse. Then to a smaller neighboring wing.

It seemed empty. The wing they'd come from had also been devoid of other guests. "Is anyone else staying here?" Tiller asked.

"The auditors," said Carnelian.

"They got assigned rooms this far away from us?"

"Yep."

"Seems like a lot of extra work for the cleaners."

"Almost like someone wanted us to be far, far away from any potential witnesses," Carnelian muttered.

She rapped at an unmarked door. The roof was lower in this wing, and the rain sounded twice as loud.

After a protracted moment, Auditor Aeris popped his head out. He held a pair of knitting needles and the beginnings of a pale green shawl. Upon request, he summoned Lapis from a room across the hall.

Carnelian explained the situation. Even expressed as tersely as possible, it sounded quite lurid. A huge and violently dead animal—a mass of biohazards. Masked hunters dressed to blend in with civilian staff. Sophisticated magical tools. A precisely targeted ambush.

The auditors seemed thrilled to help. A little too thrilled, maybe. Both were clad in cozy knitwear from head to toe—seemingly crafted by Auditor Aeris himself. Their relaxed-fit sweaters, which didn't appear to be part of an official uniform, still bore the spiral symbol for Central.

Carnelian handed them her room key and sent them off to inspect the crime scene for themselves. They would take care of alerting the commander afterward. She wanted them to see it with their own eyes first.

Meanwhile, Tiller and Carnelian waited in a downstairs sitting room. It was lit like a romantic restaurant. Heavily shaded lamps colored the air a peachy hue. Rain whipped at the windows, tireless.

Tiller flipped through an album filled with old historical images of the outpost. The groundbreaking ceremony. Past commanders. Visiting dignitaries. Open-base events and ceremonies for the Feast of Chalices.

"Didn't expect you to give them your key so easily," she said to Carnelian. "You trust them not to snoop?"

"They'll snoop, all right. If they find my underwear and tampons and toiletries titillating, so be it. I didn't leave anything incriminating in my luggage. No signed confessions of murder."

"Too bad," Tiller said. "I was so careful to put murder confessions on our packing list."

"I don't trust them one bit, if that's what you're wondering. But they're perfect for playing against the commander."

A double-sided clock protruded from the wall on a bracket. The sort you might normally see at a train station. Midnight was fast approaching.

Tiller tried to remember the last time she'd given Carnelian maintenance. It had been a very long day. Just yesterday, they'd visited the Temple of Combat and Chains.

When she suggested that now might be a good time to perform some much-delayed maintenance, Carnelian turned from the rain-smacked window and said: "You need your head checked."

"Excuse me?"

"No, seriously. I may have been out of it, but I still saw what happened. You rammed your head into the side of the door. You might have a concussion. Or whatever it's called."

"I feel well enough to detangle your magic," Tiller said.

"Feeling that way doesn't make it a fact. For all I know, you might be out of your mind. You might start weaving my magic branches into a cute braid. Put your health first, okay? I'm not about to go berserk."

Right around the stroke of midnight, the auditors came down to discuss their findings. Colonel Istel joined soon afterward, looking even paler than usual. Carnelian spoke to him with the cruel indifference of a socialite taking revenge for a petty slight.

At Carnelian's insistence, Colonel Istel took Tiller to see the outpost's nighttime doctor.

At Tiller's insistence, Carnelian submitted to the bare minimum of necessary magical maintenance.

Everything came together with remarkable speed. If nothing else, the commander ran a tight ship. By the time Tiller got back from her medical check, Carnelian's room had already been cleared of the wind-deer carcass and the captured hunters.

The entire mattress was gone, too, together with all its bedding. It would most likely be deemed unsalvageable.

Carnelian demanded that they get moved to a room in the same wing as the auditors. Far from any lingering odors. "We'll need a few extra days here just to air out my clothes," she said.

She and Tiller collected their things. It went much faster once Carnelian saw their new room. After that, she could help port everything over. (She'd released her shields once outpost authorities apprehended the hunters.)

"We could've asked for two rooms again," Tiller pointed out. "They've got plenty of vacancies."

"We'd best stay together," Carnelian said. "For safety reasons."

"We could still have asked for a room with two beds."

"At some point we have to learn to act like a couple," Carnelian said evenly. "If you're worried about me getting amorous—don't. You think I'm in the mood for a long night of sensual loving? Lord, no. I may never indulge my fleshly appetites again."

"Yesterday you said that about eating."

"Yeah, and how much did you see me eating today?" Carnelian pulled pensively at her gloves. "It's been a rough two days, huh?"

"We aren't even in the Forest yet."

"Surely the Forest can't be any worse."

"Famous last wor—"

"Keep the rest of that thought to yourself."

Carnelian had one final demand before they turned in for the night. She ordered Istel to get them a private audience with the commander.

He pointed out how late it was. How fierce the storm had grown. How nothing else could possibly happen to them before daylight. Not with the intruders in custody, and the auditors on the watch.

Carnelian looked at him without smiling. Without saying anything more.

It was rare to see a mage face an operator with such an imperious attitude. Both she and the auditors were outliers in that respect, though probably for different reasons.

Eventually Colonel Istel buckled. Thus Tiller and Carnelian ended up visiting the commander once more: in her private office, in the witching hours of the morning.

# 24

THE COMMANDER'S NAME was Mariabel Bloodwood. Tiller knew this from their past correspondence.

But in spending time with Carnelian, who never referred to her by anything other than her title, Tiller too had found herself thinking of the commander as nameless.

The filtered air of the commander's office was as scentless as a plain paper towel. Here the wallpaper had a monochromatic design: vines that might look either light green or gray, depending on the light. Their leaves bore an uncanny resemblance to stylized human eyes.

A scarwood table in the middle of the room held a detailed map of the island, from the Amber Strait south of Nui City to the eternally stormy seas north of the Forest. Extensive markings showed how the Forest had expanded its range over the years.

Despite the late hour, the commander was still dressed for daytime, with her prodigious skirts and precisely laced top and the badge of honor worn by all military operators: the mark of the snake. The glue-white scars cupping her face gleamed as if she'd applied a special cream to them.

"Nellie," she said when they walked in.

"Don't." There was a warning edge in Carnelian's voice.

The commander, in contrast, remained calm. She waited before speaking again, as if watching the subsiding of ripples from a rock thrown in a pond.

On the wall behind her desk hung long vertical scrolls painted with exotic flowers. The windows all had their curtains drawn.

The rain sounded more muffled here than it had anywhere else, irrespective of architecture. As if it didn't dare disturb the highest-ranking officer on base.

"Mage Silva," said the commander. "You needed to speak with me?"

"They were from the Parasite Guild," Carnelian said without preamble. "Same as our attackers in the city."

The commander folded her fingers below her chin. "Did they wear the guild's emblem? A little eight-legged tick, is it not? Easy to mistake for a spider."

"They used the same tools," Carnelian said. "I know their methodology. How could I not? I've seen them up close. I've worked alongside them, inside and outside the Forest. Always at your direction. You really love farming out work to them, huh? They're your favorite contractor."

Tiller turned to examine the decor as she listened. She had questions of her own, of course, but she'd let Carnelian say her piece first.

Alcoves built into the walls held all manner of curios. Intricate ships inside rotund bottles. Scale models of chalices and other war machina, painstakingly painted and distressed. Statuettes of legendary national heroes: a gritty-looking woman in a chalice suit, and a crueler-looking woman with horns.

"I don't need to spell it out," Carnelian told the commander. "You hired the Parasite Guild. Yet again. This time, you tasked them with coming after us." She pointed at Tiller. "After *her*. What were you going to do with her? Sacrifice her to satisfy your own scientific curiosity? Just like—"

"Mage Silva," the commander said gently. "The two of you willingly came into my territory, onto my base, with zero backup. If I planned to murder Tiller Koya, I wouldn't have relied on subcontractors. I wouldn't have done it in a way that risked failure."

She rose from behind her desk. Her skirts creaked a warning like the sound of an intruder at a rusty gate. "Would you have brought your blue into my private office if you really thought I had any intention of harming her? No. She senses that, too. She wouldn't have come along if she suspected me of posing any real risk."

That statement cut right to the heart of the matter. Tiller still hung back, closer to the table with the map than to the commander and her desk. But she gave a brief nod of agreement.

"What was I going to do with her?" the commander echoed. "Nothing. I asked the Parasite Guild to hold her in a secure location for the next forty-something days. At which point chalices would come to burn huge tracts of Forest land.

"A solid pretext for me to withdraw my blessing. To forbid you two from going there. With luck, the chalices might change the shape of the Forest enough for you to be forced to give up.

"Why?" she went on, before Tiller or Carnelian could get a word in edgewise. "Well, I don't expect any great show of gratitude or appreciation."

She looked steadily across at Carnelian, fingertips resting lightly on the edges of her dark desk. "Please know that—as usual—I was only trying to help you."

Carnelian sucked in a breath.

For an instant, Tiller feared she might leap across the desk and slug the commander in the face. Yet something seemed to forestall her.

The commander turned toward Tiller. Again, a peculiar rasping came from her skirts.

"You must be very confused," she said.

Her tone held nothing but kindness: no animosity, no impatience, no disdain.

"Just a little," Tiller confessed.

Something shifted behind the commander's eyes. Only then did Tiller realize that no matter how soft she sounded, the commander was just as angry as Carnelian.

"As I feared," the commander said to Carnelian. "You've told her nothing."

She moved out from behind her desk. Her skirts reached the floor, wholly concealing her shoes. She faced Tiller.

"Where to start?" she mused. "There's so much to explain. How about this? Mage Silva was not, in fact, the only candidate interested in going with you."

Carnelian stirred. "None of them—"

"You shut your mouth," the commander said.

Hers was a voice accustomed to absolute obedience. The voice of a seasoned leader. The voice of an operator who knew her commands would always take legal precedence over the concerns and desires of individual mages.

"There weren't many other volunteers," she told Tiller. "But there *were* others, at one point. Not everyone in the Corps wants to see the Forest even partially razed. Some of our younger personnel might surprise you with the respect they have for foresters, and for the Forest itself."

"Colonel Istel told me only one mage volunteered," Tiller said.

"He wasn't lying," the commander replied. "By the time you met with him, all the rest had withdrawn their names. Why? Because Mage Silva plied her dear friend Istel for information on the other candidates. She worked diligently to ensure they backed down. One by one. Quietly."

"How?" Tiller asked.

Carnelian took a step back.

"Don't think of leaving," the commander warned. "You think she'll respect you for running away?"

Carnelian turned to stare into one of the wall nooks. She looked much as she had on the guesthouse roof in the rain. Lovely and rigid and as empty of life as one of those heroic figurines posed right at eye level.

"Bribery and intimidation," the commander told Tiller. "That's how she stamped out the competition. She's never hesitated to use money to further her own ends.

"Now, the others weren't ideal candidates, either," the commander admitted. "Overall younger and more hotheaded than I would have liked. But if they'd stayed in the running, I could have appointed one of my choosing. Or I could have held an audition.

"Mage Silva is a known loose cannon. A dilettante—not even a full members of the Corps. She has numerous black marks on her record. To have any hope of being the one to go with you, she needed to make sure you had no other choice."

This was a lot to sort through.

"Sorry," Tiller said. "Can we clear up a few things first?"

"Yes, of course."

"Will anyone come after us later? From the Parasite Guild, or anywhere else."

"No," said the commander. "Not tonight. Get all the sleep you need."

"And tomorrow?"

"No. Certainly not now that you've put those auditors on the case. Well played."

Carnelian deserved the credit for that, not Tiller.

"You wanted to stop us from going to the Forest," Tiller said slowly. "Why didn't you just say no when I first wrote to you?"

"Would you have accepted that? Wouldn't you have attempted to go over my head? If all else failed, wouldn't you have sought to sneak into the Forest without the Outborder Corps' knowledge or authorization? Poachers do it all the time, I'm afraid."

"Maybe," Tiller said. "Probably."

"Same goes for Silva," the commander said. "She's been determined to follow you. She would've tried to help, one way or another. Even if you outright refused her."

"But she demanded payment." Tiller was growing increasingly bewildered. "We cut a deal. She only wanted to come as long as there was something in it for her."

"Ah, yes," murmured the commander. "A promise of marriage?"

Carnelian raised her head. She stared at the commander with narrowed eyes. "We never told you anything about—about any sort of engagement."

"I had your bags searched during dinner," the commander said smoothly. "A basic security measure. Whatever the case, I can't think of any other reason why Tiller Koya would carry around a necklace of teeth."

"You could have just claimed you heard about it from Alder."

"I did. You should know I like to double-check my sources."

She pivoted the conversation with the finesse of a fencer.

"You wrung that promise out of Tiller Koya because you needed her to believe you were coming along for selfish reasons. You couldn't afford to have her wondering why this strange mage was so strangely eager to join her on a dangerous mission with no other takers."

Tiller wished fervently that she hadn't banged her head on the door quite so hard. Each disparate piece of new information swirled around in the bowl of her skull like ingredients in a sodden pot, never quite melding.

"Mari," Carnelian said roughly.

The commander seemed amused. "Oh, so now I have a name?"

"I just don't understand," Tiller said. "I don't understand why you had to go to such lengths to keep us out of the Forest."

The commander's skirts squeaked as she came over to join Tiller by the table with the map.

Tokens were positioned at various points along the coast and the edge of the Forest. The layout made Tiller think of a game board.

The commander picked up one such pawn and tapped it on the area representing Outpost 24. "As a leader in the Outborder Corps, and a protector of the general public," she said, "I would very much like to see your stated mission succeed. When you contacted me to request my support, I offered it with full sincerity. I meant it with all my heart."

She placed the pawn just inside the Forest. "It does sound like fairy-tale logic. The idea that a prodigal blue might be able to convince the Forest to retreat. To end its decades-long advance. At the same time, the Forest itself is very much like something out of a fairy tale. I wouldn't be surprised if it works."

She picked up another pawn and turned it thoughtfully in her fingers. "That's truly how I feel. Believe it or not, I also feel that Mage Silva is an adult woman capable of making her own choices. My only requirement was that she explain to you the full, unflattering truth. Then you in turn could make an informed choice about whether or not you really want to bring her with you."

"What choice is there to be made?" Tiller asked. "Even if she bullied every other prospect into dropping out, she's still my only option."

The commander set her second pawn down right at the border. Touching Forest territory without fully crossing over.

"No matter how driven you feel to return to the Forest," she said quietly, "and no matter how motivated that makes you to tolerate her quirks, you might change your mind after learning the rest of her story. You might decide that never seeing the Forest again is a far preferable fate to going in there with *her*.

"You have the right to know who she is. You have the right to make that choice. That's been my position from the beginning. That's why I asked her to tell you."

"You sound very enlightened," Carnelian said from behind them. "Very virtuous. But nothing you say now can change the fact that you sicced hired killers on us."

"Hired killers," the commander repeated. "You've always been a bit overdramatic. Did anyone make a serious attempt to kill you, Silva? Did anyone cause either of you a direct injury?"

"Her head," Carnelian snarled, gesturing at the spot where Tiller had banged herself. "Who knows how many brain cells she lost to that!"

"Head injuries are always unfortunate," the commander conceded. "I am sorry about that."

She lifted her eyes from the map and looked at Carnelian. It was a gaze bereft of sympathy.

"You refused to obey my one and only stipulation. I waited as long as I possibly could to take action. I gave you as many chances as time allowed. I didn't harass you to hurry up and tell her. I didn't even discipline you for how you bribed and manipulated your competition.

"Weeks passed. You evinced no interest in meeting your end of the bargain. I could have sent Tiller Koya a letter detailing everything you refused to reveal to her. Instead I sought to give you a way out. A way to save face."

Carnelian came up to the table and looked down at the map as if she wanted to set it on fire.

"You were trying to break my will," she said. "You wanted me to think I couldn't even stop a handful of human hunters. You wanted to hide Tiller until I thought I'd lost her."

Her gloved right hand smacked tokens off the map. Tiller saw it coming soon enough to avoid outwardly flinching.

The commander, too, remained unmoved, even as tokens smacked her skirt and then bounced to the floor.

"You're treating me like a child," Carnelian said in the ensuing silence, a heavy rage in her voice. "Your concerns are entirely fabricated. I've been in the Forest countless times, and you know it."

"Not as deep as Tiller Koya proposes to take you," replied the commander. "Never that deep."

"I've been—"

"You haven't been that deep in the Forest since the kidnapping."

The kidnapping.

That word had only ever meant one thing to Tiller.

Could it mean something different to the commander and Carnelian?

*We've met before.*

*We've met before*, Carnelian had said after they got off the train.

She hadn't offered any explanation of where or when. She'd watched to see how Tiller responded. She'd agreed with whatever Tiller said, her voice light and breezy.

*I had a brother, too. Also long gone*, she'd said on the roof.

*I had red hair. Used to, anyway*, she'd said in the shower room.

Memories turned like the delicate machinery of a mechanical clock. Tiller had the distinct feeling of drowning, of sinking under the weight of lightless waters. She looked from the commander to Carnelian. Neither seemed eager to reach a hand out to save her.

# 25

"There's no point." Carnelian sounded very tired. "There's no point in digging up the past."

"Why don't you let Tiller Koya be the judge of that?"

"You're just like your father," Carnelian said to the commander. "You make everything seem rational and compassionate. Like you're only acting out of neighborly concern. You intervene just to show how important you are, how very useful. I won't play along."

"My darling girl," said the commander, "you might appear be living as you please, without a care in the world. That would be wonderful, if true. In that case, you wouldn't need anyone to look after you.

"But have you ever really cared about your own well-being, or your own freedom? To say nothing of your future. I know you. I don't buy it for a second."

Tiller, listening, rubbed the back of her hair. She'd removed her wig when Istel took her to have her head looked at. By then it had been in a sorry state. The hair below wasn't much better off: it felt stiff and dirty.

The commander and Carnelian looked nothing alike. But when they argued, they sounded like family. Sisters, or mother and daughter, or stepmother and stepdaughter. Relatives close enough to wound each other with skill cultivated through years of practice. They drew blood as if they knew no other way to fight.

Tiller fake-coughed into her fist until she had their attention.

She cleared her sore throat and said: "It's late. The doctor told me to take it easy. I'd love to get some sleep."

She looked the commander in the eye. "You wanted Carnelian to tell me something. Let's save some time. You can tell me instead."

Carnelian—lips pressed tight—displayed a renewed interest in the curios lining the wall.

She must want to flee this conversation, Tiller thought. Yet she stopped short of doing anything and everything in her power to halt it. She'd knocked tokens off the table. But she hadn't grabbed Tiller and tried to make a run for it.

It was almost as if part of Carnelian agreed with the commander's premise.

"It would be better for Mage Silva to explain in her own words," said the commander, "but I can certainly provide a summary. Let's see."

She stooped to collect two pawns from the floor. She placed them on the part of the map depicting Nui City.

"The first big donor to the Koya Foundation," she said. "Your anonymous patron. Their donation was more than enough to get the Foundation off the ground. During a period when refugee foresters were in dire need. And no one else would give you the time of day."

"Yes," Tiller said, with the sensation of walking into a trap. "We owe that donor everything. What's that got to do with—"

"Your mystery benefactor was Carnelian Silva."

This didn't compute.

"I was a child at the time," Tiller said. "She would've been around the same age. How could she...?"

Carnelian studied a ship in a bottle. She kept her back turned, as if they were speaking of someone who had nothing to do with her.

"She was young at the time, yes." The commander spoke with a touch of amusement. "She had lawyers. She'd just come into an enormous settlement from the government."

This tripped Tiller up. "She's a mage."

"Indeed."

"A mage? Winning money from the government? That seems—"

"Unusual? Unprecedented? Yes. But it happened. Some of the experiments on her got taken a few steps too far. Her settlement was granted in recognition of that. As compensation. Of course, you know who ran those experiments."

"I know," Tiller echoed blindly. "I know?"

"A man who had an obsession with twins," the commander said, "and who specialized in working with children. Some called him the Scholar."

She gazed down at the map on the table. "His last name, by the way, was Bloodwood. Nowadays, very few know or remember that."

"Bloodwood," Tiller said. Then, stating the obvious: "Like you."

"We're an example of how fortunes can change within a family. He was an unusually respected and privileged mage, at least until he died in disgrace. After that, they called him proof of the inherent viciousness and inhumanity of mages in general.

"The government did nothing wrong by attempting core extraction and implantation. Their one fatal mistake was trusting a mage, no matter how brilliant, to oversee the project. Or so people said."

The commander spread her hands. "Yet here I am, his biological daughter. Trusted to oversee the Outborder Corps. I'd like to think it's because people consider me my own person, separate from the sins of my father. And they do. But really, it's only because I'm an operator."

She touched the mark of the snake on her lapel.

Tiller searched for signs of a resemblance. The commander's scars kept her from seeing it.

The Scholar's face in her memory was a warped thing, anyway—a face not belonging to any real human. A collage out of nightmares. Something plucked from the depths of a hundred funhouse mirrors. That was the shape he'd taken after ensconcing himself deep inside her brain.

She felt as if she'd slipped into another reality when she slammed her head on the door frame. As if she'd tripped and fallen into an invisible vorpal hole, and this—rather than death—was what awaited her on the other side: absolute nonsense.

It was like the sort of dream that felt too real yet was still undeniably a dream, cleverly weaving together threads of long-buried past stress.

Carnelian had been the Foundation's nameless savior?

Carnelian and the commander both had ties to the Scholar?

*We've met before.*

Tiller stared at the crown molding where the top of the wall met the ceiling. She stared without really seeing it.

She'd suspected that the Scholar kept other captives. Once in a while, she and Gren had heard their voices. But no one outside their cell ever answered Gren's attempts to make contact.

Only the red-haired boy in the cage stuck in her memory.

"The Scholar led the project to build Carnelian up into some sort of super-mage," Tiller said. "Before he kidnapped me and my brother. She was still in his custody when he went rogue and abducted us. She was somewhere nearby. Out of sight. Maybe just a few rooms away."

She went over to Carnelian and plucked at her sleeve. "Is that right?"

Carnelian's only response was a jerky nod.

"There was a boy with red hair," Tiller told her. "Your brother?"

"My brother," Carnelian said. A whisper without any hint of emotion. "My twin. Just like you and your Gren."

She contemplated Tiller with an air of resignation. Her eyes were glassy. They had the same otherworldly shine as the commander's vivid alabaster scars.

"I could see you from the neighboring room," she said. "I was alone in there. The whole time, I could see you, and your brother, and my brother. The magic on the wall worked like a one-way mirror."

She laughed to herself, low and dry. "Yes. It might be stretching the truth a bit to say we *met*."

"I always—" Tiller didn't know what she was trying to say until the words left her mouth. "I always thought I was the only survivor."

"Silva lived, too," said the commander. "And yet only one of you received a life-changing settlement from the government."

Her eyes flicked to where Carnelian's nine cores lay hidden, their magical light artificially smeared together to give the appearance of only one.

"Well. She's always been a special case. The compensation wasn't for being abducted. It was for the irreversibility of what the Scholar did to her."

"My brother's death was irreversible," Tiller said.

"Originally she wanted to give you the entire settlement. She said she'd donate her whole fortune to the Koya Foundation.

"I myself was still near the start of my career at the time. What did I know about anything? But I convinced her not to overdo it." The commander managed to make shrugging look elegant. "Extremely disproportionate donations aren't always a good thing for smaller nonprofits. You had sharks circling, didn't you? Anyway, I told her to hold some back for herself. To keep enough that she could decide to help you and your Foundation again in the future."

Tiller and Doe and Baba Sayo used to banter about how to thank their secret first donor. If they ever got a chance.

Obviously their benefactor wasn't seeking any sort of public recognition. Perhaps they were very shy. An agoraphobic heiress. Or perhaps they were in fact someone incredibly famous. A celebrity of such stature that they hid their identity as an act of kindness: to avoid drawing undue scrutiny to the Foundation, and to refugee foresters in general.

Doe suggested collecting handwritten messages from all the foresters who'd gotten new housing. Baba Sayo suggested that the elders come together to craft handmade gifts, whittled and woven and dyed with the kind of forester artistry that seemed likely to die out within a generation. But the necessary ingredients were very difficult to find in the city.

Naturally, Tiller had imagined the donor as someone much older. Someone closer in age to Baba Sayo, an entire lifetime away from her. Maybe someone without much of a life left to live.

She'd imagined gently taking hold of a fragile withered hand. She'd imagined saying all kinds of things to thank them.

Those words fled her now. It was as though she'd never thought about it before in her life.

A blockage in her ears made the incessant rain sound more distant than ever. The air in the room felt weirdly pressurized. Like the air in the bypass tunnels truncating time and space below Nui City.

Carnelian's averted gaze—and the fixed neutrality of the commander's expression—said that this was not an occasion for gratefulness. This was not an occasion to celebrate.

"I'm not so brutish as to tell you everything against her will," the commander said. "I've at least set you on the right path, though." She glanced meaningfully at Carnelian. "Nellie … Mage Silva. The Scholar didn't abduct you to the city, or to the cultivated countryside. He took you and your brother—and Tiller Koya and her brother—to a house he'd carved out in the Forest. Very, very deep in the Forest.

"He did something to you there, Silva. You in particular. Implanted your last few magic cores, yes—but that's not what I'm talking about. I think he did something more. He always had ambitions that went beyond what others were capable of imagining or even guessing at. That's why he succeeded in taking things so far before anyone stopped him."

One by one, she pushed the remaining pawns on the map into a small cluster around Outpost 24.

"Maybe I'm just paranoid," she said. "I've pored over all his papers, again and again. I still have no idea what he really wanted to accomplish, in the end. But I've always had a bad feeling about sending you all the way back in there. To the parts of the Forest where a normal Corps operation would never venture."

"A bad feeling," Carnelian replied. "That's how you justify hiring the Parasite Guild to hound us. That has to be breaking all kinds of regulations. Even if you paid out of pocket."

"Care to report me?" asked the commander. "Oh, but you essentially already have, what with the auditors sniffing around. Good thing I've always had a gift for dodging scandal."

"A bad feeling," Carnelian said again, bitterly. "Bad feelings can come on for no reason at all. You wake up hating your lover because your brain concocted a dream about cheating. You fall into a funk on your day off, on a beautiful afternoon, just from knowing you have work tomorrow.

"You let your thoughts stray in the bathroom, and suddenly you're horrified by how tree roots spread out so deep and far in the unseen earth. Suddenly you remember that death is always with us, and everyone and everything is just killing time until they perish. Anyone can have a *bad feeling*. Don't inflict your nebulous fears on the rest of us."

She strode behind the table and knelt, collecting the rest of the tokens she'd smacked to the floor. She dropped them back on the map as if tossing a fistful of dice.

The commander put out a hand to keep them from tumbling off the edge again.

"Thanks for your time," Carnelian said, without a speck of gratitude.

"My pleasure." The commander didn't sound tired at all: her voice had the bright ring of morning. "Don't neglect to tell her the rest."

Carnelian's hands formed taut gloved fists at her sides. She inclined her head sharply at the door, a signal to Tiller. She left without another word.

# 26

Carnelian spent a long time washing up before joining Tiller in their new bedroom. She reappeared with wet hair tucked behind her ears. She'd changed into a short turquoise night robe printed with colorful animals: sloths, parrots, tropical sharks.

Tiller regarded her with bemusement as she put her mantle and gloves on (a new set; not the same ones from earlier today). She needed to wear them to prevent sleep-maging, yes, but it made for quite a contrast. Her hollow gray eyes. Her flashy little robe—Baba Sayo would've loved it. Her professional military outerwear.

"Sorry," Carnelian said. "Didn't pack anything more morose to wear."

"I saw some neutral colors in your bag."

"Sure, if you want me in just my undies."

The words were playful, but her tone remained distant.

Tiller had already tucked herself in, taking the left half of the bed. A glowing water-light clock on the nightstand indicated that they were well into the haunted hours of the morning. The rain continued in capricious fits and starts. Sometimes dying down to almost nothing. Sometimes spraying directly against their windows like a vengeful gardener with a high-powered hose.

Tiller had tied the curtains back. So Carnelian wouldn't need to request it.

"You'd think this would be a happier occasion," Tiller said.

"What? Sharing a bed?"

"Meeting the Foundation's most important donor."

An indescribable expression crossed Carnelian's face. She swallowed visibly, one gloved hand at her throat.

"I *am* grateful," Tiller continued. "Then and now. All the other Koya villagers in the city—almost seventy people—they lived more comfortably because of your gift. Other foresters, too. Those who died had much better deaths than anyone could've expected, stranded so far away from home."

She smoothed the geometric bedspread over her legs. It was quilted in various shades of navy blue. The pattern resembled dark entrances to a series of octagonal tunnels.

"You aren't happy, though," she said to Carnelian.

Carnelian sat on the opposite side of the bed. Just on the very edge. Atop the bedspread, without getting beneath it. "Yesterday we got our fortunes inscribed on oracle leaves."

"Two days ago," Tiller corrected. "It's past midnight."

"Same difference. You got Life-Changing Luck."

"You kept yours hidden."

"Mine said Supreme Misfortune."

"Never seen anyone pull that before," Tiller commented.

"My leaf told me: *You are your own god of destruction.*"

"What's that supposed to mean?"

"Whatever it means," Carnelian said, "it's true."

Her fingers pressed the bedcover as if to keep a tiny trapped animal from squirming free.

"All right." Tiller sat up straighter and crossed her legs beneath her. Sleep still seemed far off.

"Why didn't you want to be known as the mystery donor? Why didn't you tell me you'd remembered me all along, ever since the kidnapping? Why didn't you tell me you were another one of the Scholar's victims?"

"Those would've been some heavy topics to raise in the middle of a cocktail party," Carnelian said dryly.

"You had plenty of chances to bring it up later."

Carnelian rose to her feet. The bed shifted with her absence.

The bed alone took up most of the room. If their luggage were any larger, it would've begun to feel claustrophobic.

The lamps were shaped like crystal balls. They cast a strange irregular light at the ceiling and walls, as if they'd been tricked into thinking they belonged in a planetarium.

"I already had seven cores before the kidnapping."

Carnelian looked Tiller in the face. It didn't feel like they were making eye contact here and now, in a shared present. It felt as though Carnelian spoke to her from a different time and place.

"Of my last two cores, one came from my brother. One came from the Scholar."

Tiller's gaze went straight to the nine lights clustered low in her abdomen. They shone like fragments of a fallen moon buried at the bottom of a lake.

The Scholar was in there.

No—not the Scholar. Just his core.

A magic core was not a soul. It was no different than if he'd bequeathed her a physical body part: one of his kidneys or corneas, or even his heart.

"I never understood how he died." Tiller's words came out slowly. Her pulse stayed very fast. "I thought he killed himself, at the end of it all. I thought maybe he just forgot I was there."

"My brother—the boy from your room—he died the instant his core got extracted," Carnelian said. "The Scholar lasted somewhat longer. He extracted his own core next. He needed to stay alive to oversee the process of his core's implantation. In me, his failed masterpiece."

"Mages can only survive core extraction through luck," Tiller said. "Life-changing luck. You can't survive with sheer force of will."

"No. He planned for it very carefully. He scheduled a miracle."

At last Tiller understood.

"He sacrificed a blue," she heard herself utter.

The air of the too-small room seemed to crumple in around her.

"He made me—" Carnelian stopped.

Rain knocked like a fist at the window.

"I performed the sacrifice. With my clear sword. It was well over half my height at the time. More than half as tall as your brother, too.

"I killed him," she said. "I killed your brother. Magic made it possible. Magic made it as easy as cutting a cake. All that came of me murdering him was that the coreless Scholar got to cling to life for a few extra hours. That's all it came down to.

"No one would prosecute me. No one would convict me. When I petitioned for it, they refused. Instead, for some godforsaken reason, they pitied me. The paid me off. Of course I gave my blood money to the Koya Foundation. You shouldn't rejoice over it. You shouldn't be grateful."

Twenty-one years ago felt like a lifetime away.

Twenty-one years ago, the auditors would've been infants.

But that time twenty-one years ago also stayed right there with Tiller in every waking moment, a stowaway making a permanent nest in the unfilled chambers of her heart. The shadow Gren cast had only thickened and darkened over the years, an indelible inkstain.

"The commander was right." Tiller's voice sounded scratchy. "Would've been very hard to forgive you for not telling me."

"*That's* what you single out as being hard to forgive?"

Tiller started to slide off the side of the bed. She would leave the room. Carnelian could have it. She needed to go somewhere she could breathe, and think.

But something stopped her. A suspicion, perhaps, that her legs would give way like wet paper. That they'd refuse to take her weight.

Carnelian's demeanor shifted in the space of a second.

She tightened the sash of her turquoise robe. With the subtlest adjustments to her posture, she suddenly looked as if she could fit in at any elite party in any town. Like her slicked-down, just-showered hair and bare face were both styled that way on purpose. Like her flamboyant sleepwear was a gift from an upcoming designer.

This was the Carnelian who had shown up at a sedate Corps gathering in a glittery bodysuit, who had looked Tiller over with practiced curiosity. Who had successfully pretended that she didn't already know about the deepest parts of Tiller's past.

"Stay," Carnelian said, and her voice sparkled again. This was the voice of a seasoned actress. A voice ready to dance all night, ready to start throwing back drinks. "I'll be on guard nearby. Just in case. But you won't have to see me. The room is all yours."

She had her hand on the doorknob by the time Tiller managed to squeeze out a response. "You can't just sleep in the hallway."

"I'm a creature of the night," Carnelian replied grandly. "Who said anything about sleep?"

And she was gone.

*I killed your brother.*

Carnelian, too, had been a child at the time. A child under the thumb of the Scholar. A child who, with her multiple cores, had practically been handcrafted by the Scholar himself.

Did it matter exactly what had made her manifest her icy sword and run Gren through? Threats, lies, torture, brainwashing—was it fundamentally any different from the Scholar taking that sword in hand and killing Gren himself?

Tiller lay sleepless in the patchy freckling of light cast by the room's crystal balls.

Every symptom the doctor had warned her of seemed to come on all at once: headache, dizziness, languor, irritability, a painful sensitivity to the sound of rain slapping the window.

She stumbled out of bed. She dug out her containers of ash—of crumbled and pulverized bone.

They felt heavier than earlier in the day. As if something invisible had started growing in the soil of Baba Sayo and Doe.

There had never been any container for Gren.

She asked them what she was supposed to do. No answers came. The ceramic remained cold to the touch.

# 27

Tiller wore a blond wig on the day after the storm. It didn't suit her features, and she knew it. But people would expect to see her with the usual plain black hair. At least from afar, she might temporarily hope to get mistaken for someone else.

"New look?" Auditor Lapis asked in the hallway. Tiller gave her a noncommittal nod.

The sky dawned with a deep-cleaned brilliance, almost sapphire in its richest parts. The outpost grounds were littered with twisted-up umbrellas and fallen branches.

She only saw Carnelian twice that day.

First: napping on a bench next to one of the practice arenas. The gray sheepdog lay stretched out nearby, eyes alert, guarding her sleep.

Second: teaching the auditors how to do tricks with her fighting pipe. The same one she'd used for making smoke sculptures on the day they first met. (The day, that is, they first met as adults.)

Tiller asked herself how she felt.

In truth, she couldn't begin to describe it. Maybe this was the closest she'd ever come to the sensation of being a mage in need of maintenance: branches all knotted, seizing up and snarling for no reason, bequeathing a pain divorced from the physical workings of her body.

She'd gotten a pinch or two of sleep, curled up on the left side of the bed. Yet her fogginess lingered. Her skull kept throbbing. The light outside felt too glaring.

This all lined up neatly with the supposed aftereffects of banging her head. But she suspected it of originating elsewhere. She was well accustomed to physical distress seeping into the fabric of her mind, and vice versa.

What the hell was she supposed to do with Carnelian?

Later in the day, Colonel Istel came to find Tiller. He did a double-take at her blond hair.

She asked him point-blank: "Were you in on it?"

"In on what?"

He sounded guilty. But he also sounded like he knew far less than the commander.

"The Parasite Guild," Tiller said. "Sending them after us. After me."

His eyes wandered. "I wasn't—directly involved in making arrangements."

"No?"

"I wasn't ... entirely oblivious, either."

Tiller didn't press him further. Judging by the way Carnelian had addressed him last night, that friendship already lay in tatters.

He made a small noise in his throat—a stifled plea to move the conversation along. Tiller let him continue.

"Asa Lantana wanted you to have this," he said.

He handed her a metal brooch. It was molded to resemble a flower with six pointed petals arrayed in the shape of a pinwheel. A type of clematis. Magic cuttings clustered at the center of the flower like a miniature bird's nest.

"Use it to consult with her," Colonel Istel said. "If you ever have need."

"When did she give you this?"

"She had it mailed ahead to the outpost. Same as your weapons and such." A curious note entered his voice as he added: "She specifically instructed for it to be handed to you on your second day here."

Tiller wondered how much Asa Lantana knew, or had guessed. She seemed like she'd be good at setting things up to make herself look as clever as possible.

Colonel Istel excused himself. He seemed relieved to be done with her. Tiller tacked the clematis pin to her shirt and went wandering along the perimeter of the practice arenas. Her stomach turned at the thought of holing up indoors. Despite the fact that it might be the best way to seek privacy.

Everywhere she went, puddles the size of small ponds reflected the sky.

She didn't see anyone training, but they had to be somewhere nearby. Wooden swords smacked protective padding. Instructors yelled orders in vocabulary that tumbled past her ears like a foreign language.

Behind a wooded area—the part of the outpost meant to simulate Forest conditions—she found an equipment shed. Tacked to it were about ten tattered notices, with many underlines and exclamation points, begging people to lock the shed between uses.

For all that, the door remained unlocked. Tiller suspected it of having been unlocked for a very long time.

Shriveled sunvines crawled over the inside of the structure, their dying light blocked by crowded plywood shelves and metal lockers. Large wheelbarrows formed a herd in the middle.

Any actual training or combat equipment appeared to have been carted elsewhere. The shelves held only a couple dusty packs of balloon skins, and a triangular metronome with dark stains dotting its wooden base.

Tiller reached for the clematis pin.

Asa Lantana's voice resounded somewhere deep in her head. "Took you long enough."

"I only just got your pin," Tiller said. "Who made it?"

"The metal part or the magic?"

"The magic."

"The cuttings are from my mage," Asa explained. "So it's a rare treasure. At least here in your country. Don't lose it."

"You've never said much about your bondmate."

"What's there to say? She's been busy in the southern islands." A pause. "Wait. I might have mentioned a partner. But I wouldn't have mentioned being bonded. I'm very private. I've been working my ass off to cultivate an air of mystery. You can't just—"

"The string of your eyepatch," Tiller said. "Carnelian told me it's a—what people on the continent call a bond thread."

"That cheeky little...."

She proceeded to insult Carnelian with a variety of colorful phrases. At least that's what Tiller assumed she was doing. Her mental voice, mediated by the flower pin, couldn't have been clearer. But it was hard to understand her accent without seeing her face or vivid gestures.

"Did the auditors come to bother you?" Asa asked suddenly. "The young ones. They look like college kids. A shame about their teeth."

"You know them?"

A snort. "They tried to speak with me a few times. Mostly before you and I met. I pretended to forget all my Jacian."

"And it worked?"

"It always works," Asa said. "People think you're dim when you can't pronounce their language perfectly. Forget the fact that there's a whole world of other nations out there, and none of them speak a lick of Jacian. But I divulge."

*I digress?* Tiller thought.

"Long-distance communication doesn't go well in the Forest," Asa continued. "Or so I hear. If you've got anything else to ask, better bring it up now."

"Do you have any siblings?" Tiller asked.

"What is this, a newspaper interview? People tell me I'm a classic only child."

All right then. "If you were me, what would you bring to the Forest?"

"Already told you, didn't I? Fast-acting—what do you call it? Se- ... se- ... sedition? No. Sedatives. Fast-acting sedatives."

"Sedatives," Tiller repeated.

"The emergency kind. Packed in an autoinjector. See if your military can get you anything strong enough to be useful."

She made Tiller go through a thought exercise. Pretend you're alone with Carnelian Silva in the Forest, she said. Pretend Carnelian starts going berserk.

The maintenance needed to fix that would be way above Tiller's skill level. No one could help her in the Forest, either. Porting and most transceiver-type skills would go haywire.

If Tiller couldn't tame her as an operator, the only way to save both their lives would be to put Carnelian under.

It might not buy much time. It might not work well on her if she were too far unraveled. But Tiller might at least seize a chance to flee. Better than Carnelian going fully berserk and immediately exploding her head. Or otherwise slaughtering her.

Tiller agreed to see if the colonel could get her sedatives.

"So you *are* still heading to the Forest together," said Asa Lantana.

"Did you think we weren't?" Tiller asked, although she wasn't entirely sure herself.

In the silence that followed, she thought she saw movement. She turned abruptly before realizing that it had been her own shadow, her own fidgeting.

A trio of moldy straw practice dummies huddled in a corner as if whispering to each other, fenced in by an accidental cage made of orchard-style ladders.

"I don't actually know much about Carnelian Silva," Asa said eventually. "Nor about you. Hey—I love gossip. But other people's deep dark secrets can be kind of exhausting. Already got my hands full with my own.

"Anyway, if you're still going through with it—then let me give you a warning. Nothing concrete. Pure speculation. Take it as the idle rumbling of a foreign operator with too much free time."

"Idle rumbling?"

"Yes. Rumbling."

"Rambling?"

"Sounds like the exact same word to me," Asa retorted.

She stopped speaking for so long that Tiller wondered if she'd abandoned the conversation.

The clematis pin still felt hot to the touch, like a coin left out on the sidewalk in the sun. Maybe she simply needed more time to organize her thoughts in Jacian.

"A magic core is not a physical organ," Asa said. "In some ways, though, your Carnelian is like someone walking around with a bunch of transplanted body parts. How many people have you heard of with multiple organ transplants? What's the mortality rate? How long does the average transplant last before failing?"

"I don't know," said Tiller. "I've never—"

"Because you're ignorant," Asa told her. "But in her case, there are no answers. Unless your government is hiding some really gnarly secrets, there's never been anyone else like her.

"For corporeal organs, transplant rejection can happen out of nowhere. Years after surgery. What about transplanted cores? No one knows. There's no anti-rejection medication that works on magic cores."

"You think she's at risk of dying young," Tiller said.

"The more transplants, the greater the risk. Whether we're talking about squishy organs or metaphysical magic cores. And the more magic she uses, and the more she ages, the greater the risk. Probably.

"More so than other mages, there might come a time when her life depends on the ability of an operator to keep her branches sorted out. Especially the ones that weren't hers to begin with.

"That's why I'm telling you, and not her," Asa said with finality. "It's only a hunch. Nothing she hasn't already thought of on her own. Just—be careful when you untangle her magic. Keep an eye out for branches from different cores getting all mixed up together."

Tiller reached without thinking for the dirty metronome on the shelf. She stopped just sort of brushing its pendulum. It kept waiting patiently and soundlessly for someone to set it in motion.

"Would Carnelian last longer with someone else?" she asked.

"Someone else?"

"Another operator. One more experienced than me. Or more skilled."

"If it were just a matter of maintaining her magic branches in perfect condition, I could do it," Asa answered. "I'd keep her alive to a ripe old age. "Even that might not be good enough, though. And I'm just passing through. I don't plan on staying in your country forever. Talking this much Jacian gives me a headache. I don't even know what I'm saying half the time."

That makes two of us, Tiller thought. But she held her tongue.

# 28

A DAY LATER, Commander Bloodwood invited Tiller to breakfast.

They convened on a glass-covered terrace attached to the commander's private quarters. It was still cold in the morning—cold enough to merit the use of lap blankets and porcelain braziers.

"Isn't this nice," said the commander, breathing in steam from her drink. "Like bathing in a hot spring in the heart of winter."

She inquired about Tiller's head injury. Tiller dutifully described the arc of her symptoms.

"Good to hear that your headaches are getting better." The commander sounded sincere. "Of course, fatigue and malaise can have many causes. All the drama with Nellie can't have helped."

"Getting chased by the Parasite Guild didn't help, either."

"I suppose not. Although that's a type of stress you've already lived with for years."

Perhaps the commander had picked this terrace because, like her dining room, its window-walls showed a sliver of the Forest. In past years, the Forest would've been much further away. But if you sat here morning after morning, sipping hot soup, and faced the right direction—little by little, the very edge of Forest would have come into sight. A slow-moving invasion.

The commander told Tiller to take as much time as she needed to decide on her next steps.

"That's very generous," Tiller said. "What if I settle down here for good?"

The commander laughed. "You're welcome to move in. But if the chalice strike on the Forest fails, you'll have to find another home before the end of the year. No—even if it succeeds, this base might end up being collateral damage."

"You must have mixed feelings about that."

Most of the serving plates had magic embedded in their design. Probably something meant to keep their contents from cooling.

The commander dragged bread through a saucer of spicy oil.

"I'm fond of this base," she said, "but it's just a place. All places age and eventually die. Just like people. Plenty of rural towns have faded out without the Forest coming anywhere near them."

In asking Tiller to breakfast, the commander had made clear that Carnelian would not be joining them.

Despite the fact that they ostensibly shared a room, Tiller had yet to encounter Carnelian there. Not since the night she'd confessed to killing Gren.

She did spot occasional evidence of Carnelian passing through. A closet door left slightly ajar. A single silver hair fallen in the corner.

There was none of the unbridled, unrepentant sort of clutter that had filled Carnelian's ruined guest room in the other wing of the building.

Tiller had steeled herself for chaos, but apparently Carnelian could choose to be tidy. If she so desired.

The commander patted her scarred mouth with a cloth napkin. "I take it that Nellie did tell you the rest."

"She told me about my brother," Tiller said. "If that's what you mean."

The commander looked down into one of the braziers off to their right. It really didn't give off very much heat.

"On paper, Nellie has no family," the commander said. "She and her brother were wards of the state. But in using them for his projects, the Scholar essentially raised them."

"The Scholar," Tiller uttered. "Your father."

"Yes. My father. He never saw them as his children. He never introduced Nellie to me as a sister.

"I felt that we were, though. I felt it very strongly. One way or another, we grew up under the influence of the same man. With him dead—and Nellie's brother dead, too—she and I were the only ones left with that shared background. The only ones left in all of Jace."

Something shifted beneath her signature skirts, as if she were crossing her legs. Her chair groaned like a living creature, then went quiet.

"Nellie cares very little for me, but that's fine. She cares very little for herself, too. I can hardly accuse her of being unfair.

"Nor can I blame her for being more interested in marrying elsewhere than in having her name added to my family register. My father got struck from the register after how dishonorably he died, but a Bloodwood is still a Bloodwood. I've extended an open offer to adopt her. I don't expect she'll ever take it."

Tiller hadn't eaten much of substance yet. She mechanically plucked princess strawberries from a bowl with a strawberry print on it. Perhaps it never held any other type of fruit.

The princesses lived up to their name: little red jewels, intensely flavored. Their heady fragrance filled the whole terrace. Her appetite failed to awaken. "I have questions," she said.

"I'm happy to answer."

"Why does Carnelian work with the Corps?"

"Why doesn't she just live off her settlement, you mean?" The commander reached over and helped herself to a few princess strawberries, too. "She gets more personal time than most unattached mages. But she still has some degree of obligation to make herself useful."

"Why wouldn't the Bureau of Mage Management reassign her closer to Central?"

"Ah, yes." Now the commander got her point. "Other branches of the military did show interest in claiming her. But her skills don't mesh well with existing strategies.

"More than that, much of her value lies in her mere existence. If she moved to Central, she'd be treated as a test subject. They're already running a longitudinal study on her cores, regardless."

"So she asked to stay in Nui," Tiller said.

"Yes. She fought very hard for it. She wanted to serve in the Nuian division of the Corps. She wanted to stay near the Forest. And, in a roundabout way, near you."

"Since when has the Bureau given much weight to requests from any individual mage?"

"She's an exception in every way," the commander acknowledged. "The government actually admitted wrongdoing with regards to her upbringing by the Scholar. She won substantial compensation in court. That's a case with no parallel. Now, if you want to talk Jacian judicial history with respect to mages—"

"Might be in over my head there," Tiller said. "Never had any sort of formal education. I bet you helped, though. With her staying in Nui. With her trying to get at least partly assigned to the Corps."

"Maybe so."

The commander kept taking strawberries. But she didn't eat them. She arranged them in red constellations on her plate.

"You didn't try to keep her off the front lines?" Tiller asked. "Couldn't she work more in training, simulations, that sort of thing? Can't think of why she'd need to specialize exclusively in dangerous expeditions."

"She volunteers for it," said the commander. "Someone needs to go on those Forest missions. May as well be someone who wants it. The Scholar envisioned her as a combatant, after all. A kind of human chalice."

"She wants to live up to his vision?"

"She does have extraordinary battle instincts. I suspect she long ago gave up on the idea of trading her skills in for other magic. Hard to replace all those years of unconventional training."

The commander looked up from her plate. "More than that—Nellie seems compelled to return to the Forest again and again. Cooperating with the Outborder Corps is the most efficient way to get there."

Tiller spent some time digesting this. The commander seemed unbothered by silence.

However long Tiller ended up staying here, she doubted she'd have many other chances to speak to the commander at length.

Outpost 24 was but one of multiple bases under her command. Vorpal beasts plagued the Nuian countryside. The Forest continued its creeping advance.

Someone had to prepare for the arrival of chalices, together with their short-lived pilots and other prestigious visitors from Central. Meanwhile, the auditors kept prowling about with bright eyes hidden behind their lavender-tinted glasses.

Tiller, for one, was glad to be a private citizen. Leading the Koya Foundation from the shadows—and, over time, getting it stable enough that she could transition herself to a more peripheral support role—had been enough of a headache for one lifetime.

She leaned back in her chair. She asked the commander about Istel's involvement with the Parasite Guild attacks.

"Don't be too hard on him," said the commander. "He was very reluctant to help. All he did was share a few tips about your travel plans and whereabouts. Nothing the Guild couldn't have found out on their own."

"You seriously trusted the Parasite Guild not to do us any lasting harm?"

"They're dedicated to staying on good terms with the Corps. They wouldn't have turned around and sold you off to the mafia."

"That's reassuring," Tiller mumbled.

The commander favored her with what was probably intended to be a munificent smile.

Stray bits of strawberry juice stained Tiller's white napkin. She folded it briskly into the shape of a rose (a trick she'd learned from a friendly caterer at a Koya Foundation fundraiser). She placed the red-streaked rose next to her plate.

Next she gathered the woolly outdoor blankets off her legs; she'd been using two at once, for extra warmth. After getting up, she left them bundled on the seat of her chair.

"I thought you'd be dying to ask me more," the commander remarked.

"I'll ask Carnelian," Tiller said. "Your time is too precious. Oh, but there is one thing."

"Hm?"

"Why the mark of the snake?"

The commander glanced at the emblem on her breast as if she'd forgotten she was wearing it.

"I'm in the military," she said, "and I'm an operator."

"I mean, why is it a snake? Why not a mosquito? A barracuda? A phoenix? A tick?"

"Some of those examples sound more like the Parasite Guild's shtick." The commander scanned the horizon as though expecting the flashed signals of a far-off heliograph to feed her the answer. "I'm not quite sure, to be honest. Snakes are good at staying untangled. Or they had better be, if they want to survive."

"So you think it's something very literal. A reflection of the work operators do to manage mages. Keeping everything from getting fatally knotted."

"Perhaps," said the commander. "Operators used to be associated with weavers, come to think of it. But weaving isn't very warlike. At least snakes have venom and fangs."

They should've used a spider as their symbol of pride, Tiller thought. Or some other creature known for spitting silk, for pulling strings.

In the following days, she went back to the on-base clinic in order to get clearance to leave. Her headaches grew sparse enough that she had no qualms about pretending they'd stopped altogether.

She didn't have a single run-in with Carnelian. The closest she ever came was hearing a hint of quiet singing from one of the auditors' rooms. But it would inevitably stop the instant she tried to listen harder.

Colonel Istel wouldn't be able to offer much help. Carnelian avoided him just as thoroughly. In the end, Tiller resorted to asking the auditors.

"Nellie?" said Auditor Lapis. "She keeps crashing with me at night. Want to come lie in wait for her? We could arrange quite a surprise."

There were still many hours left before sunset. "I'd rather corner her now," Tiller said.

Auditor Aeris had been doing handstand push-ups next to a nearby wall as he listened. "Nellie's a slippery one, isn't she?"

He took one of his arms off the ground. Tiller was fairly certain that a one-handed handstand push-up would be close to impossible even for a trained acrobat. She stepped back out of range. Just in case he was about to come toppling down.

Lapis walked over and kicked him casually in the side. He caught himself, but it looked like a close call.

Tiller couldn't begin to understand their relationship. Would she and Gren have ended up like this if they grew older together—play-fighting like springtime wolves?

Lapis instructed her to wait outside the entrance to the guesthouse. It was an unusually warm day, much warmer than when she'd had breakfast with the commander.

A knot of people in the civilian staff uniform surrounded the usual sheepdog, lavishing it with pets and scratches. The sight of that uniform made Tiller jumpy, though half the personnel around here seemed to wear it.

Were the disguised Guild hunters still locked up somewhere nearby? Had they gotten sent back to the city?

The cover story, as Tiller understood it, was that their assault had been a training drill gone wrong. They'd been hired to do a penetration test, and ended up coming after Tiller—rather than the actual soldiers on base—wholly through a series of regrettable accidents.

She wondered how they would explain the attack at the Temple of Combat and Chains. But she didn't doubt that the commander had some plausible-sounding scenario up her sleeve.

The auditors had asked if Tiller would like to press charges. She swiftly refused. She had no interest in making a real enemy out of the commander.

A wise forester knew how to pick their battles.

Ten minutes later, Auditor Lapis came bounding back over. "Aeris can lead you to her," she said. "You'll find him by the gate to the forest arena." She adjusted her glasses and shot Tiller a gap-toothed grin. "Don't scream once you see it," she added. "This is normal. At least for Nellie."

# 29

THE WOODED training grounds had little in common with the real Forest.

The trees looked much too similar, as if they'd all been planted together. Every single one was the same species and the same height, with long vertical stripes of green and yellow bark.

"Careful, now," Auditor Aeris said. "Stay back behind the fence."

He'd clapped his gloved hand over Tiller's mouth as soon as they reached the center of the training grounds. He removed it only once he seemed assured that she wouldn't start yelling.

He put a cautionary finger to his own lips instead. "Just imagine," he murmured, "what terrible things might happen if you distract her."

But who would hear Tiller even if she shrieked at the top of her lungs?

A film of magic covered the fenced clearing like a circus tent. It extended beyond the fence posts, beyond the stretch of buzz-cut grass where Aeris had brought her to spectate. It made every crack of sound seem as distant as summer fireworks going off on the opposite bank of a river.

Without that magical interference, everyone here would've risked serious hearing damage. The veil protected Tiller's ears, but also misled them. The staccato pop of gunfire felt somehow divorced from the scene before her.

Soldiers shot at Carnelian like a firing squad.

Her shields materialized to meet each bullet with inhuman precision—some multifaceted, some as small as a single hexagon.

Granted, Tiller had no way to tell if they were shooting standard flesh-ripping physical bullets. It might've been something else altogether. She'd never learned much about firearms, icearms, or other guns in general.

Carnelian stood on the other end of the clearing. Not so far away as to make the soldiers miss her. Definitely too far for her to read or react to the subtleties of their body language, to guess the timing and location of each shot based on how they tensed certain muscles.

Yet, holding herself as still as a paper target, she nevertheless managed to block every projectile.

The shooters paused to reload. Carnelian raised a hand. They yelled something back and forth.

Then it started again, almost without warning. They seemed to fire at random. Carnelian couldn't have been deploying her shields based on any kind of predictable pattern.

This time she walked toward them. An easy, straight stroll. No zig-zagging.

Focus solely on Carnelian, and she'd resemble the star of a futuristic fashion show. Shield fragments bloomed and vaporized with each step, an ever-shifting escort.

She had her gloves on, but not her mantle. In a muscle tank and shorts, she looked dressed for rock climbing. She'd pulled her hair back off her face with a clip shaped like a claw.

She was smiling.

The more they shot at her, the more her smile broadened.

She was empty-handed. Tiller mentally traced the outline of her magical sword, bright and clear. Wherever she went, she carried the potential to manifest it.

Tiller thought of Gren. Of how assiduously he'd attempted to communicate with the boy in the cage. That boy had been virtually mute.

That boy had been Carnelian's brother.

At the same age, would Carnelian have looked more like her twin—red hair, large eyes?

If Tiller knew nothing of the past, she'd have assumed Carnelian used to be the kind of spoiled kid adored by all for her charm and her preternaturally pretty face. Her capricious exuberance. Her willingness to ham it up and put on a show for whoever would watch her.

But she couldn't picture Carnelian as a child. She could only picture the magic sword—not a child-sized weapon—and Gren.

Carnelian looked past the shooters. She looked at Auditor Aeris, casual in his spiral-pattern hoodie.

She looked at Tiller.

Their eyes met. Carnelian's smile vanished. All the while, shield fragments bobbed about to protect her.

She made a hand signal. The shooting ceased again.

Thanks to the sound-absorbing magic on the clearing, it had not been nearly loud enough to leave Tiller's ears ringing, or stuffed with an illusory fullness. Yet for the next few seconds she still felt as though someone had reached in her head and switched off her hearing.

Carnelian turned as if intending to slip off in a different direction. Right on cue, Auditor Lapis popped up outside the fence to block her path.

Lapis waved vigorously. Carnelian stopped dead again.

Apparently the threat of dual auditors was enough to keep Carnelian in check. She trotted over to speak briefly with the shooters.

After packing up to leave, they filtered out past the fence, nodding politely at Tiller and the auditors as they went.

All wore neon mesh scrimmage vests over their uniforms. Carnelian had one, too. Rather than pull it on the way it was supposed to be worn, she dangled it from the back pocket of her shorts like a garish orange tail.

The two auditors loped closer. They halted once they appeared satisfied by Tiller and Carnelian's proximity: on opposite sides of the fence, but only an arms-length apart.

"Good luck," called Auditor Lapis. She seemed to be addressing Tiller, but she could have meant either one of them.

Auditor Aeris saluted. The two of them vanished into the woods.

"I'll get my mantle."

Nothing about Carnelian's tone suggested that these were the first words they'd exchanged in days.

"So long as you come back," Tiller said.

It turned out to be hanging from the outside wall of a nearby storage shack. Carnelian shook it out, making the fabric snap like a wind-tossed flag. She slung it over her shoulders.

"Who gave you permission to remove that?" Tiller asked.

"Everyone's favorite colonel."

"Thought you weren't on speaking terms."

"I'm on speaking terms with anyone who'll get me what I want." Carnelian grinned at her like a singer prepared to sign autographs.

That face invited her to forget about the sword that had emerged from nothingness to slaughter Gren. The Scholar, and how tall he had seemed from a child's perspective. The malformed walls of the room where he'd kept them. His magic core living on as a transplant.

Tiller had seen that core close up. Every time she gave Carnelian maintenance, she'd unknowingly smoothed out magic branches that once belonged to the Scholar.

Carnelian caught at her shoulder. She hadn't felt herself swaying. "You see," Carnelian said neutrally, "this is why I've been keeping my distance."

She removed her hand. She stepped back.

Tiller looked away. She looked inward. She seized the wheel of the ship inside her. Many, many years had passed since the last time she came so close to losing sight of her path.

If she let emotion steer her, she'd have smashed to smithereens a thousand times over.

She cocked her head at the fenced arena. "Keeping your distance," she said. "And all the while, you've been throwing your magic around like this? Without getting maintenance?"

"You and the colonel aren't the only operators on base, you know."

An electric bolt of sickness lanced down through Tiller's body, brief and blinding.

She realized with dismay that no matter how it repulsed her to think of touching magic branches that came from the Scholar—the thought of surrendering that task to other operators was much, much more revolting.

Carnelian continued without any change of tone. "I can grovel if you want me to grovel, by the way. I don't have any qualms about prostrating myself.

"I'll be whatever you want me to be. I can beg for absolution, or I can shut up and never mention the past again. If you tell me to go away, I'll go away."

"And if I decide to go to the Forest alone?" Tiller asked.

A skeptical bird squawked somewhere outside the vast tent of sound-sucking magic.

"I would ask permission to follow from a distance," Carnelian answered.

"And if I say no?"

"Then I guess I'm stuck," she said. "I would have to find a replacement. I would have to go back and bargain with the other mages I scared off."

"Might even have to prostrate yourself before them."

"Right. They'd savor a chance to kick me when I'm down."

Carnelian removed the claw-shaped clip from the back of her hair. She clicked it in her hand like a pair of tongs. She looked more as if she were speaking to the claw than to Tiller.

"I don't think you would go in the Forest alone. You're not like me."

"What's that mean?"

"You wouldn't put yourself in a situation guaranteed to bring grief to your loved ones. Your grandmother, your brother, your previous bodyguard. You wouldn't do it even if they're gone now. Even if they would never find out."

Tiller watched the clip open and close like the mouth of a carnivorous plant catching flies. "You think you know me so well," she said. "Why? Because you stalked me for years before I ever approached you?"

This was meant half in jest. But Carnelian winced. "I'd prefer not to call it stalking. Guess I'm in no position to quibble over definitions, though."

"What would you call it, then?"

"I kept tabs on you from afar." Avoiding eye contact, Carnelian clamped the claw-shaped clip onto the bottom hem of her shorts. "I paid a private eye to send me regular updates."

"That's how you knew the perfect time to donate." Another mystery solved. "Your PI must've caused poor Doe no end of stress."

She'd never mentioned it to Tiller, but Doe would definitely have noticed if they were being periodically monitored.

"She called them out once or twice," Carnelian said. "Gave them a dreadful fright. But she must've realized they weren't connected to any sort of genuine threat. For the most part, she left them alone."

"Yeah. Doe already had her hands full watching out for murderers and profiteers." And there had been plenty of those to deal with. "Was it true, what you said on the train about seeing me at a charity banquet?"

"Just once. It was the same as when the Scholar held us prisoner. I saw you clearly. You didn't even know I was there."

Carnelian fastened the front of her mantle. She turned her body as if attempting to signal an end to the conversation.

"With your leave," she said, "I'd like to go take a shower."

"No."

"No?" She looked askance at Tiller and murmured: "You may prefer me sweaty and unwashed, but out of respect for the general public, I really should—"

Tiller interrupted. "As your designated operator—"

"Oh, now you decide to pull rank?"

"—I say we're not done talking yet. I'd like to give you some mainte-nance, too, while we're at it."

Carnelian laid a hand on the fence. It was a surprisingly rustic thing. The type of weathered wooden rails you might see surrounding a horse paddock.

The bird hidden in the trees behind her let out another cynical screech, then flapped noisily away.

A smile ghosted across Carnelian's face.

"Funny, isn't it," she said, "the sheer lengths we go to torture ourselves.

Why work so hard to gouge your own wound? Want to hear more about your brother? Sure." She locked eyes with Tiller. "He looked for you as he bled on me. He must've known you weren't anywhere near. But he kept looking.

"He made the Scholar swear not to hurt you. *You don't need her*, he kept saying. *Not anymore*, the Scholar agreed. *Thank you, little blue*.

"I couldn't hold your brother up for long. My legs folded under me. He slumped over my shoulder. My sword melted like ice. The Scholar came over and ruffled his hair. He had the air of a busy father. A bit absentminded, a bit distracted, but still happy to reach down and pat his little blue on the head.

"It felt like your brother was melting onto me together with my sword. It felt like lava kept coming out of him, too hot and thick to be blood. Hardly any of it got on the Scholar."

She touched gloved fingertips to the base of Tiller's throat. It felt like a threat.

"I didn't wear gloves back then," she said. "Your brother's blood got between my fingers, between every knuckle. Under my fingernails. Under my cuticles. Inside the corners of my mouth. The crook of my elbow."

"Are you done yet?" Tiller asked, as steadily as she could manage.

"I could go on. But you see my point."

"That's the picture you want me to have in my head when I look at you?"

Carnelian lowered her hand. "Doesn't matter what I say, or what I want. It's inevitable. It's the truth. It's what you *should* be seeing every time you—"

"Oh, shut up."

This actually worked, at least for a moment. Carnelian blinked at her.

Tiller took a long breath.

She'd always wanted to grow up to be like Doe, scarily patient and implacable. Eternally amused at the smallest things. Instead, she seemed bound to end up more like snappish Baba Sayo.

"Don't waste your energy," she said. "You can't drive me off like how you drove off your rivals. I know you still want to follow me to the Forest, anyway. Where can we go to talk?"

Carnelian stared down at the tips of her running shoes. When she raised her head, it was as if the previous exchange hadn't happened at all.

At least she knew when to give up.

"Obviously the real Forest would be best," she said lightly, "if you're concerned about being overheard. As far as places on base go, this"—she gestured at the woods around them—"seems like a reasonable substitute."

"There isn't anyone else using it for training right now?"

"Wasn't on the schedule. Here."

Carnelian pulled out a crumpled orange scrimmage vest, the one she'd had hanging from her back pocket. Tiller donned it with some reluctance. It smelled as though it hadn't been laundered in months. Magic tingled in the mesh fabric—a network of cuttings that made it as itchy as tulle, even when worn on top of all her other clothes.

"A friendly fire vest," Carnelian explained. "Just in case."

"You're not wearing one."

"I trust my shields."

"Sounds like arrogance talking."

She caught a glimpse of Carnelian's dimples. A precursor to a smile. "It's the gambler in me." Carnelian tapped her lacquer earpiece. "I'll get an alert if we're about to interrupt someone's exercise. Or vice versa. You like deep talks, do you? Let's go deeper, then."

She pointed out a path winding between the eerily regular trees.

# 30

DEEPER IN THE artificial woods, Tiller gave Carnelian some much-needed maintenance. As she worked, she tried to prioritize all of Asa Lantana's past tips and advice. It was a lot to keep track of.

It felt cooler here than in the clearing. Almost cold enough to get goosebumps. The perfectly uniform trees formed a canopy too dense to let through any solid patches of sunlight.

At no point did she think she might vomit. But as she eyed each of Carnelian's faceless cores, smoldering with concentrated magic, she remembered that one of them had been excised from the Scholar. By his own will. A living transfer facilitated by the sacrifice of a very young blue.

*Little blue.*

He'd called Tiller that, too.

She did a maneuver with Carnelian's magic branches that Asa had compared to finger-combing long hair.

No, Tiller didn't feel as if she were about to be sick. It was more like her organs had gotten stuck in all the wrong slots: her stomach snagged too high, her heart squeezed too low.

The Scholar wasn't alone in here, she reminded herself. The other cores belonged to Carnelian, and Carnelian's brother, and six other anonymous donors who'd probably been victims of the Scholar in their own way. Just as much as the Silva twins and Gren.

She and Carnelian had stopped in a section of the training grounds where an abundance of boulders competed for space with the ubiquitous stripe-barked trees.

All those green-and-yellow trunks blended together in the dappled shadows like camouflaged commandos. The boulders, in contrast, made no attempt to hide. They were marked liberally with a type of spray paint that had the side effect of attracting bioluminescent fungi and peculiar-smelling ferns.

Carnelian climbed up to sit on one such boulder. In effect, this put her waist right at eye level. It was nice not to have to stoop down to fiddle with her magic.

Few of the other boulders appeared suitable for sitting. One, shaped like an enormous egg, stood on its end as if held up by an invisible carton. Others were piled in precarious-looking yet mysteriously balanced stacks, some tall enough to touch the underside of the canopy.

Mages with levitation powers had built those towers for practice, Carnelian said. They would stand among the striped trees with their hands in their pockets, trying to suppress any obvious physical tells.

Sometimes they took turns to magically disassemble and reconstruct their creations. Sometimes they made a game of mutual sabotage.

"You never stacked any?" Tiller asked.

Carnelian did possess a skill nicknamed Float. A languid form of telekinesis.

"I would much rather be shot at." She sounded like she meant it.

Tiller kept her hands moving. There were a lot of magic branches left to untangle.

"Well," Carnelian said from above her, "I assume marriage is off the table."

"Why?"

Carnelian twisted to look over her shoulder. "Why?" she asked. "*Why?*"

"No one mentioned anything about breaking off our engagement. Besides, you were the one who proposed in the first place."

"The commander already covered this," Carnelian said sharply. "I only brought up becoming a magewife so you would think I was coming along for my own selfish reasons. So you wouldn't wonder why I'd enter the Forest to aid a stranger."

"You *were* selfish," Tiller countered. "You drove away anyone else who might've wanted to help."

"I thought if anyone were going to defend you with their life in the Forest, it had better be me." Carnelian looked forward again. "I don't expect you to agree."

Tiller focused harder on separating her magic branches. Some attempted to wind together like young vines curling around a support stake.

If someone with weaker magic perception came by to watch them, it might look as if she were inspecting Carnelian's back for ticks. Carnelian had her tank top pulled up out of the way, together with her mantle. All Tiller's fingers physically touched was the skin around the subtle bumps of her spine.

Magic cores were located in the body in the same way that consciousness was found in the brain. You couldn't saw open someone's skull and yank their consciousness out with your fist.

Laypeople and fellow mages could rap at Carnelian's lower back all they wanted, as if knocking on a door, and nothing would happen.

Tiller was an operator. Not a particularly seasoned one, but an operator nonetheless. Gradually, wearily, the magic branches coiled up inside Carnelian heeded her touch. They looked like a shadow network of stray veins in her torso, a vestigial organ that had forgotten its original purpose.

Half an hour later, Tiller's concentration clung to life by the slimmest of threads. She removed her palms from Carnelian's back.

"I'll explain my stance on marriage," she said.

"Please do. I'm very confused."

"You were a child. Legally blameless, for all sorts of reasons. You did take my brother, though. I appreciate your contributions to the Koya Foundation. But money alone isn't enough."

"What is, then?"

"Flesh," Tiller answered. "Think in terms of folklore. Do you have a firstborn to give me?"

"If you're waiting for my firstborn, you'll be waiting for the rest of your life."

"Then give me yourself." She paused for effect. "See? Getting married after the Forest still makes plenty of sense."

Carnelian lowered the back of her tank top. She shook out her mantle. She hopped gracefully down from the boulder covered in esoteric military symbols. Then she turned to Tiller and said: "If you actually want a life of luxury, I can give you that."

"Doesn't hold much appeal for me."

"Didn't think so. If you're looking to murder me in revenge on our wedding night—I'm terribly sorry to say this, but it won't work. You saw me deflecting all those shots earlier. I'm just too good at staying alive."

Tiller leaned on the spray-painted boulder. Sorting through Carnelian's magic always left her exhausted. Her brain felt as if it had shriveled like a raisin.

Each time she tended to the wayward branches, each stubbornly bending in the wrong direction, she came away wondering how Asa Lantana made it look so effortless.

Was Asa a genius? Or was Tiller a simpleton? A little bit of both, perhaps.

She glanced up at Carnelian. It felt as though they were watching each other from behind fanned-out hands of playing cards. Tiller's move would come next. But she was much too tired to make a game of it.

"I don't see you as Gren's killer," she said. "I see you as...."

Words left her. Carnelian contemplated her fumbling with unwavering gray eyes.

"I see you as—as a kind of classmate," Tiller finished.

An incredulous silence reverberated among the trees, with all their matching trunks clad in impressionistic streaks of yellow and green.

"A classmate," Carnelian said.

"Let me explain. I never went to school."

"Are you sure you even know what a classmate is?"

"You meet in school when you're young. You go on field trips together. You share experiences you'll never share with anyone else when you're older."

Carnelian spoke delicately, as if attempting not to wound her. "Allow me to point out that a kidnapping is nothing like a field trip."

Tiller refused to be deterred. "I never thought I would meet anyone—not in all the rest of my life—who could know exactly what it was like. Back in that house deep in the Forest.

"I thought there'd never be anyone who could tell me with absolute certainty that I'm not losing my mind. Or my memory. I used to wonder if I'd done something to Gren. If I'd somehow—"

Carnelian caught her hand. "You never did anything wrong," she said in a voice stripped of every layer of irony. "You never did anything."

"I know. That's the problem."

Carnelian's gloves were so conductive of sensation that they felt more intimate than the touch of bare skin.

"I won't order anyone how to feel," Tiller said to the pair of fine gloves clasping her right hand.

"Let me tell you something, though," she continued. "My old bodyguard Doe was like a sister to me. To both me and Gren. It was my fault that she died. Not even the Lord of Circles could convince me otherwise. Did your private investigators mention that?"

"No." Carnelian's hands tightened. "There was a time when I pulled back. The Foundation was doing well. You seemed happy. You didn't need any help I could offer—anonymously or otherwise.

"I thought I'd better make something of myself. I thought I couldn't just keep waiting for another chance to do penance. That's when I started studying for the Corps audition."

"I see," Tiller said. "And then Doe got killed."

She tugged her hand free. She could speak of it, but not like this. She crouched and plucked a few tender blades of grass from near the base of the boulder. Anything was better than the choking sensation of stillness.

She'd always been good at rolling quick little grass rings, twining the tiny stems together as if twisting a rope. She used to give them to Gren and Doe and Baba Sayo and any number of other Koya villagers. She used to know the size of everyone's fingers by heart.

"I met a girl," she said. "I really, really liked her. I liked her enough to bring her back to the house where I lived with Doe.

"I waited, of course. Nine or ten months passed before I ever told her my address. But it was fine. Nothing happened. She visited so often that Doe began to get a little sick of us. It was the happiest I'd ever been since Gren died."

All of a sudden, the grass ring was finished. It lay on her green-stained palm. Not quite a perfect circle. Tiller hadn't been paying any attention to the movements of her own fingers.

"That girl shared everything she knew with black-market hunters," Tiller said. "About me and Doe and our routines. About the inside and outside of our house. About our defenses. That's how they got to us."

She rose to her feet. She passed her grass ring to Carnelian. It was loose on Carnelian's gloved pinky, but too tight on all her other fingers.

"Did you get revenge on your girl?" Carnelian asked.

"I'll leave that up to your imagination."

"Sounds like a yes."

"The point of that story is not about how I did or didn't exact my revenge," Tiller said. "It's about the fact that no one can stop me from blaming myself. That's just how it is. So I understand you, in a way. Blame yourself all you like. But you can't convince me to join you. I'll be the judge of where my rage goes. If I can tolerate my own presence, I can certainly tolerate yours. We're both killers."

Carnelian let out a short laugh. "Yeah. That's a stretch."

"Baba Sayo—my grandmother—she thought she was a killer, too. She had more guilt than blood in her veins, by the end of it. She tortured herself with thoughts of it. But she never said a word of complaint."

"Why would she think that?" Carnelian turned the grass ring around and around her pinky, as if trying to twist open a bottle cap.

"Come with me to the Forest," Tiller said. "Stick to our agreement. Then I'll tell you. Marry me when we return, too. I'll get you your freedom. It's not like I have plans to marry anyone else."

Carnelian looked increasingly bemused. "You don't need to bait me with information. I'll follow you anywhere. It's just—it's incredibly hard to believe that you're still willing to have me."

"I figured you'd have a little more faith in your own charm."

Carnelian ran a gloved hand over her shag of loose silver hair. "I can charm the pants off most people, if I put my mind to it. But I haven't killed most people's brothers."

"You better stay in our room tonight," Tiller said. "No more imposing on Auditor Lapis."

"I'll have you know that I was extremely unobtrusive." Carnelian spoke with an air of wounded nobility. "I'm a wonderful guest."

In truth, Tiller half-expected her to slip out again. To tarry on the guesthouse roof or in the hallway, if not in the auditors' rooms.

So it surprised her to come to bed that night and find Carnelian already there, cozy under multiple layers of thick winter blankets.

"You stayed," Tiller said.

Carnelian fluttered her eyelashes. She did look very cute. And also remarkably punchable.

The crystal orb-lamps cast a dappled river of light across the ceiling, a thick stream of pretend stars. Tiller's grass ring, now a bit ragged, rested peacefully next to the clock on the nightstand.

For better or for worse, the bed felt unnecessarily wide. The mattress stirred whenever Carnelian fidgeted, but neither of them ran any risk of crossing the invisible line in the middle.

Carnelian took up so little space.

Tiller was fast asleep when she felt something graze her upper arm. A gloved touch, wispier than skin. The rest of her remained enmeshed in nonsensical dreams. But that skittish brush of gloves seemed real enough to send her heart pelting away into a far-off dimension.

The bed shifted.

In the brief confused moments when she woke, every now and again, she always saw Carnelian lying with her back turned, inhaling so quietly that her body looked utterly motionless.

Then sleep sucked Tiller down deeper. Much too deep to remember how her breath hitched, seized by a nebulous neediness.

Subsequent dreams dragged Tiller to distant times and places where she found herself even more alone than she was in reality. Quite a feat, considering that in reality she was the last surviving member of her family register.

So much for those phantom gloved fingers. The far side of the bed may as well have been on a different continent. Carnelian lay locked tight inside herself, unreachable.

# 31

ALL IN ALL, Tiller and Carnelian ended up staying over a week at Outpost 24. By the time they got ready to leave again, there were only thirty-six days left before the scheduled chalice assault on the Forest.

Carnelian complained more than once about Tiller invading her side of the bed—chasing her to the very edge of the mattress. Tiller had no recollection of this. She was always right where she belonged when she woke.

As per Asa's advice, she got Colonel Istel to bring her a pack of sedatives. He gave her a compact heliograph, too, explaining that Carnelian would know how to use it.

"Sunlight is much more reliable than communication magic in the Forest."

The day before their departure, the commander requested another meeting. They joined her in a room off to one side of the dining hall. Here, too, sunvines criss-crossed the walls and ceiling and windows like an elaborate privacy screen. "I hear you've been drinking my subordinates under the table," the commander remarked to Carnelian.

This was news to Tiller. "When?" she asked, puzzled.

"I've always been renowned for my time management," Carnelian said primly.

Tiller coughed. So did the commander.

"I have no idea what you're implying," Carnelian continued, undaunted. "It's perfectly possible to sneak in some carousing even when you've got to be snug in bed by eleven."

"You're a terrible influence," the commander told her.

"Then you should be glad to get rid of me."

This reminded Tiller of how she'd griped at Doe and Baba Sayo during her teenage years in the city.

She kept that thought to herself. Next to her, Carnelian tore a paper napkin into strips and began methodically braiding it.

The commander pivoted to face Tiller. "You're very forgiving," she said. "Your brother—now, that's a highly personal matter. But if it were me, I would struggle to get over the fact that she kept so many secrets."

Tiller laid her hands on the polished wooden table, fingers splayed as if to play chords on a keyboard. "The secrets are out now. Which is what you wanted, correct? And I still want her to be my mage in the Forest. Better than starting over with a stranger."

Commander Bloodwood nodded slowly, then took a sip from her glass of opaque green juice. It had a pungent vegetal scent.

"A very happy ending for Nel- ... for Mage Silva," she said. "Which reminds me. I almost forgot to congratulate you on your engagement. I suppose I won't ask what you see in each other."

"We're desperately in love," Carnelian said coldly.

"In your case, I'd believe it. Anyway—to reiterate, you don't have to worry about the Parasite Guild any longer. The Forest contains dangers far worse than hunters." This was perhaps not the most encouraging thing she could have said to them. But it was undeniably true.

The commander drank from her glass again, or tried to. The lower half of her green juice had morphed into a sludge as thick as pudding.

"I really do think you can stop the Forest's spread," she added, her eyes on Tiller. "For example—I'm speaking hypothetically here, mind you—the sacrifice of a blue is said to work wonders."

Carnelian stopped twisting at the shreds of her napkin. "Are you telling my wife to kill herself?"

"She's not your wife yet," the commander said sweetly. Her skirts creaked like an old wooden floor as she rose to walk them out.

Colonel Istel assumed responsibility for escorting them to the edge of the Forest. He'd been the one who brought them to the outpost, and he would be the one to lead them away from it.

He insisted that Carnelian wear her military ID necklace and field scarf. He stopped Tiller, too, and gave her the same insignia she'd seen on him and the commander and every other operator in the Corps. The mark of the snake.

"You're a civilian," he said. "But Nellie isn't. Not completely. You've got authority over her in the Forest. By proxy, that makes you a kind of temporary officer.

"You shouldn't run into any Outborder squads—much less any local constables. But if you ever need to prove you've got the right to be out there, start by showing them this mark." He tapped the snake's complex coils.

"Hopefully they don't attack us before asking questions," Tiller said.

"Catastrophe ROE is still in place. Do your best to look human."

"If you're paranoid enough, anyone can appear like a phage from afar," Tiller pointed out. "Or like a shape-shifting vorpal beast."

Carnelian had at first stood behind them looking bored and aloof, in much the same way that a high fashion model might be trained to look bored and aloof.

By the time Colonel Istel finished delivering a rote lecture on Forest safety practices, she'd begun juggling small rocks from the side of the road. One almost landed smack on his head. He shot her a glare.

"Did you try my gift yet?" she asked, all innocence.

"The roeberry liquor? No."

"How ungrateful."

"Come back alive, and we can all share it."

"Very well," Carnelian said haughtily. "That's a promise."

At ground level, the entrance to the Forest was not a conspicuous borderline, like a road or a river. Were it not for the persistent warning signs planted acres away, a layperson could stumble inside without noticing anything wrong.

Tiller and Carnelian parted ways with Colonel Istel at the military portal positioned nearest to the current border. The portal was disguised inside an otherwise empty farmhouse. It must've been sold to or seized by the government quite a few years ago.

Colonel Istel stood on the porch and watched them go without waving. They stepped past fences that led to nowhere, past sagging barns and grain silos.

No reasonable person would've looked around and declared that they were in the woods. Trees remained sparse, though their roots bulged in the way of chemically enhanced veins. The sky above remained a light disinterested blue. Keep your problems far away from me, it warned.

Yet the instant they entered Forest territory, Tiller knew it in the soles of her feet and the palms of her hands. In her ear canals and her sinuses. In the way her throat seared as if rending itself.

The moment passed. The same chilly breeze still wafted through stiff grasses. Thorny weeds loomed as tall as sunflowers. Tiller adjusted the bags on her back. The heaviest parts of her load were the two precious containers of ash.

Up ahead, the trees grew broader and denser. The air tasted both fresher and older, all at once. It was reminiscent, somehow, of a centuries-old castle cellar.

The temperature simultaneously rose and dropped. They skirted pockets of startlingly sweaty air, like a stranded patch of last year's summer, and a few seconds later would find themselves inexplicably shivering. It was the same feeling as wading through random currents of hot and cold water in the ocean shallows.

The Forest was not a collection of hoary trees. It was an eternal presence that enveloped them, neither hostile nor welcoming.

Likewise, there was no hostility in the drowning waters of a lake, or in the flesh-eating parasites waiting for someone to come by and accidentally snort them, or in the neverending lightning storms that terrorized the northern seas above Nui.

You might find the Forest malicious if you lost your farm to it. But the Forest itself had no notion of malice.

Carnelian reached out without saying anything and tugged Tiller a step closer.

Tiller made no mention of how she could feel the Forest rising up invisibly in the air around them, jostling like a crowd at a stadium, siphoning down into their lungs as if making them drink the essence of a million trillion bustling ghosts.

Could only foresters sense this? Or only blues? Either way, it filled a starving hole in her—reconstituted a part of her so dessicated that she'd thought it was dead.

# PART THREE

## *The Devouring Forest*

# 32

CARNELIAN SANG a buoyant medley of hiking and battle hymns.

The songs were not to Tiller's taste, but she didn't complain. She didn't want to say anything that might result in hearing less of that voice. She had the urge to close her eyes and fill herself up with it, to gulp it down like water until no more wayward thoughts remained.

Normal conversations with Carnelian didn't affect her like this. Something fundamental changed when Carnelian sang. The very taste of the air around them. The natural speed of Tiller's heart.

Until now, it wouldn't have occurred to her that one might become just as infatuated with a singular voice as with a beautiful face.

She would have to be careful not to lose herself.

The first landmark they encountered was the Market at the Edge of the Forest.

Needless to say, that name had not been true for many years. The Market lay in ruins, fully swallowed by the woods.

It had already been on the verge of abandonment twenty years ago, when Tiller and the other Koya villagers passed through one last time on their way out of the Forest.

She'd held Baba Sayo's hand as they walked. A weary wind swept fall leaves and stray bits of paper through stone-paved squares.

Even back then, the Market had been far quieter than at its peak. No voices bawling about one-day-only discounts. No pregnant dogs barking. No knock-knock of carnival ball games. No jeering from kids trying their luck at beaten-up dartboards. No fresh stink of fried leek pancakes.

Instead, a vague odor had wafted from piles of old vegetable peels behind shuttered food stalls. That odor seemed to trail after them until the Market was well out of sight.

Now, two decades in the future, reddish-purple bamboo had shattered every last paving stone.

Tiller stopped to remove her wig. Today she'd only used pins to attach it. No glue. She took off her stocking cap, too, and dragged her fingers through the ends of her hair.

Carnelian looked at her strangely. "Thought your hair was a lot shorter than that."

It was still too short for Tiller herself to see much of it. But it did fall past her ears now.

"The Forest might be making it grow," she said.

"Does the Forest normally do that?"

"Maybe. My brother and I had longer hair as children."

"Hmm. Let me know if you need a hair tie."

The Forest had seasons, but they tended to be more localized than those in the world outside.

Besides, its seasons weren't bound by things like the proximity of the sun and moon and stars, the turning of time. The Forest's seasons came and went as they pleased. Perhaps because of this, there were none of the summer flake-flies or winter fireflies you might see elsewhere in Jace.

For now, the Forest gave them the cool earthen air of late April or mid-May. A month or two ahead of schedule, yes, but preferable to an excess of ice or mosquitoes.

Still, there were plenty of other hazards to watch out for. Tiller steered Carnelian through a labyrinth of icicle-shaped stalactite fungi. They dripped numbing toxins: a single drop would suffice to fell a grown adult.

"When's your birthday?" Carnelian asked out of nowhere.

"Does it matter?"

"Just trying to think of things to look forward to if we survive the Forest."

"I don't really have one," Tiller said.

"You must have some kind of date listed on your family register."

"It's a day in summer. But calenders weren't important in the Forest. We didn't celebrate anyone's birthday."

"Not even children?"

"My brother and I were the only children in Koya Village," Tiller replied. "And no one saw us get born. Baba Sayo found us wandering in a summery part of the Forest. You already knew that, didn't you? Your PIs must've told you."

"They said you might be a year or two older or younger than your recorded age."

"There you go," Tiller said. "Don't throw me any big parties."

Carnelian stopped speaking as they navigated a complex outbreak of wrinkled roots. The air was stale with the musty smell of wind-deer. Living ones, thankfully.

"I don't celebrate my birthday, either," Carnelian said afterward. "Not since the kidnapping."

Not since losing her twin, Tiller thought.

There were places where wading through plant life felt like trudging through waist-high snow. The underbrush dragged far more at Carnelian than at Tiller, despite them being very similar in stature. They made faster progress when Tiller walked first.

"The Forest really does go easy on you," Carnelian observed.

"All part of being a blue."

It took another hour for them to reach an area that outsiders might identify as looking like a proper part of the Forest. Each great cedar was as wide around as a fancy townhouse in Nui City. They stood generously spaced out, roots warring underground, branches fencing for dominance high overhead.

The canopy was an average of forty stories tall. From the ground, it resembled a vague dimness papering over the sky.

The sunvines that hung from the highest branches grew thicker than a human torso. They tapered like serpent tails, coming to an end ten or twenty feet above the Forest floor. They could kill you if they fell.

Fecund dwarf trees clustered around the giant cedars. Tiller and Gren used to beg to join harvest parties, groups of workers heading out to fill waist-high baskets with pulpfruit. This zone would've been a prime destination for harvesters. Or any hungry forester, really.

Carnelian eyed the hanging pulpfruit with longing.

"No," Tiller warned.

"Don't scold me. I didn't even say anything."

"You know what'll happen if you eat that. Stick to your rations."

Tiller had been tempted to pluck some pulpfruit for herself, but she decided not to rub it in yet.

"The most common type of hazing in the Corps," Carnelian said thoughtfully, "is convincing new recruits that it's safe to eat certain

Forest foods. Berries from a particular bush. Or anything taken from just inside the border."

"Ever fall for it?"

"Nah."

Carnelian stopped to fuss with the fit of her backpack. Heavy-duty straps encircled her chest, hips, and shoulders.

"The Scholar tried mixing Forest food in my meals," she explained. "I was sick for months. But it didn't last nearly long enough to push through and develop a tolerance."

"I'll eat enough for both of us," Tiller said.

"How kind of you."

A tiny part of Tiller did wonder if, all these years later, her stomach might have issues digesting Forest produce. That would certainly throw a wrench in their plans. Carnelian had only packed one person's worth of rations.

Tiller had never heard of a native-born forester falling ill from things that grew in Forest soil. Even after living on the outside for years and years.

Still. Two whole decades.

As they hiked onward, she reached out to break off a small pinch of a bread mushroom. She cleaned it on her jacket before tucking it in her cheek.

"I saw that," said Carnelian. "You were getting a little worried, weren't you?"

Chewing made the flesh take on a gummy texture. It tried to glue itself to Tiller's molars. She swallowed and said: "I just kept it low-key to spare your feelings."

Something eased in her when Carnelian chortled. It had been a very long time since she'd wanted to make anyone laugh.

Six-legged rabbits scooted up and down both the trees as wide as buildings and the smaller stands of growth that clustered beneath them. The rabbits didn't discriminate.

"Spider bunnies," Carnelian said.

"Spiders have eight legs."

"Well, what do you call them?"

"Crabrabbits," said Tiller.

"Most crabs have eight legs, too."

"*Most*," Tiller emphasized. "Still more accurate than lumping them in with spiders."

"You'll be really mad once you hear the other name we soldiers call them."

"Do I want to hear it?" Tiller asked.

"Arachbits."

"We should never have let you lot inside the Forest."

Carnelian laughed again.

But an odd hush followed.

Carnelian stopped in place, her head tilted back.

Tiller squinted.

A dull spot clung monkey-like to one of the dazzling sunvines. Far below the distant canopy, but still about three or four stories above them.

It was human-shaped. Light-skinned. Shredded clothing hung off it like cobwebs.

Their first phage of the day.

The first phage Tiller had spotted in a full twenty years.

She sucked in the odor of damp moss and ripe earth.

The fat vine swayed with the phage's weight—slowly, slowly. The creature stared down at them with large, fixed, lemur-like eyes. From this distance, they looked like brilliant holes in its face.

The phage tilted its head in the manner of an owl, more crooked than any human could comfortably bend. The gesture made its neck appear broken.

Down on the ground, Tiller held herself absolutely still. So did Carnelian.

Two minutes passed. Three minutes. This lack of movement would soon become torturous.

The phage turned and climbed higher. Neither of them said or did anything until it had vanished from sight.

"They don't always attack." Tiller kept her voice low.

"They don't always attack blues, maybe," Carnelian said. "I can promise you that they always, always attack the Corps."

Unlike vorpal beasts, phages were not bizarre monsters who'd accidentally wandered over from other worlds. They were as much a part of the Forest as glassfish and pulpfruit trees and crabrabbits and wood urchins.

They wore the shape of human beings. Yet unlike human foresters, phages could never simply choose to pick up and leave.

Tiller had her basher staff lashed to her bags. She reached back to check its fastenings.

"Yeah," Carnelian said, watching her. "Might want to have that ready." She wiggled her fingers. "Permission to remove my gloves?"

"We're alone in the Forest now," Tiller answered. "I said it before, and I'll say it again. Take off anything you want, anytime you want."

Carnelian rubbed her bare hands together as if it tickled them to touch raw air. "We'd best stay alert. Phages rarely move alone."

# 33

THEY STAYED ALERT. But they didn't see any other phages until late afternoon.

During one of their breaks, Carnelian ate a heavily spiced and salted meal from a tight-sealed pack. She didn't complain about the taste, but she didn't seem overly thrilled by it, either.

Tiller, meanwhile, scraped marmalade-colored Forest jam off a tumble of damp rocks.

Carnelian watched her lick her fingers with a hint of envy. "What's that?"

"A slime mold," Tiller said.

"Oh. Delicious."

"My brother and I used to eat it like candy."

They crossed through the remains of another military outpost. This one had been fully operational up until about a decade ago. Carnelian claimed she'd stopped by a couple times before it went defunct.

"Came here for my Corps audition," she said. "And just look at it now."

The ruins might as well have been nine hundred years old, not nine. Only a few stony walls remained recognizable as the work of human hands. Voluptuous roots poured like lava flows down through the shells of old barracks.

A few Forest bison raised heavy dark heads. Tiller and Carnelian were careful to keep their distance.

When the bison were no longer watching, Tiller took some pulpfruit. Back in Koya Village, a little old one-armed woman had been the fastest at picking it. She could almost swear she still heard the incessant soft plunk of fruit hitting fruit inside harvest baskets.

Further along, they exchanged wary looks with a mottled ermine. Fat wild turkeys scratched the ground for acorns, leaving behind a jumble of tracks and curls of scat. Chameleon peafowls rippled like a mirage atop low branches.

At the base of a lonely heliograph station, Carnelian attempted to use her pointy lacquer earpieces. The magic cuttings welded to them emitted an obedient firefly glow.

No voices came in response.

"Figures," Carnelian said. She lowered her pack and bent this way and that, stretching her back. "I'll climb up to send a signal."

"Is it safe?"

They craned their necks to see the top. The station was shaped like a water tower, albeit one as tall as a skyscraper. It needed to be that tall simply to breach the tops of the trees.

"Should be fine," Carnelian concluded. "Looks more intact than the old outpost we passed."

"I know you don't like to use Float," said Tiller. "But you might not have any choice."

"If I fall, I'll consider it."

"Or if the tower starts to come down on my head."

"Right, right." Carnelian pulled the pointy caps off her ears and dropped them in Tiller's palm. "Guess these are useless now."

Tiller held one up in the light of the sunvines. "Why are they shaped like this?"

Carnelian blinked as if seeing her own ear cuffs for the first time. "Always figured it was to pay tribute to our national heroine."

"Who?"

"You know. The demon. The lady with horns and pointed ears."

"Ah."

"One wonders," Carnelian mused, "where the legendary guardians of old have run off to. Why can't they come tame the Forest for us? They did it before, didn't they?"

"Allegedly," Tiller said. "Hundreds and hundreds of years ago."

Carnelian folded up her mantle and left it on top of her pack. She put her gloves on to protect her hands. She splayed her fingers like a tree frog.

She added Istel's portable heliograph to a smaller bag at her waist. There ought to be more impressive equipment at the station up top, but best to go prepared.

"We aren't obligated to flash a message," she said. "Might as well do it as a courtesy, though. At least once. The stations located deeper in have probably all collapsed by now."

She grabbed the ladder bolted to the base of the tower. The rungs were painted metal, albeit with little paint left. They looked liable to snap like rotten wood.

Carnelian started climbing. The ladder whined, but held firm.

Tiller let out a breath. She crouched and tucked the ear cuffs in one of the front pockets of Carnelian's backpack.

Here, too, the Forest canopy blocked the sky better than blackout curtains. The requisite sunvines dangled down like long glowing snakes, drinking up outside sunlight and regurgitating it in the Forest all day and all night.

She would've expected sunvines to tangle with the heliograph tower, too, but they let it be. Perhaps some manner of magical repellent had been built into the structure in hopes of protecting it.

While waiting, she tested her silver clematis pin. She'd clipped it to a spot near her collarbone.

"What?" demanded Asa Lantana.

The voice came from somewhere behind Tiller's eardrum. It sounded clouded, as if Asa were speaking through a mouthful of toothpaste.

"It works," Tiller said, taken aback.

"Damn right," Asa said archly. "You're in your Forest now?"

"As of today. Just wanted to see if the pin would still—"

"Well. No promises about it working much longer."

"You change your tune quickly," Tiller said.

"Change my what? My tuba?"

"Never mind."

Asa didn't seem particularly interested in learning Jacian idioms. "How long will you be stuck in the woods?" she asked.

"Could be two weeks. Could be two months."

"You don't have that much time left."

"Hopefully we'll be on the faster side."

"Two weeks or two months...." Asa sounded dissatisfied. "Do you have any idea where you're going?"

Tiller attempted to explain that the amount of time it took to reach a destination in the Forest often had little to do with its physical distance. She and Carnelian would first aim for Koya Village, then cross over to the closest of the sacred mountains.

(The house where the Scholar had held them captive lay further north. No need to venture so far.)

Asa made a noise to indicate that she'd understood about ten percent of this. "You're clueless about how long it'll take you in practice."

"Yeah. Basically."

Tiller looked up. By now Carnelian had climbed high, high out of sight. No sign of encroaching phages.

Their bags nestled amid a cluster of knee-high dwarf trees. As Tiller spoke to Asa, she'd used the tapered end of her basher to grind small round depressions in a greenish slick of mud that probably hadn't dried out for centuries.

"One last word of advice," Asa said.

"You could've given me all this advice in one go, you know. Just a thought."

"Would you have re- ... reigned it?"

"Retained it?"

"Yes. That."

"I'd have taken notes."

"Carve some notes on that brain of yours," Asa said briskly. "Carnelian Silva isn't listening, is she?"

Tiller glanced up again. "She's out of earshot."

"First time I saw her, I picked through her cores and branches as if looking for lice."

"Find any?"

"No. But I did notice some...."

The pause that followed was so long, Tiller wondered if she'd wandered off to flip through a dictionary.

"Some ... impurities," Asa finished.

"Not magical lice."

"Magical lice don't exist," Asa said. "This is a different kind of hitchhiker. Stray dreams and desires. The memories of others. Small fragments. Nothing active enough to make a difference in her everyday life. Not at this stage."

"You think her cores need to be cleaned?" Tiller asked. "Of—their original owners' leftovers. These impurities."

"No. Might provoke a rejection response. You just focus on keeping her branches from getting all crinkled. She's in a very delicately balanced state right now."

"Then why'd you bring it up?"

"In the future," Asa said, "you might have no choice. You might have to mess directly with her cores. If some alien element in them starts to contaminate her. If you begin losing sight of her."

Over the next few minutes, she elucidated her theories about how an operator of Tiller's capabilities might endeavor to cleanse Carnelian's cores. How she might strip out any remaining evidence that they'd ever belonged to another human being.

Tiller was left with more questions than she'd started with. "How can I tell if it's needed? You're talking about something completely different from the typical signs of a mage going berserk. Anyone can act unlike themselves from time to time. I don't know her well enough to—"

"If you aren't confident, then don't do it," Asa declared. "Simple as that. Don't die out there."

The magic in the clematis pin lost its warmth. Tiller's eardrums went silent. She tipped her head all the way back to check on the tower. Carnelian was starting to climb down.

A heart transplant wouldn't make you fall in love with the donor's husband. But magic core transplantation was a type of surgery performed in a whole different dimension—with, perhaps, a whole different set of risks.

Carnelian had said offhand that her other cores had a way of getting pushy with her. Even though they'd been part of her for most of her life now. Who knew what abstract scraps of humanity might still cling to them, growing like a silent film of bacteria in an unwashed water glass?

After descending from the ladder, Carnelian declared proudly that her mission had been a success.

"I flashed a long message. Got a brief acknowledgment." She mopped sweat from her neck. "At least they know we're alive."

"Good thing you aren't afraid of heights," Tiller said.

Carnelian sidled up beside her. "Would you have come to rescue me if I were?"

"You don't want to hear me answer that."

Later in the day, the light piped in via hanging sunvines turned a luxurious, sleepy orange.

The Forest would remain bright all night long, but everything took on a different tint from before. The cedar trunks shifted redder. The shadowed earth became interpolated with a pinkish-blue aura like someone's lost memory of a fading sunset.

Tiller's hands moved before she became consciously aware that something was wrong.

She looked down and found herself making the old forester signal for phages. For danger. She'd covered her right wrist with her left palm.

Carnelian wouldn't know what it meant.

"Nel—"

It was more like a spasm at the back of her throat than a proper attempt at speech. She swallowed. She dropped her bags. She called out Carnelian's full name.

At this point, Carnelian had only been wearing one glove. She whipped it off faster than Tiller would've thought possible.

Then Tiller heard the swarming phages. A rising whisper. The sound a million cobwebs would make if they could leap from one tree to the next.

Up ahead, Carnelian drew her long transparent sword. It glittered like a golden icicle in the light from the sunvines. She'd positioned herself to take on the bulk of the horde.

Tiller adjusted her grip on her basher. Her arms faltered as if wishing they had an excuse to drop it. "I'll watch your back."

"First and foremost, watch out for yourself," Carnelian said tensely.

There were plenty of more modest trees below the absurdly high canopy. Some of the younger and less ambitious varieties filled out at around seven to ten stories. Their leaves and needles shook as if in a restless wind as the phages rustled closer.

Tiller didn't get a chance to see what Carnelian did next.

A lone phage—an adult male, separated from the rest of the herd—charged out of the bushes like a lynx pouncing. Hands extended.

It looked gray and wet and gluey. It would melt Tiller's skin if it touched her.

Greedy creatures, all of them. They had no purpose except to absorb humans. They had no purpose except to be fruitful and multiply, to recruit more people to their side.

Sweat made her hands slip. She almost lost hold of her basher. She met the phage with a hard kick. It bounced up off the moss-coated ground as though it felt nothing.

Because it didn't.

Magic flared at the corner of her awareness. No time to look. At least Carnelian seemed to be holding her own.

Her boots slipped as they crushed moisture from the moss. The phage bent itself backwards to avoid her basher. It flung itself at her again and again without tiring.

She flipped her grip and rammed the stone edge of the basher with all her might into the phage's head.

It failed to lose its pasted-on smile.

She hit the vertebrae on the back of its thick neck. Then the side of its skull. The crack of stone and scarwood on bone trembled down the length of her basher.

The phage folded up on a bare patch of ground, its head misshapen. Clear liquid dripped out to mat its once-human hair and glisten its once-human skin.

Before it could get up, she struck it again and again.

It stopped moving.

Once, when Tiller and Gren were nine—only a few months before the Scholar abducted them—a child-sized phage had grabbed Gren with both hands and nearly absorbed him.

Tiller had jumped across a ravine to reach Gren, breaking her ankle as she landed. The phage swiped hungrily at her left arm, at the crook of her elbow. It left a sticky melted gunk on her skin that stung like acid.

She'd smashed the phage with rocks until its head hung limp as a sock. Its mushroom-white fingers had forever stained the right half of Gren's brown face.

It was the bravest she'd ever been. Back then, she'd thought that if she could throw herself at phages, nothing else would ever scare her. Back then, she'd thought she'd be able to do anything for her brother.

She'd ripped the phage off Gren and hurled its body down into the ravine behind her. She'd been too gutted with rage and pain to stop and think.

Even at that age, she should've known better. You couldn't just crush a phage's skull and call it a day. Without proper treatment, a broken phage would always come back for seconds.

Tiller was thirty now, and she no longer had a brother. She knew what she had to do next, though her stomach clenched at the thought of it.

She had a set of yo-yo knives. She had a sheathed machete strapped to her hip.

She went for the knives.

She stopped just before cutting into her left hand (she'd aimed for the meaty part at the base of her thumb). She held still, her small blade poised at the ready.

She'd been so utterly focused on her one opponent that she'd missed the silence suffocating the rest of the Forest.

# 34

She didn't understand what Carnelian had done.

Carnelian stood like the statue of the swordswoman in the hotel where they'd met Asa Lantana.

Phage bodies sprawled on the ground around her, dozens and dozens of them, their heads mangled, their water soaking the earth. Some were pale. Some were varying shades of deep gray. None held any living color in their skin.

When Tiller first turned, she'd glimpsed a blaze of red hair. By the time her eyes focused, it was gone without a trace.

Carnelian's sword impaled the face of the phage closest to her. It lay right at her feet. Her blade drove a path between its eyes and through its skull and out the other side, staking it to the dirt below.

Her hair hung silver around her lowered face. Her fingertips rested lightly on the end of the sword hilt as if she'd just discovered it there, a natural mineral growth.

Tiller assessed their surroundings. No darting movements at the edge of her vision. No hints of dripping gray skin in the trees. No susurration of disturbed leaves.

She stepped closer, avoiding the maze of immobilized phages.

"Carnelian?"

Carnelian still wouldn't look her way.

She tried again. "Nellie?"

The magical sword burst apart like a powdery snowball. Fine frosty particles billowed, then faded to nothing.

Carnelian's hand lowered itself to her side. She gave Tiller a searching look.

"I won't use that name if you don't like it," Tiller said.

"I like it," Carnelian said quickly. "I love it. Just didn't expect to hear it from you."

Together they eyed the fallen phages.

"Phages rarely move alone," Tiller recited.

"You're quoting me."

"When I was a child, I saw plenty of lone phages. Is this something new? This—herding behavior."

Carnelian grimaced. "I meant that they usually come in twos or threes. Not giant stampedes."

"None of them touched you?"

"Nope. Still got a perfect track record." She wasn't out of breath, either.

"Now I understand why they wanted to put you up against entire armies."

Carnelian seemed skeptical. "Phages are physically superior. But humans are scarier. Anyway, it helped that they nearly all targeted me from the start. Fighting while protecting someone is a lot harder than fighting to save your own skin."

"Phages don't go after blues as much," Tiller said.

"I noticed."

"They'll try to absorb me if they see an opening. But the majority will always go for you first."

"Just the way I like it."

Tiller reached for her knives again.

Carnelian put a hand out to halt her. "There's still time. Let's take a closer look at them first."

"What's there to see?"

"I may be a troublemaker," Carnelian said, "but I'm still capable of following the appropriate military procedures. Indulge me."

"Military procedures," Tiller uttered as Carnelian knelt to poke at the oozing corpses.

"Yep. That's what this is. Not looting bodies. No matter how it looks."

"Dead phages don't bother you?" Tiller asked.

"What's a dead phage, really? They're already dead before we bash their skulls in. Do they stink of decay? Are they decomposing?"

No, and no. Like any other animal born in Forest territory, phages did not rot in the usual way. It had been a shock for young Tiller to leave the Forest and realize that people on the outside thought it was normal for garbage to stink, for bodies to bloat, for flesh to degrade.

"No indeed," Carnelian said in conclusion. "Phages never bothered me."

Together they studied the nearest phage. An adult. Its telltale crackled complexion became easier to make out when it wasn't moving. A spiderweb of tiny lines covered every surface of its skin, like the deliberately cracked glaze of certain ceramics.

The dead phage's sacred water seeped steadily into the soil beneath their toes. It was very similar in clarity and consistency to the cerebrospinal fluid of a living human being. Or so people claimed.

Carnelian pointed to a cluster of white stitches on the front of the phage's dark shirt. Embroidery in the shape of an eight-legged tick.

This phage had once belonged to the Parasite Guild.

"Nothing nefarious," Carnelian said. "They must've joined in on some ill-fated mission to the Forest. Might even have been one with me.

"There were plenty of times when I had to flee for my life without taking along any bodies. Or when I could only spare the energy to haul away one of many."

Some phages bore the same modest tick emblem. Others wore the field uniform of the Outborder Corps. Still others appeared to be poachers. Plus a few lost-looking children.

Carnelian approached them all with an equal dearth of sentiment. She rooted through the poachers' clothes to locate coin purses and money clips. She collected ID tags and tattered field scarves from former Corps soldiers.

There was nothing to borrow from the children.

From the Guild members she took magical tools, some familiar-looking and some esoteric, all still lustrous with an abundance of active cuttings. Tiller saw her stash away a gun—the icearm type, which Tiller would've had no clue how to use herself.

She showed Tiller what appeared to be a tin of breath mints. "Listen to all these little friends."

She rattled the container next to Tiller's ear.

"Immobility ticks?"

"You got it." Carnelian tucked the tin in Tiller's pocket. "You hang onto these. Keep them with your sedatives." Later she also passed Tiller a compact bubble wand. It looked bizarrely similar to a tube of mascara.

"I remember the Guild's bubbles from the temple," Tiller said. "But what do they actually do? They never touched us."

"Their entire purpose might be to serve as a foamy cage of magic. Very fast-acting. Like using a net gun to capture wildlife." Carnelian tapped the black tube with her fingernail. "If it's not written on here, and you're really curious, there's only one way to find out. Blow a bubble and touch it yourself."

"I'll pass."

"So cautious."

"It isn't really my style to start playing roulette alone in the Forest."

Carnelian went right back to pawing at phage bodies.

She'd been telling the truth about coming out of her battle unscathed. None of them had landed so much as a single swipe on her uniform. The fabric would've shown if it they'd touched her: bleached-looking handprints, faded stretch marks.

Cloth could only offer so much protection. Given enough time, a phage could fully absorb anyone. Clothes and all.

After you vanished, it would regurgitate you from its body. Your new phage self would climb out of your killer's back like a starfish growing anew from a severed limb, like a worm budding off to make offspring.

Your phage would be clad in the same outfit and accessories as before, curiously lacking in stains and damage. At least at first.

After Carnelian finished inspecting her victims, Tiller suggested that they divide up the labor of anointing each phage.

"No," Carnelian said immediately. "I'll take care of it."

"It'll go twice as fast if we both help."

"If we both shed blood, I'll have to use First Aid on two people instead of just one. Thought you wanted to keep my magic use to a minimum. Let me do all the anointing."

She drew a combat knife she'd pilfered from a soldier-phage. She flicked a cut across her palm. No hesitation.

Tiller backed up out of the way while Carnelian walked around sprinkling her blood on the phages' smashed faces. Even a single drop per phage would technically be enough to do the trick. But it was best to err on the side of generosity.

This was the only way to keep a phage from resuscitating: crush or break open their head, then salt the remains of their skull with your own blood. Living human blood.

Blood would have no effect if you simply splashed it on them before killing them. Likewise, they could recover from any manner of head wound if you forgot to anoint them after they died.

It might take months. It might take years, depending on how thoroughly you'd obliterated them. But without the anointing ritual, a broken phage would always find a way to come back.

Carnelian's blood mingled pinkly with the sacred water still trickling out of the brutalized phages.

Once she'd made the rounds of every single carcass, she pressed her hands together as if trapping a fly. Stifled healing magic burned between her fingers, then went out like a candle.

When she pulled her hands apart, the cut on her palm was gone.

"I'll give you a tune-up," Tiller said.

Carnelian waved her off. "Maybe once we turn in for the night."

Tiller rallied, ready to convince her.

A sound she'd never heard before filtered down from high in the treetops. So high that she probably shouldn't have been able to hear it.

An insect?

An aural hallucination?

She saw the moment when Carnelian heard it, too. Carnelian raised a hand to shade her eyes.

No matter the time of day, the sunvines shone bright.

Carnelian's face changed. Her arm lashed out as if to strike down an invisible enemy. The type of blow that would knock teeth loose, fill a mouth with blood. More than enough blood to doubly consecrate the massacred phages still slumped underfoot.

Tiller went rigid. Her body locked up, and she had no idea why.

It took an extra second to sense the magic that had rolled overhead like a fatal wave in open water.

A crumpled sunvine hung suspended in the air above her. One as girthy as a full-grown tree trunk.

Carnelian was choking. "Please—"

Tiller darted out from beneath the floating sunvine.

The instant she moved, a phage leaped down off the vine's folds. She felt a crashing impact by her heels. Half a second slower, and the phage would've broken her back.

The magic in the air snapped like a cut string. Behind her, the titanic severed sunvine dropped with the weight of a toppling building.

The ground shook. Tiller foundered. The phage rocketed at her. If it were human, it would've shattered far too many bones to move like that. But it was faster than any living human being.

Long damp fingers grasped at the nape of her neck, sticky as the toes of a gecko. Her breath froze inside her lungs.

Her basher rested together with their bags. Piled neatly out of the way. Out of reach. She groped for the machete sheathed at her waist.

The phage's touch seared as if it had already melted finger-shaped holes in her.

Before she could get her machete out, a blade whistled past her ear. The weight of the phage dropped off her shoulders.

Carnelian strode past. She slammed the phage to the ground, her boot on its chest. It struggled to rise again. She pulled her translucent sword from its body—smoothly, and without any apparent effort. She put both hands on the hilt and stabbed down again.

And again.

And again.

"I think you got it," Tiller said hoarsely.

The sword turned to mist. Carnelian stood there, still stepping on the phage. Its torso had gone concave. Her hands remained curled, as if paralyzed.

Bit by bit, she opened her fingers. She looked over her shoulder at Tiller as if she'd forgotten what to do next.

"My turn," Tiller told her.

She took out a yo-yo knife and pricked her thumb. She let a few drops of blood fall on the remnants of the phage's forehead. Carnelian seemed inordinately fond of stabbing faces.

She put the pad of her thumb to the tip of her tongue. The bleeding would stop soon enough if she sucked on it.

Carnelian, saying nothing, took her wrist. The warmth of First Aid leached up toward Tiller's fingertips. It spread in other directions, too, seeking the burning patches of skin near the base of her skull.

When she pulled her hand away from her mouth, and away from Carnelian, the tiny cut had disappeared.

"That was exciting," Tiller said.

Carnelian released an abrupt whuff of breath. Not quite a laugh, but close enough.

She turned Tiller around and lifted the ends of her hair to stare at the back of her neck.

"How bad is it?" Tiller asked.

"...You'll have several new scars."

# 35

THEY BEGAN investigating the fallen sunvine.

Judging by its size, it might have hung there shedding false light for hundreds of years. Sunvines never grew to such ripe old ages outside the Forest.

"No way this fell on its own," Carnelian muttered.

It glowed in the way of embers clinging to life—mottled and cracked, already fading. Its sheer mass and weight would've killed Tiller if it dropped on her head.

"Your Float skill saved my life," she said.

Carnelian didn't preen. She stepped past Tiller to examine the sunvine more closely.

They discovered a sawed-off edge where someone or something had put in significant amounts of labor to sever it. Cutting down a mature sunvine would have been no easy task.

Still—did phages understand how to use tools? Why would a phage work to slice through a sunvine when it could skip straight to chasing after you and grabbing your face with gooey fingers?

Phages didn't plot murder. Phages didn't do anything in a roundabout manner.

There might be some element of stalking, of biding their time, of gauging the right moment to strike. But if there was any strategy in phages' behavior, it was something purely instinctual. Like stray cats hunting songbirds. They didn't invent whole new tactics from scratch.

Or so Tiller had always believed. She asked Carnelian if phages had learned to use weapons in recent years.

"No. Never seen anything like this." Carnelian dug a warped combat saw out from beneath the thickest coils of the felled sunvine.

Old magic cuttings still glazed the sawteeth. She dropped it next to the corpse of the phage who'd jumped at Tiller's neck.

"Any chance," Tiller said, "that a human being did it?"

"Someone hiding in the treetops? So the phage coming along for a ride on the vine would be pure coincidence?"

Carnelian scanned the sunvine. It looked like a giant sea serpent cast up on a beach.

"Zero chance," she said decisively. "Either this phage or some other canopy animal cut it down. Not a person. Even if a human being managed to climb that high, phages would've found them before they made an inch-deep dent in the sunvine."

Carnelian prodded the phage in question with the side of her foot.

"Look at these clothes," she said.

"Not a lot of clothes left."

"Enough to see that they weren't a soldier, though. And they were a phage for a very long time. Might be a forester. You know them?"

Tiller shook her head. "This might surprise you, but I'm not familiar with every forester who's ever lived here."

Carnelian flipped the bent saw over with a deft flick of her boot-covered toe. "If they weren't in the Outborder Corps, that makes it even stranger. There's military magic all over this saw."

"Must've gotten it from another phage. Or an abandoned outpost."

"Do phages know what saws are? Do phages trade goods and services?"

Neither of them could answer.

They went back to their bags, winding a path among dozens of other dead phages. Less than half an hour had passed since their anointing.

Emerald grass already sprouted from their parted lips (or from the mashed-open holes in their ruined faces, if they had no recognizable lips remaining). The blades of grass were too rich and heavy to stand up straight. They overflowed down the dead phages' crushed chins and cheeks like a mouthful of baby garden snakes.

Crenelated moss invaded the ground where the phages lay, nuzzling up against them on all sides. Some had stalks of purple-green bamboo bursting from their chests, tenting shreds of old clothing.

By this time tomorrow, the bamboo would be as tall as Tiller. Soon there would be nothing left of the phages but vegetation.

It wasn't always bamboo. Properly anointed phages might morph into fresh honeysuckle, or fungi, or thorny bramble, or dwarf trees, or oracle trees, or other young saplings. The anointing ritual tricked them into returning as something other than empty-eyed humanoid shells.

"Didn't think I'd ever see you use levitation magic," Tiller said as they shouldered their packs again.

"You were about to get turned into cold-pressed human juice."

"I know. And it came right after you fought off an impossible number of phages. I owe you my life several times over. I'm glad I brought you."

An uncharacteristic discomfort entered the set of Carnelian's shoulders. She spent a very long time adjusting her various straps again. "I ... I could've done better. The last phage still touched you."

"I stood there like a dolt while you fought to keep that vine in the air. Can't imagine how much magic that took."

"It was nothing," Carnelian said shortly.

They chose to keep moving a little longer before turning in for the night. Carnelian seemed drained, but she refused to take a break.

"Forest navigation is always tricky for the Corps," she said, trudging after Tiller. "How do you know which way to go?"

"How do you know which way is up and which way is down?"

"That simple, huh? Can all foresters navigate as well as you?"

"I never heard about other villagers getting lost."

Tiller deliberately set a slower pace. She asked multiple times if Carnelian was sure she didn't need immediate maintenance.

She could've flat-out ordered Carnelian to stop and submit. With just the two of them alone in the woods, Carnelian could theoretically say no. But most mages wouldn't.

And most operators would pull rank as soon as a mage began to look like their magic needed serious grooming.

That was the job of an operator, after all. Their responsibility. Their birthright. To override the self-destructive impulses that plagued fickle mages. To know what was best for mages—and to see it through before their charges' mercurial inner magic could lead them astray.

Yet Tiller was a forester before she was an operator. Unlike operators born outside the Forest, she hadn't been schooled all her life in the art of proper mage management.

She lacked the inherent conviction that if she uttered a command, any mages in earshot would leap to obey her. The same conviction you might hear in the voice of an experienced dog trainer.

People said mages were born to be mastered, tormented by the wildness of the magic within them. They secretly craved structure and order and direction. Why wouldn't they obey? It would bring them relief from their own chaos. Besides, most mages found maintenance incredibly soothing. Or downright euphoric. Addictive, even. Just like other types of powerful pain relief.

Carnelian didn't fit anywhere in this narrative. The act of magic maintenance didn't leave much of an impression on her, compared to other mages. Although she was still very much in need of it.

As for Tiller, she hadn't grown up around mages. She hadn't been socialized to regard them as an unruly underclass. Giving hard-line orders would never come to her naturally.

"You didn't sneak any Forest treats, did you?" she asked.

Carnelian grinned weakly. "What if I did?"

"I'd call you an idiot."

"No Forest food passed these lips. If I seem like I'm about to keel over, blame it on the levitation magic."

"You really should let me look at your—"

"Using it brings back bad memories. That's all. On the bright side, I'm extra beautiful when I'm sick. Ah, to be a poet with consumption. Watch how exquisitely I waste away."

She wasn't wrong. But Tiller wouldn't be caught dead giving her a single syllable of validation.

"I see that smile." Carnelian sounded triumphant.

"I'm not smiling," Tiller said. "I've never smiled before in my life."

"I could prove otherwise."

"Prove it in court. I'll sue you for all you're worth."

"No need," Carnelian said slyly. "We're betrothed. What's mine is yours."

"Does that make me a gold digger?"

Carnelian wiggled her eyebrows in answer.

Their conversation gave way to the sound of running water. They climbed down into a minor ravine to cross a brook, then heaved themselves back up the other side. Glassfish—nigh invisible when not in motion—faced the current to feed. Some were so corpulent that their backs protruded above the surface like little icebergs.

A pair of giant salamanders, dark in the rocky shallows, observed them warily as they passed. These human-size salamanders weren't known for having excellent eyesight. They must've scented a disturbance in the water.

Later on, Tiller and Carnelian picked their way gingerly through a sucking bog full of carnivorous pitcher plants. As they went, they traded stories of the innumerable ways one might die in the Forest.

For instance: parasitic larva. Treatable, but intensely painful and gory.

Hungry grabber lilies arrayed to guard their queen—an organism large enough to digest full-grown aurochs.

White long-armed monkeys that lived impossibly high in the treetops. No one ever saw anything of them but their hands shooting down to snatch children and small women.

"When we first spoke at that party, I thought you were a very serious sort of person," Carnelian said, apropos of nothing.

"Me? Why?"

"Everything I said seemed to annoy you."

"You kept trying to provoke me." Tiller shot her a look. "You already knew who I was, and how to unbalance me."

Carnelian glanced around innocently. "How long till we reach your village?"

"What's left of my village," Tiller corrected. "Another day or two."

Saying this helped her convince Carnelian that it was about time to set up camp. First they bathed on the banks of a deep, narrow creek. Carnelian used First Aid to soothe their aching legs and feet. Which were already rife with blisters, though her magic soon erased them.

For a time, Tiller zoned out and listened to the water as she cleansed herself. Magic could cure these early blisters, but it didn't penetrate deep enough to purge her overall exhaustion.

Droplets sprinkled from Carnelian as she tossed her hair back with a great sigh of delight. She hadn't wasted a moment in taking all her clothes off.

It was certainly warm enough here by the creek. Summertime insects raged on both sides of the water. But Carnelian seemed to be having a little too much fun letting light from nearby sunvines gild every glistening inch of open skin.

"Like what you see?" she asked merrily.

Tiller made an ambiguous noise in the back of her throat. After a rough internal battle, she averted her eyes again.

Carnelian, who had far more familiarity with high-tech gear, did most of the work to prepare their campsite. In the meantime, Tiller foraged for dinner.

She returned to find that their shelter packet—originally the size of Carnelian's fist—had unfurled into a sturdy orange geodesic tent.

The criss-crossing poles were glossy with pre-applied magic, as if they'd been thoroughly oiled. Those magic cuttings were what enabled it to fold up so compactly for storage. They might've helped cut the total weight, too.

Somewhere in Jace were mages who did nothing but pump out these cuttings for Corps equipment. Pruning and regrowing their magic branches, day after day after day.

The same could be said of every freestanding magical tool they carried. Carnelian's military ear cuffs, for instance, and the gun she'd confiscated from a slaughtered phage. The tin of immobility ticks in Tiller's pocket, and her tube of mysterious Guild bubbles, and the nausea pellets she'd packed as an extra safety measure.

Outside their tent, a miniature cup spun itself like clay on a potter's wheel. When it finished whirling, it had swelled up to become a full-size fire pit.

After Carnelian warmed her rations, Tiller settled down to cook.

"What'd you get?" Carnelian asked.

"Wood urchins. Tree kidneys. Eggs."

"What kind of eggs?"

"From an egg plant."

"Eggplant? Like the vegetable?"

"No. An egg plant."

She sliced open one of the fruits she'd collected, then squeezed it till carrot-colored yolk-like globules plopped out one after another onto the cooking pan.

Carnelian went to fetch more water from a nearby spring. Unlike all the flora and fauna of the Forest, pure water would not—thankfully—make outsiders dreadfully ill.

She'd still have to treat it before drinking any, but so would most anyone going camping like this. Whether on Forest territory, or out in the rest of the Nuian countryside.

Night fog began to curl up from the ground as Tiller cleaned after dinner.

According to Carnelian, Corps members would use the fog (predictable as it was), to decide when to sleep. Although they were usually under strict orders to avoid staying overnight in the Forest.

It looked like the earth itself was exhaling. On some days the fog would feel cold. On other days it would feel like the hot humid breath of an animal.

The Forest remained bright even while the rest of the world went dark, but the rapidly thickening fog made it difficult to see anything beyond their orange blob of a tent.

The heliograph station they'd previously passed would by now be wrapped in night, given how it poked above the canopy. Light born of the Forest confined itself to the Forest, never spilling out.

From afar the Forest should've glittered like a city skyline on the horizon. Yet it remained stubbornly shadowed. Closed off.

Tiller bent over to slip inside the tent. It was a relief to find that Carnelian had at last resigned herself to receiving maintenance.

Carnelian lay on her stomach, arms folded under her head, as if awaiting a thorough massage. Tiller sat cross-legged beside her and tended to her magic.

A water-light that looked and functioned very much like a stress ball rested near the curved tent wall. Carnelian had taken it out and squeezed it until it deigned to illuminate them.

The light was soft and full of shadows. Hints of fog had snuck in whenever one of them fussed with the flap leading outside.

Tiller asked if Carnelian needed the flap tacked all the way open. Like how she'd always fling open curtains on bedroom windows.

"It'll let too much fog in," Carnelian said.

"You'll be able to sleep with it shut?"

"I can cope with a closed tent. I know what I need to put up with to travel in the Forest."

The tent was designed to provide a modest bubble of false night for those unused to sleeping surrounded by the everlasting glow of sunvines. Once the squishy water-light got put out of its misery, the interior would turn at least as dark as a city alley.

Carnelian kept her head turned away. For a time, she remained so quiet that Tiller assumed she'd fallen asleep.

Yet Tiller sensed a quivering awareness in the uncovered skin of her back. In the skittish threads of magic that darted to and fro to evade Tiller's meddling.

Snatching at them felt like sticking a hand in an aquarium and grasping clumsily at a family of minnows.

"You called me Nellie," Carnelian said, muffled.

"Want me to say it again?"

"I used to get angry when people called me that."

"I thought you liked it."

"It was my brother's name for me. I hated when others stole it. Like those auditors. And the commander."

She turned her head. "Years later, I started to miss hearing it. I started to make more people say it. Don't have much else to prove that my brother ever existed."

"Except his core in you," Tiller said.

"There was no body. Nothing to take home. Not even ashes. Was it the same for you?"

Tiller tried to say *yes*. That one word refused to leave her mouth.

"What was your brother's name?" she asked Carnelian instead.

"...Rozen."

"Did I ever tell you Gren's name? Well—you'd know all about him even if I didn't."

"I've known of your Gren for twenty years now."

"Don't boast about it," Tiller said acidly. Then, in a more experimental tone: "Nellie."

She immediately knew she'd made a tactical error.

From the moment they left Outpost 24, Carnelian had carried herself with the neutrality of a veteran bodyguard.

Her tone might turn flippant. Her comments might take on a provocative double meaning. But on a fundamental level, her body language and bearing had been strictly professional.

Carnelian sat up and, for the first time, gazed at Tiller as if they were two brides-to-be alone in a tent late at night.

# 36

It was humiliating to realize that Carnelian had been deliberately shutting off her considerable charm.

The tent should have been adequately sized for the two of them. No complaints there. Yet now it seemed very small.

Carnelian looked utterly relaxed. Like she'd never felt out of place in her own body. Like she'd never felt self-conscious in her life. Like she'd never fretted irrationally about strangers seeing through her girdle, gaping at the cluster of magic cores simmering low in her abdomen.

Tiller had forgotten how little Carnelian wore beneath her mantle to sleep. And she'd cast the mantle off during maintenance.

There was nowhere safe for Tiller to put her eyes except the oppressively low ceiling of this imprisoning tent.

Carnelian reached out and laid three fingers on the side of Tiller's jaw. Her meaning was clear.

*Look at me.*

Against her better judgment, Tiller looked.

No dimples. No smile. Carnelian leaned forward on her knees. The graveness of her expression made the air between them feel that much thinner.

"I'm still the same person who put a sword through your little brother," she said.

"Big brother," Tiller said hastily, seizing on her chance to nitpick. "Gren was the older twin."

Carnelian canted her head. "How can you know? Your grandmother found you two alone in the Forest. No one saw your birth."

"We decided it," Tiller replied. "It felt right. It felt true. Everyone agreed. They couldn't prove us wrong, anyway."

"Rozen was younger than me," Carnelian said. "By seventeen minutes. But now you're trying to distract me. Want me to back off?"

"I—"

"It would help if you didn't do that."

"Do what?"

"Look at me that way, for one thing."

Tiller would have sworn on her forester ancestors that every muscle fiber in her body had been working to inch back, lean away, carve out a tiny pocket of extra breathing room.

She and her harried ancestors would, however, have been dead wrong.

Tiller herself was the one who'd moved closer. She was the one who'd made it feel claustrophobic. She'd drawn near enough that she could almost taste the scent of Carnelian's neck.

She had no excuse. The night fog of the Forest seemed to lick every corner of her dumb slow-moving head, filling her to the brim, crushing out other thoughts.

This must be what it was like to get lost in the woods or the mountains, to lose your ability to judge distances, to go in circles without realizing it, to be drawn back to the same inevitable place again and again. No other way to explain why her hand had crept across the tent groundsheet to find more of Carnelian. Her fingers closed down on Carnelian's naked ankle as if trying to take something that had always belonged to her.

She forced herself back.

She groped at Carnelian's mantle, wadded up in a corner. Carnelian watched with an air of silent amusement. She could feel the lingering warm phantom of Carnelian's hushed breath by her cheek, very near the corner of her mouth.

"Here," she said harshly.

She thrust out Carnelian's long silver pipe. Her wrists shook minutely, and not just from the weight of it.

Carnelian looked curiously at the etchings on her own pipe. "Planning to knock me on the head?" she asked. "No need. I understand when to pull back."

"If you want to put on a show," Tiller told her, "use this."

"What did you think I was about to do, give you a striptease?"

"You aren't wearing enough clothes for that."

Carnelian scoffed. "Oh, very funny."

"Try drawing on the fog from outside," Tiller said.

"Not quite the same as the usual vapor."

"Forest fog is different from fog in other places. Much richer."

Carnelian's skepticism remained unassuaged. But she gave it a try, filling her lungs with fog from beyond the tent flap. She pulled her head back in, then exhaled through her slender metal pipe.

A convoluted snake took shape. A perfect match for the one on the temporary insignia Tiller had received from Colonel Istel.

Tiller praised the fog sculpture—she was genuinely impressed—but Carnelian snorted.

"That's the easiest one there is," she said.

"You can show off more if you want."

"Maybe another night." Carnelian waved a hand to break up the snake. Beyond the scattering clouds of its corpse, she looked pensive. "The tent's already getting too misty."

When they woke the following morning, the fog had cleared. Both inside and outside their shadow-trapping tent.

Tiller had been dubious about Carnelian's ability to rouse herself for long days of trekking through the Forest. Yet today she got up with remarkable speed.

"Your hair grew," Carnelian blurted.

Indeed: it fell past Tiller's shoulders now. Once they finished packing up their campsite, she asked if Carnelian could give her a trim.

"I could," Carnelian said. "And a very cute one, at that. I told you about studying cosmetology, didn't I?"

"You pretended that was why you knew about my wig. During our so-called first meeting."

Carnelian breezed past this. "I could give you a pro-quality haircut. But I didn't think to pack shears."

Tiller dug out her yo-yo knives. "Try with these."

"I've got a better idea."

Carnelian pulled her magical sword out of nothingness—except that this time, it was the size of a letter opener.

"You can shrink it?" Tiller asked.

"Or grow it to absolutely ridiculous proportions," Carnelian confirmed. "For real-life use, I mostly stick to the size I'm accustomed to handling."

"Still nothing like a pair of shears, though."

"The edge is sharper than any razor. I can work with that."

"In theory," Tiller said.

"In theory, yes. Go sit on that rock, and we'll put it into practice."

Tiller cautioned her against spending too much time on it. Her hair might grow out again a day later.

Carnelian, undeterred, appeared determined to service her like a licensed stylist. Bits of blue hair fluttered to the ground like lost feathers.

Upon reflection, it occurred to Tiller that she'd never gone to a real hairdresser in her life. When she was a child in the Forest, Baba Sayo had cut her hair. Doe took over after they moved to the city.

Neither had been interested in the intricacies of cutting hair to a specific style. Outside the Forest, the main priority was making it easier for her to wear a wig cap.

Doe had used clippers to crop Tiller's hair short. She'd been careful to collect and burn the trimmings, too. Doing so produced a hideous stench, but it also reduced the risk of someone discovering telltale blue hairs in their trash.

After Doe got murdered, Tiller kept the clippers. She taught herself how to use them. She collected and burned the trimmings, just like Doe. She told Baba Sayo not to worry. She didn't need any help.

No one else had cut her hair for twelve full years. Not until today.

No one in her entire life had ever touched her hair with this kind of tender expertise, unhurried, taking pleasure in the act of shaping it.

Baba Sayo and Doe—and Tiller herself—had seen haircuts as an annoying necessity, a task to complete with the no-nonsense briskness of washing dishes.

She closed her eyes.

"Don't fall asleep," Carnelian said from behind her.

"If you want me awake, better go faster."

"Can't rush perfection."

After finishing, Carnelian attempted to show her the outcome. The only mirror they'd packed was a small compact.

With some maneuvering, Tiller got the sense that Carnelian had given her a kind of crisp pixie or short bob. She didn't know the right terminology. Either way, it was cropped high enough to feel morning air on the fresh phage-scars all over the back of her neck.

She closed the compact and found Carnelian still assessing her, leaning this way and that to scrutinize her head from every conceivable angle.

"I do love your hair." She made it sound quite matter-of-fact. "You'd hear that all the time if more people could see it."

"I'd have ulcers if everyone could see it," Tiller said. "You'd better enjoy the view on their behalf."

"Already am." Carnelian pushed a few pieces of her hair this way and that, then backed away for another look. She nodded to herself, self-satisfied.

"Totally worth it," she declared.

"Even if it grows long again tomorrow?"

"Even better. Next time I can try something different. You're a stylist's dream come true."

"You're doing this for free," Tiller said. "I'd think a stylist would dream of getting paid."

"What fun we'll have," Carnelian said blithely. "I can cut your hair every day."

# 37

Inside the Forest, it started to feel like the rest of the world had never existed. The Forest went on forever.

Tiller still knew exactly where they were heading. She felt the pull of Koya Village. She sensed upcoming new zones of the Forest before the temperature rose or dropped, before the scent of the wind changed.

She nicked her hand while vivisecting pulpfruit for a snack. Ivy-green dragonflies trailed after her, lured by the smell of blood, until Carnelian slathered on First Aid magic to seal the wound.

There had been no such dragonflies back in the area where they'd anointed dozens and dozens of phages.

Despite her full-coverage uniform, Carnelian kept getting gruesome bug bites. They pierced straight through the fabric. She had some tart words to say about the fact that nothing similar happened to Tiller.

As Carnelian scratched at her arms, Tiller spied a hulking ground sloth. They stopped to watch it rear up on its hind legs and paw at a tree. Carnelian leaned toward Tiller and asked: "How much do you know about Asa Lantana's bondmate?"

"Thought you were going to say something about the sloth."

"What's there to say? It's big. It's a sloth."

"I don't know anything about Asa's bondmate," Tiller said. "Except that she has one. Does her bondmate resemble a ground sloth?"

A bird concealed somewhere close by kept repeating the same cry. As if worried that no one was listening. Indeed, no other birds of the same type seemed willing to answer. Its distress signals began to sound increasingly desperate.

"In effect," said Carnelian, "I'm a bad imitation of Asa's bondmate. She has far, far more magic branches inside her than I've got from all my cores put together. Hers stem from a single core. And she didn't acquire her power through artificial means. She was born with it."

They left the ground sloth to its meal and pushed forward.

Carnelian was in a chatty mood. Tiller chewed spicy bark as she listened. It lacked the texture of gum, but the flavor lasted for hours.

"How ironic," Carnelian continued. "A backwards place like the continent birthed a mage way more powerful than any from Jace."

"Is Asa's mage that well-known?"

"As a symbol of the foreign threat, if nothing else."

*The foreign threat.*

No wonder Asa Lantana stayed cooped up in her hotel suite. Some would feel menaced by the very existence of a woman speaking Jacian with a Continental accent. Even on the more cultured southern islands, Jacians would expect to go their entire lives without ever seeing a single foreigner in person.

"You've heard of her, too," said Carnelian.

"I have?"

"Asa Lantana's bondmate is the mage popularly known as the Kraken."

"The most powerful mage on the continent?"

"The most powerful mage in the world," Carnelian answered. "Just don't get caught admitting that in front of anyone from Central. Like our friends the auditors."

"You met Asa before I did," Tiller said. "Ever meet her ... Kraken?"

Carnelian pushed aside a skein of vines, making a tunnel for the two of them to duck through.

"Asa offered to introduce us. I declined." She laughed a little. "What would I even do if I met a mage that powerful? Clasp her hand and tell her how she's everything I've failed to become? How she embodies every expectation and ideal I ever fell short of?"

Carnelian explained that the Scholar had started work on her cores long before the general public knew a thing about this modern-day Kraken. Intelligence analysts might've heard of a formidable foreign mage, but not regular people. No one called her the Kraken back then.

She wasn't that many years older than Tiller and Carnelian. But the Jacian government had marked her as a threat all along. Perhaps even before her own country recognized her potential.

This in turn made everyone want the Scholar's projects to succeed. It had been remarkably easy for him to get funding.

"So you don't know what the Kraken is like in person," Tiller said.

"I'm sure she's perfectly nice. She must be something of a saint, actually, to get along with Asa Lantana. But it's not like I could learn anything from her."

"Why not?"

Tiller tugged at the back of Carnelian's elbow. As they paused their step, petite deer fled away through the underbrush. They were delicate creatures, hardly any larger than a well-fed city rat.

"She can't tell me how to be something I'm not," Carnelian replied. "She can't help me sprout extra magic branches or merge my cores into one. That's just not how magic works, is it? Even for the strongest mage in the world.

"Her branch count is so far beyond mine. There's practically no limit on the number of skills she can acquire and keep. And unlike me, she can use multiple skills at once. Any great mage wisdom she might attempt to teach me would be like explaining proper grammar to a dog. No point in even trying."

"You don't aspire to live up to the Scholar's dreams for you, anyway," Tiller said.

"No. I'm an incurable slacker."

"Then there's no need to compare yourself to Asa's bondmate. Or any other mage."

"It's just odd to think that a stranger somewhere out there has more magic than the Scholar could cobble together by making me a chimera."

Carnelian patted her lower belly. Gingerly, as if it belonged to someone else.

"People died so their magic cores could be placed in me. Including my own brother. The Scholar himself died for it, too. *Your* brother died solely to facilitate the Scholar's final transplant. All that murder culminating in little old me? What a joke."

"If the Scholar failed to engineer the mage of his dreams, that reflects poorly on him," Tiller said. "Not on you."

Carnelian halted. She put a hand up. The self-deprecating note left her voice.

"Is that your village?"

Tiller immediately denied it. She already knew without looking. Even if Koya Village lay in ruins, even if the Forest had swallowed it without a trace, she wouldn't ever mistake it for anywhere else.

She surveyed the scenery. The air wasn't warm at all, but the humidity had shot up. Sweat clung to her like an extra layer of underwear.

A solid gate loomed before them, its shape reminiscent of the gates to city temples. On either side tumbled the remnants of a wall now covered in a colorful explosion of mushrooms. They puffed out of cracks as if feeding on mortar.

"This isn't forester architecture," Tiller said.

Carnelian stood on tiptoe to peer past the wall. "Might be left over from one of the resettlement projects."

"This far in?"

"Ten or fifteen years ago, it would've been much closer to the border."

True.

For a time, the government had attempted to bribe foresters into going back to the Forest. They'd rounded up volunteers—mostly those too poor to have any other options—and tasked them with establishing resettlement zones.

Many intellectuals had theorized that the Forest would slow its spread once enough humans returned. Living foresters, they claimed, were a key component of the sophisticated magical ecosystem.

From start to finish, Baba Sayo took a strident stand against it. We left for a reason, she said again and again. Her opposition convinced the other former Koya villagers to avoid participating in any resettlement projects.

A few years later, everyone would say that Baba Sayo had been right all along.

All the settlers were native foresters. All were simply returning to the land of their birth. Yet, for reasons unknown, it never went well.

Some got massacred by phages, and subsequently became phages themselves. Some went mad and killed each other. Without anyone left to take care of the bodies, they too turned into phages after death. Very few survivors made it out of the Forest.

The resettlement projects resulted in exactly one lasting accomplishment:

vastly increasing the population of newborn phages. All the while, the Forest continued its steady march south.

There were no forester trails left truly intact. Not around the empty resettlement village, nor in the beginnings of Koya territory.

Here, however, there was little undergrowth to tangle their steps. The magnificent pines and cedars soared even higher than elsewhere in the Forest, some maxing out at over fifty stories overhead.

Down below grew the familiar Koya finger-trees. At only a couple stories tall, they stayed far closer to the ground.

Lichen painted their bark sage green. Thin pastel yellow leaves fluttered about like the fingers of an invalid waving for help.

Sunvines hung down from the canopy: a thicket of emergency escape ladders. Their tapered ends wound in strangling spirals about the arm-boughs of the finger-trees. Slender fallen leaves formed moist golden heaps underfoot.

Carnelian inhaled sharply. There was something very wrong about the sound of it. Like she'd been stabbed.

Tiller traced her gaze to a stand of blighted finger-trees. Their branches were bald and crumbling, their bark the charred greyish-white of fireplace ash. The ground, too, had been singed bare of moss or mushrooms or clover.

The Forest was not devoid of fire. Deep fire caves smoldered in the sacred mountains; they never went out. A few of the oldest cedars housed magical flames that Baba Sayo used to call demon-breath. Bright green illusions, colorful as an aurora come to earth.

But this grove had not been scourged by fire.

No—

Carnelian lingered outside the clump of naked trees. She used the end of her mantle to cover her nose and mouth. She appeared to breathe rapidly through the fabric.

The finger-trees stank of death.

Tiller stepped closer to the source of the stench.

A cold drop hit her cheek. She wiped it off with her thumb.

It was a blackish smear. Too dark to be new blood. She drew back quickly, before more could fall on her face.

She stared up at the human body lying twisted among leafless branches.

Phages only bled clear water. Phages never gave off this kind of fetid stink.

Any human that died in the Forest would become a phage, no matter what killed them. Unless you first carried them up to the mountaintop fire caves. The place where foresters took all their dead.

No human or animal that died in the Forest would rot.

But Tiller had smelled a decomposing body in the Forest before. At least once.

Doe had warned Tiller and Gren not to touch it. Someone killed that poor soul outside the Forest, she said, then dragged their rotting body across the border.

Perhaps they'd meant it as a form of anti-forester harassment. Or perhaps they were just a simple murderer desperate for a place to hide the evidence.

If you imported a body from outside the Forest, it wouldn't transform into a phage. Nor would it continue breaking down. It would stay half-rotten, poisoning the area around it, preserved as an eternal snapshot of partial decay. Never fully liquefying or drying up. Never reduced to mere bones.

This corpse poised above Tiller might have been dumped in the finger-trees just yesterday. Or it might have been tangled up there for decades. Dribbling out a slow yet seemingly infinite supply of red-black fluid, viscous as sap.

Even phages would give a body like this a wide berth.

She wiped her wet thumb on deadened bark. Then she turned and pushed Carnelian away through the healthier finger-trees. Long plaintive leaves brushed their shoulders.

She stopped only once the ashen copse had passed far out of sight. Together with the long-dead woman. The trees had borne her up as if on a warped parody of a funeral bier.

"If there were more of us," Tiller said, "we could try to carry her out of the Forest."

Carnelian was sitting down, her forehead pressed to her knees. "Can't," she mumbled. "I'm sorry. I can't."

"Even if we wanted to, we don't have enough time. Got to keep going."

"You've got a strong stomach," Carnelian said feebly.

"Guess I should've been a soldier."

A minute or so after Tiller shut her mouth, Carnelian asked her to keep talking.

"About what?"

"Anything."

"This can't be the only rot-frozen carcass still stranded in the Forest," Tiller said. "But I wouldn't expect to see others. Unless we're really unlucky."

"Wow. I'm so comforted."

Carnelian had begun sounding moderately less liable to faint, but not by much.

"I found a dead body as a kid once," Tiller said. "Same type of thing. A bludgeoned woman. A circle of dead earth around her. A farmer's wife, it turned out. She lived and died in the Market at the Edge of the Forest. She'd already been dead for a couple of days before someone deposited her near our village."

"You didn't know who did it?"

"A couple of the stronger villagers banded together to carry her back out of the Forest. They left her body with the Market officers. Didn't ask for any follow-up info."

Maybe this wasn't the best topic to expound on. But as soon as she trailed off, Carnelian motioned for her to keep going.

Tiller picked a finger-leaf off her shoulder.

"For us, it felt the same as how someone outside the Forest might feel when stumbling over a dead wind-deer," she said.

"Maybe the deer got killed by a pack of wolves. Maybe it got killed by a tiger. Maybe it died of illness or old age and got scavenged. A hunter might form an educated guess about what happened. But would they try to solve it like a mystery? Would they search for the killer?

"People die for all kinds of reasons inside the Forest. People die for all kinds of reasons outside the Forest, too. Not our place to question it. But rotting flesh doesn't belong in the Forest. So we had to remove it."

She sat down next to Carnelian. "I'd better stop babbling."

"I like listening to you," Carnelian said into her knees. "I could listen to you for ages. In fact, I was listening to you since long before you ever knew me."

A white room. Misshapen walls. Gren. A boy in a cage. A boy who did have a name, after all, though they hadn't known it at the time.

And—hidden on the other side of the walls—Carnelian.

Something bumped Tiller's shoulder. Carnelian had tipped over to lean against her. "You haven't asked much about my hang-ups."

"Asking won't cure you," Tiller said. "Maybe you just have a weak stomach."

When Carnelian spoke again, the teasing note had left her voice.

"The Scholar did a lot of experimentation with corpses," she said plainly. "Before the abduction. He had me use levitation magic to float them across the border and into the Forest. He made me drop them in random places. Just to observe what would happen."

"Wouldn't a single experiment have been enough to find out?"

Carnelian wore an odd little smile.

"The Scholar was a man of science," she said. "He wanted to test bringing in cadavers at different stages of decomposition. Human and animal. Sometimes both together."

"The woman we saw in the trees—was she one of yours?"

The Forest was enormous and highly changeable. Even a body placed relatively close to Koya Village could've gone unnoticed all these years. Especially if it had been left there not long before the kidnapping.

"Might have been," Carnelian acknowledged. Her weight left Tiller's side. "I don't ... I don't remember them all in detail. Of course, the Scholar took meticulous notes. He pinpointed the exact amount of rot that the Forest would react to most strongly."

"True to his name."

"As always. Once he had it all figured out, he made me carry more bodies. Much further in. All the way up to that secret house of his.

"The funny thing is, I was totally fine with it at the time," Carnelian added. "I ignored the smell. And the look of them. Didn't gag much. My floating magic became very efficient. I was like a waiter at a busy restaurant. It's amazing what kids can get used to under duress."

"The Scholar's body was never found," Tiller said. "Did you—"

"What do you think?" Carnelian asked.

They had a staring contest.

They both lost.

Carnelian rested her chin in her arms. "Before he died, he told me to dump his body in one of the Forest fire pits. He had no interest in becoming a phage. I followed his orders.

"It was only years later that stuff like the smell of old food in garbage started to get to me. One fine fall day, I saw a dead hedgehog in a garden. Just some random person's little suburban garden. All the horror and disgust and nausea I'd deferred as a kid came back for me, all at once. I've been squeamish ever since."

"So that's what happened to our brothers," Tiller said.

Carnelian looked at her as if she'd started speaking in tongues.

"To their bodies. If you dropped the Scholar in the fire caves—"

"Ah. Yes."

Carnelian got up. She stretched one limb at a time, readying herself to take up her heavy bags again.

"I'll be honest," she said. "I don't remember much of it. I just did as the Scholar said. I did everything he told me. I must've cleaned up every last bit of his mess."

She shouldered her backpack. "When the Corps rescuers came, the first thing they did was get you to safety. They didn't find me till later. After a more detailed sweep of the bunker.

"They also found the room he'd used as a substitute morgue. They found traces of unspeakable experiments. But for all that, they never found any bodies."

# 38

WHEN A VILLAGER died in the Forest, the very first order of business was to carry their body up to the sacred mountains. Everyone would drop all their tasks and all their plans to make it happen.

There was no hope, of course, if a phage had already killed and absorbed them. For any other cause of death—cardiac arrest, a hunting accident, the frailty of old age—at least twenty-four hours would pass before the deceased became a reanimated phage. In some cases, the metamorphosis could take days and days.

So foresters bore their dead to the nearest of the sacred mountains. To the nearest of the caverns that blazed with a neverending fire.

A cadaver transmuted to bone and powder by those flames would never need to rise again as an insatiable phage.

The fire caves were deep and deadly. Unlike man-made crematories in the city, they offered no way to recover the ashen remains of those they burned.

But foresters knew not to expect anything in return. All they needed was the assurance that their father or mother or sister or daughter had gone where every other forester belonged in the end. That they would be blessed with peace in the sacred mountains, rather than the mindless, homeless hunger of a phage.

If ten-year-old Carnelian had thrown Gren's body into one of those caves, that meant Gren had already been sent exactly where he was supposed to go.

He'd burned away to nothingness surrounded by remnants of past foresters. He wasn't lost and alone, abandoned in death while Tiller and every other villager fled to the city.

Beyond the Koya finger-trees awaited a wild growth of stinging nettles. It stood eight feet tall, dense as a formal hedge and as long as a castle wall. No visible breaks.

Carnelian made a face.

"The leaves are delicious if you prepare them right," Tiller said.

"That's one Forest food I won't be jealous of. Do we have to hack a path to the other side?"

"It'll let us through."

"How?"

Tiller moved over to a separate cluster of shrubbery with long wild tendrils sticking out every which way. She snapped off a tender young branch.

"What's that?" Carnelian queried.

"A witch stick."

"From a witch bush, presumably."

"You're starting to catch on."

Tiller thrust her witch stick at the wall of nettles. They rattled in their eagerness to shrink away.

She gestured for Carnelian to follow close on her heels. As she menaced the nettles with the (thin and harmless-looking) stick, a narrow path opened to the other side of the hedge. Just wide enough that they could avoid getting snagged.

More witch bushes grew on the far side of the nettle barricade. Tiller planted her twig in the dirt nearby.

"Will it grow back?" asked Carnelian.

"It might. Broken sticks take root a lot easier in the Forest."

Behind them, the nettles stopped bowing out of the way. The tall spiky stems rustled rapidly back into place.

"We never built stone walls," Tiller said. "We made these nettles sprout high and thick. We cultivated witch bushes on both sides for convenience. Good to see that it all kept growing without us."

"Is this the Forest, or is it your garden?"

"We did live here. It would be strange if we didn't leave some kind of mark on the landscape."

After another fifteen minutes of walking, they reached Koya Village.

Tiller unwittingly came to a halt. The weight of twenty whole years gripped her ankles like deadly swamp mud, denser than water or blood.

By the grace of the Forest, the village remained largely unchanged.

It was nothing like the other abandoned places they'd passed: the empty military outpost, the doomed resettlement zone. Both of which had fallen into ruin well after Koya Village. Both of which had employed far sturdier material in their architecture.

There was no logical way to explain it. The Forest destroyed what it wished to destroy, and preserved what it wished to preserve.

That said, Koya bore little resemblance to villages outside the Forest, those little townships dotting the Nuian countryside. It looked like thirty miniature hills of blue moss. The hills congregated around a couple of the usual colossal cedars.

Here the canopy-high trees wore fewer leaves. Their bald crowns let more light fall to ground level than in other parts of the Forest. Hints of real sun warmed Tiller's neck for the first time in days.

The sunvines around the village were scrawny. They had the look of earthworms dried up on a hot street.

Originally, neat-trimmed moss had furred every roof. In the dim mildness of midnight, it glowed bluer than Tiller and Gren's hair, far outshining the local sunvines.

It had been their job to thin the roof-moss. Most of the other villagers were over sixty, after all. Tiller and Gren liked to help, and they'd had energy to spare.

Tiller used to climb up and plunge her arms in the moss. She'd yank out giant tufts and toss them down around the cottages like fluff from a wolf's winter coat.

Gren, following her, would collect the fallen moss. He stuffed it in the shoulder-high clay jars that lurked outside every door.

They'd speculated about what would happen if no one groomed the roofs. Tiller had imagined the moss growing so shaggy that it'd hang in curtains from the cottage eaves, thickening its way down wooden outer walls. A blue snowdrift to lock the elderly villagers in their homes.

She could see now that she'd imagined correctly.

"It's beautiful," Carnelian said quietly. "Want to stay here tonight?"

Tonight?

Tiller's sense of time had gotten uncharacteristically skewed. They'd already traveled another full day.

By the time they took their next meal, the faraway patches of sky over the village would go dark. The famished-looking sunvines would squeeze out a light like a candle with hands cupped around it. (They gave off that light even now, but there was no way to discern it.)

"Show me around," Carnelian suggested. "Or would you rather have some privacy? I can entertain myself while you explore."

"Stay," Tiller said, surprising herself—not with her response, but with how quickly it sprang out of her.

"If you insist," Carnelian said lightly. "Anything for my bride."

In her mind, Tiller stripped the excess moss from the cottages. She slipped back to the period of her life when she and Gren would run circles around each other in the fighter paddock.

The village's sixty-two-year-old combat instructor was the same woman who'd once taught Doe. She did her best to channel their boundless enthusiasm into an age-appropriate training regimen.

Old villagers would hunch around the paddock fence. They'd heckle Tiller and Gren as they battered scarecrows (or each other) with child-sized wooden staffs.

When the Scholar came to claim them, he'd left their instructor's body in seven pieces.

Someone from the village must have carried the pieces of her body to the mountains. Someone must have thrown her remains in the nearest fire cave.

Tiller ran a hand over the fence posts, cracked and weathered. Overgrown grass and weeds overflowed from inside the fighter paddock.

"When the Scholar took us," she said, "no one knew where he went. No one guessed that he'd actually brought us deeper in the Forest."

After all, the Scholar wasn't a forester himself. Everyone—from the villagers to the Corps—thought he must've hidden his victims somewhere far outside Forest territory.

"Search magic works almost as terribly in the Forest as porting," Carnelian remarked. "That probably didn't help, either."

They moved along. Tiller pointed out Baba Sayo's cottage, nestled against a cedar with an especially swollen trunk.

Out back languished the slouching remnants of a moonflower garden. Baba Sayo had rigged a system of mirrors to give them extra sunlight during the day, and all kinds of coverings to produce a simulacrum of legitimate darkness at night.

She'd never tried to grow moonflowers in Nui City, come to think of it. Even though it would've demanded far less effort than in the Forest.

They checked a couple of other dwellings and found them shockingly intact. Forest magic, no doubt. As if the seamless coatings of blue moss had somehow preserved every interior in pristine condition. Better than a museum vault.

There was hardly even any dust. The tight-woven mats plastered over dirt floors appeared as if they'd been neglected for two days or so. Not two decades.

Old undyed clothing rested in neat pyramid-shaped stacks, along with other belongings that the departing villagers had opted not to take with them. Their trinkets looked like offerings to a sleeping god.

Tiller didn't need to touch the folded piles of fabric to remember how it felt. The sensation of it covered her, a childhood ghost on her skin.

Carnelian leaned past her to poke at ancient jars of lingonberry jam.

In another room they found looms for weaving bark cloth, still set up for use. As if Baba Sayo might stump through the door and get back to work at any moment.

Back outside, Carnelian said: "I recognize a lot of this."

"How? You never—"

"I never came in person. But I always heard you and your brother talking to Rozen."

"In the Scholar's house," Tiller uttered.

"In the Scholar's house. You told Rozen how to thin the roof moss. How to kill and anoint a phage. How to pick the ripest pulpfruit. How to get on your grandmother's good side."

Gren had wanted so badly to find a way to communicate with the boy in the cage. Tiller's throat went tight. "He never said anything back. We weren't sure if—if he ever understood us."

Carnelian looked at her nails. "I wouldn't say I coped particularly well with how the Scholar treated us," she said. "Look at how I turned out."

"What's that mean?"

"Whatever you think it does. My point is that Rozen coped far worse. He wasn't always mute. But by the time the you first saw him, he'd stopped talking to anyone."

"Not even you?"

"Not even me."

The most infuriating part of this trip home was how much it made Tiller think of the Scholar.

She collected rolled-up bamboo shades from inside several houses. She unfurled them and laid them out flat in the light. Stripes of dried sunvine wove their way down through the slender wooden slats.

She told Carnelian about how Gren had been the first to encounter Rozen in the woods.

"It started happening a few weeks before the Scholar kidnapped us. Gren kept saying he'd seen a boy near the village."

"Did you believe him?" Carnelian asked.

"I believed him—but he was afraid to tell anyone else. He was afraid they'd think the boy was a phage."

This had made sense to them as children. The village almost never saw visitors. Not even other foresters.

More importantly, Baba Sayo—the village's unofficial leader—had vowed to never take in another stranger again.

If the boy turned out to be human, and not a forester, surely the villagers would've given him a safe escort to a border outpost. Or to the

Market at the Edge of the Forest. No one would have attacked a child on sight. Not unless they knew for a fact that the child was already a full-blown phage.

But Baba Sayo's fierce warnings about outsiders must've made too strong of an impression. Gren remained determined to keep the boy a secret from everyone but Tiller.

They went darting through the Forest from branch to branch. They were children, but they weren't defenseless.

Tiller, who had just turned nine, kept daggers at her hip. In secret pockets she'd stashed miniature knives that she could juggle like bean-sacks.

Gren wasn't so good at knife-juggling. Hand him a blade, and Gren would prefer using it to help Baba Sayo with supper.

They both knew where to thwack sunvines to make them glow a brief reproachful red. They could traverse the tree-paths as easily as solid ground. They could hide from most phages, if needed.

They crouched like crows on a high-set branch and watched the red-haired boy meander below them. He wore a white shredded garment, filthy with mud.

Gren would call out to him carefully, gently.

All he ever did was gaze back without responding. He looked lost. But he didn't seem particularly worried or thirsty or hungry.

"What was the point?" Tiller asked. "Why would the Scholar set your brother loose like that? Why go to the trouble of arranging for us to meet him?"

"Worked, didn't it?" Carnelian said. "When the time came, Rozen led you straight into a trap."

"But we fled. We made it all the way back to the village—"

"And the Scholar was ready. Waiting nearby." Carnelian shrugged. "He had plans on top of plans."

Enough talk of the Scholar, Tiller decided. For the time being, anyway.

Together they hand-washed the worst of their clothing. Carnelian had packed magic cleaning sheets that could suck all excess water out of even the wettest of fabric.

This would save them from needing to wait around while their laundry hung to dry. Which definitely wouldn't happen overnight, after the arrival of the inevitable fog.

As night fell in the outside world, the air in Koya Village turned a muted twilight gray. The blue moss went incandescent, as if lit from within. As if the cottages were full of hidden fire.

The skinny sunvines around the village perimeter made no serious attempt to compete.

Carnelian kept pausing to stare off into the trees. Tiller asked her what was wrong, but she didn't have a concrete answer.

It felt like they were being watched, she said.

No matter how they searched, neither of them could locate any phages.

Sand-colored bats flapped overhead, small enough to be mistaken for moths. Tiller pointed out other animals as they caught her eye, too. A civet cat. Raccoon dogs. A pair of panicking crabrabbits. An extremely lengthy (but otherwise harmless) snake.

"No," Carnelian said. "No. It's something larger than any of those."

"But you don't know what."

"I think we'll be fine as long as we stay near the cottages."

"We have to get going again tomorrow," Tiller said.

"Ah—tomorrow is tomorrow. No use in getting all paranoid now." Carnelian heaved an eloquent sigh. "Wish I could wipe it from my mind."

Then she turned back to Tiller, eyes bright again, and cheerfully demanded a continuation of her tour around the village.

# 39

After foraging for her evening meal, Tiller showed Carnelian the village demon.

It was a humble statue of an androgynous figure. Lace-fine purple lichen coated its stone skin in a manner that suggested a network of capillaries. Stone sunvines grew from its scalp, twining all the way down to its ankles.

Carnelian dug a coin from her bags. One hundred grails: enough to buy a small juice box.

Together they compared the Koya Village demon to the coin's proud horned woman embossed in a bicolor mix of silver and gold.

"They aren't at all alike," Carnelian commented.

"The word *demon* can mean a lot of different things."

"Did you worship it?"

"We didn't even have a name for it," Tiller said. "But this might be what you felt glowering at you from the shadows."

Carnelian considered the small demonic figure for a few moments longer. "If only it were. Like an overprotective parent. Bet your village demon thinks I'm not good enough for you."

"Hah."

At last there was nothing left to do but retreat to Baba Sayo's cottage. Tiller's gut kept trying to resist going in.

She admonished herself: where else could they possibly spend the night? They had their pick of the whole village, sure, but it wouldn't feel right to crash at any other house.

Carnelian exclaimed delightedly over the voluminous nest left indoors by an industrious spider. (They searched, but the architect was nowhere to be found.)

Tiller brought in the bamboo shades she'd left outside to soak up the last of the daytime sun. The strips of dried sunvine in them emitted a weary light—and, curiously, a grassy scent reminiscent of fresh tea.

Carnelian leaned over and sniffed the shades as if she'd never smelled anything like it.

Tiller took out the ceramic containers that held Baba Sayo and Doe. She placed them in an empty alcove. Just for tonight.

She couldn't quite remember what used to go there. Gren's old pine cone and acorn sculptures? The mushroom etchings that now hung in Baba Sayo's city apartment?

Carnelian bumped her shoulder. "Look what I've got."

She waggled a bottle of roeberry liquor.

"All the weight you're carrying," Tiller said, "and you still wanted more?"

"All for a good cause."

It appeared to be the same style as the bottle Carnelian had given Colonel Istel. Only with preserved petals heaped at the bottom, rather than berries.

"This is from that souvenir shop in the city," Tiller said.

"Yep."

"How come I didn't see you buy it?"

Carnelian grinned wider. "Got the clerk on my side. Made them think I needed to arrange a special surprise. Want any?"

"It's your bottle. You're welcome to sit there and glug the whole thing right in front of me."

They found a pair of small chipped ramekins on a lonely-looking shelf. Tiller rubbed at them with her sleeve, inside and out, until they seemed decent enough to drink from.

The bottle rested on an uneven low table. They sat on woven floor mats (the cottage had no chairs). Dense blue light from the moss-covered windows submerged them.

It felt like being trapped in an underwater cave. That drowning sensation only began to retreat once Tiller tasted the warmth of the alcohol.

She asked if Carnelian wanted to go back outside and remove the moss blocking the glass.

"Seems like a lot of work," Carnelian said. "No—I like this better than regular curtains. Somehow."

She reached over to refill both of their ramekins. Tiller bobbed her head in thanks. She watched idly as Carnelian's fingertips traced the frilly floral pattern on the side of the bottle.

There was really no good reason for any of these houses to still be standing. For the air to smell the same as it had when Gren was alive.

Had the Forest saved the village for her as a gift, or a punishment?

Tiller toyed with an old bamboo flute she'd found in a corner. A child-sized instrument. This one might have belonged to Gren.

She could still play it, albeit clumsily. She was way out of practice.

She stopped, startled, when she heard Carnelian softly singing along.

"You know this?"

"Not the words," said Carnelian. "Just the melody."

It was one of the traditional tunes played by street sharpeners. There were lyrics—some did sing, instead of tooting it—but Tiller had always preferred to use a flute.

"You look shocked," Carnelian said.

"Because I am."

"Hasn't everyone heard this song at least once? Same with the music you hear from carts selling autumn potatoes. And bean curd."

"To be honest," Tiller said, "those are all dying trades."

Carnelian kept singing wordless vowels while Tiller noodled around on the flute. Eventually Tiller offered to teach her the words.

"You could sing, too." Alcohol had made Carnelian's speaking voice warm and throaty.

"No, thanks. I'll be your accompaniment."

They mastered an entire suite of knife-sharpening music.

Somehow this evolved into teaching Carnelian other things, too. Village songs that Tiller hadn't thought about in years.

She was amazed to find that she still remembered them. Lullabies for phages. Carols for morning chores. Pulpfruit harvesting songs. Bark cloth weaving songs. Well-digging songs. Songs made up of mysterious syllables; no one knew their meaning. Songs that allegedly hailed back to the lost kingdom of blues.

Carnelian was a quick study. She fudged some of the words, but she picked up each and every melody after a single repetition.

They kept going until Tiller's fingers cramped.

She set the flute down. "Did you ever want to be a singer?"

"Ever heard of a mage making a career in the arts?"

"You could try," Tiller said. "If you ceased to be a ward of the state. Isn't that part of why you sought marriage?"

"So I could make it big in music? Nah."

If you had magic, you were expected to use it.

If you were an unattached mage, you were expected to use it in ways dictated by the needs of society. Or, more specifically, by the Bureau of Mage Management.

Carnelian was something of an edge case. A semi-failed experiment. A leftover prototype for a standalone warrior. She fit poorly in a military that prized seamless cooperation.

In an all-hands-on-deck crisis, she would nevertheless find herself drafted to help.

Perhaps she liked having a gift that, if she wished, she could keep entirely to herself. No one would ever claim she had a duty to sing for the sake of the nation.

"It feels so surreal to be here in person," Carnelian murmured.

"The Forest is a surreal place."

"To outsiders, you mean. To you, it's just home."

Carnelian swirled the liquid in her ramekin. Originally Baba Sayo would've used it as a dish for serving dipping sauces. Or little stacks of sliced preserved radish.

"Don't suppose you ever got many tourists," she added.

"We never got a single one. Except—"

Tiller stopped herself before she could continue that thought. Why ruin the mood?

They spoke of how the latent magic of the Forest seemed so very different from the magic found in human mages.

No one knew why mages were hardly ever born in the Forest. Or what exactly might spur the birth of a blue.

It would be a mistake to ascribe any particular intent to the nature of the Forest and its phenomena. Phages appeared in the Forest—their sole habitat—for the same reason that the air might get thinner at the top of a tall mountain. For the same reason that meteoroids might fall from a clear sky. This was the way of things.

Nothing about the Forest felt unfamiliar to Tiller. After twenty years away, though, she'd gained a much better understanding of how outsiders saw it.

She knew now what was considered strange—according to the rest of Nui, and the rest of Jace—and what was normal.

If you weren't a forester, this land might strike you as being like something from another world. Closer to the inexplicable magic of vorpal holes and vorpal beasts than to the more systematic (and more heavily documented) magic of human beings.

"I was just thinking that we haven't run into any vorpal holes yet," Carnelian said.

"The Forest might be trying to keep them out of our path."

"Excellent service." Carnelian raised her ramekin. "Five stars."

Even the Forest would struggle to completely erase a vorpal hole. But unlike all the rest of the land in Jace, it could be self-healing. To a certain extent. It shrank and covered its vorpal holes, making them difficult to notice.

Whenever vorpal beasts did emerge in the Forest, though, they tended to be unusually dangerous. Even by the standards of vorpal beasts. And unlike phages, they had no qualms about venturing out beyond Forest borders.

Carnelian had several gnarly stories about such encounters.

"You'd think it was a phage that got the commander," she said, "judging by the scars on her face. Obviously she had a lot of tussles with phages, too. But it was a vorpal beast that took her legs."

"Her legs?" Tiller echoed.

Carnelian scrutinized the rim of her makeshift cup. As if it had done something to betray her.

"Slip of the tongue," she said at last. "Not that it matters. We have better things to talk about than our dear commander."

Tiller drew a mental picture of skirts falling bell-like to swish against the floor. Thick as winter curtains. They'd creaked whenever the commander moved.

"If you're going to insist on looking that curious—"

Tiller took exception to this. "I didn't say anything."

"You had questions written all over your face."

"Even if that's true, all you have to do is not read them."

"Well, you'll never see for yourself," Carnelian said. "Unless you stick your head up the commander's skirts. And as long as I'm alive—"

"Would you have a problem with that?" Tiller inquired.

She didn't harbor any romantic interest in Commander Bloodwood. On the other hand, she did find Carnelian's vehemence a tad amusing.

"I'll tell you, then," Carnelian declared. "So you don't go probing for yourself."

"I would do my best to resist temptation."

"Wooden legs," said Carnelian. "Limbs, rather. More than two. About as many as a spider. That's what she's got under there. The Scholar designed them."

"For her?"

"No. For me."

Tiller's eyes fell to Carnelian's legs. But there was no question of her wearing prosthetics. Tiller had already seen her stippled with bug bites from ankle to hip.

"The Scholar was long dead by the time she lost her legs," Carnelian clarified. "He meant for me to use it as a kind of supplementary equipment."

"Like a weapon? Or an exoskeleton?"

"More like a bonus second body. There was a time when he wanted to try implanting human magic cores in animals. In machines. In artificial vessels."

Carnelian made a dismissive gesture. "Didn't keep his interest for long. He kept getting drawn back to the Forest. Years after he died, the commander pulled some of his lost experiments out of storage. Those old wooden limbs—she figured out how to repurpose them."

"The Scholar didn't try to leave you anything?"

"In his will? No." Carnelian tapped the side of her stomach like a drum. "He saddled me with his core. That's already enough of a curse."

They spoke of many, many other things, too. Self-defense tools. The perils of catastrophe ROE. The legality of the Parasite Guild, as well as less scrupulous groups.

Only select people could carry lethal weapons in the city. Licensed beast hunters. Soldiers. Security officers. The occasional constable.

But any of them might take side jobs going after less legitimate prey. Tiller had seen them all come after her. First with Doe there to guard her, and later on her own.

Without any fanfare, Carnelian used the hexagonal texture of her magical shields to conjure up stick figures. Each about the height of a finger.

They marched across the table like a paper doll chain given life. They shimmied up the sides of the liquor bottle and battled to straddle its mouth, playing king of the hill.

"You'd make a good entertainer," Tiller said.

Carnelian dissolved her animated shield fragments. She took another long drink. She appeared to be smiling behind her ramekin.

A mage like the Scholar might succeed in getting authorization to run human experiments. But no state-sponsored mage would ever win permission to devote their magic to the arts. To putting on a good show.

Commercial cosmetic magic had been outlawed for the same reason.

Every branch a mage allotted to mastering a frivolous skill was one less branch that could be assigned to fill the endless grinding needs of the government and the military and public utilities like the postal service. And every other vital industry.

Mages formed a very small percentage of the population, and few of them possessed multiple branches. They could neither be farmed nor manufactured. (Although this hadn't stopped people of the distant past from trying.)

The skills attached to each available magic branch needed to be allocated strictly and wisely.

"I have a confession," Carnelian announced.

"Uh-oh."

"I never did pass the Outborder Corps audition."

"You fraud," Tiller said in tones of false shock. "Why'd they authorize you to come on missions?"

"I'm just so special."

There was something provocative about the mocking way Carnelian pointed at her magic cores. Or maybe that was just the alcohol in Tiller's blood talking.

At the back of her mouth she could still taste the greens she'd thrown in her dinner soup, most of them bitter: butterbur, fiddlehead ferns, mustard greens, mugwort. Carnelian had looked on with a now-familiar gaze of envy as she simmered bamboo shoots.

There were no hints of nighttime fog invading the cottage. Nor any moss sprouts, for that matter.

Only a few impudent weeds had germinated in the cracks between floor mats. An exploratory vine curled its way around books on a tilted shelf.

Considering how much time had passed since anyone last tended to this place, it should've been far worse.

A wicker tray near the hearth was still covered in withered peppers, ones shaped like skinny scarlet talons. The walls were still lined with glass containers and earthenware pots storing moonshine and pickled vegetables, now unidentifiable, their liquid gone darker than the darkest of beer.

The air around the jars only held a sticky mustiness. Nothing ever went bad in the usual way in the Forest.

Tiller started to stand up, then realized this was a terrible idea. She stayed put.

For a time, the room moved about her like water in a fish tank.

"I'm jealous," she said.

"Of what?" Carnelian asked cautiously.

"Part of your brother will always stay with you. For the rest of your life. Wish I could've kept part of mine." She thought this over for a minute. "I'm not blaming you. I just—"

"Tiller," Carnelian said, as if addressing someone hard of hearing. "Tiller, I think you are very drunk."

Tiller recalled the operators who'd been draped all over Carnelian at the Corps party. Or had it been the other way around?

Right now it was startlingly easy to imagine herself doing the same. If the room would only twist a few more degrees in the right direction, she'd fall over into Carnelian's lap without even meaning to move.

But she refrained. She wasn't so far gone as to miss the unusual wariness in Carnelian's bearing. She had a very strong feeling that Carnelian would turn her down.

# 40

IRONICALLY, TILLER'S DREAM took place in the city. A turtle dove flew down to lay eggs in her hand. Then it flapped off, entrusting her to raise them.

She did her best to protect the eggs. But when she looked away for half a second, a worm-sized snake came and stabbed holes in them. By the time she caught the tiny snake and flung it away, there was nothing left to hatch.

The dream had no connection to her present situation. Except for the fact that she kept grumbling to someone nearby. About not knowing what to do with the eggs. About how difficult it was to keep them safe. About the snake.

She couldn't see who was with her. They were a presence like her own shadow.

In the beginning, she assumed it was Gren. As she woke, she thought it might be Carnelian.

Some of the birdsong she'd heard in her dream turned out to be real. She listened to them with her eyes closed. Green jays and azure-winged magpies and numerous others whose names and voices she hadn't thought about for a good two-thirds of her life.

They sounded muffled. As if a friendly ghost had stooped to put hands over her ears, trying to help her sleep longer. Must be the insulating effect of the blue moss growing like shaggy fur all over the cottage exterior.

She found herself covered in a heavy crochet blanket. One from the cottage, not anything they'd brought with their camping gear.

She slowly sat up. The blanket remained intact.

So far nothing from the village had dissolved into dust, scattering like the remnants of a soon-forgotten dream. Yet she couldn't shake the feeling that it was only a matter of time. As in old myths, she might blink and see it all reduced to a pile of leaves.

Someone had placed the blanket over her. Someone had put a pillow—one stuffed with hard dried beans—below her head. Someone had bound her hair in a stubby braid.

She looked blearily at Carnelian.

Carnelian lounged on the floor with her back to the wall, one knee up. Her hair was a steely color, curling wetly about her neck. She must have gotten up early enough to pump water for bathing.

"You tried to chew your hair in your sleep. That's why I braided it." She offered Tiller a porridge bowl full of water. "You didn't get much hydration last night."

"I think I had quite enough to drink."

"Don't be obtuse. It isn't becoming."

Tiller lacked the energy to roll her eyes. She drank gratefully. She'd dodged the agony of a full-fledged hangover, but she wasn't in the best shape of her life.

"Need any food?" Carnelian asked.

"What if I did?"

"I'd go pick mushrooms, I guess. Or share some of my rations."

"You might poison me either way," Tiller said. "No—I'm not hungry."

"If you feel settled, then, I'd like to register a complaint."

"What's there to complain about?"

"Several things, actually."

"Between the two of us, I thought I was the one in a position to give you performance reviews."

Carnelian leaned forward, arms on her knee. "Hear me out. You conked out right in the middle of a conversation."

"What were we talking about?"

Carnelian frowned.

Tiller waited. She waited some more. "Must not have been very important."

"Hey. Maybe we were planning our wedding. Anyway, there you were, snoozing face-down on the table. Snoring like a puppy with a stuffed nose."

"Sounds kind of cute when you put it that way."

"Speak for yourself," Carnelian said balefully. "I laid you out to sleep. You seemed cold. Hence the blanket."

"Then it came my turn to call it a night. I look over and see you with the blanket kicked away and your shirt pulled all the way up to your chin. Drinking sure does change people. I didn't expect you to flash me."

"Must've gotten overheated."

"You were shivering! And you"—Carnelian gestured rather crudely near her chest—"well, it was all hanging out. Which I'm fine with. But I thought you might have reservations."

"How gallant," Tiller said dryly. "Thanks for protecting my modesty."

Carnelian got up. "No thanks needed. It was my choice to ply you with alcohol. I could tell from our time at the outpost that your tolerance isn't too high."

"...Did you want me to fall asleep first?" Tiller asked.

Carnelian walked over to the wall-mounted bookshelf.

"I'm sorry," she said. "I snooped."

She didn't sound sorry.

Tiller tried to swallow. She failed. She set down the porridge bowl, still half-full of water.

A young vine had snuck its way up the wall to caress Baba Sayo's book collection. Carnelian lifted wire-thin green tendrils. She extracted a bound pamphlet.

"I looked through this entire shelf while you slept," she said. "These chapbooks are all signed by the Scholar."

She took the one in her hand and opened it to the blank page on the underside of the cover. She thrust it out in the air.

Tiller saw a tall block of beautiful characters. Most likely produced with a proper calligraphy brush. The sort of writing that would do a poet proud.

"Bloodwood." Carnelian jabbed the name at the end of the inscription. "Look at that. It's not just some generic autograph. Every single one has a personal message. *Dear Miss Sayo of Koya Village.* I don't understand."

The birds outside sounded like echoes reverberating from another world. More and more, the moss-wrapped cottage took on the feeling of a sealed tomb.

Tiller pushed the crochet blanket aside and rose to her feet.

Even the best private investigators in Nui City would've struggled to learn much about events that happened deep in the Forest. Foresters kept to themselves.

Carnelian did know an awful lot about the kidnapping. But only because she'd been there in the house with Tiller and Gren, watching through her magical wall.

What about before the kidnapping? What about before the Scholar started extracting and transplanting magic cores? What about before anyone might've thought to fear him?

He had simply been a mage with a keen interest in intellectual pursuits. A mage who hadn't minded all the mockery this invited. An outsider who wished to study the ways of the Forest. He'd been proud to call himself a would-be scholar.

There were some things about that time that only the Scholar knew. And Baba Sayo. Plus other villagers of her generation.

And Tiller, too. Though she'd only heard about it from Baba Sayo much later.

She took the chapbook from Carnelian's hands. The paper felt powdery to the touch, but it seemed to have retained its structural integrity. For the most part.

The front cover bore line art of a pulpfruit divided in half. *Legends of the Kingdom of Blues*, said the title. *Oral Tales From the Devouring Forest*.

She returned it to the shelf, laying it flat like a roof atop the other lined-up books.

"How's it feel?" she asked.

Carnelian's eyes seemed darker than they had been the previous day. But of course it was only a trick of the light.

"You knew so much more about me than I ever knew about you," Tiller said. "You knew it for much longer, too. But I guess there are still some areas where I've got the advantage. Where I know things you don't. How's it feel?"

Carnelian kept looking at the spines of the books. "I'm not angry."

"You sound angry."

"You'll make me angry." She laughed without humor. "I'm just—disconcerted."

"Did you know the Scholar used to visit the Forest alone? Before he became a kidnapper."

"The commander shared his personal papers with me. Her inheritance." Carnelian pushed at the books as if trying to fix their alignment. The shelf itself was not entirely even.

"He obviously sought a connection to the Forest. He dug out a secret house at the heart of the Forest to hold us. But he was very coy about what he left in writing."

"Years before any of us were born," Tiller said, "Baba Sayo found a man collapsed among the finger-trees near Koya Village. A mage. An outsider. He'd made himself deathly ill from eating Forest fruit."

She turned her back to the bookshelf as she told Carnelian the rest of it.

Baba Sayo brought the sick man to the village. It was right during the season of fire festivals. Many villagers had gone to the mountains.

There was no one who could carry him to the border. No one who could visit the Market at the Edge of the Forest and fetch food for him to keep down without vomiting.

Baba Sayo nursed him. She assumed she'd have to starve him. But he'd eat Forest food whenever she had her back turned. Anything he could get his hands on. Sweetened black beans, perilla leaves, dried slowfish.

She thought he was crazy. Eventually she managed to escort him out of the Forest. But he kept coming back.

Baba Sayo didn't tell Tiller about it until several years after everyone left the Forest. She never dropped any hints, either.

Tiller could never have made a connection between the chapbooks that helped her learn to read and the nameless man who'd stolen her and Gren right out of the middle of Koya Village. After all, the books had stayed behind in the Forest.

One day, in their first city house, they opened the kitchen windows. Tiller had gotten very good at wearing wigs. Even at home.

The room smelled of early summer. Morning birds piped warnings in a multitude of incompatible languages.

"I should've left him to die," Baba Sayo said as she folded dumplings. No context.

Then, for each new dumpling she folded, she explained more. Her rheumatic fingers expertly pleated the wrappers.

Until Tiller felt as if she too had been there, years before her own birth. Back when many Koya villagers remained hale enough to form adventurous harvest parties and fight off phages.

Now it was her turn to tell Carnelian.

"He returned to the village month after month," Tiller said. "Baba Sayo gave up on chasing him out. He seemed harmless at the time. Friendly and eccentric.

"The elderly loved talking to him about forester traditions and stories. He scribbled it all down in his notebooks. He always brought lots of gifts from outside."

Like the moonflowers that Baba Sayo had worked so hard to cultivate. They weren't native to the Forest. Still, she'd loved how wide and bright they bloomed in the dark.

"But you never met him," Carnelian said. "Not before—"

"Not before the kidnapping. His visits became less frequent a few years before Baba Sayo found me and Gren. After a while, he stopped coming by altogether. Must've gotten busier back in the world outside the Forest."

He still sent a few letters. So the villagers had known he wasn't dead.

After discovering Tiller and Gren, Baba Sayo was glad to have him out of her hair. She didn't think it'd be safe to let an outsider meet blue children.

She'd heard stories of past blues getting dragged out of the Forest, never to be seen again. Tiller and Gren were the reason she became strictly opposed to letting strangers enter Koya territory.

That being said, no one other than the Scholar had shown up for decades. Fellow foresters always preferred to stick to their own home villages.

Tiller's throat was parched. She went back for the rest of the water in her porridge bowl.

"Right when everyone had forgotten him, he made his grand return to abduct you," Carnelian finished. "Killing any villagers who stood in his way."

A wordless understanding passed between the two of them.

A promise that once they left the cottage, closing the door on the Scholar's beautifully autographed chapbooks, they would speak of him as little as possible.

He'd left his core deep inside Carnelian. But on its own, a mere magic core contained no more significance or sentience than a peach pit.

A fuller portrait of the man emerged as they pieced together their respective fragments of knowledge. Carnelian's came from herself and from the commander—his daughter. Tiller's came from Baba Sayo, the reluctant host of his Forest homestays. As well as from Doe, an occasional witness.

The Scholar had been an irrepressible optimist.

Despite being born a mage, and growing up with all the usual restrictions, he truly believed he could be anything and belong anywhere.

In a way, he was right. He ended up getting married to one of the highest-ranking officials in all of Jace.

(Jace was not a dictatorship. But sometimes it came very close.)

Through marriage alone, he won the sort of far-ranging freedom—and soft power—that no other mage could realistically hope to replicate.

Never for a moment did he doubt he deserved it.

He even believed that he could belong among native foresters if he put his mind to it. He gradually immunized himself to Forest food via long-term exposure, though it made him extremely sickly for years. Gaining such immunity was thought to be borderline impossible for a grown adult.

And sure, he pulled it off. But only because Baba Sayo, out of the goodness of her heart (and despite all her grumping) diligently tended to him for months and months. Again and again. She could've left him alone to wither and die, a victim of his own arrogance.

He didn't become her patient as part of some brilliant plan. He didn't engineer the situation out of sheer cleverness.

No—the whole thing was born from pure dumb luck.

He simply assumed someone would *have* to take him in. He assumed that if foresters saw him staggering about, ill and delirious, they would sacrifice their time and space to save him.

One way or another, people had always learned to make room for him.

Ultimately, the Scholar was a mage who'd dreamed of bigger things than other mages. But not for mages in general. Only for himself.

He saw himself as a designer. A craftsman. An engineer. An architect. Especially with respect to Carnelian.

People complimented him by saying he had the mind of an operator. He loved hearing that.

And the more people said it, the more onlookers came to trust him. They saw him as a mage too intelligent and enlightened to be driven by the base emotional instincts that hounded other magic-users.

In that sense, they considered him peerless. A mage who understood the world through the rigorous logical framework of an operator. A mage with preternaturally peaceful magic branches; rarely did he ever need serious maintenance. A mage who knew how to experiment and iterate and get results. Even if the results weren't yet perfect.

He'd succeeded in jamming multiple cores into Carnelian, after all.

He used to boast of having two daughters.

Mariabel, his daughter by blood.

Carnelian, his daughter by artifice.

"I've wished I could reach inside myself and rip out his core," said Carnelian. "I'm glad I'm not the commander. I've never had to fantasize about ripping out all the blood in my veins."

"Baba Sayo wished she'd never shown him our village," Tiller said. "She wished she'd let him die in the dirt. She wished she'd dragged him up to the fire caverns and dropped him in headfirst. Good riddance."

"Good riddance," Carnelian concurred. "We could go back even further. We could blame his spouse. His parents. His grandparents. Every last ancestor. The founders of the nation. The Lord of Circles. But I suppose maybe that doesn't seem entirely fair."

# 41

THERE WAS NO real need to tidy up the cottage. But they did it anyway, putting everything they'd touched back in its original place.

They left behind only one sign of their visit: the empty bottle of roeberry liquor, which Carnelian rinsed clean. It sparkled in the kitchen.

The whole room, tinted by what little light managed to penetrate the moss over the windows, was awash with watercolor hues of blue.

Tiller packed up her jars of ash. The frame of the front door was a touch too short for both her and Carnelian.

"Don't bang your head again," Carnelian warned.

"I'll do whatever I want," Tiller said.

"Out of sheer spite? Lovely."

The Forest didn't feel any smaller in scale than the last time Tiller had been here. An extra handspan (or two) of human height wasn't nearly enough to make a difference in comparison to forty-story trees.

But the houses were far humbler than she'd remembered. None had a footprint much larger than a low-end city apartment. In her memory the ceilings were higher and more mysterious, the shelves harder to reach. The clay storage jars had looked large enough to nap in.

Carnelian teased her for being slow on her feet.

"Next time you can just drink the whole bottle yourself," Tiller muttered.

"Sounds lonely."

Later Carnelian commented on how everyone had left so much behind in each of the cottages, from clothing to utensils to furniture. Even little mementos: whittled ground sloths and aurochs and bears.

It looked as if they'd been planning on coming back.

"Well," Tiller said, "there weren't any moving companies we could ask to come schlep all our earthly possessions out of the Forest."

As they walked through the village, she explained the other half of it. They'd ended up leaving the Forest rather abruptly.

After sixty-plus days of abduction, Doe finally got the Outborder Corps to come find Tiller and bring her home.

Shortly after Tiller returned to Koya Village—minus her brother— local phage attacks began escalating as never before.

Soon they received word that it was getting worse for foresters in other territories, too.

Doe quit the Corps. She stayed behind to protect the village. Doe was only one person, though, and a layperson at that. She had no magic to fight with, and none of the specialized tools she'd used as a Corps member.

The villagers went foraging in larger groups than before. Even that wasn't enough. Several died to vicious phage ambushes.

Carrying them up to the fire caverns now seemed inconceivably risky. After all, Doe would have to choose between escorting the corpse-carriers and defending the remaining villagers.

Mutilating the dead bodies might delay their phage transformation, but not for long. And who had the stomach to do such a thing?

Eventually they built a pyre a short distance from the village.

Not far away enough, it turned out, to avoid breathing smoke.

Baba Sayo made Tiller stay indoors all day and all night. She could taste it in the air anyway: the burnt hair and fat, the smell of roasting.

The worst part was that even those they cremated would still become phages in the end. Only the supernatural fires of the sacred mountains could permanently burn away every last possibility of regeneration, of reanimation.

Which was why Baba Sayo declared that it was time to leave. They'd tried to wait out the attacks for several months. They couldn't wait any longer.

Perhaps some villagers did think they'd be able to return in the future, after this strange season of violence receded.

But—quite independently of each other—the residents of every other village had begun trickling out of the Forest, too.

Soon there was no one left in the Forest at all.

The already elderly Koya villagers aged even more in Nui City. Years passed. It became impossible to imagine ever successfully moving back.

"We should've brought a camera," Carnelian said.

Tiller had a hunch that standard photography wouldn't work so well in the Forest. But it might be worth a shot. One day, she'd like to share the village scenery with everyone back in the city.

"We'll have to try it out another time," she said.

"And now to the mountains," said Carnelian. "Right?"

"Follow me," Tiller told her.

Carnelian only followed her for about five minutes.

They snapped off witch sticks to pass through the protective hedge of nettles. Gradually the sunvines thickened, and gave off a far heartier light than they had within the village proper. The oldest megalithic trees glistened with rivulets of deep ruby-purple sap, the precise color of blueberry jam. Among their roots clustered plants with fleshy leaves that looked confusingly similar to tumbled gems.

A waterfall whooshed sleepily in the distance.

"The birds," Carnelian said.

She'd spoken in little more than a whisper. But Tiller heard her clearly.

Because she was right: the birds had ceased their chatter. Nothing rustled among the stubby sago palms.

Tiller relaxed her eyes in an attempt to pick out movement, but she failed to spot a single moth or bee or ant or fly.

"I thought it stopped watching us." Carnelian sounded as if she were in a trance. "Wrong. It was waiting."

Tiller lowered her bags. She'd been using her basher as a walking stick. Now she took it up in both hands.

She expected to see a phage. Or a whole crowd of them. She couldn't imagine Carnelian reacting that way to any other predator.

"Your hood," she said. "All your limiters. You can—"

Carnelian's backpack hit the ground. Followed by her mantle and gloves.

One step further, and it came into view.

A vorpal hole.

Not so much a hole as a giant rip in the air. A kind of metaphysical tent flap.

But this, too, was a true vorpal hole. Even if no painted vortex signs had been posted on poles to warn them off.

Something indefinable was in the process of emerging. Spilling from the lips of the vorpal hole. Slowly and leisurely, with an air of the inevitable.

Pale tentacular shapes. They appeared more conceptual than corporeal.

Tiller blinked, and it began to resemble a bundle of bloodlessly severed human legs. The next second her focus wavered, it switched to looking like a trapped starfish of mythic proportions. Then like horse-sized slugs welded together in a listless imitation of a six-fingered hand.

Carnelian had not drawn her sword yet.

"This is the kind of beast they use chalices to drive back," she said. "This is the kind of beast that would make the army sacrifice multiple pilots. This is the kind of beast that only the Kraken could defeat one-on-one. We've got no chance."

If all else failed, they'd have to ditch their bags.

"We'd better run," Tiller said.

"I can't." Carnelian lifted a hand to her face. She forcibly turned her own head to one side, as if by no other means could she look away from the beast. "It's hungry. It wants my cores."

"You can hear it?" Tiller asked. "It's using words?"

"Not words. I just—know. I can feel its hunger all though my body. You can't?"

"I've got no cores to eat," Tiller said. "I feel nothing."

The beast didn't appear to be in any rush. It was still a good sixty feet away.

No—fifty feet?

No—forty?

She and Carnelian hadn't moved an inch. Nor, surely, had the vorpal hole.

But the beast slinking out of it suddenly seemed that much closer.

Sometimes its wet pallor brought to mind the glassy gray or whitish skin of phages, which lost all color as they aged. Sometimes it bore a closer resemblance to thick swirling clouds of Forest fog.

She tried using her basher to push Carnelian backwards. Away from the hole in reality, and away from the beast. It felt like trying to push over a tree.

"Where do you keep your girdles?" she asked.

"You've got to leave," Carnelian said, her jaw set. "Those tentacles are already deep in my head. It doesn't want you yet. It only wants me. You've got to—"

"Tell me where you keep your girdles." Tiller spoke loud enough for the monster to listen in. "That's an order."

"Tiller, don't—"

"That's an order," Tiller ground out, "from your operator. And the sister of the boy you killed as a child."

Carnelian told her.

Tiller dove at her bag.

Never would she have guessed that one day she'd find herself frantically dressing a mage in the middle of the Forest.

All the while, the vorpal beast undulated closer.

The two of them kept standing there, open targets. And for what? So Tiller could hook the magical equivalent of a corset around Carnelian's middle. Right on top of her tactical uniform.

Carnelian's backpack was an open mess at their feet. It looked like the aftermath of a garbage bag plundered by crows.

"You could've escaped by now," Carnelian said as Tiller tugged at her girdle. "You're wasting time."

"And you're wasting your breath."

"Go as far as you can. Go back to the heliograph tower, if you can make it." She reached back and tapped out a pattern on Tiller's thigh.

"Memorize that." She tapped again. "Flash it with the heliograph. Flash it at least three times. Then get the hell out of the Forest."

Tiller was too busy to react.

Serpentine white shapes wormed out of the vorpal hole and through the trees. They groped curiously at sap-bleeding bark, and at bushes bristling with long woody spines.

The tentacles—or oversize feelers, or pasty cellulite-stippled limbs—did not follow a straight path. They split apart, veering gently to both sides, biding their time.

They aimed to form a complete circle around Tiller and Carnelian. A wall thicker and taller than the village's hedge of stinging nettles.

"It's surrounding us." Carnelian's voice broke with urgency. "Tiller—this won't work. One core might look less delicious than nine. But that won't take its mind off me. It won't make the beast less hungry."

Tiller had already hooked a second magic-dampening girdle on top of the first. Carnelian, to her credit, remained physically cooperative. She raised her arms when needed, and didn't attempt to squirm out of reach.

"I'm only supposed to wear one," she protested. "They aren't made to—they won't even fit!"

"You don't use these as shapewear," Tiller countered. "There's enough give."

She yanked harder, straining to fasten on a third layer.

Carnelian grunted pitifully. "The beast sensed me from all the way back in the village. There's no way a few extra layers of specially treated fabric could—"

"Could what?" Tiller asked pointedly.

The limbs of the beast seemed confused. Or at least less certain of where to go next. They wandered further away rather than closer, fondling sunvines and sago palms.

Carnelian, trussed up in three separate girdles, looked wildly uncomfortable. But Tiller struggled to detect even a single trace of her cores. Any magic lingering near her lower back seemed like an afterimage, a trick of the senses.

"The beast doesn't have eyesight," Tiller said. "It's tracking you with magic perception. Is it still pulling at you from inside your head?"

"Its hold feels a lot weaker," Carnelian admitted. "But—"

"You said only chalices could battle a beast like this. Even if I escape by myself, days will pass before any chalices arrive from Central. And that's assuming they get authorized to come as soon as they can."

"Right. I'll be a goner regardless. That's not the point."

"So I'll stay," Tiller said. "You think I'm the type to just abandon my future wife?"

"This really isn't a good time for jokes!"

"Is our engagement a joke to you?"

Carnelian sputtered. Tiller pressed onward. "You better come up with an alternate strategy. A way for both of us to survive. I'm not going anywhere, Nellie. You'll just have to do your job and protect me."

"I think I hate you," Carnelian said with wonder.

"Because I'm making you work?"

"I also hate wearing three corsets."

"The faster we get rid of the beast, the faster you can take them off."

Easier said than done, of course. Attacking would instantly serve to refocus the beast's attention.

"Or, consider this," said Carnelian. "It's drifting the wrong way now. We've got an opening. We could just leave."

"Are you serious?"

"I'm always serious."

Tiller looked her in the eye. "Even if it seems slow at first, even if we sneak away out of reach, what'll happen the second you remove your girdles to breathe? What's to stop it from catching up with us in the mountains? Or following us out of the Forest?"

Carnelian, listening, heaved a sigh.

The roaming tentacles looked creepily raw, as if their slick white surface had no protective membranes or skin. No suckers or scales to be seen, either.

Fibrous whiskers—each at least the length of a human arm—sprouted and retracted with a cadence like breathing.

"Don't vorpal beasts have magic cores, too?" Tiller asked.

"If we can find one, we can crush it," Carnelian answered reluctantly. "But they don't all have a core."

Tiller ran her magic perception over the beast's moist crenelations. All the way back to the far-off vorpal hole.

No core.

"This one's only come partway out," Carnelian said. "Either it's hiding its core in the hole—which would make it unreachable—or its entire body is a sort of core."

"What would the Corps do for a beast without a core?"

"No use trying to destroy it. We'd force it back inside the nearest hole."

"It doesn't pop straight out again?"

Carnelian spoke very fast. "A vorpal hole isn't like a simple burrow for a fox or a crab. It isn't like one of the bypass tunnels, with a set beginning and end.

"Once a beast passes fully through, it gets lost. It might end up somewhere completely different from where it originated. It can't find its way back to us. That's the theory, anyhow. Pray for it to be true."

At long last, Tiller realized that the sound she'd thought was a waterfall was in fact the sound of the beast.

She'd dropped her basher when she went fishing in Carnelian's bags. She didn't bother picking it up again. Against a beast of such scale, it would prove about as useful as a toothpick.

Instead she reached in her pocket. She got out a small black tube.

"Your shredding claw," she suggested. "It tears up magic cuttings. The vorpal beast itself is magical, isn't it?"

"That skill doesn't work as intended in the Forest," Carnelian said grimly. "Trust me, I've tried. It's worse than porting."

They had a whispered discussion of strategy. The beast's limbs were beginning to reorient themselves, to writhe steadily closer. Now they resembled a herd of albino earthworms, segmented bodies and all. Worms the size of sea serpents.

Terse instructions were engraved on the tube in Tiller's hand. The tick-shaped mark of the Parasite Guild adorned the lid.

The tentacles laced themselves back and forth through the trees like the horrific beginnings of an eldritch basket.

Tiller twisted the tube open.

The tentacles trembled, as if scenting magic.

She drew in a long breath. She began blowing bubbles.

# 42

Endless soap-shiny bubbles streamed toward the beast.

The text on the bottle warned that contact with the bubbles might result in faintness, debilitating pain, hallucinations, even seizures.

If you were human, that is. No guarantee of them having the same effect on a vorpal creature.

Next to Tiller, Carnelian raised her right hand and curled it shut around empty space.

A few bubbles passed through the beast as if it had no more substance than a smoke sculpture. Yet as it shifted from one form to another—tentacles, fleshy feet, monstrous salamander tails—there were brief moments when the bubbles appeared to actually touch it. They glued themselves to its greased-looking surface.

"It passes in and out of tangibility," Carnelian said under her breath. "Between forms, it'll be invincible."

"You think its whole body is its core?"

"Might as well be."

"The bubbles aren't doing much good," Tiller said.

The beast's whisker-hairs were longer than porcupine quills. They erupted one by one, an inquisitive percussive beat, skillfully lancing each bubble adhered to it. They'd failed to induce any discomfort.

The beast quivered with gelatinous delight. Its tendrils spiraled in corkscrew paths through the air, deliberately bumping more bubbles. It popped them with the enthusiasm of a child at play.

Carnelian finished drawing her crystalline sword. "At least it's distracted."

Tiller blew more bubbles. The tube was already beginning to feel dangerously light in her fingers. It wouldn't last forever.

For now, the bubbles had dazzled the beast like an explosion of magical confetti. Bright enough, hopefully, to keep it from peering too closely at Carnelian's sword.

The blade grew longer. And longer. Longer than Carnelian was tall, and then longer still. If it were a normal sword forged by a blacksmith, there was no way she or any other mere mortal could've lifted its weight off the ground.

This, however, was a sword forged by magic. Carnelian held it up with zero difficulty.

In fact, she let go.

Her sword remained poised in the air beside her like a twenty-foot arrow nocked on the string of an invisible bow.

Tiller tried to keep blowing, but the tube was all out of bubbles.

Carnelian gestured as if ordering an army to charge.

The tentacles twitched. They destroyed every last remaining bubble in a simultaneous eruption of newly grown thorns. Some were as short as a thumbtack. Some were the size of a spear.

At the exact same moment, Carnelian's ridiculously long blade angled itself so as to narrowly avoid decapitating any trees or hanging sunvines. It slashed once, then twice, cutting countless tentacles off at the root.

Despite their visual heft, the severed limbs fell like feathers.

Now all that remained was the sticky-dough bulk of the beast's body. (Or was that supposed to be its head?) It overflowed from the vorpal hole, shapeless and whitish, bristling with tentacle-stumps.

Another sweep of Carnelian's hand, and her waiting sword flung itself like a javelin. Deep, deep into the soft pale mass of dough. So deep that—even with the blade having grown to a good twenty feet long—the hilt all but vanished in the vorpal beast's folds.

Carnelian was panting. Her sword had hurtled forward at breathtaking speeds, a razor-edged battering ram. Its momentum almost forced the beast all the way back through the tall ragged hole.

Almost.

The last visible hint of the sword winked out of sight, and out of existence. Carnelian had released it.

Her shields rippled into being instead, wrapping around and around the vorpal hole. And around the beast still straining to emerge from it.

The air bore an acrid, anxious scent. The shimmering shields crunched tighter and tighter against the captured beast. It was oddly reminiscent of the girdles Tiller had cinched shut around Carnelian, one after another.

"Can you push it through?" Tiller asked.

Carnelian clutched at her shoulder for support. "It might—it might shatter my shield first."

Despite the surreality of their slow-motion descent, the tentacles she'd hacked off had shown no subsequent movement. No indication of pain or desire or intelligence.

They lay draped over thick tree boughs or curled on the ground. They shed neither blood nor the clear sacred water that fell from phages.

Their naked slick whiteness, devoid of all those ephemeral whiskers and spikes, made them look like monuments molded from animal fat.

Carnelian fought to breathe. The diaphanous hexagons of her shields rattled as though caught in an earthquake.

Tiller reached forward to unhook the uppermost girdle—trying to give her more air. If Carnelian shoved the floundering beast all the way through the hole into nothingness, there would no longer be any need for camouflage.

Both of them saw it coming too late.

The nearest amputated tentacle leapt at Carnelian like a constrictor snake.

She shoved Tiller back.

Tiller tripped over their bags. Stumbled. Raised her head just in time to see how all the scattered appendages of the walled-off beast had begun quivering, quivering like wind-swept water. Quivering as if they wished to inch closer.

Yet only the one coiling around Carnelian had mustered up the strength to attack.

Keen needle-hairs pulsed out of its mucilaginous surface. They stabbed straight through all the tough layers of Carnelian's corsets and uniform.

She didn't scream. But the bulging shield around the vorpal hole seemed to falter.

Tiller drew her machete.

The tentacle didn't bind Carnelian to the ground, or to a nearby tree. It just wound tighter and tighter, crushing her in place, its sightless needles piercing and immobilizing her like the teeth of a python.

"Don't—come—any—closer," she said, each syllable shot through with pain.

Tiller approached anyway. The tentacle remained wholly focused on its current prey. It didn't loosen or switch its target. Not even when Tiller attempted to cut it open.

Every other second, it morphed into chains of mist. Even then, something about it held Carnelian trapped.

Tiller couldn't hack away at the coils fast enough to strike them in the precise moments when they embodied pure vulnerable flesh. Nor could she put sufficient power into her blows. Not without decapitating Carnelian in the process.

"I need your sword," she said.

The longer it took to free Carnelian, the harder it would be for her to answer, or breathe, or harbor rational thoughts. Or to keep using magic.

"Can't," Carnelian choked out. "My shields—"

She could only use one skill at a time.

Her magical sword would cleave flesh as if cutting through water. Zero resistance. Tiller could use it to slice up the binding limb of the beast much more effectively than with her plain old machete.

But to manifest her sword, Carnelian would first have to lower her shields. She would have to unleash the body of the beast.

"You were already afraid of it breaking your shields," Tiller said rapidly. "Let them fall. Give me your sword. The second I'm done, you can dismiss it. Then—"

The tentacle tightened. There was very little of Carnelian left visible. Just her head and part of her shoulders.

Tiller winced as if it were her own body being crushed. Her ears braced for the sound of ribs cracking.

Yet it went no further. Carnelian was still breathing, albeit shallowly. The immense appendage that imprisoned her kept flickering back and forth between the texture of a cumulus cloud and the texture of a slug.

It wasn't actually trying to suffocate her or break her body or stop her heart. What, then, was its goal? She looked like the prey of a spider swathed in silk, in a half-formed cocoon. A treat to be stored for later.

Her left hand poked out of the cobwebs. Or snake coils. The piece of the monster that bound her was still constantly changing.

Tiller caught at her fingers without a single thought for how this might help them.

Carnelian's hair flashed red.

Her fingers tightened on Tiller's. There was a life-and-death ferocity in her grip, the kind of strength that welled up when no ordinary strength remained.

"Promise me you'll run," she said hoarsely.

With her free hand, Tiller extracted yo-yo knives from her pocket. She picked frantically at the beast's flesh. She timed each stroke of her blade to the rhythm of its transition from untouchable mist to total solidity. And then back to mist again. Unyielding even in its moments of intangibility. And much too fast to follow.

"Tiller." This was the sound of Carnelian being desperately serious. "Tiller, it's right here inside me. It'll make me go berserk. You have to—"

"*I'm* your operator," Tiller snapped. "Not—not this hideous cosmic squid."

She struggled to remember what Asa Lantana had told her about throttling.

Something to the effect of: don't bother trying. Not with Carnelian.

The brawn of the beast blocked her access to Carnelian's back.

Carnelian's hair was turning red again, this time more slowly. It flowed down like blood from the top of her scalp. She cried out as if hidden quills had plunged deep into every spot they could reach, ardently tenderizing her meat.

Her hand seemed to be getting pulled back inside the white cocoon, together with the rest of her. Tiller clenched harder.

A strange frustration crossed Carnelian's face. "I'm trying to let go."

"I'm not," Tiller said.

The air smelled of ozone. Like a storm coming, like lightning yet to strike. Like wild magic brewing.

Tiller had never been face to face with a berserking mage.

She knew the warning signs. And she knew she lacked the skill to neutralize a berserker. She had no hope of expertly coaxing frenzied magic back into a state of calm.

She could sedate Carnelian. This precise situation was why she'd packed sedatives in the first place. But that would be tantamount to surrendering their lives—or, at minimum, Carnelian's life—to the beast.

"Please." Carnelian was all but begging now. "Please go. Before it makes me hurt you." Her eyes had begun to turn the same bloody red as her hair.

They heard a sound like a window shattering in a distant room of a haunted house.

# 43

CARNELIAN'S SHIELDS had fallen. The vorpal hole lay exposed, a vertical crack in vulnerable space. The body of the beast extruded itself, skinny new limbs telescoping out of old stumps.

This really was like fighting a living magic core, Tiller thought dimly.

The beast had no eyes or ears or mouth or blood or voice. Its body was an irregular lump, a corpulent hunk of magical essence. Its inquisitive tendrils—its branches—went exploring with a mind of their own.

These were the kinds of slowed-down thoughts she would've expected to consume her on the verge of death.

The severed tentacles began to shrivel and deflate. They came to resemble skin from a molting snake. Fine white flakes rose into the air as they shrank, streaming toward the main body.

The coils around Carnelian gave way, too.

It took all of Tiller's strength to catch her.

She felt Carnelian looking at her. Her own eyes stayed riveted to the regenerating beast. It drank down the powdery ash of its many, many lost limbs.

She was in much better shape than Carnelian at the moment. And it would be a dire mistake to ask a half-berserk mage to activate a branch skill. No faster way to drive her over the edge.

Tiller couldn't count on any of it: not the icy sword, the faceted shields, the homing pearls—nothing.

She had sedatives meant for use on humans. A tin of immobility ticks. A handful of nausea pellets. Her basher. Her machete. Her knives. Bags full of travel gear. Clothing, soap pellets, sunvine glowsticks, medical supplies.

She could throw all their soap at the vorpal beast. Perhaps the taste would give it pause. Perhaps the immobility ticks would weigh it down for a few extra minutes.

The beast still hadn't finished extracting its mass from the hole. It looked like a giant octopus swelling out from a microscopic fissure in craggy rock. Like a cat flattening itself to slink beneath a gate.

Blood darkened the needle-holes dotting Carnelian all over, from calf to shoulder. Wounds left by the beast's whiskery spikes. Thirsty green dragonflies circled closer, scenting her warmth.

The emergent beast loomed larger and larger. Its regrown feelers tangled hungrily with high-up branches, criss-crossing overhead as if weaving a net.

The wild magic in the air was thick enough to coat Tiller's teeth. Icicles of crimson-brown blood twirled up out of the mossy ground around them.

That wasn't the beast at work.

That was Carnelian, her magic slopping over its boundaries.

Tiller wondered if she could be trusted to lie still when the beast inched close enough to cover them like a crashing wave.

Probably not.

She grabbed Carnelian's discarded gloves. The restrictions woven into them had no effect on Tiller; she wasn't a mage.

With newly gloved hands, she clicked open the tin of immobility ticks. Given how the beast had responded to the Guild's bubbles, she didn't have high hopes.

But unexpected magical stimulation might shock it into retreating from Carnelian's head. Even just for a second. Before she completely lost it.

"The problem with going berserk," Carnelian murmured distantly, "is that you hurt the ones you love. Although they do say you enjoy it."

Tiller flicked ticks at the beast as it drew closer and closer. Its squirming appendages, freshly regrown, remained strung up in the trees. Its faceless body leaned forward ever more steeply. It would squash them as soon as it burst free of its crooked vorpal crevice.

At first the ticks appeared to fall short. Yet once the flesh of the beast slithered forward, they shot up and latched on.

Tiller had flung them too far to follow them with her eyes. They were so very small. She could detect them only with her magic perception, a transient brightness like sparks from clashing metal.

Carnelian paid no heed to any of this. She kept talking. "They say that going berserk is the best feeling in the world. How unjust."

"You're bleeding," Tiller said shortly. "You're full of holes. Save your breath."

"Oh, these?"

Wild magic rippled over Carnelian, head to toe. When it receded, she looked as if she'd never been injured. No blood, no stained clothes, no puncture wounds, no torn fabric.

The swarm of blood-seeking dragonflies flitted off.

Carnelian kept going. "I've done all kinds of atrocious things, and I wasn't in berserk mode for a single second of it. I didn't get to enjoy it. I didn't get the excuse of being out of my mind. Out of control. A whole different self."

The vorpal beast showed virtually no reaction to the immobility ticks. It might've slowed down a fraction. But it was nowhere near immobile.

Tiller's insides felt leaden. Like she'd poured those stupid ticks down her own throat instead.

She pitched nausea pellets at the beast next. Three in a row, one after another. At least she didn't need to have good aim. Not with a target that was beginning to balloon up as tall as a castle.

The beast swallowed her pellets like candy. It slurped its way closer with each passing second.

Carnelian's fingers touched Tiller's side as if discovering her for the first time.

"I was my real self when I killed your brother," she said wonderingly. "I'm glad I won't be my real self when I kill you."

This would have been a lot more alarming if they weren't already about to die.

Truth be told, Tiller couldn't remember how she was supposed to talk to a berserking mage.

"Direct some of that murderous energy at the beast first," she said. "That one. The really big one. Right in front of us."

"But I like you so much better," Carnelian said.

The beast's shadow had grown very dense now. So dense that Tiller could sense it through her clothes, a cold layer of paint.

The sunvines were rapidly dimming to strange sickly colors. As if the tentacles caressing them had found a way to turn them off.

Up close, the beast appeared to be the same hue as the wet white part of an eyeball.

The beast let out a noise that Tiller heard with some organ other than her ears. The sound of an invisible mouth opening impossibly wide.

Her joints buckled. Empty snow filled her mind.

Carnelian, beside her, looked unfazed. She put an arm around Tiller and pulled her closer. With her other hand she groped for her fighting pipe.

For a moment she held the slim pipe pointed out at the vorpal beast, as if warning it not to lurch any closer.

Then she flipped her grip on it. She tapped the heavy metal bowl of the long, long pipe on Tiller's breastbone. She kept tapping it lightly here and there, with the air of an explorer searching for a secret entrance.

The vorpal beast had paused its slouching decent, as though in deference to Carnelian calling dibs.

It curved so far over and around them that its amoeba-esque body formed a shape like a pale gaping cave. Like the irregular white walls and roof of the room where the Scholar had locked up Tiller and Gren and Rozen Silva.

Carnelian stopped tapping her pipe. She raised it higher. There was a very gentle look on her face: framed in red hair, all tender shadows, picturesque as any classic painting.

Too late, Tiller realized that berserk Carnelian was a woman of her word. She knew how to wield that pipe to kill.

She would land fatal blows on Tiller—all with one arm still cradled lovingly around her. She would show no sign of straining to lift the heavy pipe one-handed.

The vorpal beast politely awaited its turn behind her. She would kill Tiller with her beautiful silver pipe. She would make sure to do it before the beast lost patience and descended to claim them both. She would kill Tiller, and as she'd predicted, she would be sure to enjoy it.

# 44

Tiller's brain crawled through mud to scream at her: *Get away!*

No. Not just that.

Get away—or strike back.

*Give me my forever death*, Baba Sayo had written on the paper Tiller was never meant to read. They were still a long way from the mountains, from the fire caves, from the sacred pools and waterfalls.

She couldn't die before taking Baba Sayo and Doe up the closest mountain. But she didn't know how to live.

Her body jackknifed. She couldn't break free. Carnelian held her there with inhuman strength, a berserker's strength, her hair and eyes the burnt-down red of old embers.

It was too late for half-measures. All the immobility ticks and nausea pellets in the world couldn't deter a berserking mage.

She'd have a better chance with regular sedatives—those not reliant on magic—but her stash languished well out of reach.

In the last prolonged second before the metal pipe came down hard enough to fracture bone, Tiller remembered her yo-yo knives.

They lay in the dirt. But she still had her fingertips hooked through their string: a strand stronger than wire, and as smooth to the touch as waxed floss. If she tensed her fingers just so, she could send the blades flying up at Carnelian's face and vulnerable throat.

No time to worry about whether the knives or the pipe would be faster.

The end of the pipe gouged a divot from the ground by Tiller's head. Her knives flew awry, too, scoring fine red lines along Carnelian's cheek and throat.

Afterward, they swooped like sparrows to Tiller's hand. For the first time in years, she fumbled catching them. She almost cut herself worse than she'd cut Carnelian.

They stared at each other. Carnelian raised her pipe slowly and rested its length on her shoulder.

Both of them had been aiming to kill.

A sound had made them miss. A sound much like the hissing waterfall noises of the waiting beast.

It came from behind them, from all around them. From beyond the network of limbs that the beast had threaded cleverly through the trees to cage them.

Phages.

An army of color-drained phages.

More phages than Tiller had ever seen or dreamed of in her life. More than the dozens they'd battled before reaching the village. Too many to even understand what was happening.

They rushed past Tiller. Close enough to feel their wind on her skin. Yet none of them touched her. They swarmed the vorpal beast like a river of scavenger ants overtaking a corpse.

With their sheer numbers, they had enough weight to push it back toward the jagged vertical hole in time and space. Its tentacles—spangling the boughs above—stretched and stretched and stretched and then tore apart, once again resembling uncooked dough pulled too thin.

The beast began absorbing the phages as they punched it through the vorpal hole, inch by fleshy inch. A sticky film grew to envelope them. Their hands and feet bulged out, straining at the membrane from within, as though struggling to rip free of a placenta.

They grabbed Carnelian, too. They hauled her off Tiller. She snarled and burnt them with gusts of a wild magical fire, both deep blue and hot scarlet.

They didn't scream in pain. They didn't flinch. They didn't fight back. They left her and ran madly toward the beast, still burning bright.

Tiller had visions of the rest of the Forest going up in flames, too. But the fire consumed only the phages Carnelian had lashed out at, and not a single stray blade of grass.

With endless torrents of phages rushing past her, bumping her hard enough to make her stagger, Carnelian faltered.

The magic crackling around her body sank back inside her with the finality of water circling a drain. She put a hand to her forehead as if expecting to find her cranium cut wide open.

The raging stream of phages covered the vorpal beast faster than it could possibly absorb them. Some began dragging over the snapped-off remnants of its tentacles. Others joined the pile surrounding the vorpal hole, a massive dam of human-shaped bodies, bodies without any interest in leaving themselves room to think or breathe.

Carnelian looked at Tiller with wide gray eyes and said: "They tore the beast clean out of my head." Her gaze fell to her pipe. Her fingers jerked, almost dropping it. "I would've smashed all the bones of your face. I would've opened new holes in your skull. I would've—"

Tiller cut her off. "I tried to knife you. Don't worry about it."

"*Don't worry about it?*"

"You were berserk," Tiller stated. "Now you're not."

Carnelian sucked down a breath. "They saved us."

"Very helpful," said Tiller. "Very convenient."

"Too convenient," Carnelian bit out.

She stared over at the phages. They'd succeeded in shoving every last swollen polyp of the beast back through the hole in the air.

Plenty of phages had gone with it, fully or partially. Stray legs and feet and forearms and half-missing heads lay strewn about the base of the hole, drenching the ground in sacred water.

The survivors began to shimmy up tree trunks and sunvines. They climbed as comfortably as lizards. They didn't spare another glance for the narrow crack of the vorpal hole, or for their fallen comrades.

A few stayed. They ringed the vorpal hole, their backs to it. The sort of formation that Forest bison would use to protect young calves. They trod placidly in puddles of bleeding fluid and on unidentifiable shorn-off body parts.

"Ever seen a phage act as a sentry?" Tiller asked.

"No." Just one syllable, but she managed to make it sound extremely sardonic.

Carnelian peeled off her extra girdles. They gathered and repacked their weapons and scattered belongings.

All the while, the circle of phages did nothing but gaze blankly out into the depths of the Forest.

Maybe some aspect of the battle with the beast had satiated their hunger. For how long, though? No one could guarantee that these phages wouldn't ever develop a renewed interest in absorbing the nearest human prey. Which made getting out of here the most imperative order of business.

Tiller and Carnelian didn't need to exchange many words to agree on that. They shouldered their packs again, grimly efficient. They skirted a path around the vorpal hole. They stayed far away from its mysterious ring of guardians.

Seized by paranoia, they kept glancing back (and up, and all around them) till they could no longer glimpse any skulking phages.

The normal sounds of the Forest began filtering down to them. Scolding monkeys. Dripping water. The distant whispering song of high-up wind.

For now, Carnelian's hair was still red. Its fluctuations seemed like something unique to her and her many cores. Not a symptom of berserking. A shift in eye color, on the other hand, was the single most tell-tale sign of a mage on the edge.

Her eyes had already gone back to their usual limpid gray. The knife-scratches on her face had stopped bleeding.

Her brush with berserking had not stemmed from an internal loss of control. It had been artificially induced by the beast. It had retreated from her like an outgoing tide as phages drove the beast away through the vorpal hole. Out of the Forest, and out of this world.

If she'd gone berserk in the usual way, uninfluenced by the pull of the beast, sabotaged purely by the tangling tendencies of her own magic—she might've ended up in a state far beyond Tiller's ability to mend her.

Luckily, her branches didn't appear to have gotten irreparably snarled. Tiller asked her to stop for maintenance anyway.

For once, Carnelian made no attempt to argue that she didn't need it.

"Fabulous start to the day," she said brightly as she turned to give Tiller her back. "I went berserk. We almost killed each other. Great trust-building exercise."

"Ever been that close to berserking before?"

"Not that I know of."

A strange answer. If her magic ran rampant, she would inevitably have found about it afterward. She would've killed people, or at least caused extensive property damage.

"You've been in the Forest on Corps business," Tiller said. "You've put down your share of phages."

"A gruesome business. But yes. I'm a real veteran."

"Have phages evolved that much over the past twenty years?"

"You asked me something similar once before."

"Are they known to attack vorpal beasts?"

Humans were supposed to be the only animal that phages saw as prey.

"No one I know has ever witnessed a group of phages acting with purpose," Carnelian said. "Ever. A couple might jump out at the same target if they happen to be in the same area. It's still a free-for-all. They don't plan their actions. They don't use tactics."

Tiller thought back to the first throng of phages they'd fought in the Forest. They, too, had seemed unusually coordinated.

In the absence of human inhabitants, had phages gained some degree of consciousness? Learned how to communicate? Or was it an emergent group behavior, the deceptively complex outcome of intersecting base instincts?

She had never considered phages as being similar to worker ants or bees. They were their own singular creature, unlike any other organism. Inside or outside the Forest.

"Maybe," Carnelian said, "the Forest is just that happy to have a forester back inside it. Maybe the Forest sent phages to save you from the beast. And from me. You saw how they rushed to drag us apart."

Carnelian's magic branches kept curling together. Some like angry summer snakes warring for dominance, others like pitiful winter snakes huddling for warmth. Tiller meticulously separated the muddled strands.

"You think phages act according to the will of the Forest?" she asked. "Last time we crossed paths, they were trying to make us phages, too."

"At least they don't seem malevolent. Even when they're doing their best to kill us."

"Right," Tiller said. "Phages and the Forest don't love or hate us. They don't hold grudges. They don't have goals."

"You say that, but the phages that tackled the beast were definitely acting with a purpose."

Neither of them could explain it. The phages that pulled Carnelian off Tiller had gone for her uniform, not her neck or face or other tempting swathes of bare skin. They'd let go so soon after grabbing her that the fabric was only faintly discolored.

"Do we have good luck?" Carnelian inquired. "Or bad luck? What're the odds of encountering a beast like that one?"

"The vorpal hole must've formed after everyone left the village."

"Anytime in the past twenty years, then."

"The beast might have begun emerging anytime in the past twenty years, too," Tiller said. "Maybe it snuck a couple tentacles across the threshold and then lay there waiting. Dormant."

"For decades?"

"Could be. You felt it craving your magic cores. You might be the very first mage to pass close by. Maybe your presence awoke it."

"Like a fly vibrating the strands of a spiderweb." Carnelian tilted her head up as though seeking wisdom in the faraway canopy. "I suppose I'll chalk it up to good luck."

"We did get away with our lives."

"Exactly. To encounter a vorpal hole in the Forest, and a beast of such caliber, and to escape unscathed—"

"—defended by phages," Tiller added.

"The Lord of Circles would be amazed by our good fortune. We'd get accused of cheating in the roulette of the heavens."

"Remember what my oracle leaf said?" Tiller asked. "The one from the temple."

"I remember being jealous of it."

"I never learned much about religion outside the Forest. But your Lord must approve of at least one of us."

"And it sure isn't me," Carnelian said wryly.

# Part Four

*A House in the Mountains*

# 45

How much further till the mountains at the heart of the Forest?

Tiller's inner compass never led her astray. But she couldn't calculate how long it would take to get there.

They threaded a path around clusters of carnivorous sundew plants. They crossed half-frozen brooks, shiny with melting ice, and ducked under humid floral bowers bristling with upside-down toad lilies.

Before leaving the Forest, Tiller had grown up thinking of seasons as a type of weather, or a type of place. Spring might blow through the village like a brief storm. Winter might last forever in a single icy grotto. The leaves of the finger-trees were always yellow, and always falling.

She gave up on cutting her hair each morning. Once it crept past her shoulders, Carnelian helped her tie it back.

"How about pigtails?" Carnelian asked hopefully. "That'd be cute."

"Maybe another time."

"A simple braid, then." Her fingers were quick and gentle.

It still felt peculiar to have Carnelian standing behind her, combing and plaiting her hair. Usually Tiller was the one at Carnelian's back, patiently picking out tangles in her magic.

Now that they were past the village and back in their tent, Carnelian siphoned off the night fog to make more smoke sculptures. She crafted playful foxes, tumbling balls of string, wide-winged geese.

She'd seemed surprised when Tiller requested it (under the pretext of lacking entertainment).

She took her pipe out, holding it with one hand by the small bowl and her other hand at the end of the long stem, near the mouthpiece. She looked as if she were offering up the sword of an enemy soldier.

"I almost used this to open a hole in your head."

"Almost," Tiller said.

Carnelian chuckled, dry as bone.

She sang, too. The village songs Tiller had taught her—and others as well.

A ballad about the heroes who'd protected the islands of Jace from myriad attempts at invasion.

A timeless Nuian folk tune heralding spring winds from the south. (Which was also the very first thing Tiller had ever heard her sing, back at the Corps gathering.)

When she was in a weirder mood, she switched to modern love songs. An ironic lilt would enter her voice.

Tiller didn't understand half the slang in the lyrics. Carnelian, leering, volunteered to demonstrate what it meant.

But she would change the subject immediately thereafter, pivoting seamlessly to a stream of commentary on her latest collection of bug bites. Or a recap of near-fatal encounters with overgrown grabber lilies.

Another day, she coughed out homing pearls and dropped them in a rushing stream. They pierced the brains of quick-moving fish, instantly killing them. Dead fish soared from the water. They flew through the air into Tiller's arms, cold and wet, pulled by the magical pearls still buried deep in their heads. They were small dappled specimens, somewhat longer than her hand.

She roasted them whole on skewers. Carnelian couldn't risk trying any.

"You said you wouldn't help me hunt," Tiller reminded her.

"I had a change of heart."

"Why?"

"We've been hiking here for around a week now," Carnelian said. "You could probably use the protein."

"Worry about your own diet before you worry about mine."

"Diet aside, it's a thousand times faster than angling for them on your own."

"Weren't you supposed to be a super soldier?"

Carnelian sniffed. "I don't see anyone showing up to complain about me using my powers for fishing."

Originally, she told Tiller, the Scholar had meant for her to pull munitions long-distance. From a designated armory. So she would never run out of supplies.

But she never quite mastered the skill for it, and there were several obvious drawbacks. She'd be left empty-handed, for instance, if someone managed to sabotage her arsenal.

The Scholar came up with a new vision. He'd make her as independent as possible, capable of materializing her own shields and weapons at any moment.

Carnelian said all this without mentioning the Scholar by name.

Tiller didn't bring him up, either. Yet the past followed like a second shadow as they drew closer to the first of the sacred mountains. The one where Koya villagers would carry their dead.

The trip must have been much faster—courtesy of the Forest?—for those who bore corpses. If it always took days or weeks to reach the fire pits, dead villagers would become phages long before anyone could lay them to rest.

Twenty years ago, the Scholar had brought Tiller and Gren to his bunker in the sacred mountains. They remembered nothing of the trip. He seized them from Koya Village, and then they awoke in a locked room.

Seeing how as they were still in the Forest, he couldn't have brought them by porting.

Had the Scholar thrown them over his back to carry them? Had he summoned Carnelian out of hiding and made her float them up the mountain? Just like how she used to float around carcasses imported from outside the Forest.

Carnelian had been completely under his sway back then. Enough so to unhesitatingly murder a child the same age as her.

Either way, the Scholar must have traveled in the same direction as they were traveling now.

He'd spent months—years—inoculating himself until he could consume Forest food without collapsing and puking his guts out. Perhaps this long and painful process had made him good at navigating Forest land, too. Almost as good as a native-born forester.

Tiller had no desire to follow in the Scholar's footsteps. But there were only so many ways to reach the mountains.

Twenty-something days remained before chalices would swoop down from the sky. Enough time to achieve her goal and then make their way out of the Forest—even if they ran into occasional trouble. Not enough time, however, for massive detours.

In a pocket of steamy summer, they found themselves surrounded by cicadas and stag beetles, some as long as a loaf of bread. The beetles crawled over Tiller's shoulder and back like affectionate cats. Carnelian kept a respectful distance.

A sprawling aspen colony brought them close encounters with crabrabbits, wind-deer, and huge feral stock-elk. The animals industriously gnawed all the bark they could reach. They paid passing humans little heed.

Tiller's mind kept flitting back to the Scholar.

For thousands of years, Jacian civilization had been built on a foundation of scrupulously controlling mages.

As a mage, the Scholar should've been closely monitored and managed from birth. He should never have gotten away with so much.

He'd been married to an elite politician, yes. But that wasn't the only reason for his astonishing freedom. He'd built up a prestigious record in core extraction, a field of magical research spanning millennia.

(Despite its long history, core extraction had always had a devastatingly low success rate.)

Above all, he was a genius when it came to selecting his victims. The bulk of his human experimentation centered on unattached mages. Wards of the state. Like Carnelian and Rozen.

In the view of Jacian society, the entire point of a mage was to be rigorously mined for resources. To contribute their magic to the greater good of the community, and to do so with maximum efficiency.

The Scholar was a mage uniquely gifted at exploiting fellow mages. And when he needed other catalysts, he turned to the Forest.

As Tiller got older, Doe and Baba Sayo shared more about what had happened while the Scholar held her captive. They told her how the investigation of the kidnapping had been infuriatingly opaque.

Doe, who never got visibly angry, had cracked a water glass in her hand as she spoke of it.

Koya Village had been filled with eyewitnesses. Adults of sound mind who knew exactly who the Scholar was and where he'd come from. They'd first met him years and years ago. They could testify in gruesome detail about how he'd chopped up the village combat instructor, how he'd abducted two screaming children.

Outside the Forest, their word counted as little more than unreliable hearsay. Rumors concocted by an insular people. Slander born of primitive superstition.

No one said this to their face. They made every pretense of writing detailed notes on the villagers' testimony. But their actions—or lack thereof—suggested that they didn't take a word of it seriously.

The Scholar was known far and wide as an eccentric genius. It wasn't unusual for him to vanish for long stretches of time. Sometimes to the Forest, but just as often to other Jacian islands. He was quite a metropolitan and well-traveled man.

He could be anywhere, people said. He'll turn up eventually.

Besides, the (allegedly) kidnapped children barely even existed in official government records.

Baba Sayo had reported their existence on a census once. But that was it. Like other foresters, at the time they'd had no family register.

No constables patrolled the Forest, either. Crime among foresters was a matter for the natives to resolve themselves. They scared off poachers and other unsavory trespassers on their own. They couldn't rely on outside forces.

The Outborder Corps, meanwhile, was not well-suited to acting as a detective unit. From the start, they seemed reluctant to assume responsibility for the investigation. Perhaps, they suggested, foresters themselves had jurisdiction.

When they finally began to investigate, they refused to treat the Scholar as a suspect. They explored every other possible angle first. They wasted countless hours building up hypotheses about the abduction being an operation run by evil human-trafficking foresters from other villages.

They even pursued the possibility of an inside job. Maybe, they said, the elders of Koya Village had made the whole thing up. An elaborate cover story to obscure the fact that they'd murdered their local combat instructor in cold blood.

All the while, the Scholar's house deep in the mountainous parts of the Forest remained a matter of public record. He'd drawn heavily on Corps and government resources to get it built.

The Forest had been moderately less violent back then. But it still must have been a difficult, time-consuming, and highly dangerous endeavor. He received permission to proceed only because he was so respected—and because he declared it necessary for the next stage of his research.

Doe, a low-ranking Corps member, had to beg for a month before she learned more about the Scholar's house in the Forest. She had no hope of obtaining a warrant.

Only after two months of utter silence from the Scholar, along with multiple failed attempts to reach him at his other residences, did a small squad get sent to the sacred mountains.

Even then, their ostensible mission was to check on his welfare. Not to search for missing children.

If the Corps had believed the people of Koya Village from the start, the Scholar's reclusive Forest bunker would have been the first place they went to investigate.

Tiller and Gren and Rozen and Carnelian—and any other children trapped with them—could've been rescued in a matter of days.

No one would have needed to die.

Sometimes Tiller wondered where anger went. Did it flow downward like water? Where did it spill to? What would happen when it became too much for any one human body to contain? Could anger make a body rend itself apart?

Like how the Scholar's magic had rent their trainer. Seven pieces.

Sometimes she wondered if foresters' anger flowed back to the Forest. They could live in the city for the rest of their lives—and still, those who knew where they'd come from would perceive them as visitors.

The city might serve as a vessel for other people's rage, but not for foresters.

The rage that she and Baba Sayo and Doe kept dammed up behind sealed lips—did it trickle its way home to the empty village guarded by a hedge of stinging nettles? Did it travel underground like blood pumping through the veins of the earth? Did it pool in all the beloved lost places where no one could live anymore?

Sometimes she wondered if the Forest had spread its roots as a form of vengeance. Not for them leaving—for how they'd been treated.

Sometimes she wished the Devouring Forest would devour the world.

Foresters knew better than to breathe a word of that. But from time to time, all of them thought it. And all of them knew it. They could hear it in each other's voices, behind the platitudes and the gratitude they offered up to the government, to the military, to their neighbors. They could see it in each other's eyes.

# 46

THAT NIGHT, the same as every other night, Carnelian took out her etched silver fighting pipe to put on a show.

Something in Tiller whispered that this would be the last night before they reached the mountains.

By tomorrow, they might be able to climb to the fire caves. They might be able to turn around and start heading back the way they'd come.

They hadn't sighted a single phage since passing the vorpal hole outside Koya Village. Nor, thankfully, had they run into any other vorpal beasts.

But they were both afflicted by a nagging sense of being followed. A sense that phages still lurked in the trees and bushes, under riverbanks and behind rocks. Never attacking. Just watching.

Phages weren't supposed to do that, though. A phage might stalk its prey for short distances, but they had no concept of surveillance.

And yet the sensation persisted.

It was a relief to close themselves up inside their cheerful orange tent.

The fog outside felt especially thick tonight. Dense enough to choke all the sunvines. Carnelian's squeezable water-light looked rather worse for wear, too.

The nighttime Forest still didn't turn dark. But the white fog obscured their vision so thoroughly that it felt as if they were floating in a cloudy nothingness.

Take a couple steps away, and even the bright dome-shaped tent might threaten to disappear.

They hooked a long, long rope to one of the tent poles. If one of them needed to go pee in the middle of the night, they could hold the rope to avoid getting lost. (Disorientation was always more of a risk for Carnelian, but Tiller didn't mind playing it safe.)

Tonight's fog quashed all sound beyond the tent, too, like a vast pile of cottony insulation. It almost seemed to have a weight to it. As if they were huddled together beneath a shelter carved from snow.

Usually they heard at least some subtle scraping or chirrups from nocturnal animals. Although one did have to wonder what *nocturnal* really meant in the Forest, with its constant sunvines.

Even on weaker nights, the fog provided sufficient cover for shier creatures. Some plants and fungi only fruited at the touch of its moisture.

Tiller would've done more nighttime foraging if she were alone, but it didn't feel right to abandon Carnelian for long stretches.

No.

No. That wasn't it at all.

She didn't want to leave the round tent that each night got filled to the brim with the warmth of their sleeping breaths.

The past—and the present outside the Forest—belonged to another world when they closed themselves up in that tent. Every circumstance that had led them here felt as far removed as the absolute void that could only be glimpsed in a vorpal hole.

Tonight, she put a hand on the thin silver shaft of Carnelian's elegant pipe.

"You said you were running out of ideas for sculptures."

This was true. Last night, Carnelian had warned that they were about to reach the end of her repertoire.

"Tired of watching?" Carnelian put her pipe aside. "I can't complain. You've been a very good audience."

"I'd hope so. I'm the one making you entertain me. You almost lost your voice from singing the other day."

"Didn't bring any cards," Carnelian said. "Or dice. In case you were hoping for other types of games."

"Brush my hair."

For a time, Carnelian regarded her without blinking. "I can believe that you aren't used to braiding your own hair. But surely you know how to brush it."

"Brush my hair," Tiller said again.

Whenever Carnelian cut or tied her hair, Tiller found herself wishing it would last longer, wishing there didn't have to be a pretext for it. Wishing that something in her would require mandatory maintenance. Like Carnelian's magic branches. No one would ever argue with the necessity of grooming mages' magic.

Carnelian got on her knees and circled behind Tiller. She even produced an actual brush. Semantics aside, Tiller had thought they'd only packed a comb.

She removed the tie from Tiller's hair. She loosened the plait with her fingers. She caught the ends in her fist to brush out tangles without pulling them.

Her hands were always confident, and so very careful to avoid causing pain. She worked her way up until at last she could run the brush smoothly down from the crown of Tiller's head.

Tiller's scalp and ears buzzed at her touch. It was a feeling so concentrated that it overloaded her to the point of numbness. It flooded down into the nerve endings of her neck and shoulders and spine, places that Carnelian hadn't so much as grazed by accident.

She leaned her head back.

Carnelian's hands stopped moving. "I can't brush if you do that."

"I thought you were supposed to be a womanizer," Tiller said.

An unreadable look crossed Carnelian's face. Though maybe any expression would be difficult to read when viewed upside down like this.

"Who told you that? Alder?"

"The colonel implied it. But I'm speaking more of my own impressions."

Carnelian's fingers were still in her hair, not quite cupping the back of her head. Carnelian gazed down at her and said nothing.

"You haven't made a move on me since that first night," Tiller said.

"No," Carnelian agreed. "Did you want me to?"

"Do you not want to?"

"You seemed to prefer my singing. And my smoke sculptures."

"I'm allowed to change my mind, aren't I?"

Carnelian spoke in the tones of a diplomat. "Thought it'd be best to avoid leaving you with more unpleasant memories."

She tilted Tiller's head upright again, a brisk professional touch, and swept Tiller's hair forward over her shoulders. Then she backed off.

"Would it be unpleasant?" Tiller asked.

A certain asphyxiating quality began to infiltrate the silence filling the tent.

Behind her, Carnelian reached out to lay a single finger on the bone at the base of her neck. That finger felt as if it were poised to press a button to launch chalices. A button that, once pressed, could never be undone.

"Tiller Koya," Carnelian said, soft and cynical, "I think you understand exactly what I meant. If you must know, though, I could show you a very good time."

Her finger traced a line down to the middle of Tiller's back.

There was no point, Tiller discovered, in waiting for her heart to calm down. It might never happen.

The light tip of that finger felt as if it could effortlessly penetrate the walls of her body, skin and flesh alike, with a single soundless push. Just like Carnelian's sword.

"In fact," Carnelian said by her ear, "I would love to show you a good time."

Tiller twisted around, and not a moment too soon. Her body was on such high alert. She seemed about two breaths away from going into cardiac arrest.

Not that any of this showed in her voice. She managed to sound so collected that she felt divorced from her own lungs.

"You've had a lot of partners," she said.

A droll smile, dimples and all. "I'm not picky."

"Well, that makes me feel very special."

"You are special," Carnelian said simply. "If I go home with someone I've met at a club, it's usually safe to assume that I haven't murdered their brother."

"Or spied on them with a gang of private investigators. For two decades running."

"Or that."

It had grown difficult to look her in the eyes for long. It was easier to hide her face in Carnelian's hair—back to gray again, though this time it had taken days to regress. It was easier to press so close that her heartbeat became camouflaged by Carnelian's heat.

Carnelian's arms drew her in.

"You know," Carnelian murmured, "I'm used to being wanted."

"If you do say so yourself."

"I've got a lot more to offer than pure personality. Anyone I meet, I can understand them wanting me. No matter how they dislike me. Never comes as a surprise.

"Except you. I see how you look at me, but I can't understand it. Knowing what you know."

"Do you really want to get into that?" Tiller asked. "Now of all times?"

"Not the sexiest topic, I suppose."

A lingering pause.

Carnelian pushed Tiller down on her back.

"Well," she said from above, "don't blame me if you get completely obsessed."

# 47

TILLER SLEPT SO DEEPLY that she forgot not who she was, not where she was, but *when* she was.

Before opening her eyes, she heard morning birds. She heard the whistling snakes that expertly imitated their calls, luring them in. The most musical snakes had feathered protrusions on their hoods—false wings or tails—that they fluttered enticingly as they sang.

She knew she was in the Forest. But for a few addled moments, her consciousness transposed itself to a time before she had ever lost anyone she loved.

Carnelian put an arm around her and sleepily pulled her closer, mumbling something that never quite reached the level of coherent speech.

Her body molded itself to Tiller's back. Her mantle covered them both like a blanket. Her gloved hands were jarringly cool to the touch, but the rest of her warmth more than made up for it.

There were questions Tiller might ask herself if she had the benefit of unlimited time.

Was it right to luxuriate in this kind of affection? Given freely, yes, but given by someone who'd convinced herself that she owed Tiller a lifelong debt.

Or: had Tiller succumbed to temptation because she was all alone now, the very last of her close kin? (Blood-related or otherwise.)

Long ago she'd learned to accept herself as the world's last living blue. She'd also known that, minus outside interference, she would likely outlive Baba Sayo and even Doe.

Still, she hadn't been prepared to find herself bereft of family at thirty. She might never have been prepared for it at any age.

After years of holding herself apart from others, would any warm body in the woods have been enough to sway her?

Had she let herself fall into Carnelian's arms because of the intimacy of the situation: camping together, lives in danger, merciless memories dogging their steps?

Or had she stumbled forward because of something irresistible about Carnelian herself?

She let these questions pass through her like flotsam swept away by a stormy river.

Carnelian, still sleeping, squeezed her with the insistence of a phage trying to sneakily absorb her.

In response Tiller's heart squeezed inward, too. As if attempting to annihilate itself. As if closing like a fist.

While Carnelian packed up the tent, Tiller foraged for her morning meal. She found a clump of parasitic land clams in a glowing tree hollow, their shells tinted yellow and gray and blue with lichen.

She licked her fingers, then crouched to harvest a second batch. She was slow to detect the burning spot on the front of her shirt.

Her clematis pin had heated up like a blade getting tempered by a blacksmith. She hastily poked it.

"Still alive?" asked Asa Lantana.

"For now," Tiller said, after blowing at her seared fingertips.

It took considerable effort to parse out what Asa said next. It seemed to be something about how she was continually amazed by the docility of Jacian mages. Most of them, anyway.

"That's just how society is built," Tiller replied.

It felt strange for her to be the one saying this. She was only an exiled forester—far from an integral part of Jacian society. Why should she speak for it, much less defend it?

"Guess I should understand it as well as anyone," Asa said obscurely. Then, with startling fluency: "When government and culture and history and the entirety of society are a sophisticated engine, a perpetual motion machine devoted to keeping you compliant...."

"Is that a quote?" Tiller asked.

"It's something I heard you Jacians say about my own country."

Suddenly she let out a betrayed-sounding yelp. "Oh! Almost forgot. I have a message for you."

"Yes?" Tiller said warily. "From who?"

"One of your military people. They moved up the timeline."

"What timeline?"

"For the chalices. You've got seven days left."

Tiller, reeling, did the math in her head. She had no memory of ending her chat with Asa Lantana, but at some point the clematis pin went silent and cold.

She checked her calculations over and over before bringing it up with Carnelian.

If the return trip went twice as fast as their travel to the mountains, they'd make it out of the Forest with a day or so to spare.

Yet she knew of no way to guarantee that. She could point them in the right direction. She could set a tougher pace. Ultimately, though, all matters of time and distance would hinge on the caprices of the Forest. She couldn't control it.

What if the Forest wanted to keep them longer? What if the Forest, too, had developed a craving for human warmth?

"No point in stressing over it," Carnelian said briskly.

Tiller gawked at her.

"Realistically speaking," Carnelian continued, "they have no hope of razing the entire Forest. They'd have to sacrifice way too many pilots in the process. They'd lose their entire roster."

"But—"

"If we find ourselves cutting it close, we can hunker down in your village for a bit. Something will have gone seriously wrong if we see chalices there. It's far past the original Forest boundary. Isn't it?"

True. Then again, the Forest might respond very poorly to being attacked. Deep in the Forest could end up being the worst possible place to take shelter. Even if it sounded preferable to getting burned alive or stepped on by an unfeeling chalice.

Carnelian put a hand just below the nape of Tiller's neck. "If you need a distraction, I'm happy to oblige."

Tiller punched her in the arm.

"Ow!" But she was grinning.

"No need to look so happy about it," Tiller said. "Daytime is for business."

"I'd argue that life is too short to take pleasure only at night."

"It'll be even shorter if we get blasted out of existence by rampaging war machina."

Carnelian nudged her as if trying to trip her. Tiller nudged her right back, and much harder.

"Seriously, though." Carnelian danced a couple steps out of reach. "You're good at compartmentalizing. Now's a great time for it. Fretting won't make things any better."

Indeed. Tiller put a lid on further thoughts of the coming chalices. She wouldn't envision the Forest screaming as they scourged it.

She set aside other things, too.

Like how much the light of the sunvines loved Carnelian. Pouring gold through her silver hair, coaxing an answering radiance from her infuriatingly symmetrical face.

Like how Carnelian had taken to touching her to get her attention, as if they'd known each other all their lives.

Tiller didn't dwell on any of this. Not for a second.

Around mid-morning, they halted for a hydration break at the bottom of a cascading waterfall.

The water was so clear as to render itself borderline invisible. Yet even after being treated, an alien quality permeated its taste.

Nothing outright foul. Nothing so alarming as to make Tiller concerned about their health. Just—something subtly and undeniably foreign to her tongue, to her esophagus, to her skittish stomach.

"Maybe it's all water from phages," Carnelian said. "Phage-water runs perfectly clear, doesn't it?"

"I never want to learn what it tastes like."

"Maybe we'll find a giant pile of them at the top. That'd make for a nice little horror story. Do you have ghost stories in the Forest?"

"Who needs ghosts when you've got phages?" Tiller asked.

She tried and failed to swallow down the aftertaste.

The scenery changed drastically as they approached the foot of the mountain.

In an oasis of scorching heat, conifers ceded ground to even taller scale trees: stark tufted towers without any real branches to speak of.

They took off their packs to squeeze past shoulder-high spherical cacti. Yet minutes later, the temperature dropped like a guillotine.

They spent much of the rest of the day navigating a semi-frozen log jam. It choked the river that veered away from the base of the mountain—an elderly relative of the waterfall they'd drunk from earlier.

This was one of the rare areas of the Forest with open skies. At night it would go dark, making the billowing fog an even deadlier hazard than elsewhere.

"Odd," Carnelian said. "The Forest hasn't forced these logs to regrow as anything else."

"Maybe they serve a purpose."

"It's like a desert of tree bodies. And so many—almost as far as the eye can see. Have they always been here?"

"Not sure," Tiller admitted. "I only came this close to sacred land on special occasions."

She had no recollection of this immense barren log jam. The older Koya villagers might've taken different paths up their mountain.

Here their only companions were standoffish mountain goats. They stood on cliffs and high branches and stared judgmentally down at Tiller and Carnelian.

Still, it was markedly less unsettling than getting stared at by hidden phages. Carnelian waved at the goats as if they were adoring fans.

"Other than people dying," Carnelian said, "what sort of special occasion would bring you to a forbidden mountain?"

"Coming-of-age rites. Gren and I never had ours. Fire festivals. Self-sacrifice—although I think Baba Sayo forbade that. Don't know anyone who actually did it."

Carnelian nodded. "A fading tradition. Like magewives pulling out teeth."

"Also," Tiller said, looking straight ahead, "marriage."

"How perfect for us."

"Knew you would say that," Tiller muttered.

The mountains closest to the village were relatively low, as if the Forest had dragged at their roots to ensure they stayed within its sphere of influence.

Their peaks failed to breach the treeline. Although the treeline in the Forest was much, much higher than what you'd find among other mountains on the island of Nui.

Still, even here there were rocky areas where trees grew further apart. They didn't always form an unbroken canopy.

Sunvines did their best to make up for it. In patches where they had no great towering boughs to dangle from, they twisted up from cracks in boulders like drill-shaped stalagmites.

In some places they almost seemed to imitate trees, sending long branch-like offshoots this way and that to cling to stony precipices. The most ambitious of the rising vines snapped like broken arrows, collapsing under their own weight.

Tiller caught a whiff of the fire caves well before seeing them. Clean and heady, unlike any other scent from either the city or the Forest.

The ineffable way it filled her lungs did remind her of the odor that might precede or follow rain. Not that they really smelled remotely similar. It was more about how even a hint of it could trick her into breathing deeper. Seeking out the source.

<h1 style="text-align:center">48</h1>

"Is THIS A TEMPLE?" Carnelian asked.

"You could call it that."

Natural monoliths peppered the crest of the mountain. The people of Koya had never tried to improve on them by erecting measly human structures. As far as Tiller knew, other sacred mountains—affiliated with other Forest villages—looked much the same.

The two of them spoke little as they climbed near-vertical rocks scored with uneven grooves. At one point in time, those grooves might have done a much better job of passing for stairs. That time was now long past.

"I'll have to use Float if we fall," Carnelian said shortly.

There was a distinct queasiness in her tone. Tiller held her tongue and focused on the (rather difficult) work of not falling.

They breathed easier after ascending to a plateau. The scent of the fire caves intensified, lending a mysterious intoxicating texture to the air. Linger long enough, and their noses and tongues would go blind to it.

A black eagle coasted high in the sky over the mountain, its wingtip feathers splayed like fingers.

Trees and scrub covered a slope to their right, but the left half of the plateau offered a semi-open view. From here the Forest appeared to have eaten the entire world. As if nothing else had ever existed. As if every Jacian farm and town and fishing port were a made-up dream.

"Feels strange to look straight up to the sky again," remarked Carnelian.

"I used to be scared of it," Tiller said. "It gave me nightmares after we left the Forest."

There were minor gaps in the canopy over Koya Village, making it more akin to a colander than a solid roof. But nothing like this.

"You didn't crave open skies? Clear blue days and beautiful stars?"

"Remember your first time seeing a vorpal hole?" Tiller asked.

"I don't think anyone ever forgets it."

"Unbroken views of the sky gave me the same feeling."

"That bad, huh?"

Tiller set her backpack down by a cairn-like mound of rocks. Wild plum trees, short and hunchbacked, bloomed stubbornly from crevices with scant visible soil.

Carnelian hung back. "Should I do anything?" she inquired.

"It's fine to look around," Tiller said. "Just don't climb the monoliths."

She pointed at the largest monolith on the plateau. A long fat column of rock, milky-white with hints of green. It rose up high over its surroundings, casting a shadow like a lumpy dimpled lighthouse.

The base tapered to a frighteningly fine point. It seemed as liable to topple over as a pencil balanced on its tip.

"Remind you of anything?" she asked Carnelian.

"Is that a trick question?"

"Looks just like a big white radish, doesn't it? Getting pulled all the way out of the ground."

"Oh," Carnelian said. "Right. A radish."

"We call it the Radish Monolith."

"How wonderfully self-explanatory."

Tiller unwrapped her two ceramic jars of cremated remains. Carnelian shaded her forehead with a hand to watch the circling eagle.

Her eyes widened when Tiller placed one of the containers in her lap. (Doe's container, which was noticeably heavier than Baba Sayo's. A muscular woman in the prime of her life would naturally produce somewhat more ash than a wizened grandmother.)

"You don't mind me touching this?"

"Carry it for me," Tiller said. "It's weightier than you'd think. Cumbersome, too. If I were on my own, I'd be making two trips."

Carnelian crept along behind Tiller with Doe's sealed jar cradled gingerly in her arms.

Entrances to the fire caves came in many different shapes. The one here was an irregular gap in otherwise solid-looking red rock. No wider than the village well. It led straight down into an almost perfectly vertical shaft, rugged on the inside like the lining of a living throat.

Concentrated firelight seethed at the bottom of the shaft. One might expect the air above the opening to be dangerously hot, too.

Yet the heat of the flames never reached that high. They boiled down below like a long-cooking sauce getting reduced to its essence. They were magical in nature—magical in the ineffable way of the Forest.

The heart of the cave burned impossibly hot, and the odor it pumped out remained impossibly immaculate. The ethereal fire was too clean to produce visible smoke.

Tiller breathed the mountain air that no other forester had inhaled for decades.

She peeled protective packing tape off the jars. She removed their lids.

She dropped the jars one by one through the opening.

It was little more than an unguarded hole in the ground. No warning signs. No railing. Bring a curious child here, and they'd tumble in headfirst the moment you turned your back. There would be nothing to stop them from falling.

Maybe she heard the pots shatter. Maybe not. It happened so long after she let go of them, and it was over so quickly.

The fire itself gave off a sound all its own, a hollow deep-sea throbbing. Wouldn't that have swallowed up the far lighter and far shorter-lived noise of ceramic breaking?

"I thought..." Carnelian searched for words. "I thought maybe you would lower them in on a rope."

"Normally you would," Tiller said. "You should. There's a special type of rope. Only a few people in the village knew how to make it. You lower the body with it, then throw the rope in after. That's how it's supposed to go."

"No one taught you how to craft the rope," Carnelian said, as if this answered all her questions.

"There would've been a stash back at the village. They always had extra on hand. No time to twist a new rope from scratch if someone suddenly died in a foraging accident."

"You didn't want to bring it with us? I'd have been glad to help you search."

"You can't just use it like any old bit of string," Tiller said sharply. "You have to tie certain knots. There's a whole procedure. The right way to secure the body."

She'd never asked to learn the knots. She'd imitated them a few times as a child, together with Gren. Then she forgot it all.

Even in the city, she could've petitioned a knowledgeable villager to teach her. But she pretended to be too busy with the Foundation.

The older villagers took care of each other instead. They sought out substitute materials to make their own ropes. They came to a special agreement with the owners of a local crematorium. They used all the correct knots.

They did it for Baba Sayo, too. A man and a woman in their late seventies came over to help. They had Tiller hold the rope for them, but she couldn't tie a single knot. It was like her ears went deaf and her hands went mute.

They were very patient. They told her exactly what to do. And she still couldn't do it.

She'd brought Baba Sayo to the sacred mountain. But to this very day, she wasn't doing it right. She hadn't even tried.

Carnelian crouched next to her, arms around her knees. Between them rested the lids of the two now-vanished containers.

Carnelian peered at the opening of the deep, deep cave as if she could actually perceive what lay at the bottom of it. Beyond just an eye-scorching glow too bright for human sight. Like gazing into the face of a god.

Some aspect of Carnelian's quiet presence made Tiller painfully aware of how emotion had rushed through her like sewage.

She felt it happening again.

"I'll throw the lids in, too," she said. "Didn't bring any rope to toss in after. These are all I've got."

She reached for the lids.

Carnelian put an arm out to block her—but she put it out with her palm open. Tiller, quite inadvertently, ended up clasping her hand.

"It's probably fine to keep one little thing for yourself," Carnelian said.

Tiller stared down at their joined hands.

She had no reason to listen. And yet she did.

She took the two jarless lids, one for Baba Sayo and one for Doe. She wrapped them up again and placed them safely back in her pack.

*Give me my eternity in the Forest*, Baba Sayo had written. *Give me my forever death together with every forester who came before me.*

Tiller wanted to ask if she'd done a good job. Or at least an adequate job. At least the bare minimum.

She wanted to ask if she'd done the right thing. If she'd done right by Baba Sayo and Doe.

But even if she'd taken the worst path in the world, even if she was dead wrong, there was no one left to tell her. No one left to disappoint.

# 49

AT THE FOOT of the Radish Monolith, they built two markers for their lost brothers. Gren Koya and Rozen Silva. Short stacks of stones; humble pine cones and acorns. Nothing guaranteed to be permanent.

But Tiller would always remember exactly where they'd placed it.

Carnelian stepped back from the markers. She gazed up at the full length of the monolith behind them.

"Tiller," she said steadily. "We're not the same."

This felt like it came out of nowhere.

"Did I ever claim we were?"

"You see us as victims of the Scholar. His only survivors. The thing is, I'm more of a co-conspirator."

"You were a child."

"Everyone says that."

"You should believe them," Tiller said, caustic.

"Age can't excuse anything and everything, can it? Look—I'm not bringing this up to be an asshole." Carnelian fiddled uneasily with the ends of her gloves. "Maybe the timing makes me one anyway."

"Go on," Tiller said. "Tell me how I should feel. Tell me how I should look at you."

"I went right up to the edge of the fire pit. I left myself wide open. You missed your chance to shove me in."

"You think I've never wanted to kill anyone before?" Tiller demanded. "You think I'm too soft on you? You think it's my job to agree with your—"

"No," Carnelian said, stronger than before. "No. I'm sorry. Bad habit. Shouldn't make this all about my guilt."

Tiller exhaled her indignation. "Then we have no reason to argue."

Carnelian crouched in front of the twin cairns again.

"The Scholar taught me that the sacrifice of a blue could work miracles."

She prodded the ring of acorns around each cairn, fixing the parts where they had ended up less then perfectly circular.

"After he put Rozen's core in me, he brought your—he brought Gren to my room. He laid a hand on Gren's shoulder. He told me: *We'll give you back your brother.*

"Those were his exact words. Then he explained what I had to do. So I did it. I summoned my sword, and I killed your Gren. Because the Scholar said it'd bring Rozen back."

"He lied," Tiller said.

"He lied."

"If the Scholar weren't already dead, we could've teamed up to get our revenge."

"If only," Carnelian said.

The nearby plum blossoms bristled at the touch of a stiff, sweeping wind. Just by existing there in her uniform and her crooked smile, she made the mountainside scenery look like part of a painting.

They ate a makeshift picnic lunch right there on the plateau, facing the Radish Monolith and the uneven stones they'd dedicated to Rozen and Gren.

The pristine fragrance wafting from the caves had the inexplicable side effect of making Carnelian's rations smell edible. For the first time, Tiller deigned to take a bite. (Carnelian always offered her some, but never before had she felt inclined to accept.)

The packaging for the rations crushed down into a tablet the size of a fingernail. Carnelian compressed it between her palms as if hoping to make it even smaller.

"The Scholar told me how blues are born," she said. "Not sure if it's true."

Tiller looked up from a palmful of spicy wild strawberries. "The sacred spring."

"Oh. Makes sense that you'd know."

"Not necessarily," Tiller said. "No one in Koya Village had ever met a blue before we came."

Baba Sayo had learned much of what she knew about blues from the Scholar's writings. The pamphlets on her tilted bookshelf. He'd collected a whole bunch of folklore and oral history from faraway settlements.

Every mountain in the Forest had at least one sacred spring. In older and harsher times, when there were too many phages and too little food, desperate foresters from each village would drown themselves as a sacrifice.

This was the only way to die in the Forest without any fear of becoming a phage. A body sacrificed to a sacred spring would disappear on its own. No need to drag it to the fire caves.

A week or a month or a full season (in Forest time) later, a young blue would appear somewhere in the woods. As if the Forest itself had birthed them. They bore no resemblance to those who drowned in the spring. They kept no memories of any other life. But clearly there had to be some sort of connection.

Carnelian kept toying with her trash pellet. "The Scholar ... he made it sound like he had a hand in your arrival. You and your brother."

"Our arrival?"

"Your emergence. Your birth. You were the first blues anyone in your village had seen for generations?"

"Something like that."

"He talked to me about all kinds of things," Carnelian said. "The way you might talk to a pet. He talked to me about sowing the seeds for blues. Lots of failed seeds."

Her voice turned hesitant.

She described how he'd convinced people to die in the sacred spring on this very mountain. Or maybe he'd made them enter the water under duress. He may even have murdered them and pushed them in himself.

He never did mind a high failure rate. He'd cut his teeth extracting magic cores. Most of his subjects died from it—and even so, his techniques were considered wildly successful. At least compared to how it got done in the past.

Carnelian rested her face in her arms, looking sideways at Tiller. "Out of all those seeds of blues he planted, he saw two germinate. He waited ten years. Then he came to collect you."

"To harvest us," Tiller said dully.

"He took credit for creating you, but it's not as if he could prove it. Maybe your birth in the Forest had nothing to do with him and his manslaughter."

"Only the Forest knows the truth."

Carnelian made a sound halfway between a laugh and a sigh.

They rose together, as if responding to an invisible cue from the skies. They finished cleaning up.

Tiller's pack felt disturbingly light now, minus the two containers of human remains. They'd been heavy enough that it was like carrying along a pair of living animals—small lemurs or six-legged rabbits.

She suggested to Carnelian that they rebalance their respective loads. They lifted and lowered each other's bags, trying to figure out an equitable distribution of weight.

It took some minutes for them to reach an accord. Carnelian kept accusing her of trying to take on more than her share.

"You're projecting," Tiller said tartly.

The blue sky and the mottled Forest appeared equally infinite. Sweet mountain breezes stirred the silver of Carnelian's hair.

They had stacked ten stones for each brother in the shadow of the Radish Monolith. One for every year that Gren and Rozen had lived. And one extra, to stand for all the years they'd lost.

"Why you?" Tiller asked.

She hadn't really meant to say it. She wouldn't have expected Carnelian to notice, either—except that Carnelian was always listening. Even when she appeared lost in her own distant thoughts.

As proof, she'd tilted her head like a puzzled hunting dog.

Tiller forged onward. "I understand why the Scholar needed me and Gren. He wanted blues so badly that he tried to grow us like a farmer.

"But of all the mages he experimented on, why did you end up being the one to get transplants? Instead of having your core taken. Like the rest of them."

"Ah," Carnelian uttered. "I always asked myself the same thing. Why me?" She stooped by Rozen's stone pile as though to assess its structural integrity. Just one final check. Although the Forest could very well open a sinkhole and swallow it whole the moment they turned their backs.

"Part of it must've been his interest in twins," she began.

She kept speaking. In Carnelian's view, the rest came down to pure process of elimination. She hadn't been the only transplant recipient in the Scholar's care. But she did end up being the only one who survived with her mind mostly intact.

Others—their cores didn't take. Or their cores attacked each other. It got ugly. The longer Carnelian lasted, the greater the Scholar's interest.

"I was just a stupid kid," she said. "I had nothing to do with my own survival. My extra cores got integrated through sheer luck.

"It hurt so bad. Every time. I wished it wouldn't work. I prayed to be a failure. I hated the fact that I was becoming something more and more different from my brother.

"I thought maybe if it went horribly wrong, the Scholar would have to take out my transplants. Put me back to normal again."

Tiller's immediate reaction: "He wouldn't have. Never. Not if he let your predecessors die from it."

"You see the flaw in my logic," Carnelian said. "I did bring it up once. I asked him if he'd remove my cores to save my life. Core extraction is risky, he told me. And observing the rejection process can be extremely informative."

"He didn't attempt any transplants on your brother," Tiller said. "Or did he?"

"That's how he kept me compliant. If he couldn't use me as a vessel for transplants, he'd try it out with Rozen next."

Their packs secured, they began maneuvering back down the mountain.

On a technical level, Carnelian was living evidence of the Scholar's brilliance. After centuries of unproven theories and crackpot experiments, he'd been the first researcher in recorded history to succeed at magic core implantation. Carnelian spoke dryly about all the failed attempts that had come before him—a history familiar only to specialists.

"But enough of that," she said crisply, eyes on the ground. They both had to look down to avoid tripping over a strangled mess of rocks and roots. "Let's talk marriage."

"Big change of subject."

"Didn't you say foresters go up in the mountains to get married? We were just there. We forgot to plan our ceremony."

"What a shame," Tiller said in a monotone.

"Ever get taken to a forester wedding?"

"I only know what it's like from stories."

"What's the ritual?"

Tiller racked her memory. "...They—the couple getting married—they'd go past the plateau where we stopped. They'd go alone to the sacred spring and drink its water from each other's hands. Then they'd bathe in it."

"Just bathing." Carnelian sounded incredulous. "Really?"

"No one would do anything untoward in the sacred spring," Tiller retorted.

"You sure about that?"

"It feeds water to all the rivers and ponds and falls downstream. Anyway, they'd spend the night up on the mountain after bathing."

"That's more like it," said Carnelian. "Shall we give it a try?"

But the sacred spring—the one Tiller knew, the one claimed by the people of Koya—filled a caldera on the far side of the mountain. The exact opposite of the direction they needed to go to make their way out of here. It was also very close to the place where the Scholar had held them captive.

She didn't want to set foot anywhere within sight of his bunker.

She didn't want to check and see if the structure still stood intact (like Koya Village), or if the Forest had digested it (like the lost resettlement camps).

She especially didn't want to look at the spring waters and picture the Scholar planting his seeds to grow blues. Pushing in men and women, foresters and outsiders.

No—it must have been almost all foresters. It would've been so much easier for him to get away with making foresters disappear without a trace. Huge numbers of them, even. Who would bother to investigate?

At Carnelian's urging, they took a brief break beside a kumquat tree. More of a bush, really. Slender fruit-studded branches protruded next to their faces and necks.

The little oval kumquats were perfectly ripe, their skin a sallow glossy orange. Tiller plucked them and popped them in her mouth whole, one at a time, as if gobbling up grapes.

"All right," Carnelian said. "One last thing." She bent to fish a single coin from her bag. "Demon or swords?"

"What's on the line?"

"The winner gets to ask one favor."

Very suspicious. "Like what?"

"Something that can be done right here, before we reach the foot of the mountain. Something that can be given or denied easily. No hard feelings."

"Swords," Tiller said on a whim.

She lost the coin toss.

Carnelian wore an irrepressible grin. "I'm not a seasoned gambler for nothing."

"Did you cheat?"

She raised her chin. "I am a woman of honor, I'll have you know."

"That doesn't sound like a *no*," Tiller said sourly.

"Can you guess what I'll ask for?"

This game was a blatant ploy to leaven the mood. Tiller chewed and swallowed one last tart-sweet kumquat as she considered the context.

"A kiss?" she guessed.

Carnelian folded her arms. "Explain yourself."

"You asked about forester marriage traditions."

"And?"

"Figured you were feeling romantic."

"Actually," Carnelian said, "I was going to ask for a nice hard slap across the face."

Now it was Tiller's turn to fold her arms. "Explain yourself," she parroted.

"You may have already guessed this," Carnelian said delicately, "but I'm quite a degenerate."

"No. Really?"

"It would be a gift to *me* if you hit me, or whipped me, or choked me."

"You never mentioned a word of that in our tent," Tiller said.

"There's a proper order to this sort of thing, isn't there? You undress each other with your eyes before you undress each other with your hands. You establish a bit of rapport before confessing your tawdry secrets."

"So which will it be?" Tiller asked. "A kiss or a slap? It's all the same to me."

Carnelian looked genuinely torn. "...I'll take the kiss."

"At least remove your gloves first."

"You don't like them?"

"I like variety."

At this point Tiller's mouth was just shaping words for the sake of it.

She took Carnelian's gloveless hands and found them colder than she remembered. Colder out here beneath warm sunvines than in the fog-swaddled tent.

"You're nervous," she said, startled.

Carnelian's fingers curled through hers as if frightened of letting go. "I—"

Tiller kissed her.

Perhaps Tiller would also have enjoyed the catharsis of delivering a good solid open-handed smack. But it was not, in fact, all the same to her.

She didn't think about what she would've asked for if she'd won. She didn't need to. She kissed Carnelian as if they'd seen the coin toss end in swords. She kissed Carnelian as if she were claiming her prize.

# 50

"I THOUGHT," Carnelian said accusingly, "I thought you'd go for a little peck on the side of my mouth."

"Not chaste enough?" Tiller began to pry her fingers free.

Carnelian let go with a start.

"That was more of a favor than I earned. It was only one coin toss."

"You'll just have to live with it," Tiller said. "No time for a redo."

The tang of kumquats still lingered on her tongue. Carnelian must have tasted it, too. Hopefully sharing the mere taste wouldn't count as feeding her Forest food. A sudden bout of illness would slow them down far more than a couple of kisses.

The birds sounded different from before. Tiller had stopped hearing them altogether when her eyes closed and she swallowed the gasp at the back of Carnelian's throat.

Now songbirds chorused from all sides as if angry at being forgotten. In this part of the Forest, it was mating season.

They discussed their new deadline as they retraced their steps down the mountain. Carnelian's pointy ear cuffs remained useless. Tiller tried fidgeting with her spiky silver clematis pin, but it too maintained an obstinate silence.

Nothing to be gained by agonizing over it, Carnelian reminded her. There were limits to what the military would be willing to communicate through a device provided by a foreigner, anyway.

Here and there, the canopy opened enough to see the quilt of the Forest blanketing the rest of the mountainside. Old green and new green; vibrant fall hues oozing down into valleys like a magma flow.

What season was it supposed to be in the rest of Jace? Spring? By now the cherry blossoms of Nui City might have fallen to carpet streets and waterways. The pale pink petals would soon turn to a brown trodden mush like dirty snow. It might be time for roe flowers to begin budding instead. People would take that as their cue to start putting up decorations for the Feast of Chalices.

In the Forest, all such thoughts felt like a tale from another life.

They traversed a stand of topsy-turvy trees with leafy roots down below. Their wide naked branches supported cake-like shelves of dirt, aerial gardens that held miniature replicas of Forest bowers. Trees the height of a finger. Dainty growths of moss that resembled a sprayed-on coating of sapphire dust.

"Do you think I did enough?" Tiller asked.

Carnelian gave her a questioning look.

"I just dropped the jars in there," Tiller said. "No speech. Nothing else. You seemed surprised."

"Would foresters usually give a speech?" Carnelian kept going before Tiller could answer. "No—that doesn't matter. You did your best."

She nodded to herself, then said it again. "It's true, isn't it? You did your best."

Once or twice—very rarely—Baba Sayo had said the same thing.

*You've worked hard enough.*

*You did your best.*

She would utter it without looking Tiller in the eye. Not because she didn't mean it. Because there were times when, for both of them, eye contact felt like staring into an open wound.

Tiller had started working from the age of ten. As soon as they fled the Forest. So had all the villagers, even those already battling to cover up early signs of dementia.

Tiller was the youngest of them by many decades, and the only child. Compulsory education went up to the age of twelve in Jace, though a majority of children stayed in school until their late teens.

As with many things, foresters seemed to be an exception. Tiller never set foot in a classroom. It took a couple years just to settle the matter of her family register.

Before the Koya Foundation took off, Doe strung together odd jobs guarding public buildings and high-risk vorpal holes.

Tiller would ply her knife-sharpening trade on the streets nearby: carting about her whetstone, piping a bamboo flute she'd brought from the Forest. She'd had to learn the melodies used by other street sharpeners. (She also had to take care not to intrude on their territory.)

Doe instructed her to stay within earshot. Or at least within the same neighborhoods where Doe worked. Even if doing so might severely limit her earnings.

Doe also told her that if anyone suspicious approached, she'd better stab them with one of her customers' knives.

Luckily, it never quite came to that. Rumors of blue hunters and threats against Tiller increased in proportion with the endowment of the Koya Foundation. In those early days, no one who mattered seemed to recognize her as a blue.

Baba Sayo, for her part, did custodial work at a penitentiary for incurable mages. Those who too easily went berserk. Or had felonies on their record. Or a diagnosis of chronic defiance.

She was more of a cleaner than a caretaker. That's what Doe said, at least. Tiller never heard much about it.

She hoped Baba Sayo had not been cruel to them. But she couldn't deny that Baba Sayo might have thought of them as proxies for the Scholar. She might have derived a cold satisfaction from seeing them drugged and disoriented, locked up, powerless.

Other aged villagers swept sidewalks. Outside rich condominiums, they filled trash bags with fallen leaves and masses of roeberry bark. They hunched over to pluck every last speck of moss from between bricks.

They would've worked till their bodies broke, and then some. They would've worked till it killed them.

They had no pension, no career history, no insurance. They had to labor with twisted backs and aching joints just to make people think they were worthy of sharing the air of the city.

The first big anonymous donation to the Foundation—Carnelian's donation—changed all that. Carnelian's donation changed their lives.

By issuing a single check, she transformed the Foundation into a powerhouse with the ability to quench foresters' suffering.

Carnelian saved them.

Tiller yanked at one of the straps hanging from Carnelian's backpack. "That thing you said by the fire caves."

"Which part of it?" Her mouth puckered as if in reaction to a foul aftertaste.

"You made it sound like I should've pushed you in. Don't say things you don't mean."

A white moth veered between them. Carnelian ducked. Afterwards she straightened with a sheepish air. She might've mistaken it for something more vicious.

"And what," she asked, "makes you think I didn't mean it?"

"You don't want me to hate you," Tiller said. "You definitely don't want me to kill you. You enjoy life too much to let go of it. You've even been enjoying this trek."

"I do have a delightfully sunny personality," Carnelian pronounced.

"Most people wouldn't like it here. Most people from outside would view the Forest as an uninhabitable and alien land. Literally sickening to them."

Carnelian fixed her with a protracted glance.

"You've got me there," she said eventually. "Despite everything, I love it. The light and shade in the Forest. The taste of treated water. The little birds that sound like alarm clocks.

"I love life in the city, too. Expensive drinks. Dank clubs. Crowds screeching when I lose a terrible bet. The smell of coffee beans roasting in a tiny shop. Waking up with or without anyone next to me.

"It's funny, isn't it? I love a lot of things."

No topic felt taboo now. They kept talking.

The Scholar was the one who'd taught Carnelian how to play cards, how to play dice, how to play all the great board games of conquest. And how to always win a coin toss.

"I knew it," Tiller said. She couldn't claim to be surprised.

If the Scholar gambled, he wouldn't win every round. However, he would always come out on top in the end.

He explained how to count cards, but Carnelian never really got it. He explained the math behind dice games, but it went way over her head.

Despite his fondness for betting, he looked down on addicts of all kinds. He would glance at them and say: *Why don't you just stop?*

"I could hear him thinking it whenever I wept," Carnelian said. "*Why don't you just stop?* That voice became part of me long before his core went inside me.

"I still hear it. At the worst of times and in the worst of places. With all my blood money, I've walked past people living under bridges and felt myself wondering: *Why don't you just stop?* He infected me like a poison."

Her eyes slid past Tiller. She seemed about to say something more, but she didn't.

The strange shadows dappling their surroundings came from clouds, Tiller realized. They were back at the edge of the wide-open log jam. Bare wood lay strewn all the way to the horizon, a scene like bodies heaped up after an endless battle.

Tiller saw the figure first.

Someone quite small stood alone in the desolate field of petrified trunks.

She elbowed Carnelian. She started to warn her that there was a phage watching them—the first phage to show itself in quite a while.

Carnelian didn't hear a word of it. She'd gone as rigid as the fallen logs.

The far-off phage looked across at them without moving a muscle.

"Rozen," Carnelian whispered.

Her lips scarcely moved. Her voice sounded like the voice of a stranger. But there was no mistaking what she'd said.

# 51

Carnelian spoke again. Tiller felt the despair of it all the way down in the soles of her feet.

"Rozen...?"

And again, though the phage couldn't possibly hear her. "*You're Rozen.*"

The phage did not have red hair.

Its face and clothing appeared weirdly indistinct. It resembled a child—a washed-out ghost of a child.

It took a few lunging steps in their direction. Carnelian trembled. Tiller knew this, somehow, without touching her.

Then the phage turned and ran away. Fleet as a deer. Toward the mountain. Tiller's pulse lurched along at a speed that made the rest of her feel fatally weak.

"It's him." Carnelian's voice had gone alarmingly calm. "It's my brother."

She was starting to move. She was starting to follow the phage that had already fled out of sight. It—he?—had vanished with the surety of a vulnerable bird accustomed to hiding in hollows and leaves.

Tiller grabbed her. "If you're right—if your brother is a phage—" She could barely get the words out. "Then what about—"

Carnelian looked blankly over her shoulder.

"You dumped them all in the fire caves. Didn't you? The Scholar, Rozen, Gren—"

"I thought I did," Carnelian said.

"You *thought* you did?"

"The Scholar—yes. At the end, my Float skill gave out on me. I dropped him on the rocks. Something cracked. I had to roll him over the edge with my hands. The fire took him."

"Our brothers," Tiller said. "What about our brothers?"

"...I don't know anymore."

Tiller wanted to hurl her down among the logs. Tiller wanted to stand over her and scream. "How can you not know?"

"The whole time we were locked up, I got almost no maintenance."

Carnelian spoke in flat practiced tones, as if this were a story she'd learned by heart. Her eyes remained fixed on the distant border where thick living woods resurfaced to swallow the log jam, where the many-colored sacred mountain rose arrogantly against a bleached sky.

"The Scholar was a mage, too," Tiller said.

"The Scholar never needed much maintenance. Compared to others. I wasn't so lucky. He made your brother treat me and Rozen. But your brother had no training."

Operators weren't born knowing how to fix a breaking mage. Just like how your average layperson didn't wake up one day with a perfect understanding of how to cook a souffle. Most people had to be taught the basics step by step.

"He drugged me to lower the risk of berserking," Carnelian said. "I was still myself. I was still in my own mind. But I was woozy. I don't remember every moment with absolute clarity.

"All the questioning after getting rescued, all their attempts to reconstruct what happened—I got lost in it. I'd believe you if you told me I made the whole thing up."

She lifted Tiller's hand from her arm.

"I'm sorry," she said with finality. "I have to go after him. Leave the Forest without me."

"I'm your operator." Tiller pointed at the mark of the snake, the badge Colonel Istel had given her. "What if I order you to put on your gloves and your mantle? What if I order you to stay at my side?"

"You want to pull rank?" There was a hint of pity in how Carnelian regarded her. "With me? Here in the Forest, where it'll take days or weeks for anyone to find us?"

Tiller tried not to look at the magic branches swishing back and forth in her belly, the quiet lashing of a predator's tail. The air by the log jam was frigid. Downright wintry.

Impotence closed up around her like a body bag. It left her light-headed. Unsure of where or how she stood. But her voice clawed out of her anyway.

Never again would she be caught doing nothing while someone braver than her turned and left.

"You're a mage," she said through her teeth. "I'm commanding you. As your operator. You know what it means to disobey."

Carnelian pivoted. She patted Tiller on the shoulder. Again that air of pity. "I'm sorry," she repeated. "I've always been a bit defective."

The old aphorisms whispered themselves in Tiller's ears.

*Magic is a fatal poison. Operators are the only antidote.*

*A mage without an operator is like a battleship without a captain.*

*There's nothing more dangerous than a mage who can't listen.*

"Before you go," Tiller said, "leave me your sword. The one that can cut through anything."

"My sword?" Carnelian sounded taken aback. "You aren't used to handling it."

"Leave it in your place. That's the least you can do, if you can't execute your duty to protect me."

"The weapons you've trained with would serve you much—"

"Maybe with your sword I'll have a better chance of surviving when more phages come. Maybe I'll get away with losing just a single arm or leg. Instead of being fully absorbed. Or maybe I'll end up becoming the next phage you insist on chasing. You can do the honors. Crack the base of my neck. Bleed on me. Watch me turn into flowers."

As Tiller spoke, she could see Carnelian imagining this—as vivid as a memory of something that had already happened.

Emotions without any word for them crossed Carnelian's face like a shadow play. Her eyes were that tenuous gray, hungry for color, that always seemed to dye themselves in the residue of her surroundings: the green and gold of the Forest, the mossy blue of village huts. There was nothing she could borrow from the devastation of the log jam.

She turned aside and coughed into her hand. A sharp ugly hacking. Unnaturally loud amidst the open space that spread like a trampled cemetery all around them.

She'd coughed out two of the small brown rocks she called pearls.

She tossed one high in the air. It zigzagged away with the swift irregularity of an angered wasp. She closed her fist around the other.

"You're right," she said. No emotion lingered in her voice. "I have a duty to you. Above all else. Not because of me being a mage, and you being an operator. I don't give a shit about that, frankly. It's because I—"

Tiller cut in. "If you saw your brother as a phage, I agree that we should go after him. Both of us."

Carnelian gaped. "You—what?"

Tiller held out a hand. "Give me that second pearl."

Carnelian passed it to her without a word. It was still damp from her mouth, and infused with the peculiar warmth of a fresh-laid egg.

It made no attempt to go flying away like its twin. Yet when Tiller curled her fingers shut to trap it, she felt a fragile tug like the death throes of an old, old magnet.

She shoved her hand in her pocket. "To me it looked like any other child-sized phage," she said. "But I believe in your ability to recognize your own brother."

"You tried to order me to stay."

"You tried to ditch me. That's no way to treat someone who carries your necklace of teeth."

Carnelian still appeared thoroughly flummoxed. She raked one hand through her hair, then another, as if surprised to find it all still there.

"He—it's a remnant of my brother," she said helplessly. "*My* brother. Tiller. There's no reason for you to—"

"There's no reason for us to separate. If we go anywhere, we go together."

"The deadline—

"If we fail to escape before the chalices come, so be it. We'll live. Somehow. You were the one who said not to worry. Anyway, you'd be lost in the Forest without me."

This was indisputably true, and they both knew it.

"Don't you dare claim I've got no reason to come along," Tiller added. "Think about it. Your brother just showed up as a phage. Twenty years after donating his core to you. Twenty years after dying."

She didn't have to spell it out in detail.

Carnelian's gaze darkened.

With a murmured apology, she slipped her hand in Tiller's pocket, making her jump. Carnelian was not a subtle thief.

"You know your way around the Forest much better than me," she conceded. "But I know way more than you about using this."

Her so-called pearl led them back up the side of the sacred mountain.

52

# 52

Soon they were back at the plateau with the Radish Monolith. A sulky breeze carried over the clean scent of the fire caves.

Rozen's phage had ascended halfway up the monolith. It clung to the gargantuan white radish with the ease of a crabrabbit. After glimpsing them, it scuttled back out of sight.

They circled the monolith—Carnelian approaching from one side, Tiller from the other—but Rozen was long gone. They moved on.

Tiller couldn't understand how the skill called Homing Pearls was supposed to work. Back on the train, she'd perused Carnelian's halfhearted attempt at a written explanation. She'd watched the pearls wound hunters at the Temple of Combat and Chains. She'd watched them catch fish for her in the Forest.

All that was days or weeks ago. This time Carnelian had deployed her pearls in a rather different manner. She'd sent one coursing after her quarry. She kept its twin close by to guide them.

Well, Tiller wasn't the one in charge of using the pearls. She didn't need to comprehend every nuance of their functionality.

It was difficult to reconcile her memories of Rozen—the mute boy in a cage—with this bloodless-looking phage. Any resemblance seemed superficial at best.

But they kept sighting the phage up ahead. Even as it scampered away from them over and over, speedy as an insect with too many legs.

Sometimes it would pause and look back, waiting for them to catch up. Making sure they were still following.

The trees thickened again on the far side of the plateau. They weren't crowded: the most substantial trunks grew much further apart than city houses. Even so, the canopy knitted shut overhead—too far overhead, as usual, to really see it.

The sunvines here were a shrewd and cautious sort. Rather than dangle freely, they wound tight around the grand conifers, tight enough to make the wood of their hosts bulge outward. The space between the all-dwarfing trees felt dim and hushed and unfamiliar.

Down at the log jam, Tiller had been galvanized by an adrenaline similar to the dread of witnessing a bicycle accident in the city. The screech of brakes, a thump, a child crying, pedestrians freezing. The stomach-clenching seconds that came before ascertaining that nobody had died on the spot. The shaky relief after everyone got up and went their own way.

A similar relief had flooded her after Carnelian agreed not to go galloping off on her own. It was a relief so deep that for a time no space remained to feel anything else. But apprehension came creeping back soon enough.

"Nel," she said. "What will you do with him?"

"Nel?" Carnelian echoed. "That's a new one."

She had not, presumably, sent her scouting pearl to pierce her brother's phage. Unlike the Guild hunters at the temple. Or the trout she'd sniped underwater.

Tiller asked the same question again.

"I'll do what I have to," Carnelian answered.

"Will you really be able to put him down?"

"I know it's not Rozen," Carnelian said. "I know it's something—something else in there. Reanimating his body. Like a parasite taking over the shell of its host. I'll lay him to rest."

She had her fist out in front of her as if holding an invisible leash. Her eyes remained on the path ahead.

"I know what you want to ask. You want to make sure I'm not wondering if maybe he's still somewhere in there. Somewhere deep in that bleached body. If maybe he isn't truly dead.

"I never wondered that about any of the other phages I've dispatched," she said. "I mean—I wondered at first. Everyone does. Then you look into their eyes. You observe their behavior. You see them scar your coworkers, or pinch their limbs off like hunks of dough. Soon you realize there's no reason to wonder at all.

"It would be the height of hypocrisy to regress from that now, of all times. Every other phage whose head I crushed and anointed used to be somebody's brother or husband or mother. They just weren't mine."

Since when, Tiller thought, had the prospect of hypocrisy held enough power to change how anyone felt at the very heart of their being?

Facing your own twin's body in battle had to be something very different from facing a stranger.

Climbing turtles bore silent witness to their passage, blending in seamlessly with the bark around them. Only the occasional slow motion of a beady-eyed head or clawed foot betrayed their presence.

The tops of the behemoth trees must have been packed with all kinds of creatures and plant life that rarely came in sight of ground. Ones even foresters were unlikely to witness, and might not have any name for.

If such animals died and came crashing down from a treetop biome, their remains would soon transform into something entirely different.

Tiller and Gren had climbed very high in the trees as children. Much higher than Baba Sayo ever knew. But it had been decades since she'd exercised those skills. She'd never attempted it with the body of an adult. And falling seemed like a far realer prospect than it used to.

"Can you tell where we're going?" Carnelian asked. "Where my—where the phage is taking us."

"Are you testing me?"

"I'm every bit as lost as you said I'd be. The only reason I don't think we're going in circles is that I figure you'd point it out if we were."

"I would," Tiller said. "We're not."

"Then—"

"We're coming up on the caldera. On the opposite side of the mountain."

"The caldera with the sacred...." Carnelian trailed off.

"The sacred spring of Koya. And before that," Tiller said, in as factual a tone as possible, "the Scholar's secret house. The place where we first met. One-sidedly. The place where you first spied on me."

# 53

If they were tracking a human being, this situation would be a trap. No doubt about it.

"I wonder which has more consciousness," Carnelian said. "A phage or a sparrow?"

"Probably the sparrow," Tiller told her. "But is it fair to compare them?"

From the perspective of the Forest, perhaps humans and phages were one and the same. Any difference between them might seem no more significant than the difference between two species of deer ticks.

The sheer scope of the cedars and sequoias reduced human-size organisms to fleas crawling about the ankles of giants.

Down at ground level, stunted oracle trees grew in scattered patches of sunvine light. Solemn storks with wide opalescent beaks studied the muddy waters of a slow-moving stream.

Gnats gathered in clouds as dense and tangible as the nighttime fog.

Tiller held Carnelian's arm to keep her from getting too far ahead. An unnerving stench pervaded the suddenly stagnant air. Even more disturbing was the fact that, after another twenty minutes or so, they both stopped smelling it.

What else had their senses gone blind to?

That wasn't the only question Tiller asked herself.

Without Carnelian's recognition to prime her, would she have made any connection between this pallid phage and the red-haired boy in the cage?

Her memories had finally come into focus. Or maybe they'd reshaped themselves to match the phage's amorphous face. Whatever the reason, she now saw the resemblance, and she could no longer unsee it.

The phage paused again, resting like a frog on a tree branch. It let them get closer than ever before.

Carnelian looked gutted. And—just for a moment—quite young. Not physically, but in the plainness and openness of her desolation.

The phage turned aside as if losing interest. It slipped around to the back of its tree. It disappeared.

Beyond that tree lay the Scholar's house.

Neither of them moved.

Because of Tiller. She had her fingers wound in Carnelian's sleeve. Her feet wouldn't budge.

Liquid dripped somewhere beyond their sight. An anemic waterfall?

The house stood at the edge of a sunken crater-shaped caldera. Like a lighthouse on a seaside cliff. Behind and below it—too deep down to glimpse from here—awaited the sacred spring.

The area around the caldera must've been open to the sky at one point in time. In an era before the lost kingdom of blues. An era too old to have a name. Now they saw only the hanging gardens of the Forest above them.

The building did not look like a house, or even like a building at all.

In Tiller's memory, the Scholar's house had no real exterior. She'd spent her time there locked indoors. She'd only seen it from the outside once, on the day Doe came to free her, and she'd retained nothing of it.

"Rozen went inside," said Carnelian.

Tiller managed a nod. They moved closer.

The house had been constructed in a hollowed-out monolith. The rock was a warm sandy color, with a redder tint than the smaller boulders scattered beside it.

The monolith was all globular curves, something like an amalgamation of half-formed clay pots. No squared-off angles.

No windows, either. Sunvines were rigged to snake in through holes bored in the rock. From a distance it looked grisly: the vines could've been a swarm of parasitic worms.

When they drew close enough to touch the surface of the monolith, Tiller put an arm out. The smooth stone yielded, soft as a marshmallow. Her hand sank wrist-deep with little effort.

Carnelian yanked her back. The hand-shaped depression in the side of the monolith vanished.

Tiller plucked a rock from the ground and pushed at the monolith again, but this time it remained hard and unbending. Her rock couldn't so much as dent it. All she succeeded in doing was scraping a rough pastel chalk-mark.

She tossed the useless rock over her shoulder. "We could try to swim through the walls. But we might drown."

"Or we could use the door."

"The door," Tiller said, sardonic. "Of course. You know how to find it?"

"You're forgetting something."

"What?"

"I was the closest thing the Scholar had to an accomplice."

Carnelian drew lines on the air with her forefinger. She seemed to be tracing angles formed by the pattern of holes drilled for sunvines. Her lips moved without letting out much in the way of real sound.

She knelt and pressed the base of her palm to a spot near the bottom of the monolith. Just above where it met the clover-covered ground.

An irregular slice of stone collapsed inward, squelching like moist strips of roeberry bark.

The shape of the opening—and the squishy slab that had swooned flat to create it—was uncomfortably reminiscent of a gigantic tongue.

Before their eyes, the fallen piece of wall prostrated itself lower and lower, blending like wet clay into the hollowed-out floor.

"We used to call this the Fertility Monolith," Tiller commented.

"Why? Wait—let me guess. Hm ... it isn't shaped like anything obvious."

"No idea. I wasn't the one who named it."

"I suppose it is rather voluptuous," Carnelian said. "I don't want children, by the way. Sorry if you got your hopes up."

"Same. Depopulation was a real problem for the village, though."

"They had you, didn't they?"

"Gren and I were the first children they welcomed in decades. And we weren't even born there."

"Must not have been any new marriages for a while, either."

Tiller gave her a sideways look, unsure of her meaning.

"No one from your town knew the Scholar was squatting here."

"Right." Tiller indicated the entrance to the monolith. "No one knew a thing about him taking it for his own."

Baba Sayo hadn't understood much about what he got up to in the rest of the Forest. When he wasn't visiting—when he wasn't bugging her.

He'd roamed all over in those days. He'd stayed in villages that Baba Sayo had never heard of. Lost cities, too. He'd been fascinated by forester history.

"He must've spent years building up his bunker," Carnelian said. "Even if he drew on government resources, or hired laborers from other forester villages. It'd still take ages.

"In all those years, if anyone from Koya got married, they'd come up to the sacred spring. They'd do the rituals you told me of. They'd have passed by this place. They'd have noticed something awry. But they didn't."

"There were no marriages," Tiller concurred. "No births. No new blood. Only deaths. For years before Gren and I turned up."

"So the Scholar could've been working on this hideout for decades."

They left their bags leaning up against the outer wall of the monolith, wrapped in a silky waterproof cloth that Carnelian pulled from a container the size of a cough drop.

Tiller laid her basher down, too. It was not meant for use in confined spaces.

She wore Carnelian's mantle, with the gloves and their cords clipped neatly out of the way.

The mantle's additional pocket space gave her room to carry the autoinjector of sedatives she'd gotten from Colonel Istel. Plus her remaining nausea pellets, and the half-empty tin of immobility ticks, and basic first aid supplies.

They brought their usual set of smaller-scale weapons as well. Carnelian's fighting pipe and pilfered gun. Tiller's yo-yo knives and machete.

Carnelian led the way into the monolith. For safety purposes, she argued that she'd better go first.

Rozen's phage had not acted particularly aggressive yet. But close quarters and phages were always a dangerous combination. There might be other phages deeper inside, too, residing in crannies of the monolith like a colony of bats.

The interior walls pretended to be regular hard stone. Tiller could not bury her fingers in them as if poking holes in a pie.

Some of these corridors preceded the Scholar. The Fertility Monolith had always had chambers hollowed out inside it. Baba Sayo used to describe it that way when she told Tiller and Gren of the sacred spring on the other side of the mountain.

No matter how it piqued their interest, she refused to take them there—as she refused to take them to the fire caves. The mountain was not a place to go on a whim.

Tiller had no direct knowledge of how crude or sophisticated the artificial caverns in the monolith had been before the Scholar moved in. Their creation predated any recorded history of Koya Village.

As with everything else in the Scholar's life, here too was another area where he hadn't been starting from scratch. He was far from the first person to think of burrowing into the Fertility Monolith.

He'd seized on what he stumbled across and claimed it for his own, as if there were no other possible outcome.

The sunvines that pierced the monolith walls so wildly were, on the inside, tightly controlled. Translucent tubes sheathed them, restricting their growth. The tubes were bound to the ceiling in neat parallel lines like train tracks.

So far, nothing looked familiar. Tiller's months here had been spent almost entirely in one single room.

The reverberation of their footsteps and breathing stimulated a vulnerable spot on the underside of her brain. A part of her that scrabbled desperately for something to recognize.

There was a strangeness to how this space handled sound. It sucked up every noise and then spat the weakened leftovers back out at them, subtly altered. Carnelian's fingers opened and closed fitfully around the homing pearl in her right hand.

They passed multiple storerooms fitted with regular sliding doors. None were locked. One contained a formidable supply of packaged rations and canned food from outside the Forest.

Tiller nudged Carnelian. "Didn't you say the Scholar used to dose you with Forest food?"

"In every meal," said Carnelian. "I was constantly queasy. And dehydrated. Made real good friends with my toilet hole."

"Doesn't look like he was anywhere close to running out of imports."

Carnelian let out a bleak little laugh. "He would've preferred to feed all of us nothing but Forest produce. Unfortunately for him, his years spent building up a tolerance hadn't exactly turned him into an expert forager."

The only taste Tiller recalled from her meals choked down in captivity was an overwhelming, tongue-coating saltiness. The flavor of food processed and sealed far away from the Forest.

Another stockroom was filled with a jumble of vintage magical artifacts. Mostly communication devices. Mirrors, masks, teeth and ear implants, glasses, hair pins, pendants, compacts, combs.

Only one or two had any perceptible trace of magic remaining. For the most part, their mage creators must have died years and years ago.

Carnelian poked at a hearing aid. "I'm surprised the government just left this. You'd think someone out there would be interested in confiscating the Scholar's collection."

"They barely spared a large enough crew to rescue living children," Tiller said.

"Guess it would've been too costly to salvage the rest of his junk all the way from the heart of the Forest."

They marched up and down stone stairs with rounded corners.

In some of the highest rooms, the walls were whittled as thin as a membrane. Thin enough that Tiller could see shadows of trees on the other side. Yet the rock refused to bend like chewing gum at her touch. It didn't even feel especially vulnerable.

Outside it must have started to rain softly. She needed a minute or two to comprehend the sound of it. Everything became distorted inside the monolith.

They ventured lower again. The mournful hissing of the rain gradually retreated.

Though made of rock, the monolith was something like an iceberg. Its body extended far underground, wide and deep. The visible portion of it might look impressive from a human perspective, but its hidden bulk was far greater.

They crossed a gallery of forester trophies—demonic statues and religious tokens from distant villages. Tiller couldn't tell Carnelian much about any of these. She knew little of what beliefs used to exist in places beyond Koya territory.

One wall showcased sliced-off ponytails of blue hair, long as snakes. They were old enough to have faded to a color like bread mold.

The largest room they encountered had the structure of a morgue.

It was empty of bodies.

Carnelian immediately backed out and shut the door to the morgue. She kept sneezing despite the eerie dearth of visible dust.

Tiller asked if she wanted to step outside for fresh air.

"Let's get it over with," Carnelian said. "This pearl is leading us all over the place. But I think I know where it's trying to go now."

She stopped Tiller in a hallway that felt far too narrow and far too tall. "I'll check out the next room alone."

"Why risk separating?" Tiller asked.

"Never mind. There's another way. We can skip—"

Tiller peeked around her.

The room behind her had a hinged door without any handle or knob.

The door was still closed. It would need to open inward. The corridor didn't have nearly enough space to accommodate it.

Tiller reached past Carnelian to push at it. Nothing happened.

"I realized something," Carnelian said conversationally. "Some of the entrances are keyed to respond only to me. Although I suppose you could get around it by blasting them open."

No real tension permeated her face or her voice. She had one relaxed hand resting on the rough stone around the door frame. The way you might place a hand on the withers of a familiar horse.

"To be specific—the doors aren't keyed to *Carnelian Silva*," she amended. "They recognize the Scholar's core in me. That's what unlocks them. I can open every last hidden room in here. Because the doors think I'm him."

"When they needed to, the Corps would've found other ways to break in. But with time, the doors fixed themselves. They scabbed over like a skinned knee."

Carnelian was making a valiant effort to distract her. It didn't work.

"I know this door," Tiller said.

"I'm telling you, we don't have to—"

"Let me in."

She felt herself pulled forward, Carnelian's arms around her.

It was an embrace of frightening intensity. And not at all like the intensity she showed in the secret world of their tent at night, cushioned by fog. More like a mountain climber clinging to their partner above a deadly crevasse. Tiller couldn't tell which of them was on the verge of falling.

Just as suddenly, Carnelian released her.

Carnelian turned and pressed her palm to the door without a knob. Something—many things—clicked in succession. Tiller's insides hitched. The door swung inward.

# 54

The walls were as Tiller remembered. Rutted organic rock like the inside of a cave, carelessly whitewashed. The coating of paint made it look even wronger. Shadow-pocked and sickly pale.

The cage that used to hold Rozen stood wide open and empty.

The room had few other identifying features.

Her eyes skipped to a far corner of the floor, half-hidden by an aggressive bulge in the wall. An opening awaited there, lidded like a manhole.

At the age of nine, she'd pried off the heavy lid to use it as a toilet. The air below was unnaturally scentless, and unfathomably deep. She'd always been terrified of falling in.

She and Gren would speak of jumping in on purpose to escape. But they had no idea where it led. The Forest, after all, had no sewer system.

The Scholar claimed that a vorpal hole lay beneath, capable of nullifying infinite amounts of waste. Or any number of little children.

That sounded rather too convenient. But neither of them dared to put it to the test.

Rozen—in the brief moments when the Scholar let him out of his cage to relieve himself—showed no interest in diving through the hole, either. It would be like leaping into an unlit well, one with no promise of a landing cushioned by water.

Tube-stuffed sunvines, bolted to the ceiling, misted the room with a fine shower of endless light. Some were swollen to the point of cracking their translucent casing.

Time flowed backwards in this room. If it flowed at all.

The craggy serrations of the walls and floor greeted Tiller like old friends. She and Gren used to perceive faces in the rock. A man with heavy eyebrows. A noble skink. A hungry hawk.

They would make up stories about their stony brethren. Just like how they—well, mostly Gren—used to make up stories to perform for the village.

Here they had no one to watch them except the boy in the cage. He had been a very tough audience.

Carnelian reached for the cage but stopped short of touching it.

"Did the Scholar ever tell you why he locked my brother up?"

"Not clearly," Tiller said. The words didn't come easily.

"It's an antique." Carnelian patted the air above the bars. "Made from materials resistant to magical intervention. Not unbreakable, but better than nothing. Berserk mages used to get kept in cages like this."

"We never saw your brother use any magic." Age and emotion might've polluted her memories, but Tiller felt sure of this.

"The Scholar stripped his skills," said Carnelian. "Before shutting us up in here. All Rozen's branches got blanked. Even if he wanted to use magic, he had no way to channel it. Not on purpose. Not without berserking. And he never actually went berserk."

"Then why stash him in a crate like a dog?"

"Why indeed." At last Carnelian looked away from the cage. "That's the really maddening part. Cruelty wasn't even the point of it.

"The Scholar shoved him in here with you like a pack of frozen chicken. The only objective was to keep the magic inside him safely preserved until the time came to use him."

"To take his core," Tiller said. "And give it to you."

"Rozen was always more prone to tangling than me. One step closer to going berserk—at least in theory. The tangling hurt him worse, too.

"The Scholar couldn't be bothered to get him proper treatment from an operator. Not this deep in the Forest. Instead he popped Rozen full of tranquilizers and locked him in a containment cage. Minimum effort."

Tiller's vision had begun blurring as they spoke. At first she thought it came from the mental effort of holding the past at bay.

She thought wrong. The air itself had grown cloudier.

Nightfall remained a long ways off. She wouldn't have expected to see fog sneak this deep underground, regardless.

Carnelian noticed it at the same time as her. She pushed Tiller back out into the narrow hall.

"It's coming from below," Tiller said.

"My pearl wants us to go deeper, too." Carnelian knitted her brows. "I never...."

The mellow pattering of rain had long since ceased to be audible. Carnelian led her to a hidden entrance further down the hall.

Here lay a room adjacent to the whitewashed cavern where the Scholar had held Tiller and Rozen and Gren.

This was the solitary room from which Carnelian used to watch them. She'd stared through a wall that, on her side, appeared as transparent as the glass of an aquarium.

Tiller's mind lingered far behind the rest of her. It kept circling back to the same question like a scavenger gnawing at a carcass already stripped bare of all flesh.

Why had the Scholar kidnapped them to a house in the Forest?

He maintained dwellings all over the country. The rest would inevitably have better equipment. Why even go to the trouble of secretly annexing the Fertility Monolith?

Did he assume the government and military would turn against him much more quickly than they had in reality? Had he hidden in the depths of the Forest as a way of delaying pursuit?

Or had he always planned on attempting something that would only succeed in this one specific location?

Had his dabbling in anthropology taught him that the sacred land of the Forest was the best place to sacrifice a blue?

"This way," Carnelian said, an unusually bitter note in her voice.

At her touch, new downward steps formed in the floor, a soundless sinkhole. Fog rose like steam from the surface of a hot spring, diluting as it mingled with the clearer air above. Sunvine-packed pipes lined the stairs as if they had always been there.

Despite their dryness, the rocky steps felt perilously slippery underfoot. They emanated a smell of festering age.

None of the rescuers from twenty years ago would've ventured down here. They wouldn't even have noticed the existence of this deeper space.

The path revealed itself only to Carnelian—to the core of the Scholar within her.

The Scholar had been adept with camouflage, magical and otherwise. Back in the day, he'd shamelessly cozied up to Baba Sayo and the rest of Koya Village. He must've endeared himself to other villages in much the same way.

The echo of their steps took on an arrhythmic cadence. Tiller's pulse spasmed in every part of her except the place where it belonged in her chest.

She groped for Carnelian's shoulder. "No one's been down this route since the Scholar."

Carnelian waited for her to continue.

"How could your brother's phage be waiting at the bottom? When did he pass us?"

Carnelian pressed the pearl into her palm. Tiller felt an unmistakable downward tug.

"I'm fine with going alone," Carnelian said.

The problem was that she really meant it. All Tiller had to do was give her blessing. Carnelian would willingly descend the rest of the steps by herself.

"I'm not fine with it," Tiller said tersely. She made Carnelian take her pearl back.

They continued on together.

These stairs would never have passed inspection in the city. They cut straight down into the monolith, not once turning a corner. Nothing to stop a long, long fall if you tripped.

The cavity at the bottom appeared half-finished. Some surfaces had been shaped into flawless smooth planes. Others, hopelessly rugged, looked like they'd never been touched by human tools.

The lopsided ceiling soared astonishingly high, with sunvines twisted to form a brilliant rosette at the peak of it.

The rock was a deeper red than in the upper levels they'd passed through earlier. Parts of it gleamed as if wet. But that sheen was merely a trick of the light. There seemed to be nothing capable of sustaining life down here, not even a meager coating of algae.

Carnelian reached for one of the unfinished walls.

Tiller interrupted her, holding her elbow. "Another door keyed to the Scholar?"

"How'd you guess?"

Tiller couldn't understand any of this. "The Scholar is dead."

Branch cuttings would die with their creator.

"Whose magic got left behind to keep this place locked up as tight as it was twenty years ago? Did he buy it from somewhere? Did he install backup after backup, different cuttings from different mages? Even then—"

"It's mine," Carnelian said. "An old branch skill. Didn't I mention it?"

In the back of her head Tiller heard the sound of train wheels numbly clacking over rail joints.

*It really only works for me, and I haven't used it in years. Great for siege situations. Not so useful for traversing the Forest.*

Her fingers slipped from Carnelian's arm.

Carnelian touched the back of her hand to the pockmarked rock.

The stone wall opened with the sound of feet squelching in mud.

The crack widened.

For a painfully stretched-out second, Tiller could not grasp what she was looking at. It was like trying to make sense of a vorpal hole.

The walls and ceiling had the look of an optical illusion. They bristled with a systematic array of deep, pointed wedges. The wedges were packed in without any wasted space between them.

She heard Carnelian take a single sharp breath. She heard it with unprecedented clarity. Intimacy, even. As if that breath scraped the insides of her own lungs.

Her throat felt as narrow as a straw.

There was little furniture. An ancient-looking spinning wheel with heavy chains piled at its feet. An old-fashioned stone bathtub, tall and deep: it might as well have been a cauldron to cook human beings like lobsters. A sleek industrial standing desk.

No one stood to work at the desk.

A boy sat atop it, legs dangling.

A boy with deathly gray skin. A gray to match the darkest bits of Baba Sayo's ashes.

A boy with pure blue hair. Long and unfaded. Bluer than the sky that foresters seldom glimpsed unbroken, living so far below the canopy.

He raised his left hand. Between his forefinger and thumb he held pinched an ugly brown pebble. One the precise size and shape of a badly stained baby tooth.

"Looking for this?" Tiller's brother asked pleasantly.

# 55

Gren—

Gren was dead.

Her ability to hope for him to be alive—to think that he never really died—was as fleeting as a shooting star.

Phages weren't supposed to know human language. Phages lost all the color from their hair. He was a phage all the same. Just like Carnelian's brother, whose once-red hair had deteriorated to a dull platinum.

She knew it with the same part of her that always knew how to navigate the Forest. Even when setting foot in unfamiliar territory. Even without a compass or a map.

Tiller could not speak. She could not move.

The homing pearl vanished from Gren's hand. Carnelian must've dismissed it, undoing her magic.

Its erasure didn't appear to startle him. He rubbed his fingertips together with a philosophical air, savoring what remained of its residue.

He cleared his throat. He cleared it several times, quite loudly. Tiller's back shivered as if at the touch of a knife.

In his stature and the roundness of his face, Gren looked exactly the same as he'd been when he'd died. A child of nine. Yet he seemed so much smaller now, so horrifically vulnerable.

Tiller had looked up to this child as her hero. Tiller had let him walk into death for her.

He cleared his throat yet again. Then: "Sorry. I was nervous to speak. It's been a while. Could you tell?"

His voice was lower and raspier than she remembered. But could memory ever conserve something as fragile as sound with perfect fidelity?

It was still very much the voice of a child.

"Gren," Tiller said. Or tried to say. At best, he might've seen her lips move.

"I do talk to myself sometimes for practice," he added. "I talked a bit once I knew you were coming down here. An emergency warm-up."

He crossed his legs atop the standing desk, hands on his ankles. He looked her over.

"Oh, Tiller," he said. "You're *old*."

The floor they stood on was covered in an airy metal grate. Slender but strong, and too well constructed for any inadvertent bouncing or rattling underfoot.

Beneath the grate lurked the same militant matrix of sharp wedges that covered the walls and ceiling with zero gaps.

No sunvines in here. A lantern rested on the desk near Gren. Another used metal claws to grip at the wide rim of the bathtub.

Water-lights, dim as candles, lit the base of the spinning wheel like an old offering. Half had gone dark.

"Wondering about the wheel and chains?" Gren asked. "The Scholar wasn't especially faithful. But he sure loved symbols of the old religion.

"He always thought the Forest was closer to the true nature of the Lord of Circles than anyone might realize or admit. Humans turning into phages. Phages turning into plants. Sacrifices at the sacred spring reappearing as blues. Life becoming life."

Tiller took an abortive step forward.

"No hugs," Gren said briskly. "I'll start absorbing you. Even if I try not to."

Carnelian wound an arm around the front of Tiller's shoulders, holding her in place. It felt, Tiller thought distantly, like the way a robber might hold a hostage.

"Where's my brother?" Carnelian asked. "Where did you put him?"

Gren shifted his gaze to her. "What will you do if I don't answer? Kill me?"

No one took a single breath.

Gren laughed hoarsely. "Just kidding." He beckoned to Carnelian. "You need maintenance," he said, all business. "Badly. Come on over and let me give you a touch-up."

"I have Tiller for that. I don't need maintenance from an untrained kid."

Gren pointed at his young face. "However I look, I'm a thirty-year-old man. Or a twenty-year-old phage. I haven't spent all that time just stewing here. I've learned things. I can tune your magic better than any human operator."

"You'll absorb me," Carnelian said.

"Yuck. No. I won't actually touch you. Afraid that I'll take my well-deserved revenge? If I wanted to absorb you, I'd already be doing it."

Tiller's emotions were a balled-up wad of paper. Crumpled in fists. Trampled underfoot. Left to dissolve in a dirty puddle. Not a trace of anything salvageable remained.

"Will you force Tiller to do the work of fixing your magic?" Gren watched Carnelian, unblinking. "Here before her dead brother? You do need it, you know. You're one bad move away from going berserk again.

"That vorpal beast really did a number on you. You're like an athlete with a permanent injury—you'll always be closer to berserking than before. Can't think of yourself as being so resistant anymore."

Tiller twisted in Carnelian's arms. Now that she knew what to look for, her magic perception told her Gren was right. He'd pinpointed the new susceptibility in Carnelian's restless branches. He'd identified it with the confidence of Asa Lantana.

But more than that—

"You saw us fight the beast?"

She hadn't even known what she was going to ask until she asked it.

"I see a lot of things," Gren said matter-of-factly. "Everything that happens in the Forest. If I wish to see it. And no, other phages aren't the same. This has more to do with being a blue than with being a phage."

He hopped down from the desk. The sound of his bare feet on the grating hit Tiller's ears like the snap of a whip.

"Can you feel the silence?" He gestured at the wedge-covered walls. "No noise from outside. No subtle echoes whatsoever.

"It's called an anechoic chamber. The Scholar put a room like this in every one of his residences. An oasis for him to do his thinking and planning.

"Most regular people would lose their minds—or at least their balance— left alone in here. For better or for worse, you really get to know yourself in a place like this. Needless to say, the Scholar loved it."

"Gren," Tiller said.

He cocked his head expectantly.

She felt old and stupid and very slow. "How do you know so much about the Scholar?"

He jabbed a thumb at Carnelian. "I was the conduit. The funnel he poured himself through to get his core in her. I know him better than any human ever knew him. Unfortunately."

His eyes narrowed. "She hasn't told you half of it, I bet. She probably doesn't even remember the worst parts. I certainly wasn't the first person he made her murder."

"That's enough," Carnelian said. "That has nothing to do with why we came here."

"You killed me," Gren retorted. "That has everything to do with it."

He reached back and took the lantern from the standing desk. He raised it up as though attempting to get a better look at their faces.

Shadows shifted across the army of tight-packed wedges surrounding them on all sides, smothering every subliminal reverberation, sucking up stray sounds with the hunger of a vorpal hole.

Tiller could hear the fullness of the air in her ears. The sound of Carnelian's arm gripping her. The sounds her own bones and insides made when she turned her head to see Carnelian's face.

Gren set the lantern down on the floor grate by his feet.

"You're overwhelmed," he said. "I understand. One thing at a time.

"Silva, you want to see your brother? Then let me give you maintenance. If you spin out of control again, who's most likely to get hurt by it? Not us phages, I can tell you that much."

"I can't do it," Tiller finally managed to say to Carnelian. "I can't do right by your magic. Not now."

She was a poor excuse for an operator even at the best of times, and she knew it.

Normally she'd be willing to try. It was the least she could do. But she saw double when she attempted to focus on Carnelian's magic, the nine clustered cores and all their dizzying branches. Her hands felt leaden at her sides, thick-fingered and dangerously clumsy.

"All right," Carnelian said. A neutral tone of assent.

She left two fingers touching the side of Tiller's wrist, as if reluctant to completely let go.

She turned to face the entrance that had seamlessly sewn itself shut once they passed. Her other hand lingered on the long reed-thin pipe she'd hooked to her belt.

It was very strange to see a warrior—even one as unconventional as Carnelian—willingly show her back to a phage.

Gren sauntered up to them and put his deep gray hand by Carnelian's lower back. He didn't directly touch her. He moved his fingers in the air as if plucking the strings of an invisible instrument.

In response, her magic branches stopped floundering inside her. They stopped trying to weave a tapestry of knots. In unison, they went flat and boneless. Relaxed and witless.

An indecipherable look crossed her face.

"You must have questions," Gren said to Tiller as he worked.

At last her voice winged back down from the stratosphere and came home to roost somewhere in her tight-pinched throat. There wasn't much space for it.

"You've always been yourself," she uttered. More of a statement than a question. "Even as a phage. You never—you've always been conscious? You remember everything?"

"The privilege of being a blue," Gren said merrily. "We don't turn into regular phages."

"You've been waiting all alone in the Forest. For twenty—for twenty-one years."

"Before he keeled over, the Scholar dumped our bodies down in the basement. Me and Rozen."

He glanced briefly at Tiller. Too briefly for eye contact. He smiled with one side of his face. The other side refused to play along.

"By the time Doe came to save you," he said, "Rozen and I had already awoken as phages. I knew who I was. He didn't. He's always been a phage like any other. Poor kid.

"We were locked up right here in this soundproof chamber. At the time, we had no idea how to get out."

He spread his fingers. It had the effect of flicking Carnelian's magic branches like the reins of a horse. A sharp, chastising flick. Nothing gentle about it.

Her hand tensed on Tiller's wrist. Tiller was reminded of clutching at Baba Sayo when they went for medical appointments in Nui City. Having blood drawn from her inner elbow. Getting the first shots she'd ever had in her life.

"The Scholar wasn't a complete liar," Gren murmured, this time to Carnelian. "Remember how he paraded me in front of you, clapped me on the shoulder? Remember what he said? *We'll give you back your brother.*

"He never claimed your brother would know you. He never claimed your brother would still be human."

He took a couple steps back. He squinted at the galaxy of magic under Carnelian's clothes and skin as though trying to ascertain whether he'd hung a painting perfectly level.

"There you go." He sounded satisfied. "That's the best shape anyone can get you in."

"Thank you," Carnelian said colorlessly.

"How can I do that?" Tiller blurted.

They both looked at her as if she'd spoken out of turn. The tyrannical silence of the room made her temples pound.

"I've been giving her maintenance to the best of my ability," she said to Gren. "You've outdone me in a single session. How can I reach your level?"

"Very simple." He slashed his forefinger across his throat. "Become a phage like me. It'll open up all kinds of new possibilities."

# 56

Only a little fog had crept into the anechoic chamber. Nothing impeded her vision, and yet Tiller's eyes forgot how to focus.

She considered what would happen if she passed out without warning. Her body would hit the grate with a terrible noise. Or maybe Carnelian would catch her.

Carnelian and Gren would look at each other over her prone body like enemy generals seated at opposite ends of a table for peace talks.

Gren didn't even come up to Tiller's shoulders. Of course he didn't: in twenty-one years, he hadn't grown a millimeter. She could look straight down at the top of his head.

He wasn't alive, strictly speaking.

But in every sense that mattered, he was the same Gren who she'd lost in this wretched prison. Back when both of them were still powerless children.

She had to close her fists to fight the impulse to touch him. To make sure his small body was real and solid. Not just an elaborate smoke sculpture.

"That rock you were holding. My pearl," Carnelian said to Gren. Her voice revealed very little. "How'd you get it?"

"A present from Rozen," he answered. "Want to see him? Open the door again. I'll show you the way."

Carnelian went over to the wall they'd originally passed through. Like every other surface in here, it was defended by a phalanx of hostile-looking wedges, their tapered tips pointing toward the center of the room. An expertly laid-out trap to capture the smallest of wandering sounds.

Tiller couldn't bring herself to look away from Gren for long. It felt like he might vanish if she got distracted.

"Only Nel—only Carnelian can open that entrance," she said. "How did her brother give you the pearl?"

"Phages can take more than one form. Me included." He placed a hand just below his collarbone. Not quite on the spot where his heart should have been.

"We can melt into solid stone, for instance. We pass through and reconstitute ourselves on the other side. But we always snap back to our default shape eventually. That's what feels best."

Once more, the wall parted like a pair of curtains. They followed Carnelian out of the anechoic chamber.

"Assimilating in and out of the monolith is extremely uncomfortable," Gren appended. "At least for me. Maybe other phages find it less nauseating. Given the choice, I'd much prefer to walk my way through open doors. Now I finally can, courtesy of Mage Silva."

He called his thanks to Carnelian. Her back stiffened. She made a blunt noise of acknowledgment.

His voice sounded so much more immediate outside of the stifling structure of the wedge-covered chamber. And not just his voice—it was as if someone had taken a plunger to Tiller's ears. No longer was she plagued by the internal gurgling of her own drifting blood.

They ascended the long precarious stairs again. Carnelian went first, but Gren told her where to go.

As they climbed, Tiller apologized incoherently. She didn't even know what she was saying. But she had to say it.

She'd believed he was gone, body and all, and she'd never doubted it.

She should have sought more proof. She should have tried to come back sooner. She—

Gren interrupted. "It's true that I couldn't just pack up and go meet you. I couldn't cross the border even if I wanted to. But think about it. There are all kinds of ways I could've sent you a message. The heliograph towers. The resettlement camps. There were plenty of opportunities."

"You didn't want to be found," Tiller said slowly. She understood what he was getting at, though she couldn't begin to understand why.

She rephrased it. "You didn't want any of us to come find you. Because you're a phage? Did you think—did you think I'd attack you on sight?"

"The Corps would," Carnelian said over her shoulder. "They'd attack even if he didn't look much like a stereotypical phage. They'd attack even if he wasn't a phage at all. Catastrophe ROE, remember? It's been known to kill innocents."

"I can testify to that," Gren chimed in. "I've seen them in action. Hilariously brutal. Once they get sufficiently paranoid, people are much, much worse than phages."

He pointed them toward a winding path that led out through the back of the monolith. Rough-hewn steps formed a zig-zagging trail down to the pool at the bottom of the caldera.

The rain from before had mostly let up. Either that, or whatever remained lacked the strength to filter all the way down from the treetops.

"The Corps rescue team never came out back," Gren said. "They were too preoccupied with what they found in the monolith."

Out here, where sunvines grew unbridled, Tiller could see that much of his clothing was the same as what he'd worn when he went to die. Bark cloth, loose and easy to move in. Years-old blood dyed the front of his top as black as mold.

Perhaps because his old clothes were not entirely intact, he'd borrowed someone's khaki green overcoat. A relic from a poacher or a would-be settler.

This too was full of holes, and would have fit very differently on a grown man. On Gren, it hung halfway down his calves. He'd rolled the sleeves up to his elbows to keep them from swallowing his hands.

Myriad skinny waterfalls dripped down past the three of them. Way down into the beginnings of the sacred spring.

Woodpeckers and magpies and toads and carpenter frogs conspired to make a racket all around the rim of the caldera.

A chameleon peacock hunched on a nearby branch with its tail dangling down, rippling in a faint moisture-laden breeze. Its colors seethed in an effort to replicate the landscape.

Dragonflies zoomed to and fro with bodies as thick as killer hornets. They were the blue of lapis lazuli, or of Gren's long unbound hair.

"Don't get me wrong." Now Gren spoke so only Tiller could hear.

Even when he sidled closer, he didn't smell anything like an unwashed human still wearing the outfit he'd died in.

He smelled like what wafted up from the fire caves: the stark spotless aftermath of something purged and forever transformed.

"I didn't hide back at the Scholar's house because I was terrified of persecution. Of being discovered as a phage and getting executed on sight. I mean, I would rather not get killed—again—but I wasn't curled up here all desperate and forlorn," he half-whispered. "Not exactly. I wasn't beating myself up over waking up as a monster. I wasn't just waiting around for a bigger phage to come put me out of my misery. I had better reasons for keeping to myself."

"Better reasons," Tiller repeated. "You—"

A cry pierced the air, or tried to. It reversed itself back into Carnelian even as it fought to escape her lips. She choked it down like a swallowed knife.

Tiller sprinted the rest of the way to the edge of the sacred spring. Gren brought up the rear, unhurried. The water was pure in hue, its surface mysteriously unreflective.

The spring was full of bodies.

Rozen crouched on damp rocks, peering down like a child watching minnows or crayfish or water striders. But there was nothing to see except submerged dead humans, dark hair fanned out like sea grass.

Carnelian stumbled back.

"What's the fuss?" Gren asked her. "You put those there. Remember? You were an expert body handler. The Scholar always used you as his gopher. Floating rotting corpses all up and down the mountain."

Rozen's phage, meanwhile, remained singularly focused on the motionless water. He held himself with the poise of an egret waiting to ambush passing fish.

"These—" Tiller stopped. She took an extra moment to master herself. "Are these ... the seeds of blues?"

"What?" Gren said. "No, no, no. Goodness, no. How could they have been reborn as anyone else? They're still right here. No—when he planted the seeds for us, the pool was still clean. His seeds were a proper sacrifice."

Gren mimed shoving the air. "They died in the pool. In Forest territory. But once we showed up, there was no longer any need for him to keep these waters pure.

"With the help of your friend there, he brought in rot from outside. Bodies slaughtered before they came to the Forest. Toxic waste—not a holy sacrifice. That's what you see now."

He waved a hand in front of his nose. "The smell isn't nearly as bad as you would expect, is it? The spring fights to overcome it.

"You might've noticed the water downstream tasting off, though. And don't get me started on that log jam. Only corruption of a sacred pool could cause that level of devastation."

He dipped a fingertip in the water. He grimaced as if he could sample it through his skin. "A parting gift from the Scholar," he said. "A bonus experiment. He didn't poison the spring right away. He stored all his extra imported cadavers in the monolith.

"Toward the end, while the spring was still pure, he siphoned out just a bit of it. A single bathtub's worth. You saw it in the basement.

"That's where he laid my murdered body. A watery coffin. Only then did he transfer the rest of his dead people—a whole treasure room full of them—out here. Of course, she was the one who did all the dirty work."

He nodded at Carnelian. She had her right hand placed like a claw on her head. As if she wished she could push her fingers straight through her skull. As if she wished she could plunge them into the pliable clay of her brain and smush all the thoughts that had no business belonging there.

"Why?" Tiller said. "Gren, I—"

"Why?" he parroted. "Let's work backwards. What drew you here?"

*What drew you here?*

Fog rising up from the bowels of the monolith. No rhyme or reason to it.

Rozen—Rozen's phage—leading them up from the log jam like an off-leash dog.

Other phages had behaved strangely, too. Attacking them in unison, as coordinated as soldiers.

Then the reverse of it: phages spying on them wherever they went, with zero hints of aggression. Phages barreling into a nigh-invincible beast for no conceivable reason. Phages standing guard around an open vorpal hole like human sentries.

And now: the way Rozen rotated his head to stare at Carnelian. No flicker of recognition in his eyes.

He still didn't move. Yet his body quivered as if he were straining to break free of invisible chains.

This was a very hungry phage.

"You can see through the eyes of other phages," Tiller said. "You can control them like a general."

Gren put his hands behind his head. His mouth curled a bit, as though he had to fight to suppress a smile. "Sacred water is the heart— the essence—of the Forest. The Scholar tainted it. On purpose.

"So the Forest took me as its heart instead. As a kind of substitute core. I hear the flapping of every fog owl. I feel the branches gripped by every phage.

"And I didn't have to," he said, spinning to face Carnelian, "but I granted your wish. I brought you to Rozen. What do you plan on doing with him?"

"What," she said huskily, "do you think?"

Her mantle felt heavy and cold on Tiller's shoulders.

"I have a better idea," Gren countered. "I'll admit that Rozen and I can't talk with words, but we get along well enough. Leave him with me. I'll watch out for him."

"That's my brother's dead body," said Carnelian. "If I don't take care of him, something else will. Other phages. A vorpal beast. A Corps squadron."

Gren sighed. "I should've expected as much. The Scholar trained you from childhood to resolve difficult problems with violence."

"Leave it be, and one day my brother's reanimated body could hurt someone. Absorb someone. Someone like Tiller."

"Who's there to hurt?" Gren demanded. "The Forest is practically empty of human life. Forgive me if I don't really count your fellow soldiers. They mostly stay quaking in the shallows anyway."

"I'm not asking for your understanding," Carnelian said formally. "It might be selfish to insist on killing this one phage myself, no matter what. It might be needlessly violent.

"That's what I am, when you get down to it. A selfish, irrational, violent mage. I can't pretend to be anything else."

Gren glanced at Tiller. "She's your mage, isn't she? One way or another."

"Nel belongs to herself."

"I strongly recommend stopping her. If you can. I know she's a rather disobedient sort."

"I'll do it instead of you," Tiller said to Carnelian. "If you'll let me."

She drew her yo-yo knives. Carnelian's eyes followed her hands.

The bowl-shaped caldera was the exact opposite of the anechoic chamber at the bottom of the Fertility Monolith. The bawling of birds and frogs—and weirder creatures, much higher in the trees—redoubled over and over as it echoed out across the water. There was a feverish quality to it, a rising hysteria.

"You *should* do it," Gren said in admiring tones. "Much as I'll miss him. A brother for a brother. How poetic. Although he's something of an empty shell."

Rozen watched Carnelian with unflinching intensity.

Not because he knew she was the sister of who he used to be. Because, in all likelihood, she was the human being positioned closest to him. If she and Tiller switched places, his attention would latch onto Tiller.

Assuming, of course, that he was the same as any other ordinary phage. Assuming that Gren didn't do anything further to manipulate his behavior.

Carnelian reached for Tiller's hands. Tenderly, one finger at a time, she took away the yo-yo knives.

"You know how to use these?" Tiller asked.

"I know how to use a lot of things." Carnelian hesitated. "May I?"

This was more than just a request to borrow some knives.

Tiller murmured her assent.

She would gladly have spared Carnelian the experience of breaking her own brother's neck. The phage wore Rozen's body, a lost child's body, even if it lacked the soul and the voice of Carnelian's twin.

If a dead villager metamorphosed into a phage before they could be disposed of in the fire caves, the other villagers would work together to kill and anoint them. Especially if it was a phage born from someone they loved.

You couldn't leave your mother's skin to roam the woods as an eternal ghoul. No matter if there remained a slim chance that the phage might run off to some faraway part of the Forest and never harm anyone you personally knew.

It was the responsibility of the living to deal with the phages of their children, their siblings, their lifelong friends.

Whether through the fire caves or through phage murder, your last and greatest filial duty was to give your beloved the unspeakably precious gift of a forever death.

She let Carnelian keep the knives. Instead she found herself touching Carnelian's sides, as though to help hold her up.

Not that Carnelian seemed particularly weakened. After her initial shock at the pool full of bodies—bodies she herself must have slid into the water, all those years ago—her demeanor had hardened.

"I really would do it for you," Tiller said, this time with greater emphasis.

Carnelian leaned in swiftly and kissed the side of her head. For a second she stayed there, her face buried in Tiller's hair. She said something inaudible.

Then she withdrew, her eyes on the small phage squatting at the water's edge.

"Have it your way," Gren muttered. "If you must do this yourself, you'll be better off not using magic. Trust me on that."

Carnelian responded by asking Tiller to give her gloves back. They would block the use of her deadlier skills. Less temptation to struggle with.

Tiller offered her the mantle, too. She declined, pointing out that Tiller needed a place to carry all the tools she'd hidden in its pockets.

She tied part of her hair back. It was just long enough to make a small silver tuft at the nape of her neck. When she pulled her gloves on, she looked like a grappler getting ready to enter the ring.

"I gave you emergency maintenance in the monolith, but that was a one-time special offer," Gren warned. "A gift in honor of our reunion. It won't happen again."

"Understood," Carnelian said in the voice of a soldier.

"Most importantly, I won't hold Rozen still for you to chop his head off. You have to win fairly."

"Understood," Carnelian said again.

Gren raised his eyebrows at Tiller, offering her one last chance to intercede. She kept her peace.

"Very well."

He put his arm out and made Tiller back up to a wall of verdant rushes.

He was so much smaller than her. His low-hanging borrowed overcoat didn't help him look any older. Yet he stood in front of her as if she were the only one who might possibly be in any danger.

"Have at it," he called out, loud and sharp and jarringly cold.

Rozen's phage sprang up faster than any human could ever move—large or small, young or old. Tiller's voice got caught in her throat.

Magpies jeered from the fern-covered caldera walls. So too did the rest of the wild audience. They screeched their approval at a steadily escalating pitch.

# 57

TILLER HAD NOT realized that Carnelian could hold her own so well with zero magic. In purely physical terms, she was a good fighter. A very good fighter. Almost transcendent.

Still, that didn't make it an easy battle. Rozen's phage wore the shell of a child, but he moved with the sinuous strength and speed and aggression of an ape.

Rocks, tree trunks, boughs, the pool itself: all served as launching pads to send him rocketing explosively toward her eyes, her neck, her hands.

Corpse water showered them as Rozen rebounded from the shallows. Carnelian flinched. Almost staggered. Tiller gripped her own wrist as if holding a friend back from leaping into the fray.

Yo-yo knives whipped through the air, slimmer than the dragonflies still heedlessly criss-crossing the caldera. They swooped like startled songbirds. They struck no target.

Rozen's bone-white fingers grazed Carnelian's bicep, then latched on like a pair of jaws. They both tumbled over watery mud and striated rocks and grassy sedges. He hung on with the tenacity of a crab.

At last Tiller saw that her knives had not missed their mark. Carnelian had thrown them that way on purpose. Their slick strings wound around Rozen's neck.

She kept a tight grip on the ends. She kicked him off her while heaving on the knife-strings, pulling them back as though in a gruesome game of tug-of-war.

A human victim would have been strangled, bleeding copiously, their throat cut like a cake with a wire.

Were these strings strong enough to slice all the way through a phage?

No. They snapped, lashing the side of Carnelian's face.

Even as she recoiled, she'd already taken another weapon in hand. And the phage was already at her throat.

She smashed his elbows with her steely fighting pipe.

Tiller felt the sound of it deep down in her stomach. She didn't see what happened next.

They'd stumbled back to the water's edge, Carnelian and the child-sized phage who no longer bore much of a resemblance to her. Or to the caged boy Tiller had met twenty years ago.

She heard the end of the metal pipe hitting something harder than flesh. A rock. Or a skull. She heard a gun—Carnelian's icearm?—going off three times in rapid succession.

Carnelian straightened up slowly, her back half-turned to Tiller and Gren.

She bled from a thin line high on her cheekbone, frighteningly close to her eye. The spot where the severed strings had struck her.

She clutched at her cheek as if squeezing juice from an orange. She bent again and pressed her bloody palm to the disfigured head of the small form below her. He lay there like a beached fish, the tips of his fingers trailing in the sacred spring.

She spent longer anointing him—and used far more blood—than she needed to.

Tiller forced herself to wait.

When Carnelian faced them, her entire left cheek was smeared red.

At first she seemed to look at Tiller—at her hands, at the mantle fastened over her breastbone. Everywhere but her eyes.

"Can I use magic now?" she asked Gren.

"You can do anything you like, Mage Silva."

"Yet you wouldn't advise it."

"Your branches might look fine," he said. "They might feel better than they've felt in weeks.

"But you just killed your little brother for a second time. One could argue that it wasn't really him. Still, it was undeniably his face that you pulverized.

"Agitation of the heart won't do your magic any favors. If you want to avoid losing your balance—if you don't want to hurt anyone human—I'd suggest holding back."

Carnelian didn't answer. Outwardly, she appeared as unmoved as the surface of the transparent sacred spring.

"Your knives," she said to Tiller. "I'm sorry. I'll find them."

Tiller hastened over to stop her from getting on her knees to search. "We can look later. I've got extra strings in my bags. The blades aren't irreplaceable, either."

Given how the strings had snapped, the parts attached to the knives were likely still wound tight around Rozen's neck.

Under normal circumstances, Carnelian would've activated First Aid to seal the wound on her face. But she hadn't made a move to treat it.

New blood still dribbled out—sluggishly, now, after how much of it she'd used to anoint her brother's phage.

Tiller fumbled through the inner pockets of her mantle. Carnelian's mantle, rather. She took out a beige hand towel to dab at Carnelian's cheek.

She only just managed to catch herself before proposing that they wash out the cut. Better not use water from a pool lined in layer upon layer of time-frozen dead bodies.

Instead she cleaned it as best she could with her little towel. Then she dressed the long thin slash with gauze and tape.

Carnelian submitted to her ministrations without comment or complaint.

It took enormous self-discipline for Tiller to avoid darting a look at the mauled phage on the ground beside them. In her peripheral vision she got an impression of puffy white skin with the texture of a mushroom. Listless limbs. A cranium shattered like a dropped bowl.

Carnelian hadn't yet put away her fighting pipe. She held it horizontally before her, balanced across her palms like a gift to be presented to royalty.

"He was empty," Carnelian said to the pipe. "Completely empty. I had to do it."

"If you showed mercy, he'd have turned you to goo."

Tiller flipped the towel around. She smoothed the less-bloodied side below Carnelian's jaw.

There were a few spots where the phage had managed to grab at her, but the contact had been quick, and swiftly severed. She pushed Carnelian's hair back to check her forehead. She lifted the short scraped-together ponytail to examine the nape of her neck.

The eventual scarring would be obvious when the light hit her a certain way. But not necessarily plain to see at a distance.

Tiller fished a tin of wound ointment out of yet another pocket.

Carnelian held still as she applied it. No wincing, although the salve must have stung horribly.

"Will these be your first phage scars?" Tiller asked.

A soundless nod.

Gren meandered over. He crouched next to the corpse of Rozen's phage. His overlong overcoat trailed on the ground behind him.

"Rozen was the phage I knew best," he said. "Insofar as you can know any creature that lacks a mind. Don't think I even learned his name until the Scholar and all his knowledge traversed my body. As part of his quest to put his core in you." He tipped his head at Carnelian.

"You and Rozen were together from the moment of your birth. So you should understand what it's like. His phage and I were together from the moment of our rebirth.

"But"—Gren straightened his knees—"he'll still be part of the Forest. The Forest has no reason to grieve individual lives. Do you mourn every spark that goes flying away from a bonfire?"

A rhetorical question.

A bright blue kingfisher perched in a willow dangling over the lifeless spring. He exchanged glances with it as if acknowledging an old acquaintance.

Tiller wondered if she was as much of a stranger to Gren as he was to her.

She'd retained her humanity, albeit not through any virtue of her own. But twenty-plus years would be enough to change anyone. Especially if you were a child at the beginning of it.

How much remained of the girl who'd cried in that room with unfinished white walls?

She put a hand on Carnelian's upper back. Carefully, so as not to startle her.

"We don't have to rush to go anywhere," she said.

Carnelian took a seat on the rocks piled up around the perimeter of the spring. She caught Tiller's fingers in hers. For an ambiguous moment, she seemed as though she might be on the verge of asking Tiller to stay close.

Then she let go. Her eyes dropped to the pitiful phage body lying sideways in the mud. She leaned forward and placed her military-issue pipe on the ground beside him.

Tiller backed away. She took Gren with her.

"Good idea," he said under his breath. "Give her space."

They circled toward the base of the trail that led down from the upper rim of the caldera. Far enough from Carnelian that they could speak without disturbing her. Their voices would be swallowed up by the shadow chorus of birds and insects and animals.

"I thought you did have to rush," Gren remarked. "The—what are they called? Those machina are coming."

"Chalices," Tiller said.

"Chalices, yes. Just a few days left till they show up."

If Gren heard and saw and tasted and felt everything that transpired in the Forest, then of course he would know about the planned chalice strike.

"You're not worried?" Tiller asked.

"The Forest always wins in the end."

"Won't it hurt you?"

"Not in this body. And it's far from the first time people have turned on the Forest. Back in another era when phages ran rampant, the Forest got completely sealed off from the outside world. Together with every living forester."

He spread his hands. "Our national heroes got praised high and low for this marvelous feat. The seal lasted for centuries. But it still gave way in the end. Now most people have forgotten that it was ever a thing."

"Gren," Tiller said.

He smiled, open and childlike. "Yes?"

"You're the core of—you've become the heart of the Forest."

"Yes."

"You were the heart of the Forest when the resettlement camps got massacred."

"Yes," he said.

"When the Forest started expanding into new territory faster than it's ever expanded before."

"Yes."

"When the Outborder Corps sent in squad after squad to get slaughtered. Carnelian ended up being the sole survivor of multiple missions. You saw all that as it happened?"

No—this wasn't what she meant to ask. She clenched the sides of Carnelian's mantle.

She made herself try again.

"You were the heart of the Forest," she said, "and you made it happen. Phage encounters didn't start escalating out of nowhere. It wasn't random. You directed their aggression."

"You think so?" Gren inquired.

She strove to keep her voice down. "How far back does this go? Were you already in control in the months right after Doe rescued me? When it started getting so bad that we had to flee the Forest? Did you *want* there to be an exodus?"

The phage in the shape of her twin brother looked up at her.

Just like Rozen's phage, he never blinked. But there was a painful awareness in his childish gray face that every other phage most definitely lacked.

On some level, Tiller had wounded him. But that didn't mean she'd guessed wrong.

# 58

Gren flicked at a clump of blue moss. The same type of moss that shrouded the cottages of Koya Village. It hung down from a crack between rocks like a strange lonely tassel.

"I'm not a micromanager," he stated.

Tiller waited for him to elaborate.

"At first it was all subconscious." He pinched off a wisp of moss and rolled it between his palms. "I couldn't phase through walls yet. I couldn't watch over the rest of the Forest. I thought I'd be trapped down in that anechoic chamber forever.

"You don't know how desperate I was to be found. I don't even know how bad it got. It's been a long time. No matter how sharp it felt in the beginning, things fade."

He opened his right fist to reveal a sad compressed ball of moss. About the size of a marble. Its color had darkened to navy blue.

"Phages all through the Forest acted out because I wanted someone to save me. Their senseless viciousness stemmed from me. Like the screams of an infant. Oblivious to everything except the pain of a need unmet."

He turned his hand over and dropped the balled-up moss. It left shadowy stains on his gray palms.

"I wanted to say *I'm here, I'm alive*. It came out in the form of the Forest rampaging. Phages going wild. By the time I understood what was happening, by the time I understood my new role, everyone was already gone."

This didn't make sense. "The Forest and its phages stayed hostile long after," Tiller said. "To foresters and outsiders alike. Not a single resettlement camp managed to last. To this day, Corps members avoid Forest missions unless they have no other choice."

"What are you trying to imply?" Gren asked coolly.

"You learned to control phages. Couldn't you have made the Forest more peaceful?"

"I could have," Gren said. "I refrained. In fact—I came around to embracing it. The Forest still hasn't recovered from what the Scholar did to that spring." He pointed.

"I didn't enjoy destroying the resettlement camps. But it had its purpose. The more time I spent as a phage, the more I came to feel that the Forest needs an era without people."

Phages under Gren's command had hurt soldiers and trespassers and hunters and foresters. Some lost an eye or a leg. Some surrendered their entire selves.

Phages would try to absorb human prey with or without Gren's influence. Yet for Tiller it changed things to know that, at least in recent years, they'd been tied to a greater consciousness.

That made it less like predation and more like a war of attrition. A war that the casualties didn't even realize was happening.

"We could dredge up the bodies," Tiller said. "Help you clean the spring. We could—"

"That would be nice," Gren cut in, "but the damage is already done."

He motioned her over to the water. Some of the submerged dead had wide open eyes.

They were still a good distance from Carnelian's vigil next to Rozen.

"I never planned on seeing you again," Gren said. "You or anyone. I did miss you, though. I wished you were here. I wished precisely because I knew it was impossible, and a bad idea to boot."

"We didn't arrive at the Scholar's house by coincidence," Tiller contended. "You lured us here with Rozen's phage."

"*I'm here*," he recited. "*I'm alive*. Even once I knew better, that feeling never completely left me. The desire to be seen, to be found. Am I weak?"

A dragonfly landed on his wrist. The same way it might alight briefly on a boulder or a willow branch. He raised his arm to send it off like a falconer.

"I spent years getting used to the idea of never speaking with another human being again. I painstakingly weaned myself off my memories. I stayed away from the village.

"Then—even though I'd made the Forest as inhospitable as possible— you showed up. Together with Doe and Baba Sayo's ashes. That's how I learned they'd died. Far out of my sight."

Weeks, months, or years ago, if some greater power had given Tiller a chance to speak with Gren from beyond the grave—surely she'd have been overflowing with things to say.

The fate of the villagers. The Koya Foundation. Blue hunters. Baba Sayo's final days. The entire world beyond the Forest and its immediate surroundings. A world he'd never gotten to experience for himself.

She would've told him how much she'd missed him. How she'd left so much of herself behind in that craggy white room in the Scholar's house.

She would've brought up all the times he'd spoken to her in dreams over the years.

She would've asked: *Was that really you?*

It wasn't. The Gren who'd advised her in her dreams had been the same as he was in life. Not a phage. Not the heart of the Forest. Not real.

"I should have stayed hidden," he said quietly. "I shouldn't have let either of you see Rozen.

"But you were right there. It was so easy to convince myself that you deserved to know the truth of us. *Deserved* in every sense of the word. A punishment as much as a reward.

"I broke," he confessed. "My determination, my discipline—once you ascended the mountain, it meant nothing.

"I never stopped being that little kid, did I? Terrified of the rest of my infinite undead life. Wailing for Baba Sayo and my sister and Doe. And in the process, unconsciously sending phages to bedevil everything I loved. My cry for attention led straight to your banishment from the Forest.

"Same root problem this time. I couldn't resist using Rozen to reel you in. I came up with all sorts of excuses to justify it. But I shouldn't have."

He was no longer looking at her. "I shouldn't have." He said it again, a temple acolyte reciting mantras. "I shouldn't have."

Tiller touched his hair.

Gren jerked back as if she'd stung him. "What're you doing?" he hissed. "Are you stupid?"

She turned her hand about. Her skin had not started melting or shredding or otherwise attempting to merge with him.

Nothing sloughed off. Her nails were not loosening.

The lines on her palm remained unchanged.

"I don't think your hair will harm me." She paused, trying to gauge his reaction. "If you don't want me touching any part of you, I'll stop."

He peered suspiciously at her fingertips.

"I was wondering," Tiller said, "how so much life can grow around the shores of the spring. Usually bodies brought from outside would create a much larger dead zone."

He ceased his skeptical examination of the hand she'd placed on his head. "The Forest is very strong in this place. The poison took more of a toll downstream."

"Like at the log jam."

"Right. This injury"—he faced the pool—"this greatest of injuries served as a catalyst to accelerate the Forest's expansion. Faster and angrier and more ravenous than ever before."

"Could you make it stop spreading?" Tiller asked.

"I'm not the king of the Forest." A dubious silence followed. "Maybe if I wished for it with all my heart. Maybe if I spent the next twenty years praying for it, devoted to the cause. The Forest is a very big boat, you know. It can't change direction quickly."

He looked over at Carnelian and Rozen. Both remained as still and quiet as carvings.

"Guess you can touch my hair," he said. "Long as it's not hurting you."

"Would you actually start to absorb me if I hugged you? You can't control it?"

"Give me your sleeve," he ordered. "I'll show you."

Tiller held out her arm. Her sleeves were three-quarter length. Fairly loose. A deep ochre hue.

Gren pinched the very end of her proffered sleeve as if defusing a bomb. He made absolutely no contact with the skin beneath, not even by accident.

After a few seconds, he shifted his fingers to show her how his mere touch had imprinted the fabric with shocking white bleach marks.

He didn't let go yet.

"Thank you for bringing Baba Sayo and Doe." He'd been reduced to whispering again, eyes averted. "I never thought anyone would come back to be with me."

He was not on the verge of tears. Phages couldn't cry.

Maybe that was why something buckled inside her. Why her throat filled up to the brim.

With the utmost care, she took her other hand and stroked his hair again. Ever so lightly. She couldn't risk grazing his scalp.

When they were twins in the Forest, Gren had always been better at everything. Gren had been the good kid. Gren had been her hero.

The same number of years had passed for both of them. It wasn't right to judge based on appearances. Yet now she couldn't help feeling as though she'd grown up to become his older sister.

"Who did your hair?" he asked as she patted his head.

"Couldn't I have braided it myself?"

"You never had the patience for a nice plait." He looked pointedly at Carnelian, over on the far side of the spring.

At this, Tiller experienced a truly horrible thought. "You see everything that happens in the Forest?"

"If I want to, yes."

"Even if it's inside a closed tent?"

"You mean yours?" said Gren. "I like it. Cute orange tent. Very fancy."

She began to feel ill. The sort of cramping sensation that visitors from outside the Forest might succumb to after eating fresh-plucked pulpfruit.

Gren laughed raspily. "I know there are things it would behoove me not to see. So I just don't see them. I'm no voyeur. Especially when it comes to my own sister. Blech."

"Smart of you." It was quite a struggle to conceal her relief.

"I've always been smart."

At last he released her sleeve. The pale stains he'd left on it looked as stark as chemical burns. The fabric was visibly thinner—on the verge of forming holes.

Tiller, in turn, lowered her hand from his hair.

"Do you love her?" he asked.

Her eyes went straight to the front of his shirt. To the old inky bloodstain that had not diminished in the least over time. If anything, it appeared to have gotten darker, as if mustering its strength. It was closer to black than to the expected reddish-brown or fading gray.

"I'm just curious." Gren pulled his borrowed overcoat shut over the unaging stain. "She did murder me. But that was a lifetime ago. It was all the Scholar's fault. I myself became a lot more murderous once I awoke as a phage."

"Still," Tiller said. "You can see why it's hard to answer."

"Because I'm the one asking?"

"Not just that. There's—there's so much to sort through."

"Then simplify it. What if you were strangers?" he posited.

"That's the problem. If we were genuine strangers, we would never have given each other a second glance. The past pulled us together. Although she knew it long before I did."

Tiller moved her hands together and apart as if playing the childhood string games that Baba Sayo had taught them.

"Without the kidnapping, without her killing you, there wouldn't be even the thinnest of threads to connect us. Ever. For all our lives. How should I feel about that? Fear? Resentment? Surely not gratitude."

"Not exactly a common situation," said Gren. "You'll just have to forge your own path. We've always done that, haven't we? Everything about us is uncommon. We're blues."

He spoke at his own leisurely pace. Time felt abundant here in the green bowl of earth below the imposing monolith.

But his gaze had shifted to something behind Tiller. His left palm came down on his right wrist.

The forester sign for *watch out!*

Her body moved before her eyes knew what they were seeing. Doe had trained her well.

She threw herself forward in a last-ditch attempt to dodge.

Knives whizzed past her, broken strings trailing like spider-silk. They vanished amid a jungle of ferns and vines.

Those were yo-yo knives. Tiller's knives.

The ones that had been wound like snares about Rozen's dead neck. Tiller whipped around.

Carnelian had left Rozen's side. She stood within throwing distance, looking inquisitively at her fingertips.

Nothing about her had overtly changed. Most of her hair had fallen out of her attempt at a short ponytail. She was still aggravatingly beautiful. Even more so, maybe, with the bandage on her face. And that rueful dimpled smile.

Yet something was unquestionably different.

The way she held herself? The arrangement of her magic cores?

She hadn't gone berserk. Her eyes remained clear, her magic branches slow and languid.

"A shame," she said, nonchalant. "You could have died without seeing this. You could have died ever so peacefully."

"Yo-yo blades can't kill in a single strike," Gren replied coldly. "Especially when you try to use them as regular throwing knives. Amateur."

His face had gone hard. He no longer seemed nearly so young.

The look he wore reminded Tiller, suddenly, of the statue of the village demon. Its stony expression. The people of Koya had taken comfort in the notion that their nameless demon might do all sorts of demonic things to protect them.

Gren pointed an accusatory forefinger at Carnelian.

"In case you're wondering," he said to Tiller, "that's the Scholar."

# 59

THE SCHOLAR wore Carnelian's body like a plush designer coat.

Carnelian's lips parted to say: "Hello there, little blue."

It was her breath. Her voice. Her lively gray eyes.

But it wasn't her.

"Truly regretful," she pronounced, "to lose the element of surprise. And so quickly. But it can't be helped."

Tiller was paralyzed.

Tiller couldn't even say her name.

The Scholar inside Carnelian regarded Tiller with an unmistakable air of pity.

"Excuse us," Carnelian said placidly.

She raised her hands like a construction worker gesturing for a beam to be winched higher and higher. Her magic convulsed.

Rozen's body rose from the dirt and hovered at waist level. Just the right height for performing an autopsy.

There was a slight curve to him, as if he'd been suspended midair by an invisible hammock.

After several interminable moments, Carnelian lowered her arms. The hammock snapped. The Float magic ended. Rozen came crashing back down.

"Hmm," she said, pensive. "Not ideal."

She began peeling her gloves off, one by one. No request for permission.

"I forbid you," Tiller said. "Keep them on." Her voice shook.

Carnelian winced as if it pained her to her core—as if she were flaying the skin from her flesh. But she still managed to remove them.

She dropped her gloves on Rozen's broken face.

Tiller felt no premonition of illness. Before she knew it, she was retching. She was on her knees at the water's edge. Hard rocks and gloppy moss.

She locked eyes with one of the underwater cadavers. A man whose copious black hair wafted into his mouth, snagging on crooked teeth.

Laughter budded within her like something cancerous. She barely managed to keep the hysteria down. All the while, her stomach kept heaving. Nothing emerged except a piercing taste of bile. It felt as though she'd poured drain cleaner down her esophagus.

Carnelian's mantle seemed sodden on her shoulders. Unbearably heavy.

There was a stealthiness to how the air grew hotter and more humid, increasingly difficult to breathe. Or maybe it was just her. She felt goosebumps on her forearms. Everything had gone clammy to the touch, rife with the sweatiness of a cold glass in summer.

She was in no state to see the homing pearls veering toward her.

If she thought anything, she thought they were insects. They moved with the same dizzying speed as the bees and flies whirling all around the sunken caldera.

A phage dove down from a tree, its back to Tiller. Several others followed, crashing gracelessly in the underbrush.

She scrambled away. She searched her surroundings for anything—anything—that might help her.

Her eyes landed on petite grabber lilies, incapable of seizing prey larger than a field mouse. Stalactite fungi whose dripping toxins would do nothing to affect a phage. Heavy submerged corpses.

Then it dawned on her that the phages had formed a wall to defend her. They'd taken the flying homing pearls like bullets.

She rose creakily to her feet. She stepped up on a rock formation to see over the phages' heads. On the other side of the fleshy wall, Carnelian stood with a hand on her hip and a faintly quizzical expression.

The carpenter frogs fell silent. Every yapping bird and insect followed suit.

Feathery bamboo stirred with a sound like flowing water. More phages waited all around the rim of the caldera, clothed in rags and poised for action.

Carnelian said: "We knew we would be able to utilize her branch skills. In a basic way, at least. We wondered if we would also inherit her aptitude for them. Her years of training and experience."

She flexed her left hand. "Not so, it seems. A moderate inconvenience."

The Scholar had always referred to himself with the royal *we*. Like he had a flock of unseen assistants and followers, even when working in rigorous solitude.

Coming from Carnelian, it sounded as if the Scholar purported to speak for her—and for the donors of every other magic core collected within her.

"She was so very good at integrating new magic cores," Carnelian continued. "Yet even now she finds herself locked by her own physiology into never deploying more than a single skill at once. Tragic. We did wish we could have used the brother instead. A pity that he turned out so feeble."

She casually drew her shining sword.

Phages swarmed down from swaying willows and the contours of the lofty monolith and the lush walls of the caldera.

They surrounded Tiller as though to protect her.

They surrounded Carnelian and her sword like hungry coyotes.

"Do you want to watch," Gren said to Tiller, "or would you prefer not to see it? I'll respect your wishes."

He was angry. Angrier than she'd ever heard him in life.

"Watch what?" she asked, dreading the answer.

He looked at her as though attempting to determine if this was a serious question. "Do you want to watch me kill the Scholar?"

"Carnelian—"

"Do you really think she's alive in there?"

Carnelian, peeking past the massed phages, gave Tiller a wry smile. The phages had yet to touch her. But they were uncomfortably close, and inching closer.

"You didn't have any qualms about watching her beat Rozen to death," Gren said. "Why? Because his real self was long gone. His phage self was nothing but an ambulatory corpse."

"What makes the Scholar any different?" he demanded. "He's desecrating your mage's body just by filling it with his filthy self. Shouldn't we put him down for the exact same reason she put down Rozen?"

"People who become phages never come back," Tiller said. The words tasted ashen. "Carnelian—whatever's happening to her, she isn't a phage. She might still—"

"Look at me. I'm a phage. I'm more myself than she is."

"Other phages aren't born from blues. Other phages aren't the heart of the Forest."

Gren scoffed. "There's an exception to everything. The facts are never as morally flawless as anyone thinks. You can still use common sense. How do you propose getting her back? A kiss on the lips? Yeah, good luck with that."

"No, no," Carnelian chastised. The Scholar had never required an invitation to butt in on a conversation. "Think logically. Think like a scientist. How did we become part of this body, and how did we awaken? Replicate the experiment."

The phages had stopped closing in on her. They'd left her just enough room to keep idly practicing various branch skills, one after another.

She put her sword away and peeled the gauze from her cheek. She touched the open cut on her face with First Aid.

*How did we awaken?*

Tiller turned to Gren. "You knew this would happen."

He wouldn't meet her eyes. "I'm not a prophet."

"You knew it was coming. You were waiting for the Scholar to take control." Her head pounded. "What triggered it? Meeting Rozen? Meeting you?"

Carnelian raised her voice. "Cumulative time spent in the Forest," she said. "In the territory of our little blue. Each day and night in the Forest eroded Carnelian Silva like water eroding rock.

"Killing her brother's phage with her own hands made the crack wider. It eased our awakening. Don't blame your twin. He tried to stop her."

"If it didn't happen now," said Gren, "it would have happened as the two of you hiked back out of the Forest."

He came over to stand by Tiller. The phages parted to make way for him.

As he spoke, he stared fixedly at Carnelian, and at the Scholar inside her.

"This is why the Scholar needed a blue to transplant himself to Mage

Silva. He wanted to do something he'd never done before. Something he couldn't ever have accomplished without power borrowed by murdering me. He inserted more in her than just his core."

Carnelian's hand cupped her cheek. The open slash below her eye had dwindled to a timid red line.

"With all due respect," she said, her tone genial, "we had no interest in becoming a ten-year-old girl. We hoped to sleep till she reached adulthood. We counted on our will to drive her back to the Forest."

"It worked," Gren said flatly. "I saw Carnelian Silva again and again. She kept signing up for Corps missions. She kept coming to fight phages and vorpal beasts. Even after every single one of her companions succumbed to the Forest. You won your gamble."

"Somewhat," Carnelian allowed. She leaned on a willow, unfazed by the phages flanking her. "Certain parts could have gone better."

Bile still pricked Tiller's mouth. She didn't want to hear another word from the Scholar leaving Carnelian's lips. Yet she couldn't stop asking—

"Why?" It came out of her in an uncontrollable spasm. "You wanted to live longer? To be young again? You were so afraid of death that you—"

"We may not have experienced a true and final death, but we came close," Carnelian said calmly. "Death seems relaxing. How could any limited reality be more pleasant than the totality of oblivion?"

Tiller could not even begin to formulate a response. This philosophical air, this utter lack of concern: the person occupying Carnelian's body struck her as being far more alien in nature than Gren, who was no longer human. Who'd been turned into a phage against his will.

"We did always struggle to speak plainly," Carnelian added. "How about this? Isn't the whole point of life to seize more of it? If you see an opportunity, it would be quite senseless not to take it."

To the Scholar, time was a commodity.

He'd planned to annex the rest of Carnelian's life not out of desperate megalomania or an all-consuming yearning for immortality—but rather because, to him, it appeared to be there for the taking.

Like a trader placing an order for an undervalued stock.

"Not feeling so comfortable now, are you?" Gren said abruptly.

Tiller strained to look past the milling phages.

Carnelian still wore a smile.

There was something odd in how she rested her weight on the tree behind her. At first Tiller had taken it for a show of insouciance.

But maybe she needed the extra help to stay upright.

"The rejection response is rather more severe than anticipated," she said.

"I'm shocked to hear you admit it," Gren shot back.

"We have always been a great believer in transparency."

"Oh, that's funny."

Carnelian gestured the shape of a circle by her torso. "These nine cores were in a very delicate gravitational balance. Moons orbiting a planet. That balance has been completely upended. With good reason, of course, but the end result is—well. We've felt better."

"Wonderful," Gren told her. "I fantasized about sending my phages to rip you to pieces. Now I don't have to lift a finger. We'll watch you die a slow and agonizing death from transplant rejection. It's only a matter of time."

"There's another way," said Carnelian, unruffled. "A bit wasteful, but we can't afford to be picky."

Her eyes moved to Tiller. "We seeded your life in the sacred spring," she said. "It's only fair for you to tithe your life to us now. Or, rather—to Carnelian Silva."

"No one will ever die for you again," Gren snapped. "Ever."

Transplant rejection.

The resurfaced Scholar.

Carnelian, buried alive in her own body.

Unless Gren was right, and she'd already been annihilated. Leaving nothing behind but her original core and her branches and the low-key dimples that formed when she smiled.

Perhaps the sacrifice of a blue could undo that, too.

Blues could work miracles.

"I know what you're thinking," Gren said to Tiller. "Don't."

This accounted for why the Scholar had immediately begun targeting Tiller: the knives, the flying pearls.

The Scholar needed another sacrifice.

It was already a miracle that Carnelian's colony of nine cores hadn't destroyed her years ago. They would destroy her body now—and the Scholar with it—eating her alive from the inside.

Right up until that moment, the Scholar would seek opportunities to kill Tiller. Or to convince her to willingly offer her life.

Tiller touched Gren's hair with the back of her knuckles. Quick and soft. Just enough to make him look at her.

"You're right," she murmured. "No one should die for the Scholar. Including Carnelian."

"Life isn't like one of our plays," Gren said. "You think words of love would be enough to call her back? You think you can defeat the Scholar without laying a scratch on her?"

"I can try." Tiller felt for the nausea pellets in her pocket.

Gren indicated the army of phages surrounding them. "If the Scholar hurts you, you know what I'll do."

"You won't need to," said Tiller.

He didn't acknowledge this. "You'll die before you touch my sister," he called to Carnelian.

Carnelian drew her icearm. She studied it as if it were her first time seeing the mechanism of the trigger close up.

"A counterpoint," she said, turning the gun to and fro. The phages bristled. "There is exactly one way to subdue us. To give Carnelian Silva a fighting chance. But you don't want us saying it, do you, little blue?"

Gren's shoulders went rigid.

"Your brother is still our vessel," she told Tiller. "Our conduit. Just as he was twenty-one years ago. Your brother is and was the key to our resurrection. The miracle of his great sacrifice continues to the present moment.

"You wish to end us?" She aimed her icearm. "Destroy the conduit."

# 60

GREN SIDESTEPPED Tiller's clumsy attempt to dive in front of him. A cluster of phages blocked the bullets instead.

Unlike the phages pierced by Carnelian's homing pearls, they dropped instantly.

A good-quality icearm would never run out of ammunition. But Gren didn't seem likely to run out of phages, either. And Carnelian hadn't shot most of them dead-on in the head. The first to fall might begin recovering any moment now.

Carnelian stopped shooting.

"You wanted to silence us before we could speak the truth," she said to Gren. "You would have killed us—and Carnelian together with us—right in front of your sister's eyes. Without ever suggesting that there might be any other path."

The collapsed phages squirmed like a brood of larvae.

Closer to Carnelian, Rozen's body began germinating.

Lingonberry sprouts grew from his chest and his mouth and his ears and the other broken parts of his face. Bunches of bell-shaped flowers formed among the glossy leaves, followed by deep red berries.

Tiller had never seen an anointed phage come to fruition so fast.

Carnelian didn't spare him a single glance.

She admonished Gren instead. "If you thought it was right to kill this body, you should have done so instantly," she said. "Without a care for how it might break your sister's heart. You aren't nearly as sure of yourself as you seem."

This was the Scholar's great power. More so than any magical or intellectual gifts. The power of absolute conviction, which had little to do with moral correctness.

The Scholar's conviction exerted a magnetic force that made most people readily fall into orbit. Long ago, even Baba Sayo (and all the rest of Koya Village) had been overwhelmed by it.

Gren lifted his head. "I'm the heart of the Forest," he ground out, "and the Forest wants you dead."

Tiller hurled herself across uneven ground. Toward Carnelian. Toward the Scholar.

She made no attempt to dodge any phages. She ran like a meteor, on the blind faith that Gren wouldn't let them touch her.

It worked. Some of the phages appeared to wound themselves with how rapidly they cleared a path for her.

Gren wanted the Scholar dead.

The Scholar wanted Tiller dead.

Tiller wanted to save Carnelian. Without killing anyone.

The Scholar would betray her the instant she left an opening. But survival was the first imperative. The Scholar—and by extension Carnelian—would need Tiller's help to survive these phages.

Hence the attempt to make her turn on Gren. *Destroy the conduit.*

Despite those words, the Scholar would have to know that Tiller wasn't capable of seriously hurting her long-lost brother. The Scholar wouldn't aim to outright kill his own conduit, either.

On the flip side, anything short of absolutely massacring Gren would be just fine by him. Anything to stop Gren's interference.

Tiller used her body as a shield, sliding between Carnelian and the sticky fingers of countless phages.

Carnelian contemplated her with amused detachment—and a terrible satisfaction.

She was still braced against the trunk of an ancient willow. She aimed her icearm over Tiller's shoulder and pulled the trigger.

Phages crawled like lizards down from higher branches of the willow. They refused to harm Tiller. But that was her sole advantage. She couldn't cover Carnelian like a mantle.

Leave a single gap for a single phage, and they'd begin melting holes in Carnelian's flesh. Or, worse, they might drag her away from Tiller's protection. Once they latched on, they'd sweep her off too fast for a mere human to ever catch up.

Tiller drew her machete. Stinging drops of sacred water splashed her as she chopped.

"You've chosen a violent way to be a pacifist." Carnelian sounded strained. "Between the three of us, there are only two humans. You could end this quite quickly."

Tiller didn't bother responding. The Scholar's words meant nothing to her.

Gren answered instead. "The choice of who to kill isn't nearly as obvious as you make it sound. I'm the closest thing the Forest has to a heart. What will happen when the Forest loses me?"

The phages surrounding Tiller and Carnelian adhered less and less to the shape of their humanoid vessels. Extra arms shot out like a frog's tongue catching flies. The fabric of pretend clothing melded with their skin. Small white and gray faces formed on the backs and sides of their heads.

Faces like Rozen.

Faces like Gren.

Patchy shields materialized to block sneak attacks from elongated limbs. The field of hexagons flickered in and out of being. Nowhere near stable.

Carnelian put a hand on her side as if to suppress a stabbing cramp.

The machete grew slippery in Tiller's grasp. She strove to see past the next few seconds of dismembering phages. To imagine a solution that wouldn't involve—

She couldn't. She couldn't see a thing. Fear and grief walled her in.

Right now she was only delaying the inevitable. Carnelian couldn't even speak up with her own voice to plead for life or death.

Even if Carnelian could speak for herself, Tiller wasn't sure she wanted to hear it. Carnelian might very well agree with Gren.

"You'll have to decide soon," the Scholar said in Carnelian's voice. "We're deteriorating."

Tiller had never been trained in fighting to protect another. Everything Doe taught her had been geared very specifically toward securing her own survival, and nothing more.

She used up the rest of her immobility ticks. She used up the rest of her nausea pellets, too, though for phages they would serve as no more of a distraction than throwing rocks.

The ranks of active phages had thinned. Judging by the rustling up above, more would soon come to replace them.

"Stay still," ordered Carnelian. "We have a clear shot at your brother."

It'd be hard to beat the Scholar for sheer self-assurance, but Carnelian was obstinate in her own way. She'd watched over Tiller for twenty-one years without a single attempt to approach her. If willpower alone were enough to overcome the tyranny of magic—the tyranny of a miracle wrought by a blue—then the real Carnelian would already be back in control.

"Use your sword," Tiller said. "Stab me. Before the next wave arrives."

Carnelian looked at her as if doubting her ears. "We don't think now is the best time for that."

"Sacrifice me, and your cores will stop trying to kill you. You'll be in the best shape of your life. You'll be able to use Carnelian's magic more freely. You'll survive."

"Ah," Carnelian uttered. Her lips curved. "No need to hide your intentions. You're gambling it all on the slimmest of chances. On the baseless hope that a blue might be able to control the outcome of their own sacrifice. You wish to soothe our agitated transplants—and call Carnelian Silva back to the surface."

"There's no risk to you if you're so convinced I can't revive her."

The sword flashed into being in Carnelian's right hand. "Once you die, you think your brother will awaken you as a blue-haired phage. He'll soak you in the pure spring water saved in our basement. He'll inaugurate you as a second heart of the Forest. A moving conclusion. Twins reunited.

"But even if Carnelian Silva overcomes us, you'll still be a sentient phage. You'll be stuck as a phage for eternity. You'll never touch her again."

Fresh phages dropped like fruit from the treetops.

"So run that sword through me," Tiller urged. "The consequences are none of your concern."

Her hands formed fists in her pockets. Her chipped machete hung at her side. She had nothing else left but an autoinjector of fast-acting sedatives.

The new phages turned, orienting themselves, and began circling closer.

Gren stepped closer, too, as though his patience had worn thin. He picked his way among innumerable phage bodies. Some wriggling fishily; others comatose.

"What," he said in a voice of absolute rage, "are you doing?"

Carnelian's sword rent the air.

Phages tackled Tiller before the blade could split her open. Their touch was like magma.

The sword kept moving. Tiller screamed as she'd never screamed before in her life. It almost seemed to jar the phages into freeing her.

Somewhere in the back of her head, she heard the soft suction pop of an icearm going off. She hurtled forward. She grappled with Carnelian—who was weak and panting, and no match for her at all.

She stabbed the autoinjector into Carnelian's thigh. She held it there. She frenetically counted the seconds.

She kept Carnelian pinned to the willow until she'd finished counting.

Her hand spasmed, releasing the injector. Releasing Carnelian.

Carnelian sagged down among the roots. Her eyes stayed open. Her mouth was loose, her limbs floppy.

"Gren," Tiller said. "Please don't touch her. Please give me a truce. That's all I— ... Gren?"

"I promised I wouldn't let the Scholar hurt you," Gren said softly.

She whirled around.

He was impaled through the chest. That damn sword again. Carnelian—the Scholar—had thrown it like a spear while Tiller wrestled with phages.

He had a bullet hole in his forehead, and two others in his shoulder.

Phages milled around the edge of the caldera like ants lost on the way back to their nest.

"Turns out that even the Scholar is a decent shot from this distance." Sacred water ran in an unstoppable stream down the side of Gren's face. "Don't look at me like that. I'm not dead yet. He's not dumb enough to get rid of his conduit."

Tiller heard herself stammer something.

"The Scholar knew that if he killed you, I would devour him next." Gren's voice had gone scratchy. "Not just me. The entire Forest. He'd never make it beyond the border alive."

"You see? He needed to disable me before sacrificing you. He needed to secure himself a window for escape."

Gren beckoned. Tiller faltered.

"I won't hurt your Carnelian," he said impatiently. "Stop wasting time."

The sword in him melted, blending with the sacred water that soaked his clothing.

Tiller looked hastily at Carnelian. Her head lolled. Her eyes had gone heavy-lidded. She seemed incapable of speech.

The light of her cores waxed and waned with renewed fury. No longer drawn to each other. No longer tangling. Instead the fine branches pumped as if trying to swim straight out of her body.

For now, the Scholar was impotent.

Tiller rushed over to Gren. He'd eased himself down onto a rocky incline, one softened by lavish moss and mushrooms. Grabber lilies trembled to his left, just out of reach.

"You'll recover," she said. Not a question.

"I could." He sounded resigned. "Given time. Feels awful to shed all this liquid. Maybe not the same as how it would feel for you. I don't really remember human pain, to be honest." He probed at the wet hole punched in his forehead. "Wonder what it looks like inside here," he mused. "Wonder if I've still got a brain."

He poked harder. "Ouch."

"I can join you," Tiller said. "As a phage. As the core of the Forest."

"Nonsense."

"I abandoned you. We all abandoned you. I owe—"

"Don't talk like that. I won't listen."

"Just tell me one thing," she insisted. "As a blue, can I sacrifice myself? All on my own?"

Gren heaved a long crackling breath. "Maybe. No promises."

He shifted against the rocks. "Be warned—that won't be an option if you become a phage. Phages can't do themselves permanent harm. Not even an apex phage like me can pull it off. Trust me, I tried. Oh, how I tried."

Over by the old willow, Carnelian had begun slumping sideways.

Tiller was in problem-solving mode, thoughts rapid and flat.

"You don't have to be alone anymore," she told Gren.

"If you ever had any love for your brother, don't you dare sacrifice yourself while I lie here in torment."

"But Nellie—"

"Anyway, there's no need for me to recover." Gren stuck an experimental finger into his forehead wound. He cringed with his whole body as he withdrew it.

"Finish me," he said clearly.

"You can't mean that."

"Do we have time to debate what I meant?"

Tiller couldn't articulate herself. Words tripped out of her as if she were the one who'd gotten sedated. "You just said—you—you were so bent on killing the Scholar."

"You should be happy that I caved."

"It makes no sense!" Tiller cried. "You can't have changed your mind. Not this fast. Did—did I do something wrong?"

"Keep putting it off," he said dryly, "and your Carnelian will die."

He cast a brief look up at the peak of the monolith. "You and me and Rozen in that white room ... you used to shake in there. You nearly lost your voice. Same as Rozen. I was afraid that the Scholar would make you join him in his cage.

"The worst moments were when the Scholar came to ask for volunteers. You froze up so bad. I thought you might stop your own heart and die on the spot."

Every time the Scholar's shadow fell in the room, Gren would get up and leave. So Tiller didn't even have to consider it.

"Just now, you fought for both of us." He didn't try to force a smile. "For me and Carnelian Silva. You would've let the Scholar put that sword through you if it meant saving us. You didn't hesitate. You didn't freeze. You don't need me anymore."

"It's not about what I *need*," Tiller said fiercely.

"Then let it be about what I need. Do one last thing for your brother."

He curled his fingers around the very edge of her sleeve again, the same spot his touch had bleached earlier.

"Don't make me watch you kill yourself for love. And don't, for the love of the Forest, attempt to join me in this farce of an afterlife. I won't be grateful for the company, you hear me? I'll never forgive you."

His voice dropped to a whisper, harsh and insistent. "Give me the same gift you gave Baba Sayo and Doe. Give me my forever death."

Before Tiller could say a word, his body stiffened.

For the first time, his eyes closed. Then snapped open again.

His fingers maintained an unyielding grip on the disintegrating hem of her sleeve.

"Drink water from the room that eats sound," he commanded.

This was not her brother.

This was not his voice.

No sound traveled through the air. It bloomed deep inside her ear canals, deep as a parasite. Gren's mouth remained parted, unmoving.

"Drink within a day," he said. "Three days at most. You too can become the heart of the Forest."

His eyes closed once more.

When they finally opened, he burst out coughing and sputtering. As if he'd been hauled up from drowning at the bottom of the sacred spring.

"If I said anything in the past thirty seconds," he told her, "forget every word of it."

The end of her sleeve began crumbling in earnest. He let his hand drop. "I mean it."

"Didn't hear anything," Tiller said.

"Good. Don't be alarmed, but your Carnelian just got a nosebleed."

Tiller's gut buckled.

"If you get rid of me, she'll make a full recovery," he said. "Transplanted cores and all. Even the Scholar's core. His spirit won't linger anymore. Not with me gone. Enjoy the time you've got—she won't leave you as soon as you fear."

Suddenly he grabbed the mantle hanging from Tiller's shoulders. He grabbed two big fistfuls of it. "Remember. The Forest was here before you and me. It'll be here when we're gone. No matter what happens. It's not your responsibility. Where was the Forest when the Scholar kidnapped us? What'd the Forest do to help us?"

"Nothing," Tiller said.

"You have no duty to the Forest. Never forget that."

She took out her machete again. Her heart thumped as if trying to shatter bone. "I can still join you," she told him. "I can—"

"What, slit your throat with that machete? Bleed out on me like a stuck goat? No, thank you."

"I hated you," she said blindly. "For making me realize what a coward I was. For not being with me forever."

"I hated you—and everyone—for leaving me," he replied. "But of course it was never just hate."

She couldn't see well enough to do this. She'd slip. She'd miss. She'd chop her own hand off before she made the slightest mark on him.

Wrapped around the machete handle, her fingers felt like prosthetics.

"I loved you as much as I hated you." She could scarcely speak through the obstruction in her throat. "And I hated myself much more."

"Yes. Twins to the end." Gren rolled on his side. "Hack a path in right below my jaw," he said. "I'll talk you through it."

And he did.

He kept speaking to her, rapid and gentle and sometimes close to inaudible. He spoke to her long after it should've become physically impossible.

Wherever he spoke from, it couldn't have been his lungs or his vocal cords or any other part of his child-sized body.

His flesh was gray on the inside, too, all its color sucked away by the inexplicable laws of the Forest.

Most of his words seemed like borderline nonsense. He rambled about the best plays they'd put on at the village, the strangest deaths he'd seen among the trees. About Baba Sayo's arthritis. About forgetting the taste of pulpfruit.

Long after the machete dropped from her fingers, it occurred to Tiller that she could have told him she loved him. She could've said she was sorry. She could've thanked him.

She could've told him how nothing in all the world would ever replace the torn-open hole left by her twin.

She could've stroked his hair one last time.

She barely remembered to anoint him.

She crawled on her knees and searched among thorny vines, displacing hordes of bewildered insects.

At last she dug up one of her lost yo-yo knives. The other seemed irrecoverable.

By then her palms were bloody enough that she no longer needed a blade.

She opened a fresh cut for Gren anyway. It came out deeper than it needed to.

The sacred water flowing from him diluted her blood to a miserable pink.

She felt like a body without a heart in it. She'd felt like that for many years now, without ever fully understanding it.

She was supposed to be the lucky one, the grateful one. She was supposed to live well enough for two.

Not for one moment had she ever thought she'd succeeded. Not for one moment had she ever thought she'd done right by her dead brother. Not for one moment had she ever thought she was good enough.

She picked up her machete again. Her hands burned like mad.

She threw it as far and as hard as she could.

The machete made an anticlimactic *plop* as it sank beneath the surface of the sacred spring.

She threw her remaining yo-yo knife, too.

Blood kept trickling down her left hand, down to the tips of her fingers, down to the filthy earth and colorful fungi and voracious lilies of the holiest part of the Forest.

She didn't feel an inkling of pain until at last she made herself turn toward Carnelian. Gren's hair was already starting to fade.

# 61

TILLER COULDN'T remember how long the sedatives were supposed to last. Her memory felt like a deep dark hole, a place that had never nurtured any intelligent life.

Who had given her the injector? Colonel Istel? She couldn't picture his face.

Only the Forest and the anguish it brought her seemed real.

She went over to the willow and laid Carnelian's head in her lap. Carnelian's eyes had not fully closed, though she appeared otherwise insensate.

Tiller reached down and shut her eyelids one by one.

Had the Scholar been fully extinguished from Carnelian's body? Was it the Scholar who lay in her lap right now—a monster hiding beneath the blanket of Carnelian's hide?

No, she told herself. No. Gren couldn't have been wrong about this. Gren wouldn't lie.

But she couldn't wish away her apprehension. It would be a very long wait for Carnelian to wake up as herself again.

She assumed they would be stuck here for the next few hours, if not for the rest of the day.

Gren's legion of phages had melted away into the light and shadows beyond the tall rim of the caldera. They displayed no further signs of aggression.

Carnelian breathed evenly, untroubled. But there were still damp traces where blood had escaped her nose and ears, thin red worms like parasites fleeing a dying host.

She might have come very close to getting destroyed by her own renegade cores.

Tiller attempted to examine her magic. She kept starting over, as if repeatedly losing her place in the middle of the same page of the same book.

She still couldn't tell which of the implanted cores had originally belonged to the Scholar. Or Rozen.

Despite this, there was a welcome familiarity to how Carnelian's magic moved now. The sleepy internal stirring of her branches.

Her cores looked comfortable, mussels anchored to a safe rock. A marked contrast to how they'd acted after the Scholar took control.

*Enjoy the time you've got*, Gren had said. *She won't leave you as soon as you fear.*

Transplant rejection was still a risk, then. Even if they'd exorcised the Scholar's essence—even if Gren had succeeded in taking the Scholar down with him—that risk would remain.

It was a problem inherent to the fact that Carnelian harbored extra cores in the first place. Not something induced solely by the Scholar's post-death machinations.

How long did Carnelian have left?

No way to know. One of her implants might become incompatible with her body in a year from now, or ten years, or never.

That was the crux of it. No matter how much time passed, no one could ever assure them that there would be nothing to worry about. That nothing would happen.

Tiller listened to amber bees buzzing as she wiped the blood from Carnelian's face. She listened until the buzzing seemed to come from inside her.

Her hands tightened on Carnelian's hair. She couldn't bring herself to look across at Gren.

The light of the sunvines congealed over time, turning a rich dark orange. She shifted position every now and then to avoid losing feeling in her legs.

As Carnelian began coming to, she grabbed sporadically at Tiller—and then at her own shoulders and arms—as though attempting to catch a thief in the act.

"Rest longer," Tiller said, but she wouldn't listen.

It was her. It was really Carnelian. Not an impostor.

Tiller had no distinct evidence of this except the wildness of her own relief. It overcame her so completely that she found it hard to swallow, hard to think.

Carnelian sat up. She immediately used First Aid on herself. So forcibly that she may as well have been punching herself in the head.

First Aid wasn't designed to speed up the process of emerging from sedation, but apparently it did help ease the symptoms.

Carnelian lowered her hands from her temples. "You need treatment, too."

Was she delirious? "I'm fine," Tiller said.

"I was in here the whole time," Carnelian told her. "I was a passenger. Like a tick on a deer. I felt everything. The Scholar didn't care."

She paused. "You're not wondering if this is really me?"

"Gren told me the Scholar wouldn't be a problem anymore."

"I heard you scream," Carnelian said. "After you asked the Scholar to use my sword on you. When all those phages jumped to stop you."

She put a hand to her forehead, touching one of the new marks where Rozen had swiped at her.

"I heard you scream," she said again. "I didn't have control of myself. But I was still the one holding that sword. Those were my hands. I would have run you through. Just like twenty years ago. Just like when I killed your brother."

Abruptly, she seemed to run out of words. "Lord," she whispered. "The Scholar was in every cell of my body. I want to burn it all down."

Tiller got up. She'd left the mantle unfastened; it slid from her shoulders. Below her, Carnelian caught it without prompting.

"I'm still here. I'm still alive. No big holes in my clothes." Tiller turned to show what she meant. "The phages pulled me away to save me. They didn't touch me for long."

Carnelian rose, too—wobbly, but somehow holding herself together. "Phages can sear right through fabric."

"They didn't wound me."

"No, but—"

"You can take a look when we set up camp."

A heavy silence ensued.

Carnelian stooped to collect her gloves from the lingonberry bushes growing over Rozen's remains. She put them back on one at a time, followed by her stained mantle. She didn't pick up her fighting pipe.

Everything else seemed unaltered. The bodies in the spring. The caldera walls and their slathering of vegetation. The convoluted sunvines and the intense saffron hue of their late-day light.

"Your brother," Carnelian said suddenly.

Tiller looked.

Gren was gone.

Not sprouting. Not buried under flowers or replaced by vigorous new sticks of bamboo.

Simply gone—erased from existence, as if the Forest had finally come to collect his debts in full. Nothing left.

Nothing except a vague wetness. Maybe he'd melted away into pure sacred water. Maybe he'd drained off into the ground, or into the tainted spring. Oh, Lord. Anything but that.

Tiller felt nothing of her own body. Nothing but the crack that split her chest, and sensation of a hammer driving it open wider and wider.

She perceived Carnelian's face like a portrait hung in a faraway museum. Nothing to do with where she stood now, hearing nameless creatures holler criticism from high above.

Then her body began to thaw. Her stomach curled with hunger. Her throat went raw with thirst. She didn't understand why.

There were arms holding her too tight, almost crushing her. There was a hand caressing the phage-scars on the back of her neck. The ones from—had it been just a few days ago? It already felt like she'd had them forever.

No—Carnelian wasn't crushing her. Tiller had misunderstood the entire situation.

She was the one who'd latched on for dear life. She was the one who gripped Carnelian hard enough to hurt both of them. She was the one who refused to let go.

She was the one who'd let all semblance of control slip out from between her cramped bloody fingers. She was the one who'd started crying.

"Our worst nightmares came true," said Carnelian.

Tiller wept.

"And it was all over in a single afternoon. And now it's just us. I—"
She reconsidered whatever it was that had been about to leave her
lips. She smoothed Tiller's matted hair, half out of its braid. They stayed
there for a very long time, grabber lilies nipping futilely at their knees.

# Part Five

*The Heart of the Forest*

# 62

THEY CLIMBED out of the caldera before night fog rose to fill it. They set up camp near the corpulent Fertility Monolith, though only after venturing out to find an alternate source of water. They wouldn't bathe in or drink from the corpse spring.

All water in the Forest was connected. The stream where they washed themselves bore traces of the same taint. But here the Forest had cleansed it enough for living fish to dart about their ankles, and for giant salamanders to take shelter below rocks lining the banks.

Neither of them had the energy to speak much.

"Real cheerful pair, aren't we?" Carnelian muttered as she rinsed her face.

The salamanders looked unamused.

The water was fast-flowing and cold enough to leave Tiller shivering. Good for scrubbing off sweat.

Carnelian pulled her over and gave First Aid to her torn-up hands.

She examined every inch of Tiller's body for phage-marks. There were too many tender parts to cover them all with salve. The phages' touch had branded Tiller straight through her clothes, leaving pale damaged splotches like color-inverted bruises. Carnelian's magic soothed the skin-level pain, but in its wake came an unbearable itchiness.

In their geodesic tent, they briefly discussed trying to do something about the bodies in the spring.

"I'll be honest," Carnelian said. "I'm in no state of mind to float shit all the way out of the Forest. Especially not a lake's worth of half-rotted human bodies."

They decided to save it for another trip.

Tiller hadn't expected to get much rest. Yet sleep took her as soon as the nightly fog finished closing in.

In her sleep she heard the voice of the Forest. The same entity that had addressed her through Gren. Now it spoke in visions and concepts rather than syllabic human language.

The Forest did not need a heart. But it craved one. It missed Gren as much as she did. Maybe more—he had spent more years alone with the Forest than he'd spent growing up with his twin.

If Tiller became the heart of the Forest, she could encourage it to pull back peaceably. To stop eating up new territory. Over time, she could again make it a livable place for foresters. She could resurrect Koya Village. She could learn to command phages.

And she would gain an understanding of magic that far surpassed other operators.

(Gren had performed sophisticated maintenance on Carnelian with such easy confidence. He'd made it look as effortless as Asa Lantana.)

She only had one question.

*What do I have to give up?*

It would take another twenty years to gain a mastery equivalent to

Gren, the wordless voice told her. At least twenty years to fully rein in the Forest's pent-up aggression.

Beyond that, her ability to exist outside the Forest would diminish over time.

At first she might be able to spend a whole season outside, if she needed to.

After a couple of years, she'd risk dying if she crossed the border for more than a day trip.

Two decades later, and she wouldn't be able to leave at all.

Don't become the heart of the Forest if you plan on dying outside it, the voice warned her. The Forest would go wilder than ever if it lost its heart to another land.

Tiller wasn't tired at all when she woke. Her blood thrummed.

She picked herself up as quietly as possible. Carnelian still appeared to be sleeping.

The fog would soon dissipate. At the moment, though, it was so concentrated that she almost got lost on the way to the monolith.

She touched the rock and found it to be pillowy again, with the texture of memory foam. The sunvines piercing the monolith tinted everything reddish-gold, including masses of fog. The magical entrance was sealed.

Quite belatedly, it occurred to Tiller that she had no way to get in on her own.

"You could've woken me," Carnelian said from behind her.

"I was about to turn around and go get you."

"Hah. You would've snuck inside by yourself if you could."

Tiller didn't deny it.

Carnelian drew closer. "Thought I saw everything that happened down by the spring. What'd I miss?"

Tiller was too weary to weigh the merits of lying.

She told Carnelian about the dream she'd had that night. About the Forest speaking through Gren. About what she might gain, and what she might lose.

*Drink water from the room that eats sound. Drink within a day. Three days at most.*

*You too can become the heart of the Forest.*

"And then you'll be stuck in the Forest forever?" Carnelian asked.

"Not forever—not in the same way as an everlasting phage. I'll still be human."

"But your brother—"

"He didn't become a phage in order to serve as the heart of the Forest," Tiller said. "He became a phage because—"

"Because I killed him," Carnelian finished. "...I see. So he was already a phage when he formed his bond with the Forest. An unusually talkative phage, granted. He took on a new role as the heart of the Forest, but it didn't change his essential nature. In the same way, you think it won't make you inhuman. But over time it'll bind you to this land where no one lives. Tighter and tighter."

Tiller waved fog away from her face. It was starting to clear. "It doesn't have to remain as a land where no one lives," she said. "I can help with that."

"By the time you're in your fifties, sure. By then—how many foresters will still remember how to live here? How many will want to return?

"If people from other villages had children in the city, there'll be entire generations of descendants who've never set foot in the Forest. How many would be interested in a way of life so different from their—"

Tiller put a hand over Carnelian's mouth. "You can't believe that I wouldn't have thought of that."

As usual, Carnelian wore her gloves and mantle over her sleepwear. Gloved hands peeled Tiller's fingers away from her lips.

"I get why your brother told you not to feel responsible for the Forest."

"Can you let me in now?"

Carnelian's face twisted. "I was rooting for you to cut down the Scholar. Even if it meant killing me with him. I was all for it. But here I am. And I don't even know if I'm glad. I don't even know if I'm grateful."

"You don't have to be," Tiller said.

She released Tiller's hand. "I trust your choices. I don't necessarily like them. I doubt I'd make the same choices myself. But I trust you to choose better than I would."

She bent down to reopen the monolith. They stepped through the front door to the Scholar's house.

Carnelian mentioned that she'd been wondering if the building would still admit her. The magic locks on the monolith were indeed keyed to the Scholar's core alone, and not to the stowed-away ghost of his consciousness.

The journey down to the anechoic chamber felt much quicker now that they knew where they were going. Part of Tiller expected to find Gren waiting inside again.

He wasn't.

The chamber stood empty. Nothing rested on top of the incongruously modern standing desk. The spinning wheel failed to turn.

The lanterns still glowed. Whatever they held, it wasn't fire.

The complex walls and grated floor soaked up incidental noise like a colossal sponge. Carnelian teetered at the threshold.

Tiller felt dizzy, too, but she took the lead anyway. Carnelian followed her in, hands on her shoulders.

"Once you do this, you can't undo it. Right?"

Carnelian's voice sounded very strange, coming from behind her. Tiller twisted around in an attempt to hear better.

Carnelian watched her fixedly. "Once it changes you, will you be changed for the rest of your life?"

"I don't think the Forest would accept a resignation letter."

They went up to the stone bathtub at the far end of the room. A single lantern perched on its rim with claws like those of an eagle. The tub came up so high that Tiller wouldn't have to bend much to lift a palmful of water to her lips.

"This is the only time I've ever regretted not being able to take a bondmate," Carnelian said. "If I didn't have all these transplants—if I were more of a normal mage—"

"What're you talking about?"

Carnelian cast a bitter look at the water, flawlessly still and flawlessly clear. "It's like you're bonding the Forest instead."

"You gave me your necklace of teeth," Tiller reminded her. "It's you I'll be marrying."

"But you aren't becoming my heart."

"Please tell me you're not jealous of the Forest."

Carnelian laughed. The structure of the room ruthlessly stripped all resonance from her voice. Laughter had never seemed so parched.

"I am," she said. "Do you find that so strange? I can't talk to you in your head. I can't come to you in your dreams. I'm not your real home. I can't compete with a place."

Tiller opted to combat this with hard logic. "The Forest doesn't have romantic designs on me. Might as well be jealous of the sky."

"I know," Carnelian said. The anechoic walls made her sound soft. "I'm just whining."

No one had told Tiller how much to drink. Presumably a sip would do the trick.

She wiped her fingers on her shirt, then dipped her hand in the tub and brought some water to her mouth.

The first thing she noticed: its coldness.

The water was far colder than the air of the room around it. So cold that it ought to have frozen over. So cold that it felt like it stripped some vital coating from her teeth.

That penetrating cold slipped through her mouth and the back of her throat and down into the center of her body.

Carnelian appeared to be holding her breath. She peered worriedly at Tiller.

Nothing happened. No great transformation.

Not on the outside, anyway.

A revelation took root in Tiller's stomach. She lowered her still-wet hand, forgetting to dry it.

Once her new knowledge began to flower, she couldn't understand how she had ever been complete without it.

Gren had not vanished. Nor had he been reborn as a berry-laden bush like Rozen Silva.

While Tiller tended to Carnelian, Gren's anointed body had melted into sacred water.

His water had stolen away from the bowl-shaped caldera, creeping up the stony walls like a living puddle.

His water phased through the sides of the monolith, just as he'd been able to do as a phage.

It went on a quicksilver journey down the stairs to the basement. It clung with trembling tension to the grate covering the floor of the anechoic chamber, fighting not to fall through. It glided up the sides of the tub.

At last it rejoined the final vestiges of untainted water from the old sacred spring.

Carnelian started to say something.

Tiller heard the sounds she made, but failed to catch their meaning.

She stared at the magic—nine people's worth of magic—lurking in Carnelian's lower abdomen.

She perceived Carnelian's cores as a kind of ecosystem.

Now she could see how to keep them in balance. How to care for and protect the entire system. How to stop it from breaking down.

Eight of those cores were borrowed organs. (If a concentration of magic could be called an organ.) Not originally hers. But all human beings—mages and operators and laypeople, everyone—lived with foreign creatures colonizing their tissue. Gut bacteria. Microscopic skin mites.

Carnelian's magic was a miniature forest. Tiller could tend to this forest.

In the past she'd tried treating one core at a time, as if giving maintenance to nine different mages. She knew of no other way to perform her duty as an operator. But merely detangling each individual unit wouldn't ensure long-term stability.

She had to manage the forest as a whole. She had to learn the perspective of a steward, a gardener.

A strange tenderness welled up in her. She'd seen Carnelian and her eight ancillary cores as the equivalent of nine inmates locked in the same jail cell. No one had chosen to get thrown in there. Tiller's job was to prevent them from getting riled up, to isolate them in their separate corners.

Yet even when they avoided touching, each core and branch exerted an invisible influence on the others. Like the subtle underground interactions of tree roots.

There was a beauty to this small forest, to the way nine pieces of nine people knit together into a fragile whole. She was only just now recognizing it, but it had been there all along.

"Nel," Tiller said. "Your cores won't ever betray you again."

Carnelian blinked at her, visibly wary.

"I'm still me," Tiller appended.

Her damp hand grazed Carnelian's stomach. Muscles clenched beneath the thin nightshirt.

Carnelian sounded choked. "Tiller—"

"You'll have to keep coming to me for treatment. Once I settle down in the Forest, you'll have to visit me here. I'm sorry about that. But you won't have it hanging over your head anymore."

"Have *what* hanging over my head?"

"The possibility of sudden transplant rejection. No reason for it. Years and years and years after the fact. Nothing to do with the Scholar trying to linger. Just—"

"Transplant rejection?" Carnelian demanded.

"Did I pronounce it wrong?"

"We've never talked about that, you and I. I'd have sewn my mouth shut before mentioning it."

"I did just see it happening. Your cores almost killed you after the Scholar took over."

"How'd you intuit what you were looking at?" Carnelian's tone made it feel like an interrogation room. "Don't tell me the commander fed you some sob story about my pathetic little lifespan."

"No," Tiller said. "It was Asa Lantana."

"Of course. The barbarian. I never—"

"Even if you never told her, she could tell."

"She shouldn't have frightened you with baseless speculation."

"Is it baseless?" asked Tiller. "This is part of why you go for check-ups at Central."

Carnelian's hands closed around the high rim of the cauldron-like bathtub.

"I'm lucky to have lived this long," she said. "I'm a madman's invention.

A machine held together with rusty gears and rotting string. No one would be surprised if I just stopped working one morning. In my fifties, in my forties, in my thirties—any day now.

"I accepted that long ago. It's out of my hands. I might get run over by a skimmer on the street, but I still go outside. I don't worry about things I can't control."

"Good," Tiller retorted. "Now I won't have to worry about it, either. I see exactly how to keep your cores from eating you."

Carnelian looked profoundly defeated. "You gave yourself to the Forest to save me."

"Don't oversimplify."

"Am I wrong?" Carnelian asked.

"If you don't worry about things you can't control, you wouldn't blame yourself for the Scholar coming back. Or for anything that happened while he held your body hostage."

Each word vanished into the ether the moment it left Tiller's lips. The flat voiceless water reflected lustrous lantern-light. Plus a hint of her and Carnelian.

"We'll walk out of the Forest together," Tiller said. "No change in plans."

Carnelian's head snapped up. "You're still leaving?"

"I only just became a new heart of the Forest. Now's my last chance to leave for any significant stretch of time. Got a lot of stuff to take care of in the city."

"I do owe you a date," Carnelian said, brightening. "Sea urchin, right? The Parasite Guild messed with our dinner plans last time."

"Sure." Tiller steered her back toward the wall they'd used to enter. "We can debate logistics later."

Time to get out of here.

She didn't see double. She wasn't like Gren, experiencing everything that took place in every corner of the Forest. She didn't sense tens of thousands of phages plucking at her awareness like slavering dogs on a long, long leash.

(How large was the phage population, anyway? Might there be far more phages out in the wild than anyone realized?)

She held the back of Carnelian's mantle while they climbed the interminable stairs up out of the basement.

Carnelian kept glancing over her shoulder as if to make sure that Tiller hadn't undergone a terrifying metamorphosis in the shadows.

Someday Tiller's mind might be less securely anchored to the solidity of her mortal body.

Someday she might find herself growing more confused about where she ended and where the Forest began. The boundaries of her humanity might blur like watercolor.

Someday she might forget how sweetly it ached to see Carnelian wounded and half-smiling. How the blankness of a turned back could fill her with inexpressible tension.

But not yet.

# 63

NEITHER OF THEM could figure out exactly how many days remained till the chalice assault. The clematis pin and Carnelian's lacquer ear pieces refused to react.

It should've been possible to count the days since Asa Lantana warned them that the schedule had been pushed forward. That the chalices would be unleashed in just a week.

But yesterday alone held an impossible weight. Everything before that felt immeasurably distant.

"Who's to say they won't change things up again?" Carnelian said finally. "Might go back to the original schedule. Or they might send the chalices even earlier."

She stopped brushing Tiller's hair. "What if they've already come? We might find the borders burning. Impassable."

"I'll probably sense it when the chalices attack," Tiller said.

"That doesn't sound pleasant."

Carnelian vowed to nurse Tiller back to health if damage to the Forest made her keel over.

Tiller, for her part, hoped they might still have a chance of escaping before any chalices came down from the skies. That certainly seemed safer than lying low and praying not to get struck by shrapnel.

As they crossed the mountain, they took a route past the fire caves. They paused at the foot of the Radish Monolith.

The stones they'd stacked for their brothers had yet to fall over.

Neither of them knew what to say. Tiller's heart felt too tight.

She thought of Carnelian lingering by Rozen's lingonberry bushes. Her mind ran like water, seeking gaps in every past action, probing for weak spots. Looking relentlessly for all the things she'd done wrong.

"Rozen only died once," Carnelian said quietly. "I let go of him long, long ago. All I did on the mountain was lay his body to rest. Your brother is different."

"I've mourned him for twenty-one years," Tiller said. "Even if we never went to the sacred spring, I would've kept mourning him."

This did not absolve her. But it was her truth, or part of it.

It didn't pain her to turn her back on the twin stone markers. Not any more than it should have.

She would return here soon enough.

They came across a lone phage soon after setting off down the mountain. A tall, spindly adult.

It didn't look at Tiller. It looked through her, as if she were just another chestnut sapling.

When she pulled Carnelian right up against her side, twining their arms together, the phage began ignoring Carnelian, too. It vanished behind a tree trunk the size of a hotel lobby.

"That was easy," Carnelian said happily. "I love not having to fight."

No phages stood guarding the vorpal hole near Koya Village. The hole seemed almost closed now—it had been reduced to a pursed line like a pair of angry lips.

They kept going. Soon they stood before the great barrier of stinging nettles. Tiller reached for a witch bush to break off one of its sticks.

The nettles parted for her unprompted, forming a path far broader than usual.

"Look how they're bowing," Carnelian commented. "You're a queen."

She didn't feel very queen-like that night.

They stayed in Baba Sayo's moss-swaddled cottage again, bathed in blue light.

Everything looked blue in here. Even Carnelian's hair. Even their skin, when they stripped down to inspect each other's phage-marks.

This turned into a sweatier set of activities, which ended only when Tiller heard a voice like a crabrabbit getting eaten alive by a fox.

She seized her basher and ran naked out of the cottage.

There was nothing to fight. Nothing but chilly fog.

The screaming continued for a very long time.

It wasn't a noise traveling through the air from any particular direction. It didn't get quieter when Tiller slunk back through the door.

The screams came from something inside her. They didn't map neatly to her existing senses. Not even her magic perception. Her body had decided to translate these alien howls into a simulation of audible sound.

From start to finish, Carnelian couldn't hear a thing.

"I think the chalices came," Tiller said.

She begged Carnelian to talk to her, to give her something to listen to other than the wrath of the Forest.

Carnelian rose to the occasion. She launched immediately into an overly-detailed explanation of every card game in her repertoire. The official rules. All sorts of house rules. Various secrets and dirty tricks.

Next she began naming cocktails. Then common smoke sculpture formations. After this she proceeded to relate, in gory detail, the biggest scandals of each prominent gambling house in Nui City.

She went to fetch the empty bottle of roeberry liquor from their previous stay in the village. It was right where they'd left it, clean and dry. She blew across the top to make a series of low, wailing notes. The rhythm sounded like a military anthem.

She seemed to be striving not to speak a word of the past.

"You can talk about anything," Tiller said, head against the wall. This screaming felt like enduring a beating. "Talk about what's bothering you. I just want to hear your voice."

For the first time in close to an hour, Carnelian lapsed into silence. Blue light drowned both of them. Tiller closed her eyes.

"When the Scholar took over, I was helpless," Carnelian said. "Worse than that—useless. I wasn't strong enough to break free on my own."

Tiller groped about until she found Carnelian's wrist. "He prepared for it since you were a child. He had the power of a sacrificed blue on his side. Nothing you could've done."

Even with her eyes shut, she could tell that Carnelian didn't believe her.

"I always wondered where my drive to survive came from. I thought it was something deep and animalistic, below the level of logic. A mage's wild instinct. But maybe it was the Scholar all along."

A broken hint of humor crept into Carnelian's voice. "He never entertained doubts about whether he deserved to live. He wouldn't have wasted time wondering if there was any point in fighting after everyone else got taken by phages.

"It must've been the Scholar in me, the way I always pulled through. No matter the odds. It must've been him. I wasn't nearly that motivated."

"The Scholar's hair didn't turn red," Tiller said.

"What?"

Tiller opened her eyes. She prodded Carnelian's thigh with her toes until at last Carnelian looked her in the face.

"You said your cores sometimes band together to push you. To give you a strength you can't consciously access on your own. That's when your hair turns red."

"It's just a theory," Carnelian objected. "I might've made the whole thing up."

"None of that happened when the Scholar seized control," Tiller said stubbornly. "Your hair stayed silver. Your other cores didn't lend him any secret power. Quite the opposite. They were ready to eat each other alive. To destroy themselves, and your body in the process. Just to get rid of him.

"Maybe the Scholar's embedded will used to play a part in propelling you past your limits. Maybe he wanted to keep you alive for his sake. For his future use. But the rest of your cores were always on your side. Not his."

"Hey." Carnelian swatted her shoulder. "I'm supposed to be comforting you right now. Not the other way around."

Tiller snorted. "Your idea of comforting me was describing the time when a circus troupe let vorpal beasts loose in the middle of a busy casino."

"Bears, too," Carnelian said. "Don't forget the bears."

They lay side by side after the screaming died down. Tiller felt flattened and exhausted. Too exhausted, somehow, to sleep.

"It would be nice," Carnelian mused, "to think that everything wrong with me came from the Scholar inside me."

"Do you feel different from before?"

"I don't. I really don't. His presence or absence can't cure me of being myself. And him being wiped away from me doesn't mean he never left a mark."

Carnelian rolled to face Tiller.

She told Tiller how she had never loved the Scholar. Not as a father, or a brother, or a teacher. Not as anything.

From the moment she first saw him, something in her had been repulsed by him. As if she could smell a scent coming off him that few others detected.

Even when he trained her to reflexively obey his every word, even when she surrendered her entire sense of self to his orders, she never particularly liked or respected him.

She raised her blue-tinted hand and rotated it in the air.

"Your hand doesn't need to respect you in order to automatically do as you say," she explained.

As a child, she'd had no deep insight into his motives or character. But she never lost her instinctual soul-level revulsion.

Rozen was different. He liked the Scholar, and he wanted the Scholar to like him. He listened earnestly. He thought the best of the Scholar, at least until the Scholar broke him.

And that, Carnelian theorized, was precisely why the Scholar picked her as a vessel for core transplants.

Rozen might've looked like a better candidate: he'd had more magic branches to start with.

The Scholar, on some level, must have appreciated Carnelian's detachment. Her persistent dislike of him. He must have perceived a kind of logic to it, although she wouldn't have been able to explain her own aversion.

He must have looked down on Rozen's more affectionate nature, his irrational sweetness and goodness.

Before dying, the Scholar had coached Carnelian on what to tell the people who would eventually come to collect her. She remembered scattered fragments of their last conversation.

*Don't cry*, he'd warned her. *If you must cry, make it silent. If you come off as hysterical, if you throw a big fit, they'll think you went berserk. Even in the absence of proof.*

*Control yourself, and speak clearly. Tell them we made you do it.*

The Scholar predicted future events with remarkable accuracy. He told her that she would be rewarded a massive sum as compensation for the negligence of those who should've kept the Scholar (a mage himself) under tighter control.

"He gave me a letter to pass to his family," Carnelian said. "His real family." She nuzzled Tiller's back as she spoke. "They would take care of me, he promised. They would treat me like a princess."

"Did they?"

"They were fine. But I always wondered. Especially about Mari—about the commander. Was she good to me because she felt sorry for me? Because I had the last existing piece of her father in me?

"I swore I would never give her father back. I would never take on the Bloodwood family name. Not even to free myself from being a permanent child of the state. My spitefulness knows no bounds, you see."

"So you'd rather marry a stranger," Tiller concluded.

"You've never seemed like a stranger," Carnelian murmured to the bones at the base of her neck.

# 64

THE FOREST did strange things to human magic. Certain ordinary skills (porting, for instance) became so risky that no one would dare attempt them.

What, then, did the Forest do to the source of the magic—to mages themselves?

There was a reason, surely, that mages were rarely born among foresters.

Some excused the Scholar's crimes by saying his long stays in the Forest had driven him mad. But visitors from outside always became disoriented and overwhelmed by the sheer scale of the Forest. That was hardly an issue limited to mages.

The state of the sacred spring, the trophy rooms in the monolith—all available evidence pointed toward a single conclusion.

The Forest had not altered the Scholar. The Scholar had altered the Forest.

The morning after the screaming, Tiller and Carnelian left Koya Village.

They walked on and on. Despite their trepidation, their surroundings seemed mostly unchanged.

They stepped around fuzzy caterpillars the size of lapdogs. They trod on a smattering of spring-green ginkgo leaves, which floated down from trees covered in obscene wart-like burls.

The main difference was that the thickest of the underbrush yielded before Carnelian could so much as brandish her sword at it. (A good thing, considering that Tiller had abandoned her machete back at the sacred spring.)

Then they spotted the biggest difference of all.

They saw it at the same time.

A humongous machina.

It lay crash-landed in a stand of wild magnolia. Trees in full flower splayed out beneath it, snapped like cheap disposable chopsticks.

Their bodies reacted before their minds did. For a few moments they grappled, hearts in their throats, each trying to leap in front of the other.

"Enough," Tiller said, breathless. "This is silly."

They calmed themselves.

All the while, the chalice stayed stationary.

From some angles it appeared vaguely humanoid. From others it looked akin to a titanic crumpled-up dragonfly.

"Did you hear anything?" Tiller asked.

"On the way here? No. It might've fallen last night."

Tiller had to stretch her neck to see the top of it. Diaphanous limbs—broken wings, or broken blades—protruded from the chalice's back, slicing deep into the trunk of the nearest canopy-height cypress.

If that cypress started to come down....

"Know where the hatch is?"

"The cockpit?"

"Whatever it's called," Tiller said. "The place where they stash the pilot."

"The main pilot is definitely dead. That's just how these machina work."

"Shouldn't we check?"

Carnelian took another step toward the wreckage. "I guess there might be backup pilots still alive in there. Too afraid to take the wheel, or yoke, or reins, or joystick. I'm a little fuzzy on the details."

"If they're alive, we'd better let them out."

"As for the dead among them—wait, would dying up in the sky still count as dying inside the Forest? Or outside it?"

"Don't ask me," Tiller demurred.

"You're literally the heart of the Forest."

"Compared to Gren, I'm an ignorant baby."

She scrutinized the chalice's surface. It looked as if it had a texture like shark skin: smooth in one direction, sharp and jagged in the other.

"Either way," Tiller said, "if they died in Forest territory, we've got to do something before they become a phage. If they died outside the Forest, we've got to get them away from here before the presence of their corpse becomes a poison."

Together they gazed at the fallen machina: top to bottom, side to side.

Carnelian pulled on her gloves. "The cockpit is probably located somewhere in the upper part of the torso."

"Does this thing even have a torso?" Tiller asked.

"Its thorax, then. I'll do the climbing."

"No, no," said a voice.

"That won't do," said another.

"You beat us to it," said the voices together.

Violet glasses. Impeccable skin.

The auditors emerged from the woods around the downed chalice as naturally as a pair of phages.

Carnelian made no attempt to conceal her aggravation.

They were in uniform. A sleeker and less layered version of the one Carnelian wore. Still just a single glove each.

"Nice hair," Auditor Lapis told Tiller. "So that's what it looks like."

"Very blue," agreed Auditor Aeris.

"We're getting the pilots out," Carnelian said. "If you've come to help—"

Auditor Aeris tilted his head.

"Help?" echoed Auditor Lapis. "Oh, no. Don't open that door. There's no hope."

Carnelian ran her eyes over the angles of the chalice as if planning how to climb it. "Might not be any hope, but there should at least be a body."

"You misunderstand," Lapis said. "The inner workings of a chalice are a state secret. Your security clearances don't cover this."

"No offense," added Aeris.

"If you see what's inside there, we can't let you live."

A pregnant pause.

"Was that a joke?" Carnelian spat.

The auditors laughed. "Not at all," they said in unison.

"Dead serious," continued Auditor Lapis. "By the way, Nellie, where's your mantle?"

Tiller had it tossed over her shoulder.

"It's been warm in parts of in the Forest," Tiller said. "I gave her blanket permission to leave it off."

"Blanket permission?" Lapis went wide-eyed behind her purple glasses. "No such thing."

For a strained second, Tiller feared they might come to blows beneath the glittering wreck of the chalice.

At first glance, the auditors were commendably composed for two young mages who would hardly ever have reason to set foot in the Forest.

But the wolfishness with which they closed in on Carnelian had a sharper edge to it than back at the outpost. As if they really did want her to lose her temper. To get court-martialed.

"Catastrophe ROE hasn't been lifted yet," Aeris said thoughtfully.

Lapis put on a pious face. "It would be tragic if we mistook you for phages."

"But no one would blame us."

"We would only be acting in self-defense."

"Such a terrible shame. Still—"

"Everyone has the right to defend themselves."

"Especially in the Forest."

"A wild and dangerous place."

"A place for all kinds of sad mistakes."

Carnelian drew a breath.

Tiller shouldered her way between them before Carnelian could speak. She flashed the badge Colonel Istel had given her.

The mark of the snake.

"Do your ears work?" she asked.

The auditors blinked, perfectly synchronized.

They both wore pointy ear cuffs. Tiller tapped the curve of her own naked earlobe to demonstrate what she meant.

"Oh, these?" Auditor Aeris's tapered tips were extended to the point of looking rather impractical. "They haven't worked in hours."

"So you can't communicate with your superiors. Or anyone else from the military." Tiller showed them her snake again. "I outrank you."

"In a manner of speaking, yes. You're still a civilian," said Auditor Lapis.

"I'm also an operator."

Lapis looked troubled. "We really can't let you inside the chalice."

"Fine." Tiller backed away, taking Carnelian with her. "You go open it. We'll close our eyes."

"Ah. No need for that." Lapis petted the chalice with her one gloved hand. Apparently she knew the correct direction to stroke it. "Our mission was to find her. Not to salvage her."

"We aren't here to retrieve her equipment," said Aeris. "Nor any personnel. Not our job."

"All we have to do now is report her location."

"Her?" Tiller repeated.

"Some personify chalices," Carnelian said. "Like warships."

She lifted her mantle off Tiller. She tossed it around her own shoulders with an impressively palpable air of resentment. She glowered at the auditors as she closed the front fastening and pulled the hood up over her head.

Creamy magnolia petals curled underfoot, shaken loose from fallen trees. Tiller caught herself sweeping them into fretful piles with the side of her boot.

The auditors' bloodthirstiness seemed like a passing mood. They wouldn't seriously challenge Carnelian in the Forest just to blow off steam.

But that could easily change if the four of them got stalled here indefinitely. If the auditors had all the time in the world to jab at Carnelian until she snapped.

"There's one more thing that might work," Tiller told them.

She reached for the silver clematis pinned next to her snake insignia. "No."

Only one person spoke—in such a hard-edged voice that she genuinely couldn't tell who had said it.

Auditor Lapis: "A foreigner gave you that."

Auditor Aeris: "Didn't they?"

"I got it from Colonel Istel," Tiller said.

"It connects to a foreigner." Lapis shook her head. "We can't have that. Not with a chalice on the line."

Tiller lowered her hand.

"Tell us your grand plan, then," Carnelian said through her teeth.

Lapis looked back and forth between Carnelian and Tiller.

"I know," she said with a wide gap-toothed smile. "Let's split up. Nellie and Aeris can guard the chalice." She gestured to herself and Tiller. "You and I can go looking for the nearest heliograph tower."

Carnelian yanked Tiller out of reach. "No way in hell."

"Are you in charge," Auditor Lapis asked amiably, "or is your operator?"

Carnelian reared up. Tiller readied herself to dive between them. The chalice's insectile chassis glinted maliciously in the background.

But in the end, Carnelian looked down her nose at the auditors and responded with steely calm.

"I'll do you one better," she announced. "I'll carry this entire machina out of the Forest. Let's all leave together."

The auditors' eyebrows shot up.

Aeris: "How uncharacteristic."

Lapis: "You hate levitation magic."

Aeris: "It's your greatest weakness."

Carnelian scoffed at them. "I'm damn good at it. Don't you forget that." She inclined her head at Tiller. "Permission to remove a glove?"

"Go on."

Tiller thought she would stretch her bared hand out toward the wrecked chalice. Instead she reached down and took hold of Tiller, lacing their fingers together. She kept looking straight ahead. No dismay showed on the side of her face. As always, she had the sort of profile that sculptors might see in their dreams.

Magic snaked out of her body: a radiant spark of motion like a long fuse burning down, undulating toward far-off explosives.

Her hand tightened on Tiller's. They were both desperately clammy.

Clouds of magnolia petals billowed from crushed trees as the chalice lurched into the air, weightless.

It looked even larger in motion. It cast a shadow sufficient to cover all four of them. And far more.

Tiller heard Carnelian swallowing as distinctly as if it were something happening inside her own body.

She pictured a little girl floating half-decayed corpses through the woods. The smell and the fluids. The hostility of the Forest. The Scholar's unwavering certainty.

White petals swirled feverishly.

She wanted to tell Carnelian not to force herself. The chalice was the size of a moderate high-rise building, and at least as heavy. She shouldn't have to torture herself for the sake of getting one up on the auditors.

Yet Tiller was too afraid to utter anything that might shatter her concentration.

If that chalice slipped from the grip of her magic, Tiller suspected it might never rise off the ground again.

She settled for squeezing Carnelian's hand. A pulse beat in their sweaty palms. As if a living heart lay trapped between them.

# 65

THE CHALICE was much too large to float through the Forest like a parade balloon. To fit, it would have to bulldoze every thousand-year-old tree in its path.

Instead, Carnelian guided the wreck up toward the hole it had originally punched in the canopy. The auditors confirmed that it had come straight down from the sky—an abrupt vertical fall.

Only then did Tiller notice how the quality of light here differed from elsewhere in the Forest. There was a startling rawness to the splotches of sun on the ground. Sunvines usually played more of a role in tempering that intensity. They digested and dispersed it, making it last through clouds and rain and long winter nights.

She asked the auditors if they knew why the chalice had fallen.

Auditor Aeris shrugged. "Pilot error, probably."

"That's a matter for other investigators to figure out," said Auditor Lapis.

Working more by feel than by sight, Carnelian threaded the chalice through the hole in the canopy. As she and Tiller and the auditors walked along the Forest floor, the chalice (born aloft by her magic) followed them in the sky above the tallest treetops. Over forty stories high.

None of them could see it, naturally. Not even Carnelian. Not once the canopy closed up again.

They just had to trust that it was still there, tagging along like a kite. And that it wouldn't plummet down a second time, killing all of them in one fell swoop.

The auditors' mission was to locate the chalice's crash site. But they had no objections to bringing the entire thing back with them. As long as no one attempted to open the cockpit.

Tiller led the way. She kept hold of Carnelian's hand, guiding her through an obstacle course of thick roots. Carnelian followed obediently, her gaze unfocused. She aimed most of her attention at the unseen sky.

At first Tiller shushed the auditors when they tried to chitchat. Eventually, though, Carnelian told them it was fine to keep talking.

"I'm not listening anyway," she said under her breath.

From time to time, the auditors put their heads together over a device that looked like the second cousin of a compass.

"This is going a lot faster than our hike to find the chalice," said Lapis.

"Lucky," said Aeris. "Perhaps the Forest is kinder to blues."

Or perhaps the Forest had detected Tiller's determination to make the route to the border as short as possible. For Carnelian's sake.

The auditors repeatedly praised Carnelian's ability to elevate the chalice higher than the Forest itself, and to keep it hovering there without any breaks.

"The greater the height, the greater the struggle," Lapis intoned.

"For most mages, that is."

"Those equipped with a standard levitation skill."

True to her word, Carnelian showed no sign of listening.

"Why'd the chalices attack so late in the evening?" Tiller asked them.

Lapis looked puzzled. "You could tell?"

"The Forest gave off signs."

"There were some problems with the launch," said Aeris.

Lapis bobbed her head. "It kept getting pushed back. We had to pull all-nighters for support."

"We're exhausted."

Tiller thought they seemed as perky as ever. But she kept her opinion to herself.

"Of course, your local commander is suffering the brunt of it," Aeris tacked on.

Lapis: "It's a regular old mess."

Aeris: "One might even call it a clusterf—"

"Don't be vulgar," Lapis said sweetly.

"My apologies." Aeris turned to Tiller again. "You'll see what we mean."

In just over half an hour, she did.

Along the way, the auditors oohed and aahed over distant sightings of everything from flightless birds to Forest bison.

They maintained a decent pace, at least. Even while dodging stalactite fungi and goggling at pillar frogs, which squatted in neat stacks of three or four like bite-sized snowmen.

As they navigated past multicolored bamboo and bushy sago palms, diurnal bats flapped clumsily in the opposite direction. The air went hot, then cold, then hot again. It came at them like waves rolling up a shore.

The birds began to sound increasingly muted.

Were there even any birds in these trees at all?

Tiller stopped amid a sea of bluebells at the height of their sweet-smelling bloom. Carnelian bumped into her.

"What's that?" Tiller said.

The auditors came up beside them.

"The edge of the Forest," said Lapis.

Ahead of them, the bamboo and bluebells continued. So did the trees that stretched all the way up to the canopy.

But after a certain point—a dividing line as clear-cut as a border drawn on a map—everything turned white. Trunks, leaves, bamboo stalks. Airy hanging curtains of lace lichen. Endless bluebells.

The sunvines looked like albino serpents. They no longer gave off any light. The whole vista resembled a vast dim cave, one hewn from milky crystal rock or ice.

"Is that snow?" Carnelian asked blankly.

"Not snow," said Auditor Aeris. "Salt."

Tiller had expected fields of razed trees. Smoldering brush. Shorn-off trunks pointing at the sky like splintered pikes.

She'd forgotten that chalices were not conventional weaponry, and the Forest was not a conventional target. Even so—

"This can't have been on purpose," she said, dazed.

Lapis concurred. "I think not."

"The whole point of sending chalices was to reclaim land from the Forest. No one's going to be able to farm here."

"I'd like to see them try." Lapis covered her mouth with her hand when she chuckled. "The chalices did their job—they pushed the Forest back to its historical borders. All in one night. Funny how it backfired."

Auditor Aeris picked up where Auditor Lapis left off. "There certainly aren't any more plans for future assaults."

"No one will be too thrilled with this outcome. Hard to brag about it to the populace."

"Especially since a bunch of pilots must've died in the process."

"Someone," declared Lapis, "had better find a way to monetize all this salt."

Carnelian leaned harder on Tiller. "Can I drop the chalice yet?"

"Not yet," Lapis said. "The salt crumbles very easily. We'll die in an avalanche."

Carnelian abruptly sat down with her back to a barrel-thick stalk of bamboo. Her hand fell from Tiller's grasp.

"I'll push the chalice out a mile or two ahead of us," she said. "Then I'm lowering it. Good luck finding it again. I'm at my limit."

"No worries," Lapis told her. "We attached a beacon. Besides—the Forest ends where the salt starts."

"Triangulation magic will work much better out there," Aeris appended.

Some minutes later, Carnelian heaved a loud breath. She slumped her weight onto Tiller, still winded.

"Want maintenance?" Tiller asked.

She nodded against Tiller's shoulder. "What I really want is a nap."

As Tiller combed through her branches, the auditors explained more about the desert of salt.

Chalice magic had transformed every single being in the outer swathes of the Forest. Vegetation, phages, insects, megafauna: all converted to salt. From the depths of the soil to the tops of the trees.

For the time being, the salt structures might appear to hold their original shape. At the slightest provocation, however, they would start to collapse. At the far end of the reclaimed territory, closer to the outpost, a scouting team had been smothered to death below fifty stories' worth of granulated salt crystals.

Carnelian groaned upon hearing this. "Lord. Like drowning in a grain silo. How'd you two get here, then?"

"A combination of porting and parachuting," said Lapis.

"It was quite dicey," Aeris admitted.

"Definitely not part of our job description."

"But we're always happy to help out in a pinch."

"I, for one, refuse to strap on a parachute," Carnelian said. "Levitating that chalice already took a good ten years off my life."

Auditor Lapis tsk-tsked at her. "How uncooperative."

Leaving the Forest, it turned out, was the easy part.

All they had to do was step very, very carefully across the stark line where the flowering bluebells got bleached to white.

Tread softly, the auditors warned. Touch as little as possible.

As soon as they were officially out of the Forest, Auditor Aeris could use a porting token to whisk them to the far edge of the salt fields. Miles and miles and miles away from here.

Over the years, the Devouring Forest had eaten up an untenably broad swathe of Nui. Now that annexed land had been retaken—in a way likely to render it useless for generations to come.

Chalice pilots only ever got a chance to fly once.

Had the pilots setting out on their first and last flights understood what was happening?

Had they stayed alive long enough to witness the devastating reaction between the magic of their machina and the capricious magic of the Forest?

Aeris prepared his porting token. He would activate it once everyone took that single step out of the Forest and stood fully on salt.

Carnelian asked if Tiller needed to cover her hair.

Good question. Any number of people might be milling around when they emerged from the portal.

Tiller dug through her bag. She pinned on a fake-looking black wig, one with thick bangs.

She worked quickly; she didn't like having to do this in front of the auditors. She pulled up the hood of her jacket, too, for extra coverage.

Carnelian, meanwhile, shimmied on a magic-smoothing girdle.

"It won't hurt you to leave the Forest?" Carnelian said very close to her ear.

"Not this first time," Tiller whispered back.

The auditors observed them curiously. Carnelian's lips tightened, but she said nothing further.

With exquisite care, they transferred their packs across the border where life became salt. They held their breath and prayed for the wind to stay quiet.

A ominous noise emanated from somewhere deep in the white part of the woods. A sound reminiscent of the ocean, or of sand streaming through an hourglass.

Crossing that line where the Forest ended felt like entering a world of spun sugar candy. And sinister shadows. Salty bluebells crunched underfoot, instantly ruined.

This was most definitely not Forest territory. This land of salt belonged to the humans who'd made it, who'd cursed themselves to live with it. Tiller's blood told her that. She already missed the air of the Forest.

# 66

THEY PORTED to an abandoned farmhouse near the former edge of
the Forest. The same place where Colonel Istel had seen Tiller and
Carnelian off all those weeks ago.

What lay outside the old farm was no longer the Forest's creeping
frontier.

A desert of salt spread from horizon to horizon. Dismayed-sounding
birds whistled in the sky. Spring sunlight poured down like a punishment.

Here the salt was mostly flattened, with only a few lonely white
trunks sticking up at irregular intervals. They stood like the last broken
artifacts of an ancient civilization.

Workers in uniform shouted unintelligibly at each other. A lot of
people labored very loudly and very hard, but Tiller couldn't discern
what they were trying to accomplish. Construction equipment lined
up in rows like military vehicles preparing to open fire.

The fields of salt weren't actually as white as snow, though they managed to be just as blinding. Tiller began to perceive streaks of soft color: pinkish dunes here, a blue-gray hollow there. (The latter might have been the shadow of a passing cloud.)

Nearly all of it had the unnaturally fine-grained and sandy texture of table salt.

Would it have been better or worse for the woodlands to become solid crystals of rock salt? At least that way the trees would've been less likely to collapse and bury workers alive.

The auditors waved an irritatingly merry goodbye. They sauntered off to inform someone or other about the crashed chalice.

Tiller and Carnelian headed back to the outpost.

They thought they might be brought in for immediate questioning. That—before a chance to eat or drink or bathe—they'd be obligated to report on their experiences in the Forest.

The reality of it was that no one cared. Outpost 24 was a whirl of chaos.

Soldiers and civilian staff trooped to and from the newborn desert. Surveyors grumbled dire warnings about the fate of the freshwater rivers that flowed from the Forest.

The Forest had always felt like a world of its own. Too risky to pillage for resources. But it was not—and had never been—wholly disconnected from the rest of the island.

The gray sheepdog ran about in a frenzy, too overexcited to accept more than a couple seconds' worth of petting. With an air of regret, Carnelian watched it go jetting off across the bright spring grass.

She and Tiller strove to stay out of everyone's way. They quietly collected the extra luggage they'd left in storage.

Through judicious eavesdropping, they learned that the countryside trains were all stopped till tomorrow.

The north-south line had kept running normally right up until the night of the chalice attack. The vorpal hole that had spawned near the tracks was still there, albeit now with all sorts of warning signs and fancy alarms strung about its perimeter.

It didn't seem to be actively spitting out deadly beasts, though. At least not on a daily basis.

Carnelian sweet-talked a harried receptionist at the guesthouse into promising them a room. Tiller's snake insignia helped seal the deal.

After all those nights alone with Carnelian, it felt incredibly strange to see so many other people. Like sliding backwards through time. Like their weeks in the Forest had been a mere hallucination.

A few hours after dinner, Carnelian succeeded in getting hold of Colonel Istel. He was dressed for work, tidy as ever. He had gruesome dark circles under his eyes.

For the moment, though, he was technically off the clock.

Carnelian made him fetch the roeberry liquor she'd gifted him before their departure for the Forest. They cracked open its seal in an empty conference room with three walls' worth of glorious wide windows.

Istel turned a stunning hue of magenta after drinking less than half a glass. He rather stiffly professed how glad he was to see them.

"Say it again!" Carnelian crowed, waving her field scarf over her head.

She kept haranguing him until he got up on the conference table and delivered a whole big speech about friendship.

Soon afterward, he fell fast asleep: head in his arms, mouth half-open, snoring woefully.

Before losing consciousness, he'd attempted to question Carnelian on the whereabouts of her fighting pipe. She said she must've lost it during one of her many fierce battles in the Forest.

Now the only sounds left in the dark room were the dainty clinking of ice cubes and the feeble snores of the colonel. Carnelian smiled to herself as she nursed her glass.

Tiller kept getting distracted by the view from the windows. People and lights and equipment streamed incessantly across the outpost grounds. She hoped someone had brought that hyperactive dog indoors for the night.

"I was going to suggest moving south," Carnelian said to the dregs in her glass.

"South?"

"To one of the other islands. Past Central. As far south as possible."

"Why?" Tiller asked, nonplussed.

"The more distance between you and Nui, the safer you'd be. The rest of Jace knows next to nothing of Nuian lore.

"Even the syndicates down south won't give a fig about the obsessions of their counterparts in Nui. You could live without wigs. Especially if you had someone to—"

"I can't leave now," Tiller said.

"Yes." Carnelian drained her glass. "I do realize that."

The hushed seconds that followed seemed to cry out for a change of subject. At least Colonel Istel looked peaceful.

"Guess there's no chance of seeing the commander tonight," Tiller said.

Carnelian got up and went over to one of the windows. "I'm sure the commander won't have a free moment for days. Weeks, even."

A yellow half-moon hung low in the sky.

"Tiller," she said.

"What?"

"I think I'll stay at the outpost for a while."

"How long is a while?"

Carnelian glanced back. "What I mean is that I won't be getting on the train with you tomorrow." She motioned at Istel. "Not sure how helpful I'll be, frankly, but the situation seems desperate."

Tiller could not think of a single thing to say.

She had never pictured any outcome other than the two of them riding the train back to Nui City together. Maybe they'd be bickering. Maybe they'd be dozing off.

It just hadn't made sense to imagine herself alone.

But they were out of the Forest now. She could protect herself. If she had to.

In the twelve years since Doe's murder, she'd mostly gotten by on her own.

"You've got business with your Foundation, don't you?" Carnelian didn't seem to expect an answer. "No need for you to be stuck here, too."

"The commander will be glad to have you around," Tiller said at last.

Carnelian's mouth twisted. "I'm not doing it for her."

Tiller had only taken a few sips of her drink. No interest in ending up like poor Istel.

She turned her glass about in her hands. The lumps of ice formed a shape oddly similar to the Fertility Monolith.

"I can start work on our marriage application," she said. "But we need testimonials."

"We can ask...." Carnelian began counting on her fingers. "Alder, when he's conscious. The auditors. The commander. That should be enough. Asa Lantana might vouch for us, too. But I doubt the bureau would take an affidavit from a foreigner."

"You would really ask the auditors?"

"They'll be thrilled for me to owe them a favor," Carnelian said darkly.

"You sure I shouldn't stay, too?" Tiller asked. "Especially if we're going to petition the commander for a testimonial."

"No, I've got it covered. She didn't believe us capable of getting in and out of the Forest in one piece. I'll make her eat crow."

"You'll have to stamp the application at some point," Tiller said.

Carnelian raised her glass in the moonlit room. "I'll be back in the city for the Feast of Chalices."

The following day, Tiller began smelling salt all over the outpost. Not quite the same as the scent of the sea. Did salt even have a scent, for that matter? Maybe she was tasting it rather than smelling it—microscopic specks borne over from the salt fields by spring wind.

Colonel Istel (despite his obvious hangover) helped her get the special dispensation needed to board the train home. For the foreseeable future, ridership in both directions would be highly restricted.

Leaving the outpost seemed harder than entering it. Tiller had to swear not to breathe a word about the aftereffects of the chalice bombardment.

She gathered that the very existence of the salt desert was being strictly censored from the public. Some country folk might glimpse it from a distance. But no one would acknowledge that they'd seen anything of importance.

On her way out, she attempted to return her snake insignia. Colonel Istel refused to take it back.

"That's still yours," he informed her. "At least until the commander decides to recall it."

Carnelian helped carry her bags up to the small station platform.

When the train doors hissed open, and Tiller's hands were full of luggage, Carnelian swooped forward to kiss her.

"You'll be protected," she said. "Sorry for taking liberties."

"What did you do?"

Carnelian winked.

There wasn't enough time to demand answers. Tiller slid into a window seat, piling her bags next to her. In the spot that should have belonged to Carnelian.

As the train lurched into motion, its clacking and rocking took on the insistent rhythm of a heartbeat.

She still tasted Carnelian, together with an ephemeral tinge of Forest salt.

She had no idea how Carnelian would help deal with the man-made salt fields. Carnelian didn't seem to know, either. She'd joked that maybe they needed someone to stand guard against newfangled monsters. Shambling phages made of salt.

What was there to be done about the desert? To Tiller it seemed nearly as implacable a presence as the Forest.

She supposed Carnelian's homing pearls might come in handy for surveying—and subsequently despairing at—its breadth.

She realized too late that she wasn't alone on the train.

Two women waited a few seats down from her.

She shouldn't have been able to recognize them. They wore civilian clothing and expressions of pleasant neutrality.

The last time she'd tangled with them, they'd been masked.

The second they met her eyes, she recalled the stench of rotting wind-deer guts. Her gag reflex kicked hard at the back of her throat.

She groped for her yo-yo knives, then remembered how she'd lost them.

"Relax," said one of the hunters.

"We've been hired to guard you," said the other. Pince-nez glasses gripped her nose. She held a guidebook about wildlife of the eastern barrens.

Tiller's incredulity must have shown on her face.

"Professionals don't hold grudges," the first hunter assured her. "Your mage offered the Guild an extremely lucrative contract."

*You'll be protected*, Carnelian had said on the platform.

From the Forest to the salt fields to Outpost 24, she and Tiller had been together almost every waking moment. When had she found time to contact the Parasite Guild?

They might've already stationed personnel near the outpost. But still. Carnelian must've called on the commander's connections. It couldn't have been easy to work out a deal on such short notice.

Tiller sat back down. She strove to regulate her rampant adrenaline.

The hunter with the pince-nez resumed her reading, or pretended to. Her companion gave Tiller a smile that was friendly in shape and ice-cold in temperature. The buttons on her shirt were shaped like flat clinging ticks.

The countryside passed by like a scene from an old untouchable dream. The hunters remained quiet and watchful throughout.

Hours later, the city's greatest symbols appeared in the window next to Tiller. The chalice statue looming emptily on a cliff. The refurbished castle mounted on ridiculous stilts.

Back in Nui City, the yearly crop of cherry blossoms had all washed down into the streets. The earliest roe trees were just starting to flower instead, eager to finally take their turn.

The hunters made themselves scarce once Tiller exited the station. She thought she sensed people following her, but she didn't waste energy trying to catch them in the act.

If Carnelian trusted the Parasite Guild with her safety, then Tiller would trust them too.

She unlocked the door to Baba Sayo's apartment. She set her bags down before locking the door once more behind her. She inspected the rooms one by one to make sure no one had been there in her absence.

The apartment still smelled very faintly of Baba Sayo. She'd thought that scent was long gone. Maybe it was just that her nose had gone numb to it before she left for the Forest.

She kept breathing in deeply. She shuffled through the mail without really looking at anything. The closed curtains made it feel like being shut up in a cave with limited oxygen. Would she be able to sleep like this? Had she been infected by Carnelian's craving for unobstructed windows?

She took off her wig of the day. Her fingers moved rustily. She should've asked Carnelian to chop her hair short again before they departed the Forest.

Halfway through unpacking, she came across all she had left of her family. Two ceramic lids for the containers that had once held Baba Sayo and Doe.

She added them to the household shrine in the corner.

Without warning, regret gripped her. It shook her. It told her: you should've showed the lids to Gren. He couldn't touch your skin, but he could've touched these. He could've held them.

This would be Tiller's first night alone in weeks.

She felt no relief.

She looked up at the faded mushroom art on the walls. At the patterns she and Gren had etched with fine-honed twigs.

They'd done it back when they were both human. Back when nothing in the Forest could've scared them into hiding indoors. Not even phages. Not even wild boars.

She waited for someone to come gaze with her. She waited for someone to take her hand, to lay a head on her shoulder.

She waited for someone to tell her: *You've done enough.* But there was no one here to say it except Tiller herself.

# 67

EVENTUALLY Tiller would need to do something about this apartment.

In the short term, she still required a mailing address in the city. Not to mention a place to live.

After she finished extricating herself from the Koya Foundation, she'd have to reconsider. She could only keep paying rent for so long once she stopped taking a salary.

She didn't tell anyone her plans for making a permanent move to the Forest. It would be impossible to explain without making people think she was suicidal, or in the grips of psychosis.

Instead she couched her upcoming departure as a sort of vague sabbatical. A newfound hankering for travel.

When asked about her destination, she'd invent an answer on the spot. The metropolis around Central. The southern islands across the Amber Strait.

Everyone at the Foundation was very approving—congratulatory, even. *Your first time leaving Nui? You deserve it. You're still young. Go see more of the country.*

Tiller hurled herself back into work to ensure a smooth transition. In rare moments of free time, she traipsed over to City Hall to inquire about the process of applying for marriage to a mage.

Sometimes she glimpsed presumptive members of the Parasite Guild. An expressionless face in a window. A lone worker pretending to lay tiles on the roof of a building near her apartment. They were admirably unobtrusive.

Through it all, the Forest dragged at her in a way she'd never felt before. A restlessness like living grubs in her belly.

In fairness, that feeling didn't stem solely from her deepening ties to the Forest. She kept expecting to turn and see silver hair, a fluttering mantle, graceful gloved fingers, a prankster's smile.

A letter arrived at the apartment a few days before the Feast of Chalices.

Tiller glanced at the timestamp. It had been submitted for mailing less than an hour ago.

The Jace Postal Service did have a reputation for speed. Dedicated mages cranked out magic cuttings to nurture its serpentine infrastructure.

The envelope showed signs of having been opened and resealed. It was littered with unfamiliar markings in vermilion ink. The content must have passed inspection: on the inside, it appeared largely untouched.

Since returning to the city, Tiller had paid zero attention to the news. She wondered how successful the government's censors had been at suppressing the story of the salt fields.

This wasn't her first time seeing Carnelian's writing. She still had the crumpled list of branch skills that Carnelian had dashed off on the northbound train.

She wasn't surprised to find that Carnelian's penmanship remained as appalling as ever. She got the sense that Carnelian had put in more effort this time—and had somehow only succeeded in making it worse. She squinted. She tilted the paper to and fro. At long last, she deciphered enough to understand that Carnelian wanted to meet her at the Temple of Combat and Chains.

The Feast of Chalices would inspire events all over the city (and at the port, and in every minor rural hamlet). The temple was no exception. With luck, it wouldn't get as viciously crowded as the military parades downtown.

Holding Carnelian's letter reminded her of finding Baba Sayo's abandoned will. The unofficial version. A piece of paper shoved in a pajama drawer.

The memory came on as suddenly as a stabbing.

*Give me my eternity in the Forest.*

How incredible it was to think that back then, Carnelian had already known everything there was to know about Tiller.

She, in turn, hadn't even known Carnelian existed.

And she could never have conceived of longing for the cooped-up warmth of a small tent, cradled in Forest fog. Just her and one other, floating together outside time, cut free from all the pressures of the future and the present and the dark bottomless past.

The Feast of Chalices dawned on a cool morning after a night of half-hearted rain. Roe trees were in full bloom everywhere Tiller looked, a rich citrus spectrum of gold and orange and yellow. Turtle doves honked portentously from the temple bushes.

Children jumped up and down on mounds of muddy bark, playing a game with no real name. The goal was to stomp an imaginary villain to death. Kids of all ages went at it with unnerving enthusiasm.

The chains of the temple were festooned with strings of paper flowers. Likewise, gaudy paper chains flew from the corners and peaks of every building.

Technically speaking, the Feast of Chalices was a very sober occasion. A tribute to generation after generation of self-sacrificing pilots.

In practice, citizens celebrated it like any other festival. With street food and nationalism and commerce and rote prayers.

Members of the Outborder Corps (mostly laypeople and operators, not mages) loitered about in full dress uniform. They delivered practiced speeches to an ardent audience.

Tiller spotted traces of her usual Guild escort, too. A woman with a pince-nez. A limping man in plainclothes.

Families flew kites in an open field surrounded by roeberry trees. Some bore the goblet emblem of the Jacian flag.

Most others were designed to look like famous chalices. The strong winds of late spring bore them aloft, dangling tiny straw effigies meant to represent their noble pilots.

As Tiller crossed the field littered with turmeric-colored roe petals, she began to catch strains of a voice singing alone.

Her feet hastened.

It was a patriotic song of slaughter. The sort of song everyone knew. One about the greatest chalice ever made, with eight arms to represent the eight major islands of Jace.

The melody: piercingly beautiful. The lyrics: disturbing, if you stopped to think about them.

Tiller took up a spot at the very back of the crowd that had formed around the singing.

Carnelian had fallen in with an informal quartet of student musicians. They weren't taking donations. In fact, once people started clapping, she bowed and began handing out coins to her listeners.

They looked confused, but in the end, they cheered harder.

Carnelian prompted the audience to applaud her accompaniment, too. She then proceeded to remove herself from the scene with astonishing ease, weaving smoothly over to Tiller as if her exit had been planned like this from the start.

She linked arms with Tiller. They strolled off through a row of festival stalls. Carnelian waved to her admirers without once looking back.

"You could've kept singing," Tiller said.

"It was a good stopping point."

"I would've liked to hear more."

Carnelian preened. "I'll sing for you as much as you want in private. That way, you won't have to stand on your toes to see it."

"You won't have backing musicians in private," Tiller pointed out.

"Then I'll hire some," Carnelian said, undeterred.

She was tanner than before. Must have spent a lot of time in open air.

Rays shed by Forest sunvines would never induce burns. Hence the extreme pallor of certain foresters and the phages who came from them.

Granted, there had been few lighter-skinned residents of Koya Village, where most everyone was born steeped in earth tones.

"You sent the Parasite Guild after me," Tiller said.

"They've been keeping you safe, haven't they?"

"I could've kept myself safe. I lived here for years without hired protection."

"Sure. But doesn't having them around make it easier to focus on your work? Constant paranoia can be very time-consuming."

This was true. "Thanks."

"Least I could do. I felt bad about staying behind."

"Who did maintenance for you at the outpost?" Tiller asked.

"Jealous?"

Tiller feigned losing interest. "Never mind."

"It was a variety of operators," said Carnelian. "Whoever could be spared. I already forgot their names."

Gloved fingertips brushed the ends of Tiller's hair. Another black bob. "How's it feel to be back in wigs all the time?"

"Not great," Tiller allowed.

She'd been trying not to think about it. Their trip to the Forest had been the first time in her entire adult life that she'd gone wig-free for more than a night.

She'd never felt particularly stifled in her wigs. Not since adolescence. They reassured her. Like an extra layer of armor.

Still, after weeks of not bothering, it had proven unexpectedly excruciating to pick up all her old tedious routines. Her patience had winged far away, a migratory bird, and she feared it might never come back.

She and Carnelian spoke of the dog at the outpost. The auditors and their mischief. Feast events happening around the city.

They avoided the subject of the salt fields. Here in public, it'd be best not to touch on topics that might get them accused of loose lips.

Carnelian stopped at a booth to buy ice cream. Today, her military affiliation would earn her all kinds of discounts.

Ironic, considering that there was no such thing as a veteran chalice pilot.

The spicy ice cream came stuffed in wafers shaped like curly goat horns. Yet another way to honor the great demon guardian of Jace.

"The musicians who played while you sang," Tiller said as they ate.

"What about them?"

"Friends of yours?"

"Never seen them before in my life," said Carnelian. "We had fun, though. That's all that matters."

If not for Carnelian's singing, it might've taken Tiller a lot longer to understand who she was looking at. She'd gotten so used to seeing Carnelian in uniform.

Now here she was in lace-up sandals and an off-shoulder dress, her hair trimmed so that only a few of the longest ends came down to tickle her collarbone.

Some of the usual trappings remained in place. Her gloves. Her mantle. The mantle had permanent whitish spots left from when Tiller wore it—from when Gren and his phages grabbed it. The blotches looked like an attempt at artistic tie-dye gone wrong.

Tiller had come in long shorts and a billowy shirt. She owned no skirts except for those passed down by Baba Sayo.

"Did you get those earrings here?" she asked.

Carnelian swung her head to show them off. They were shaped like chain links.

"From that booth over there," she said, pointing. "The temple sells all kind of chain-themed accessories. You'll see half the people here wearing something."

She was right. And she was still glowing from her performance. Passers-by invariably glanced at her.

Most would not know what made them look. Most would chalk it up to her beauty.

Tiller proposed that they find a quieter spot to go through their marriage application papers. A place with fewer strangers.

Carnelian showed every sign of agreeing. The route she led Tiller down, however, took them on what was essentially a tour of the entire temple grounds.

They shimmied past a massive line leading up to a group of diviners beneath the oracle tree. After seeing how many people stood waiting, they decided against getting their fortunes inscribed on fresh leaves.

Instead they went all the way out through the winding tree tunnel. Today it rustled with flamboyant paper chains.

They reentered the temple park via a lesser-known side path. Whistles and shouts rang out from exhibition matches taking place in the old dueling ring.

Carnelian stopped to play a few pop-up carnival games. She distributed her winnings to the nearest children afterward. Cheap boxes of candy. Toy chalices with wobbly joints. A flimsy mask of a photorealistic wolf.

Tiller stood close by. She was glad she'd brought her snake pin. Parents visibly relaxed when they saw her hovering next to Carnelian.

She was surprised that more of them hadn't snatched their kids away, warning them not to interact with unknown mages.

Then again, this was a once-a-year holiday. Perhaps they were predisposed to show extra courtesy to those in the military. Even an eccentric mage who only wore a few pieces of her official uniform.

"At this rate, we'll never get those papers signed," Tiller muttered.

Carnelian tossed off an unrepentant apology.

Seconds later, her eyes landed on the next attraction: a creaky carousel. It piped out a rousing naval battle theme as it turned. The sculpted mounts within were, as usual, shaped like human beings down on all fours.

"How about we—"

"No, thanks," Tiller said. "If you want to take a ride, I'll wait out here."

Carnelian gave her a pointed look. "I'd much rather ride...."

"What?"

"I can't say it out loud."

"Why not?"

"Too inappropriate."

"So you do know how to exercise self-restraint."

"Of course," Carnelian said virtuously. "Look at all these families. I'll keep my lewder thoughts to myself."

Despite their many detours, they eventually reached a quieter area.

Benches ringed centuries-old trees. Their lower boughs dangled numerous tarnished chains, thin and light as tinsel. Light enough to stir in the breeze.

The chains made a meek scraping sound as they moved together. A corroded whispering.

"You just wanted to enjoy the festival," Tiller said.

Carnelian shook out the skirt of her spring dress. Roe petals drifted to the ground.

"You would've come here anyway at some point."

"Where? To these trees?"

"To the temple. To pay your respects to the Lord of Circles. Before leaving for Forest territory again. Like how your grandmother taught you."

"It's a bit early for that," Tiller replied. "I won't be dashing out of the city tomorrow. Or even next week."

"I wanted *you* to enjoy the festival," Carnelian said. "You haven't done anything for the Feast of Chalices since your Doe—"

"Since Doe was murdered. Right."

Ethereal white fluff grew all over the bench-encircled trees. Some kind of flower or seed? Tiller didn't know the name of it.

The sky past the treetops had condensed to a thick blaring blue. It felt much closer than the ambiguity of the Forest canopy.

Tiller took a seat. "Objectively speaking, it's creepy for you to know so much about me."

Carnelian sat next to her, unembarrassed. "Can't argue with that."

They were lucky to be here, and to be here together.

Tiller looked down and saw her hand resting against the white-bleached parts of Carnelian's mantle. If they'd stuck to their original timeline in the Forest, they would never have made it back for the Feast of Chalices. She remembered how Carnelian had called it her favorite holiday.

"This might be your last Feast," Carnelian said, as if reading her thoughts.

"Sounds foreboding."

"Outside the Forest, I mean."

Tiller hadn't intended on putting it into words. She was right, though.

With each coming year, Tiller's capacity for spending time outside the Forest would drastically diminish. Like air corroding the chains around the temple. Like a phage's touch eroding human flesh.

"Nel," she uttered.

"Hm?"

"A lot happened in the Forest."

"No kidding."

"Have there been any ... aftereffects?"

"On me?"

"On you."

"From what?"

"The Scholar's resurgence."

"He's completely gone now," said Carnelian. "There's nothing vestigial hiding inside his core anymore."

"You can tell?"

"I couldn't feel him while he slept in me. For a whole two-thirds of my life. But I can feel it now that he's vanished."

Carnelian pushed up one glove to expose her bare wrist.

"I wonder how much my body knew," she mused. "I never really had nightmares about the Scholar. Not even as a child. I only ever had nightmares about myself."

Tiller had no suitable words to give her. There was only one thing she could offer that Carnelian might want.

She took the marriage application out of her satchel and showed Carnelian the sections that required her stamp.

Tall bearded irises grew in dense concentric circles around their bench, black and blue and periwinkle, tongues flapping in the wind. They made for an attractive contrast with the saffron roe petals that came whirling in from the rest of the park. And with Carnelian, in her sunny gingham dress.

Tiller pressed down the papers to keep them from flying away.

Carnelian tucked her hair behind her ears. She took her personal seal out of a pocket-sized case made of premium elk leather.

The stamp was slender, carved from scarwood. Smaller than a tube of lipstick. She pressed one end to a lacquer ink pad that looked very much like a vintage rouge compact. The ink, however, was not scarlet.

She hesitated.

"I hope you're not doing this because you feel like you owe me," she said. "For coming to the Forest."

"Do my reasons really matter?" Tiller asked. "I want to. That's all it comes down to."

"*Do your reasons really matter?*" Carnelian recited, as if struggling to remember the lyrics to an old song. "I suppose nothing in our lives matters much. If you take the long view."

"Exactly."

All Carnelian had to do was fit her mark somewhere in the right box. A slight misalignment wouldn't disqualify it. Yet she took extreme care in how she stamped the application.

It was strangely moving. The intensity of her gaze as she adjusted her gloved grip on the wooden seal. How far she leaned forward in the process of placing it just so.

Wind combed through Tiller's wig. For the first time since stepping out of the Forest—since sensing the crunch of salt beneath her feet—the writhing in her innards went dormant.

She felt content.

Carnelian's seal turned out perfect. Indigo ink. Impeccable placement. Tiller's own stamps looked rather sloppy in comparison.

Tiller collected the papers and put them away before the wind could steal any loose sheets.

"I was thinking of swapping out some of my skills," Carnelian said. "Ones I can't use in the Forest. Like porting. And the shadow claw."

"You can do that?"

"I'd need to get permission. It helps that I've gone on a lot of Forest missions. Could use that as a pretext. Anyway—the bureaucratic hurdles to a skill set update will be much lower after we get married."

"After I become responsible for you," Tiller concluded. "Rather than the state."

Carnelian batted her eyelashes. Tiller pretended not to notice.

"The Corps keeps pretty meticulous records on which skills are proven safe for Forest use," Carnelian said. "And vice versa."

She stretched out one leg, then another, showing off how her sandals laced all the way up her calves.

"My top priority would be to acquire heavier-duty medical magic. First Aid won't cut it if one of us breaks a rib."

She stood abruptly and turned, her mantle swirling. "You know what? This calls for drinks. Wait here. I won't get distracted."

Roeberry petals landed on her shoulders and in her hair again. She strode off through the irises, humming.

Elsewhere in the temple park, children shrieked and wagons groaned. Someone yelled about ice cream horns. Someone played melodies from the southern islands on a zither.

Tiller's stomach felt like the hole at the center of a whirlpool.

Methodically, she attempted to unearth the source of her unease.

Why was Carnelian so eager to throw away branch skills she couldn't deploy in the Forest?

The mere act of assigning a new magic skill to an unoccupied branch wouldn't result in instant mastery. Carnelian had practiced her skills since childhood. Trading in even just a few of them would be like a professional athlete trying to switch sports mid-career.

The Scholar had chosen most of her existing skill set. The government would have chosen the rest. Maybe she had little emotional attachment to her current portfolio.

Still, surrendering something like her porting skill would mean simultaneously surrendering years of expertise and fine-honed instincts. She might not be able to port in the Forest, but it could prove plenty useful elsewhere in Jace.

Once they got married, Carnelian could retire from the Corps. She could go anywhere she wished.

If she craved the novelty of new branch skills, why limit herself solely to what might be workable in the Forest?

Sure, she'd come visit Tiller for maintenance every so often. She had to. But how much of her wide-open life would she spend in a place where she couldn't even nibble fresh fruit without falling unbearably ill? A place with only one person to hear her sing?

# 68

Carnelian came back with hair mussed by the wind and cheeks flushed from hustling.

"Ran into some gambling pals of mine," she said breathlessly. "Incorrigible rascals, the whole lot of them."

She handed Tiller a large paper cup printed with a chain motif.

"They sold real drinking horns, too. And souvenir goblets. But none of that seemed like your style."

The alcohol looked milky and sweet. Tiller took a wary sniff.

"Don't worry," Carnelian assured her. "It's pretty weak."

This whole scene was too beautiful. Something about it hurt Tiller's teeth in the way of too-cold ice cream. The swaying flowers with their extravagant petals. The overdramatic wind. The fiercely blue sky. The distant voices of strangers. The feeble whining of chains in the trees around them. Carnelian's springtime scent.

Most of all, Carnelian herself. Her skirt rippled furiously until she sat next to Tiller again. She tucked the excess fabric beneath her thighs to stop it from flying every which way.

Tiller took a sip of the unnamed drink. It was indeed very mild.

"Nel," she said.

Carnelian instantly went from happy and radiant to watchful and poker-faced.

Tiller made herself say it.

"I meant to go back to the Forest alone."

"You told me to come to you for maintenance."

"Occasionally. That doesn't mean you have to become a hermit with me."

"Then who'll protect you from—"

"From what?" Tiller's hands threatened to crumple her cup. She forced them to stay relaxed. "Rabid ground sloths? Panthers? Phages?

"Things are different from before. No matter where I go, or what I do, nothing in there will attack the Forest's very own heart."

Carnelian took a long drink. Then she folded her empty paper cup down to the size of a matchbox. She crushed it slowly and deliberately. Almost meditatively.

She gave it a gentle shake, testing to see whether any lingering droplets might slither out. When none proved forthcoming, she shrugged one shoulder and tucked it away in her clutch like a stolen souvenir.

She turned her body toward Tiller. "You don't want me to come with you." She didn't phrase it like a question.

"It's not healthy to survive on nothing but rations," Tiller said. "You're not a forester. It's just not realistic."

"If the Scholar could learn to tolerate Forest food, so can I."

"Are you telling me to nurse you like how Baba Sayo nursed him?"

"I'd be happy just languishing in a corner," said Carnelian. "If you'd have me."

She plucked a bit of fuzz off Tiller's shoulder. A gift from the tree at their backs.

She didn't have to blow at it to send it flying on its way. She opened her fingers, and wind came to carry the white fluff high out of sight.

Tiller's throat hardened. "When I watched you singing earlier—"

"I was good, wasn't I?"

"I watched the crowd, too. They didn't notice you were a mage. Or if they did, it didn't register. They didn't care. It didn't matter. They just wanted to hear more."

"How about you?" Carnelian asked.

Tiller wrestled with how to say this. She could already tell it wouldn't go well.

"Once we're wed on paper, no one will make a big stink about us living apart," she said. "Think of the Scholar. Think of the auditors, and how free they seem. Married mages, all of them."

"I'm not trying to be like the auditors."

"There's just no reason for you to stay in the Forest," Tiller continued. "*I* have to be there. I want to change Gren's legacy. I want to live, and I want to make the Forest livable again. None of that requires your presence. Most of all, I'm a forester. It's my home. Not a prison." She shooed a fly away from her drink. "What's the Forest to you? It's actively hostile. It's a repository for the worst memories of your life."

"If we get married, you won't be under any obligation to use magic. You have other talents. You could make people see you as more than just a mage."

"Meanwhile," said Carnelian, "you'll be all by yourself at the center of the Forest."

"Yes."

"It'll take twenty-something years to undo your brother's work. To turn the Forest into a place viable for other foresters."

"Yes."

"Afterward, you'll be bound there for the rest of your natural life. You can't take it back—you can't step down from being the Forest's heart. A day will come when you can no longer set foot on any other land."

"I don't mind being alone."

"Liar." Carnelian mimed tossing a coin. "Demon or swords? Let fate decide who's right."

"I'm not playing that game."

"I won't cheat. Not when it matters."

"I don't mind being alone," Tiller repeated. "Even if I did, is it right to take you just because you're willing?"

"Sounds like a wonderful reason to me." Carnelian wasn't smiling. "Your brother may have spent his twenty-one years utterly alone at the heart of the Forest. Doesn't mean you have to do the same. And you can't possibly claim he would want that.

"Your argument is that you don't *need* me there. Or anyone, I suppose. Not in the way you need water."

She studied her gloves as if trying to read the future in the way they hugged her palms. "I misread you." Her tone turned analytical. "I didn't realize being an operator was so central to your identity. I thought you were raised differently."

"I'm not—"

"Intentionally or not," Carnelian said, "you're approaching this exactly the way a proper operator should. Looking at the big picture. Applying logic first and foremost. Would it accomplish anything productive to bring me with you to the Forest? I suppose not.

"To be fair, my life of indulgence and idle gambling isn't all that productive, either. But you think I can make something more of myself. You think you're setting me free to be a star."

"You don't have to be anything," said Tiller.

"Isn't this your way of ordering me to sing for the masses?"

"I'm just saying that you don't have to be stuck in the Forest for decades to come."

Carnelian rose from the ring-shaped bench. She extended a hand and pulled Tiller up, too, natural as you please. The chains in the old tree creaked and whined.

"I'll take that," she said, plucking away Tiller's drink. "Didn't mean to burden you."

She eyed the remainder for a moment, then downed it. She stashed the crumpled skeleton of the cup in her little bag, just as she had with her own cup.

"Permission to remove my gloves," she said evenly.

"Granted," Tiller answered on reflex.

Carnelian let them fall to hang forlornly from her mantle. She clasped Tiller's hands in her bare fingers, forming the shape of a prayer.

"Whatever the Scholar may have wanted for me, I never actually aspired to be a timeless warrior," she said. "I love singing, but I never aspired to become a famous singer, either. And I never aspired to a long-distance marriage."

She cradled Tiller's hands against the side of her face. The ever-present wind had stolen the warmth from her skin.

"I consider myself lucky that we're even on speaking terms. You've always had the right to sent the conditions of any future involvement. I'll come visit whenever you wish, and I'll stay away for as long as you like."

"It's not that I want you out of the Forest because I can't stand you," Tiller protested. "I just—"

Carnelian's grip tightened. "I said I would trust your choices. And I do. Just please, please don't tell me you're choosing what's best for me. I don't care if you're right. I want to be with you. Please believe me. Please do me the courtesy of letting me want what I want. That's all I ask."

She let go. She stepped back. Her skirt flapped like a flag in the breeze. Cheery yellow gingham.

"Nothing to fear." She flashed her usual charming grin. "I won't say it again."

She was utterly sincere, wasn't she? She'd given up.

She would take whatever crumbs Tiller doled out to her, and she'd take them with a smile. She was accustomed to deprivation. She would expect and endure it, and probably think she deserved it.

But how could it be any better to trap her like a pet in the isolation of the Forest?

People didn't always want what was good for them. Carnelian's own brother had craved the Scholar's approval.

If the choice were left up to Tiller, how could she choose anything other than to plant each of them in the soil where they were best suited to live? Even Baba Sayo had never succeeded at making moonflowers truly flourish in the Forest.

The poet's trio never blooms together, Tiller thought.

How could she bear to tell Carnelian *come with me*, and then watch her suffer for it?

How could she bear to send Carnelian away after getting used to the immeasurable luxury of companionship? A luxury that Gren never got to enjoy to begin with.

As promised, Carnelian didn't bring it up again. Not once.

She led Tiller through the temple grounds with a playful smile on her lips. She showed Tiller how to fly a chalice-shaped kite.

She fleeced a smattering of acquaintances in a few impromptu rounds of dice. Then she lost it all in bad bets on gladiator reenactors in the combat ring. She laughed as she had at the Corps party, loud enough to make bystanders turn their heads. Spring sunlight warmed her bare shoulders, and kindled a hot shame in the pit of Tiller's stomach.

Tiller could be happy, knowing that this Carnelian still existed—still laughing, still gaming, still drawing looks—somewhere far outside the Forest. She could.

The more they saw of each other, the harder it would get. Every brief visit (no matter how necessary) would cut deeper.

Why couldn't she have turned out more like Gren? Why did she have to be so weak?

*Feed your heart to me*, the Forest whispered without words. *Feed your whole heart to me, and you'll be as free as a phage.*

<h1 style="text-align:center">69</h1>

OVER THE NEXT several weeks, the roeberry trees shed all their petals. Together with absurd quantities of soft velvety bark.

The spring winds began to die down. Tiller wrapped up her most urgent business with the Koya Foundation.

She didn't see or hear from Carnelian.

She did, however, receive a formal letter from Commander Blood-wood. In flowery language, the message thanked her for her extensive contributions to Forest research and Forest safety.

*The snake emblem is yours to keep*, the commander had jotted at the very end.

Carnelian must have greatly embellished the events of their journey. Tiller opted not to raise a fuss about it. If she ever encountered Corps personnel in the Forest, carrying the mark of a military operator might very well save her life.

By early summer, she'd distributed many of Baba Sayo's belongings to other foresters. The apartment was beginning to look and smell rather bare.

The Parasite Guild still guarded her from afar. Over time, she'd developed quite an eye for detecting them.

The pull of the Forest gave her stomach cramps at night. A feeling like stitches from sudden running. The pain ate away at her sleep.

She couldn't put it off much longer. Soon she would have to go back.

Asa Lantana summoned Tiller for a visit on the same day she'd planned on consulting with Baba Sayo's landlord. She'd have to figure out the fate of her apartment some other time.

She wasn't all that surprised to run into Carnelian outside the elevator.

She was a little surprised, perhaps, by how lightly Carnelian's eyes glided over her. How easily Carnelian waved at her. How quickly they passed each other, walking in opposite directions.

She caught a whiff of some sweet subliminal scent, gone almost before she smelled it.

Her lungs brimmed with piecemeal memories. A stew of touches and low whispers. The orange hue of the taut tent wall. The perfume of discarded clothing.

Neither of them said anything.

Carnelian was clearly on her way out. Whatever her business had been with Asa Lantana, it was over. She had no reason to hang around and wait down by the fountain in the lobby.

Tiller stopped to collect herself before knocking at Asa's penthouse door.

Asa wore a shirt that came down to her knees and an eyepatch with a doodle of an angry-looking snail.

"You've looked better," she said.

It had been a while since Tiller last heard that accent. "Thanks."

"Did that get lost in—lost in—"

"Lost in translation?"

"What I meant is that you look real bad."

"I got the point."

"I thought *she* was supposed to be the lovesick one."

Tiller had no idea what to say to this. Fortunately, Asa Lantana kept going. "Anyway—congrats."

"For what?"

"You didn't die out there in your Forest."

"Had a couple close calls."

"Haven't we all?"

Asa fell silent, her brow furrowed. Tiller attempted to give back the silver clematis pin. She declined to take it.

The penthouse windows showed a hollowed-out sky. A faint hazy blue.

Would Asa have seen chalices flying north from here? Perhaps they'd gone streaking across this very sky on the day of the strike that ended in endless vistas of salt.

No—on second thought, surely not. They must've launched much closer to the Forest.

"I'll be leaving soon," Asa said abruptly.

"Leaving the island? Or leaving Jace?"

"I still have chores in your country. Gotta go meet my partner down south."

"Where? Someplace past Central?"

"Don't be...." A long pause. "Noisy. Nosy? One of those."

Tiller kept a straight face. "I'll try."

Asa adjusted her eyepatch. "I don't have any extra advice for you about mage healing. Your magic perception's changed."

"I'm impressed you can tell."

She puffed herself up like a haughty little pigeon. "I can always tell."

The building across the street from the hotel was still wrapped up in scaffolding. The sheets that covered it were still printed with the same unmistakable black vortex.

"Have any relations?" Asa asked Tiller.

"What?"

"Relations," she repeated grumpily. "Relationships. Relativity."

"Family?" Tiller said. "No. Not anymore."

Saying it made her feel the weight of it. Far more than before.

She watched Asa strain for words. Although Asa had accused Tiller of looking under the weather, she seemed pretty tired herself.

Her Jacian was passable enough, but constantly functioning in a second language might've begun wearing her down.

"Your family," Asa said. "Your lost family."

"What about them?"

"If you had a chance to reverse yourself. If you had a chance to go back. If you had a chance to spend more time with them, would you?"

She'd had that chance, Tiller thought. At the top of the sacred mountain. She'd had a chance to spend more time with her brother.

It had passed in the blink of an eye, and she'd ended it with her own hands. She'd given up her one precious opportunity.

But if you asked her—of course she'd say yes. Of course she would want another chance to hold Baba Sayo's veiny living hand, to spar with Doe, to listen to Gren.

"Don't cry," Asa said curtly.

"I'm not—"

"If that's enough to make you watery, then don't be an idiot." She pointed at the penthouse entrance. Those grand double doors. "Your mage is still alive. *This is your chance.*"

She steered Tiller over to the doors, and to the elevator hallway that awaited behind them.

"Mages don't get to make a whole lot of choices in this country," she said as she pushed Tiller out of her suite. "Carnelian's a special case. But still. Don't brush off her attempts to choose for herself. To say what she wants. It isn't easy.

"Now get out of here," she called. "And have a good damn life!"

Stranded alone in the elevator compartment, Tiller forgot to press any buttons.

She didn't notice anything wrong until, minutes later, the lift jerked into motion. Someone must've called it from the lobby.

*This is your chance.*

In other words: one day she'd look back and wish she'd spent more time with Carnelian, too. One day it wouldn't be possible at all.

Right now she could still make miracles happen, and with remarkable ease. Right now was her chance to give that gift to her grieving future self. She couldn't buy more time with anyone else she'd ever loved. But Carnelian was still alive in this world with her, alive and human. Carnelian was still—

Right there in the lobby, looking up at the ostentatious fountain. Beneath her mantle, she had on a stylish sleeveless jumpsuit.

She drew a clematis-shaped pin from her pocket and spun it in her fingers as Tiller approached.

"She gave me a parting gift," Carnelian said. "Same type that you have. We can link them, if you like."

She held it out as if contemplating whether or not to wash it in the fountain. "I probably need explicit permission to accept any sort of bauble from a foreigner. But I was planning on quitting the Corps anyway."

"Once we're married," Tiller said.

"Once we're married. So did she call you up for one final scolding, or was that just me?"

"You got scolded?"

"Did I ever." Carnelian put away her clematis pin. "She reminded me that I owe you a date. Want to hear how she told me off?"

"Not really."

"Let me paraphrase." Carnelian cleared her throat. *"Have you ever taken her out to a proper dinner? Not even once? Dear heaven, what's the point of all your money if you can't even impress the ladies with expensive outings?*

*"Are you going to make an effort, or are you just going to mope? Are you the kind of half-baked flirt who immediately gives up when your usual charms fail to make the world turn your way? Pathetic."*

She swept a mock bow. "It was choppier when Asa Lantana said it. But she made her meaning very clear."

Tiller gazed at the fountain's long ribbons of water. She cast her mind back to their very first temple visit.

"The best sea urchin in the city," she said.

"That's what I promised you. Shall we?"

Carnelian held out an arm. Tiller took it without thinking.

They'd already left the lobby by the time she realized she had just surrendered the rest of her evening.

"Miss me?" Carnelian asked cheekily. "Did my best to stay out of your way these past few weeks."

"I lived most of my life not knowing you."

"But now you do. There's no going back."

Tiller didn't attempt to parry this. She couldn't. It was too late to forget the void Carnelian left in her absence. It was too late to pretend she felt nothing.

"Hope you've been getting proper maintenance," she said.

"Want to give me some?"

"Not here and now. Unless you're really desperate."

"Not to worry," Carnelian told her. "I went in for weekly tune-ups. I've been a very good mage."

"Should I praise you?"

"I mean, I certainly wouldn't say no."

They ate sea urchin. They ate scallops flavored with a medley of mouth-searing pepper. They ate crab drenched in a hot sauce much brighter than blood. They ate puff pastry and fresh sweet corn—not the kind used for tea. All sorts of food that would be difficult or impossible to obtain in the Forest.

Carnelian ordered a bottle of wine with a nauseating price tag. Tasty, yes, but too lofty for Tiller's plebeian palate.

"This is money we wrung from the Scholar," Carnelian said. "Or from his government backers, at any rate. I can always shunt more to the Koya Foundation if you need it."

"We're doing all right," Tiller said.

"Then enjoy the wine. Or don't. Order anything else you like."

Tiller drank a few more token sips.

They were at the far southwestern rim of the city. They'd taken a private room in a restaurant overlooking a sleepy ocean inlet. Sunset was still a while away, but the light of the sky had waned.

Once their meal wound down, Carnelian kept drinking glass after glass of lavender-hued wine.

Her tone remained steady—almost clinical—as she described the rest of Asa's message to her.

"She pointed her finger at me and told me I'd regressed into the habits of a typical Jacian mage. Waiting around for orders. For someone else to determine my direction in life, and to assume responsibility for the consequences. Don't make Tiller choose everything on your behalf, she said."

Carnelian used a dark red napkin to clean an invisible speck off the side of her glass. She wiped the vase in the middle of the table, too. It bore four stems of showy ranunculus.

"She claimed that my stance of total deference is what forces you to act like a proper operator. How'd she word it? Something like this—

*"You may think of it as your way of respecting her, honoring her, paying back your debts. Why can't you see that all you're doing is making it harder and harder for her?*

*"Because now—like a good old Jacian operator—she's got to decide for both of you. She's got to pick the best possible path, and own it for the rest of her life. If you love her, set aside whatever past you're getting tangled up in. Don't put that burden on her."*

"Asa Lantana said all that?" Tiller asked.

Carnelian's eyes followed a dark lonely bird outside the window. It could have been anything from a large crow to a small eagle.

"However she put it, she's right."

"Right or wrong, that seems unfair," Tiller said. "Who is she to—"

Carnelian stood. "Let's go for a stroll. I need fresh air."

"Don't we have to pay first?"

"We?" Carnelian's lips curled. "Are you offering to split the bill?"

"I've been planning to run off to the Forest," Tiller said, "but I'd prefer to avoid declaring bankruptcy first."

"Fear not. They know how to charge me."

No one stopped them from leaving the restaurant, at least.

They walked a long way along the water. The air smelled fishy and brackish, but not entirely unpleasant. No beach or sand or waves here. The bay came right up against stone steps that marched down into darkness like part of an old sunken stadium.

Perhaps because it was a weekday, and still fairly early, there weren't many other people around. With the exception of their Parasite Guild retinue, who continued to be exceedingly discreet.

They walked by a children's park filled with too-tall grass and wild poppies, and no children whatsoever.

Everywhere they went, faded signs warned them to beware of hawks. Said hawks circled low overhead or perched on handy lampposts, keeping a constant eye out for tourists carrying food they could snatch.

Further down, Tiller pointed out the silhouette of a waterside concert hall.

"You know," Carnelian said, "I never sang as a child."

"Never?"

"Never even knew I could sing worth a damn. The Scholar taught me and Rozen a lot of things. But he wasn't musically inclined in the slightest."

"No lullabies, then."

"Which is a good thing. Who'd want a lullaby from him?"

They came to a mutual halt some distance before the concert hall.

In a weedy lot taped off for construction, prong-tailed swallows darted about to catch insects. Much higher up, long-necked water birds glided off to destinations unknown.

Carnelian picked her way down the crumbling concrete-block steps. Tiller followed.

The semi-stagnant scent of lapping water intensified. Minuscule wharf isopods scurried about frantically underfoot, fast as roaches.

"Not the most glorious seaside experience," said Carnelian, "but I figured you might not think to come on your own."

The Forest was rumored to hold at least a couple vast lakes, though Tiller had never been there in person.

Carnelian had a point—unless she went very far out of her way, she might never again see blue-gray saltwater stretching to touch the horizon.

"How'd you discover music?" Tiller asked.

"How do you think?"

"Did you end up getting drawn to it because of the Scholar's lack of interest?"

"Trying to prove myself different from him, you mean? Huh. Never thought of that. No, it's much simpler."

Tiller waited for her to explain herself.

Carnelian, half under her breath, sang the first few bars of a knife sharpening song.

"You wondered how I knew this." Carnelian looked away across the water. "It was you."

"Me," Tiller said. Her brain felt empty. "What?"

"I made my investigators take me along once. Back in your street sharpener days." Her expression turned rueful. "Your Doe almost caught us. No PI would ever allow me on the scene with them again. But I was there, that one time. I heard your flute."

"*I* got you into music?"

"I do like singing," Carnelian said. "In the beginning, though—I only started it because it gave me a connection with you. I started it in the way of an animal biting at its own wounds.

"I turned out to be a quick learner. If only I had the same sort of talent for magic, right? I taught myself all the classic knife sharpener tunes. I sang them all the time—pure sound, no words—and I didn't even know why."

"I love your voice," Tiller said. This was the one coherent thought left in her head.

Carnelian shot her an impish smile. "I know. You're not the only one."

She turned, her back to the fence at the edge of the water. The only people in sight were a few solitary fishermen, too far away to make out their faces.

She sang the songs of the old kingdom. She hadn't forgotten a single syllable. If Tiller closed her eyes, it sounded as if this voice came from pristine speakers. As if the real Carnelian were up in a tower, or giving a concert on stage, or waiting somewhere across the ocean.

It was too rich a voice for these ragged concrete steps.

Carnelian stopped.

She said: "Without you, it would never have occurred to me to sing a note in my life."

"I didn't do anything for you," Tiller said. "I didn't even know—"

"I like attention and all, but I only ever sang because of one person. Nothing would make me happier than to sing just for you. Nothing would make me happier than to sing for you again in the Forest."

"Asa Lantana told you to do this," Tiller accused.

"Did I take her advice to heart? Yes. At least I'm transparent about it."

Hungry brown hawks still swooped close above. They emitted high ululating cries of frustration.

Carnelian didn't try to touch her.

"Look. I know it's a bad idea to feel this way. I wish I had no desire to burden you."

"I wish—I'm the same," Tiller said. "That's why it'd be better to serve as the heart of the Forest alone."

"If you can't have me all the time, you don't want me at all?"

"I didn't say—"

"I understand that," Carnelian said tenderly. "I understand."

She shifted her weight from one foot to the other. Isopods scattered beneath the wet fenced-off rocks. She laced her gloved fingers together.

"I told myself I would respect your wishes above all else, in all things. I told myself I owed you that for a lifetime. And more.

"I killed your twin. That will never change. Whether you love me or hate me. Whether you blame me or absolve me. Any relationship we ever have will be growing in soil watered by your brother's blood. Always and forever. Even if it's all the Scholar's fault."

"Take off your gloves," Tiller blurted.

Carnelian stared at her. Then she obeyed. Her exposed fingers curled gradually inward as if trying to hide from the ocean air.

Tiller felt a surge of something so intense as to be virtually indistinguishable from grief.

Grief had many faces, and she would never presume to think she'd met them all.

She cupped her hands around Carnelian's knuckles.

When they touched, the fatal weight in her vaporized like steam on hot rocks. It turned instantly to elation, bright and harsh enough to hurt.

Evening had finally begun to subsume the color of the sky.

"You killed Gren, once," she said. "So did I."

For a time, Carnelian seemed speechless.

"We don't have much else in common," she said at last.

"You're a mage. I'm an operator."

"You're from the Forest. I'm an outsider."

"You're a singer," Tiller said. "And I'm not."

"I'd like to hear you sing."

"No, you wouldn't. Trust me."

"I know what I want," said Carnelian.

Tiller ignored this. "You're a gambler, and I'm not. You can hold your drink. I can't. You've got the kind of looks that make people gawk from a block away, and—"

"Oh?" Carnelian evinced deep interest. "Do I? Tell me all about my animal magnetism. You always put on this act of being semi-immune to it."

"Am I a good actress?"

"Not at all."

"There's another difference between us."

"What were we talking about again?" Carnelian asked.

"How much you love me," Tiller said. "You're turning red, by the way."

Carnelian tugged one hand free. She pressed it to her cheek. "Damn." Her voice grew quieter. "I told myself the best I could ever hope for would be to help you out behind the scenes. To keep playing my part as a secret benefactor.

"I told myself I had no right to ever ask anything of you. To open the door wide enough to let you see me. To let you know me. I thought I'd best leave it unspoken forever."

She clutched the wispy end of Tiller's sleeve.

The Parasite Guild might be watching. But as long as Carnelian paid well enough, they would keep whatever they saw to themselves.

In the diffuse light of early evening, it was cool enough to embrace a long, long time without stickiness.

One of Tiller's arms went under Carnelian's mantle. This led to the discovery that her jumpsuit had a wide open back. She touched the stiff edge of Carnelian's magic-blurring girdle, and then the overheated skin exposed above it.

When Carnelian flinched, she ended up pressing in closer to Tiller.

"Even if all you wanted to do was spit on me," she mumbled, "I would still love you."

"You'd enjoy that."

"I'm being serious here!"

"So am I."

"You've made me weak." Carnelian took a wobbly step back. "I love you, but I can't stand this. Tell me to come with you. Don't leave for the Forest without me."

Only the ends of their hands stayed connected.

Foresters were not known for being demonstrative in their affections.

Tiller could hardly ever remember hearing such words from Doe or Gren or Baba Sayo.

How many times in her life had she said it herself? Right now she couldn't think of a single instance.

She'd never felt deprived by the lack of a few short syllables, unfamiliar to her ear and tongue. For her forester family, it went without saying.

She couldn't control whether or not Carnelian would regret this.

But she could feel the shakiness of Carnelian's gloveless fingertips. So very different from how she'd touched Tiller in their fog-wrapped tent. She could see how Carnelian's face hid nothing anymore, neither aching hope nor brittle fear.

She spoke for Carnelian's sake. And for her own. And because she wanted it. And because it was true. And because they might never view the ocean together again.

"Come with me," she said. "I love you."

# 70

The current wait times for hearing back about a marriage license seemed to range anywhere from four months to over a year.

(In cases, that is, where one of the parties was a mage. A couple of operators or laypeople could expect to get their license within a day.)

They finished collecting testimonials, proof of payment for many years' worth of taxes, copies of Tiller's family register, and so on. They sat for individual and joint interviews.

Tiller warned Carnelian not to bribe any of the officials working on their case.

Meanwhile, Tiller kept waking up earlier and earlier. The ordinary sounds of the city grated on her senses: squeaking bicycles, sneezing neighbors.

It did help that Carnelian stayed over most nights. With Carnelian there—and the Parasite Guild on patrol—she didn't mind leaving the curtains open.

The windows stayed closed, though. The streets outside had begun to fill up with the stink of early summer roeberries.

Carnelian would never win any awards for tidiness, but in Baba Sayo's apartment, she did endeavor to keep her clothes off the floor.

Hours after Tiller woke, she would belatedly shuffle out of bed and make corn tea for both of them. She served it in the mugs Baba Sayo had painted.

There were moments when Tiller could imagine this life lasting forever. Yet the Forest still pulled at her, unrelenting.

One morning, Carnelian passed her a mug and made an announcement.

"I'd like to redo my proposal."

"Excuse me?"

"We got off on the wrong foot." Carnelian's voice was still rough with sleep. "No thanks to me. I regret ever bringing up marriage in the context of bartering."

Tiller put her mug aside. She looked deep into Carnelian's eyes. "Please marry me."

"You stole my line!"

"You already had your chance."

Carnelian knocked back her own corn tea as if downing an entire evening's worth of rice wine. Afterward, she took a few preparatory breaths.

"What I'm trying to say is that I would still want to marry you even if I got nothing else out of it. As long as you're willing. Even if I had to stay a ward of the state. Even if we ended up living apart."

"We won't," Tiller said. "I learned to see reason."

"Thank the Lord for Asa Lantana."

When she mentioned her worries about Baba Sayo's apartment, Carnelian told her to keep it. "I'm already paying for multiple places. What's one more? We can hire a housekeeper to come by for check-ups."

If she weren't quite so worn out, Tiller might have resisted this offer on principle. But half her soul already felt as if it had gotten sucked back across the countryside, over the salt fields, and into the depths of the Forest.

She scraped together the last of her energy and went to visit each of the remaining Koya villagers.

Some, in the throes of senility, kept asking her to bring over Baba Sayo or Doe or Gren. Some—seeing only her dark wig—treated her as a stranger.

Carnelian was a big hit at the group home. She played games with the residents all afternoon.

Tiller didn't tell anyone that this silver-haired woman was the secret donor who, back in their early days, had singlehandedly funded the entire Koya Foundation.

The group home they stood in had been built, brick by brick, using money she'd won in her giant settlement from the Bureau of Mage Management.

No one here knew that.

They loved her anyway.

At one point, she pulled Tiller aside to whisper: "Why don't you use the forester dialect? Won't they be more comfortable hearing it?"

"You'll have trouble understanding."

"I got the gist of your conversations with your brother."

Tiller hadn't even noticed that she'd lapsed into the forester dialect with Gren.

"Up to you, of course," said Carnelian. "On a selfish note, I rather like how you sound when you speak it."

The former villagers definitely appreciated it when Tiller switched to their dialect.

Though Carnelian couldn't speak it herself, she was able to form the right sounds with extraordinary accuracy when singing. Upon request, she sang the village tunes she'd learned from Tiller.

Eventually, most everyone joined in. Others, without seeming to realize it, wept clear soundless tears like sacred water.

"You must be good with kids, too," Tiller commented afterward.

"I'm good with everyone."

This sounded like something Carnelian would normally have said with a smirk. But her face was clouded.

"What's wrong?" Tiller asked.

"Nothing."

Tiller watched her until she crumbled.

"Donating felt like paying a fine. I wasn't thinking about who would benefit. All I thought about was my own torment. And my obsession with you. I just wanted a sliver of that weight off my conscience."

"Your money saved them," Tiller said. "You saved all of us from Koya Village. You're the reason my grandmother didn't have to keep laboring till the day she died."

Tiller took her hand. Carnelian nodded mutely. It didn't seem like a nod of agreement. But she didn't argue, either.

They went back to the Koya group home several more times before leaving the city.

Then, at last, they began making their way back toward the Forest.

Just like earlier in the year, they stopped at Outpost 24. The grounds shimmered with early summer greenery. Everyone's favorite sheepdog was beginning to look a tad overheated.

Carnelian fanned herself. She didn't otherwise seem too bothered by needing to wear the shroud of her mantle over her absurdly short sundress.

"Welcome to the family," the commander told Tiller over coffee.

Carnelian protested vigorously.

Tiller sat back to let them have it out.

The commander knew the truth about the Scholar, and Rozen, and Gren. And the sacred spring full of bodies.

Carnelian's official report had mentioned the toxic bodies, but little else. She must've told the commander the rest of the story in private.

During a natural break in their bickering, Tiller jumped in. "The Corps won't object if we make more trips to the Forest. And you won't, either?"

"No one will stop you," agreed the commander. "By the same token, no one can come rushing to save you."

"That was true even before an eighth of Nuian land turned to table salt," Tiller said.

The commander's scarred face formed a pastiche of a grim smile.

A day later, she walked them to the edge of the outpost.

Colonel Istel was off helping a research team explore the far ends of the salt desert.

The auditors, to everyone's relief, had gone sailing back to Central. Together with the chalices and whatever remained of their ill-fated pilots.

(They had, however, left behind an unexpected present. A pair of light summery shawls knitted by Auditor Aeris himself. Carnelian was reluctant to accept them, but she relented after seeing the attached note: *With best wishes for your future marriage.*)

As Tiller and Carnelian and the commander crossed the outpost, the gray sheepdog came bounding across the grass. Carnelian crouched to greet it.

The dog went straight for the commander instead.

"Belladonna!" she exclaimed as she petted it. "My darling. Such a sweetheart."

"Belladonna?" Carnelian said, incredulous.

"My dog has a name, of course," the commander replied serenely. "No one told you?"

"But—you—" Carnelian couldn't stop sputtering. "Since when were you such a big animal lover?"

"All my life. You were never very interested in getting to know me, come to think of it," the commander said in a voice as dry as the salt fields.

Her skirts rasped as she rose. "Try to stick your head out of the Forest at least once a month," she continued. "I'll let you know if your marriage application goes through."

"You better not sabotage it," Carnelian said.

"I already had plenty of chances, Nellie. If I really wished to interfere, I could have written you a most atrocious testimonial."

"You—"

"Lovely necklace," the commander told Tiller. "Not quite my taste, but it suits you."

"Thanks," Tiller said neutrally.

Only later did she realize that Carnelian hadn't said a word about the commander calling her Nellie.

After several jumps through military portals, they stood back at the new edge of the Forest.

Even here, the salt had been almost wholly flattened. It formed low dunes imprinted with intricate ripple marks.

Improbably, not a grain seemed to impinge on Forest territory. Nor had the Forest attempted to invade the saltscape.

They stepped across the border. Carnelian touched the necklace of brass teeth hanging from Tiller's neck.

"Can't believe you wore that in front of the commander," she said.

"Shouldn't have given it to me if you didn't want me to wear it."

"On the contrary, I'm delighted. But where's my jewelry?"

Tiller pointed at their matching clematis pins.

"Those don't count."

"I can make you another grass ring," Tiller offered. She had vague memories of twisting one together on their first visit to the outpost.

"I've still got the one you made last time."

"Really?"

Carnelian patted her backpack. "Looks a little worse for wear. But it's in there. I carried it all the way through the Forest. And all the way out again. And then all the way back here once more."

"Sometimes I think you like me a little too much," Tiller said.

"Oh, hush."

In the Forest, she tended to Carnelian's magic.

In the Forest, she understood what to do much better than in the city. She perceived the nine separate cores as a united entity.

Caring for the whole required a different perspective from caring for individual components.

You could rub balm into dry hands, massage tired feet, offer eye drops and painkillers and throat lozenges for various ailments of the head. You could ease each part of the body without ever touching the true wounds of the person inside it.

She cared for the forest of magic under Carnelian's skin. Magic that now fully belonged to Carnelian, even if most of it had come from other people. Even if some of it had come from the Scholar himself.

Tiller wouldn't ever let these cores forget who they had taken root in, who they had become. She wouldn't ever let them regress.

In a grove of limestone and maidenhair fern, she asked if she could remove Carnelian's gloves.

"Take off anything you want."

A predictable response.

But a dazed look came over Carnelian as Tiller carefully freed her fingers. One by one. Preserving the shape of the skin-soft glove as she slid it off with the smoothness of removing a ring.

Tiller moved on to the next glove.

Carnelian was more used to dazzling people herself. She wouldn't be prepared for someone else's touch to put her in a trance like this.

Besides, part of Carnelian had always been disconnected from her own body. As if she were temporarily leasing it. As if she wouldn't be surprised to have it torn away from her at any moment.

That inner distance explained her mental fortitude in situations that would crush more sensible mages. It explained her utter lack of self-consciousness, no matter who stared at her or condemned her for improper comportment.

Gossip and resentment and the secret thoughts of others had always lacked the power to leave a mark on her.

The way Carnelian saw it, there was no one else like her in all of Jace. No reason for she and her nine cores to have survived this long.

The slightest shift in inner gravity could knock her entire system out of orbit, send everything crashing down in an unstoppable chain reaction of self-annihilation.

She'd always lived with the knowledge that it might happen a second later, or tomorrow, or never.

Nothing was certain and nothing was final except for the inerasable sins of her past.

But Tiller had learned from the Forest how to preserve her—how to keep all nine of her cores in a more permanent balance.

Now Carnelian would live in a body that no longer threatened to turn on her. Now everything she felt burning in her would be promised to last longer than she'd ever imagined.

Her old oracle leaf would wilt away, a forgotten falsehood. She was no longer her own god of destruction.

No one told Tiller this—least of all Carnelian herself.

She sensed it in the unaccustomed shyness of Carnelian's skin. In how her hands seemed to go weak simply because Tiller had been the one to strip off her gloves. In how she clung to Tiller when they kissed among the ferns.

And in the insatiable joy with which Carnelian, recovering some of her verve, attempted to flip Tiller on her back. It became difficult to tell who had the upper hand.

She tasted the old phage-scars by Tiller's elbow. Then the newer ones behind her neck. Then the newest ones striping her torso and thighs: an indelible reminder of phages seizing her at the caldera. Ripping her away from Carnelian—from the Scholar animating Carnelian's body.

Other memories clung even more strongly to Tiller's flesh. Invisible tattoos written directly on her deepest muscles.

She would never forget the feeling of killing and anointing her own brother.

But Gren, in his way, had blessed her.

Twins to the end.

Tiller, too, found the new phage-marks that Rozen had left on Carnelian—her forehead, her neck.

As they touched each other, Tiller's body began to unwind. Tension she hadn't known she was carrying flowed out of her like sacred water from a phage.

In a strange sense, it felt as if Carnelian were giving her maintenance. Untangling the cramped knots of guilt and regret that ran through every limb. Just like how Tiller would untangle the knots in Carnelian's shuddering magic.

It never would have occurred to Tiller that she, too, needed to be cared for. She, too, needed tending.

She wanted to punch herself for fighting so hard to give it all up.

With time, she and Carnelian hoped to settle in the ruins of Koya Village. But their first major task would be to dredge the corpses from the sacred spring on the other side of the mountain.

"Nice," said Carnelian. "What a cute idea for a date."

One day they would perform the forester wedding rituals. They would drink together from the recovering spring.

It might take years for the water to become clean again. But they knew they could afford to wait.

One day they would be married in the eyes of the Jacian government, as well as in the eyes of the Forest.

One day Tiller would learn to exert more of a conscious influence over phages. She would send phage guardians to escort Carnelian on trips down to the Forest border.

One day, Carnelian insisted, she would push through the pain and force her body to start keeping down food grown from Forest dirt.

One day the Forest might become as kind to Carnelian as it was to Tiller. One day it might be welcoming enough for other foresters—or at least their descendants—to live there.

If they wished to. If any remained.

One day, decades later, the Forest might become a place spoken of with equal measures of awe and horror. One day it might become a place known for more than just devouring.

But right now it was still far too early. They'd only just arrived. First they needed to follow through with their vow.

Before anything else, they had to float soaking dead bodies in a long morbid parade out of the Forest.

It took weeks. A dreary march that left a broad slug trail of ashen damage wherever they passed.

They had much farther to travel than when Carnelian had helped rescue the fallen chalice. No amount of rest or magic maintenance would make her capable of levitating all these bodies high above the Forest canopy for days on end.

They were left with no choice but to drag their miserable haul straight through the air of the inner Forest, deadening swathes of vegetation along the way.

Finally, finally, they finished cleaning the spring.

They alerted the commander, asking her to come do something about row after row after row of decades-old dead folk.

The carcasses lay stretched out on beds of salt. Their decay resumed the instant Carnelian's magic bore them out past the inimitable air of the Forest. Clocks restarting. Rot reviving.

Tiller and Carnelian fled back to Koya Village. They washed themselves over and over in streams along the way.

This water, too, bore molecules of the faraway tainted spring. But it felt much better than doing nothing.

Tiller's hair had already grown halfway down her back again. She stopped to tie it out of the way.

Later, in a moss-covered hut, she reached for her stored luggage and dug out a long metal fighting pipe. Less elaborate than the model Carnelian used to carry. But quite serviceable nonetheless.

Carnelian burst out laughing when she saw it. "Who'd you get to give you that?"

"Colonel Istel. Said he never makes much use of his."

Carnelian, in turn, passed her a bamboo flute so fancy that Tiller hardly dared attempt to play it.

"This is an instrument for a concert musician," Tiller said reproachfully. "Not for tooting all by ourselves in an empty village."

"Well, I say it's for you."

Like most foresters, Tiller had never believed in ghosts. Why fret over intangible spirits when phages were a real and proven threat?

Phages were phages, and ashes were ashes, and dead foresters never became anything else.

Her beliefs had not changed. Her breath and fingers remained disappointingly clumsy. Even so, she played as if she were playing for everyone who could not hear her. For Baba Sayo and Doe. For Gren. For Rozen Silva.

Nothing felt right until Carnelian started singing with her.

Carnelian sang songs passed down by street sharpeners. Songs of Jacian heroes and demons. Songs in a lost language; songs of the old kingdom of blues. Weaving songs and fruit-mashing songs and songs to praise the powerful winds from the south.

When night fog engulfed the village, the distant and ancient reaches of the Forest began to twinge at the ends of Tiller's nerves. A sensation like being buried in a sky full of stars.

She laid her flute down next to Carnelian's new pipe. She leaned on Carnelian to ground herself in this moment that would never come again.

There would be other moments, each new and irreplaceable, for as long as they lived.

*This is your chance.*

Tiller's voice wavered off-tune at the slightest provocation. She sang much quieter than her partner.

Carnelian's breath hitched. Carnelian squeezed her. Tiller would never sing for an audience. But here in the Forest, they sang together.

# A Note from the Author

Did you enjoy your journey to the Devouring Forest? If you have time to leave a rating or review, I'd love to know what you think!

In some ways, I see this story as being a companion novel to *The First and Last Demon*. Granted, they have very little overt overlap—although they're set in the same country, they take place in completely separate locations. Only one character makes an appearance in both books.

(In terms of the present-day timeline, *The Forest at the Heart of Her Mage* ends shortly before *The First and Last Demon* begins.)

On the other hand, the core ideas for these two stories have been with me for a very long time. Perhaps that's why they came to develop certain thematic parallels. Like siblings being raised together—although they aren't exactly twins.

As always, I'm excited to write more novels set in the same universe. It's been such a joy to explore different parts of this interconnected world.

Follow my Author Page for future updates if you'd like to see more:
**https://amazon.com/author/hiyodori**

Hope to see you again next time!

– Hiyodori

*Novels by Hiyodori*

The Clem & Wist Series

Book 1: The Lowest Healer and the Highest Mage

Book 2: The Reverse Healer Case Files

Prequel: No One Else Could Heal Her


Set in the World of Clem & Wist

The First and Last Demon (Standalone)

The Forest at the Heart of Her Mage (Standalone)